mondays with you

kj lewis

To Amber, because you asked.
And to Frankie and Shawn,
a beautiful example that love is love.

mondays
with you

West

I can't help the stupid grin on my face as I stack the last of my papers to take home and grade. And, honestly, I could care less.

All thirty-two of our students showed up today. All thirty-two students passed the exam. I cannot wait to tell Bree, my teaching partner and best friend, who's out sick today.

"Coach Connors."

I turn from packing my papers to see Julius, a student I taught last year, fly into my room on a rush.

"Here." He proudly places a rough rock in my palm.

I fucking love teaching these kids. Especially this kid. He's the reason I started teaching. Kids like this: smart, funny, broken, necessary.

"We went to the Bronx Zoo for biology class today. I know it's not the same as some of the ones in your collection," he shrugs, trying to lower himself in some way. Lower his expectations of what he thinks I'm going to think, how he's going to compare, measure up.

"Cool man." My stupid grin smiles back, reassuring him.

"I love it. Incidentally, this is volcanic rock." I hold it up and show him the coloration and the way the holes were formed.

"They use this in some of the animal exhibits."

"I got it from the tiger exhibit. They had some on the ground. I thought it looked cool."

"Thanks, man." I give him a bro's handshake and add the rock to my growing collection on the windowsill. Julius is looking over my shoulder to see what spot it's going to be given. Julius has a home life like my best friend growing up. I couldn't save my friend, but I can do my best to save some of these kids. To save Julius.

Rocks from my students have been a tradition passed down year to year since I started teaching five years ago. One student was planning a trip to visit his aunt in Boston, and he was determined to bring me something back. I tried to think of something that was cheap and easy, and a rock was the first thing that came to mind. I mean, anyone can pick up a rock from the road. Most of these kids have never been out of the city, but like Julius today, they find ways to be creative. It might seem crazy but this small gesture has come to mean something to them. And me. They are so proud to be able to give something to someone. To contribute to the collection.

I don't get many days like this. Usually when my kids take a geography exam of this magnitude, less than half my kids pass. Today no one made less than a 70.

Still proudly wearing my silly grin, I am definitely feelin' myself as I take the steps up from the 14th Street subway stop to wind my way to my apartment. The man working the stand on the corner doesn't appear to appreciate my giddiness when I stop for warm nuts. In fact, he appears to find me odd, but I don't mind. Because my kids rocked it. And not just today, but every day for the last week that they stayed after school to study, working their asses off to learn the material.

It helps they had an incentive. Without a passing score on this exam, they couldn't play sports, and sports is all some of these kids have going for them. Most won't make it past high school basketball, but if half of them make it to a junior college or better, I would be thrilled.

I shake my head as I enter my apartment building, trying not to focus on the difficult road ahead but to celebrate in what happened today. My kids fucking passed!

"West," Ari winks at me as she enters the elevator as I exit. "You're happy today."

"My kids all passed their exam," I explain, my arm snaking out to keep the elevator doors open.

"That's fantastic! I'll be back in a couple of hours. If you want to celebrate, swing by my place?"

"Sorry, can't. I have a dinner at Bar 9 tonight."

"Fancy. Did you come into some money I should know about?"

"No," I laugh. I wish. "It's a work deal."

"Have fun," Ari says as my hand falls to my side to let the elevator doors shut. "Wear the navy blue," I hear just before they close.

Right, my navy suit. It's either that or the gray. I only have two. Not much of a need for suits in my line of work.

I unlock the three deadbolts and pull open the industrial door to my apartment. The panic bar automatically latches behind me. Home.

My apartment is in the meatpacking district. It's become a trendy place to live in New York, especially since the High Line was added several years ago. I was lucky. My cousin lived here before she was married, and since it is one of the few rent controlled apartments left in the city, I am subletting it for a steal. Something I am grateful for on my teacher's salary.

It's perfect for me. The sixteen-foot ceilings and large arched iron windows make the seven hundred square-foot one-bedroom apartment seem larger than it really is. The footage is in all the right places. The small entrance is enough for a landing place when coming in the door. The kitchen, dining, and living areas are all one. Directly off the living area is a bedroom large enough for a king-size bed. One of my favorite things about this place is off the bedroom: the walk-in shower. I've stayed in some New York apartments where I couldn't fit under the shower head much less turn around. With the high ceilings in this apartment, my 6'2" frame has more than enough room to spare.

I walk behind the iron windowpanes that separate the shower from the rest of the bathroom and jump back when the cold water hits me. Fuck, it's freezing. My good mood not to be deterred, I whistle while the minutes tick off and the water warms up.

"Whistling while you shower. Someone had a good day."

"What are you doing here, Jay?" I ask, shampooing my hair, my smile faltering for the first time. "Don't force me to change the locks."

"Don't be like that, baby."

"I'm not your baby." I look at him for the first time since he's entered.

"I want you back." He crosses his arms and attempts to look like he's all in, but he should know better. We've had this conversation more than once.

"And I wanted a boyfriend who didn't fuck his way around."

"It wasn't like that."

"Really? What was it like then? They just accidently fell on your dick?" I wait a beat for an answer I know is not coming. I don't know why either, because it's not going to make a difference. Even without the cheating this relationship needed to end before it actually did.

"West." He says my name but only meets my gaze after I clear my throat. "What can I do to make this right? How much longer do I have to pay the punishment?"

"I have no idea what you are talking about. We haven't been together for months and I am not punishing you. I would have to care about you to punish you."

"Ouch." He follows me into the closet and stands behind me as I slide into my briefs. "I think I like this side of you. Angry. Hostile. It's fucking hot."

"Jay," I mutter with disinterest. "I'm not playing a game with you. I have no feelings for you. Happy, mad, indifferent. Nothing. Move on. You only want what you can't have. Once the novelty wears off, you'll be back to your usual proclivities."

"Are you saying you can't forgive me or you won't?" His breath tickles my neck as he skates his fingers down my arm. My eyes lock on his in the mirror.

"You know, Jay, when I was little my best friend's mom always told me, 'When someone shows you who they are, believe them.'"

It takes about a nanosecond for his eyes to flash in anger and show the reflection of the Jay I knew and saw often.

"You aren't blameless in this you know," he spits.

"I'm pretty sure I didn't stick my dick in anyone. Call me crazy but I'm thinking that is something I would have remembered," I counter as I button my shirt.

"Maybe not, but you've always held part of yourself back and you know it. You never gave your whole heart. There are parts of you that you always kept locked away and you can't deny it."

"I don't have to deny it. It's not true." I slide my last shoe on and stand upright. "Look, Jay. We had problems long before you started dicking around. You have a temper—"

"I was drunk that time and you know it. And I apologized."

"You have a temper," I continue. "You never respected what I do for a living. You never connected with my kids. You always wanted me to be smaller. To control me. It's over. I'm done. You need to move on."

"I could make you change your mind."

Instinctively, my hand shoots out and grabs his wrist when he reaches for my crotch.

"Do not touch me." My voice is low, but it carries a promise.

His jaw ticks and he pulls his arm free.

"When you're alone and have nothing but your impossible expectations to keep you warm, remember you're the one who said no."

"Got it. It's on me. I take full responsibility." I pull on my sports coat walking to the door, waiting for him to follow.

"My key." I hold my hand out.

He drops it in my hand and walks out. We ride down the elevator in what, for him, must be an uncomfortable silence. For me, it's just silence. Disconnected silence.

I walk a block east and catch a taxi. Releasing a breath, I take a minute to get back to the elation I was feeling minutes ago. My phone beeps a text from my dad.

Dad: Maggie made partner. Dinner details to follow.

Maggie is my oldest sister, second oldest of the seven of us, and probably the most ambitious. She's been dreaming about making partner since graduate school, and I'm glad her dream has finally come true.

Me: Let me know. I'll be there.

I'm looking out the window but not really seeing the city as it flies by. I'm a little unsure of this meeting tonight. The Foundation is an organization formed by some of the most affluent families in the world. Each family gives a large part of their fortune to the organization, and they each make up the board that collectively decides how best to disperse the funds. The article I read in the *Times* several months ago mentioned that most of the billionaires are public, except for two that wanted to remain anonymous. They've chosen simply to refer to themselves as Board Member X and Board Member Y. The board member I am working with is Emme Taylor.

I was introduced to Emme when she came to PS 1782 to talk to our staff and students about the yearly internship she helped create. It's in its second year and is now being run by Holt Raines, the son of Richard Raines, one of the board members.

The program has received a ton of publicity and numerous rewards. It was during this visit she learned they were closing the only community center in the neighborhood. The Foundation bought it, and after a much-needed renovation, re-opened it to the community. It's done wonders for the area, providing a place for kids to go besides the streets. There's a place for seniors and it employs people who live in a ten-block radius. Since the revitalization, four small businesses have opened on the block and the area has seen a reduction in violent crimes and petty thefts. It's becoming a case study for how investing in a community center can change the imprint of the neighborhood.

Traffic was heavy, which I should have accounted for but didn't, so I am running close to thirty minutes late. The hostess confirms Reid Bennett is here and sends me up the elevator to the rooftop bar, bypassing a line of people hoping to get in. Bar 9 is one of the hottest places to be seen right now. Swanky and well above my pay grade, this will likely be a unique and one-time-only experience for me.

I had the opportunity to meet Reid last week when Emme hired his team to look into what she thinks is some questionable accounting where the center is concerned. When he called a couple of hours ago hoping I could meet him, I made the time. What better way to celebrate my day than dining *al fresco* in Tribeca. And what better eye-candy to enjoy it with. Heartbreakingly straight, but eye-candy.

The elevator opens onto another model-hostess who informs me my party was just seated. I swing by the bar and grab a beer before heading to the premiere table sectioned off by black sheer panels, preserving the views of the city but allowing privacy to the table.

It takes me a minute to recognize Reid, who is sitting next to a beautiful brunette. When I met him and his brother Dean last week, he was all business. Almost stoic. Tonight, he looks…happy.

He greets me and we shake hands before he introduces me to the group seated at the table. "I'd like you guys to meet West Connors. We're going to be doing some work with him over the next few weeks."

"Southie?"

The familiar voice and the use of my childhood nickname stops me dead in my tracks. Blake Thomas is sitting in one of the booths, looking like he's seen a ghost. I echo his surprise.

"What the hell man?" He stands and wraps one arm around me, hugging me to him.

My heart misses a beat. Or three.

I don't know whether to swing him around in the relief of knowing that he is alive or to punch the shit out of him for letting me think he wasn't. For walking out on our friendship the way he did.

"You guys, this is one of my childhood best friends." One of? "We haven't seen each other in what?"

"Ten years," I manage to squeak out.

My eyes meet his and they are just like I remembered, only they look like they've seen more. If that's possible. This fucker is still alive and he didn't come find me.

"Here, have a seat." Blake shifts to the end of the booth next to the brunette Reid introduced as Elise. The table is a square-top with booth seating for two on all four sides. The only open seat is next to Blake.

Of course, it is.

Shit.

"This is so surreal." Blake looks to Elise and the others. He puts his hand on my shoulder and I have to stop myself from pushing it off.

"This guy is the only reason I made it out of my hellhole of a childhood. I used to stay with his family all the time." He smiles like he's genuinely happy to see me. I'm more lost now than ever.

"Why don't we order then you can tell us some stories about Blake," Elise suggests, motioning for the waiter.

I choose the easiest thing to order, a steak, and exchange my now empty beer for a glass of wine that the one named Dean poured once I was seated.

"So. Blake as a kid, huh?" the guy across from me says. I

think they said his name was Ryan.

Clearing my throat, I realize I need to use actual words or continue to sit here like an idiot. A stunned-beyond-measure idiot.

"So how well do you know Blake?" I ask for starters.

"These guys are my family. They know me better than anyone," Blake says smiling at them.

An unwelcomed feeling spears through me. It's a mixture of anger, hurt, and, fuck me…heat. But the prevailing feeling is anger. Even after all this time, to hear him refer to these friends as his family when I was his family, is like a blade to the gut.

I guess I missed more than a beat when it's clear everyone is waiting for me to respond.

Shackle your shit, Connors.

"Well then, it's you guys who could probably tell me stories. It's been a minute," I admit.

"Ten years? That means you were, what?" The one named Gabby does the math. "Your birthday is in two months, so… sixteen? Did sixteen-year-old Blake get laid as much as twenty-six-year-old Blake does?"

"Gabby," Elise chastises.

"Well, uh, I wouldn't have anything to compare it to."

"The answer is no," Blake interjects. "I was too busy with work, sports, and trying to keep my grades up."

"You were a dork, weren't you?" Fran, the other woman, says like the secret is finally out.

"With buck teeth and glasses with tape on them," Gabby snickers.

"Yep. I didn't become cool until I met Elise," Blake teases. The reverence he feels for that woman is evident.

"Oh, you were cool alright," Elise laughs. "It took a year

for me to convince you there was no way I was sleeping with you."

"It's never too late," he winks. She laughs and Reid growls.

"He was a force to be reckoned with," I continue when I realize they are still looking to me to provide some fodder. I give what I can remember. "Always up to something. Like the time you talked some of the football players into emptying out the locker room while your lacrosse buddies were in the shower."

Blake throws his head back in laughter. "I mean, we took everything. There wasn't even a shampoo bottle for them to put in front of their junk."

"So, when we—yes we, I was one of them, thanks for that," I cut my eyes to Blake. "We decided we'd make a run for it. When we came out of the locker room, we were met by the entire high school lined up with flash cameras snapping pictures like paparazzi. They got an eye full of a couple dozen guys running down the field with asses shining and hands over our willies."

"Made the yearbook," Blake smiles triumphantly.

"And the paper. Asses blurred in both," I add shaking my head.

"Yep. That's Blake," Ryan says with some sourness. Sounds like he's been on the receiving end of Blake's pranks.

"Dude, you're the one who crashed my room and my shower," Blake reminds him.

As much as I hate to admit it, they do seem like family to Blake, and I take a moment to observe this man next to me. Just like I remember, his sky-blue eyes still stand out against his dark hair. If you look hard enough you might find a gray hair or two. He's taller than I am. I'd guess an inch, maybe two. His face holds hard lines with a chiseled jaw covered in a light dusting of a heavy five-o'clock shadow. He's dressed in a suit that probably costs more than I make in a month and it's tailored to his body like a glove.

Shit. I'm hard.

I shift in my seat. His leg brushes mine when he pulls out a beeping pager at the same time his phone buzzes. Who even uses pagers anymore?

Blake issues some directives and Reid leaves the table. Blake and his team discuss whatever it is they must be working on. I'm thankful to have a minute to recoup from the last person in the world I expected to see tonight. My mind is still reeling.

After the team resolves the interruption, we finally move on to our dinner. Just like I remember, Blake is a magical storyteller. People have always loved to listen to him, to be a part of whatever he is doing. It's obvious his team feels the same way.

I've had more than my fair share of wine by the time Reid makes an excuse for he and Elise to make their exit, leaving us to finish our desserts, and makes plans to work at his place tomorrow. I'm to be there to go over what I know about the community center and give some insight on the staff.

It's a little after ten now and the atmosphere on the roof has picked up. The weather has guaranteed a packed house. We move from the table to the bar and from wine to liquor. For me, not the smartest choice. It's been a long time since I drank this much and by the time I realize I'm feeling the effects, it's too late. I'm more than a little drunk, and the more I spend time with Blake, the madder I get.

"I think we're going to call it a night. When he comes back from the restroom, tell Blake we'll see him tomorrow," Ryan says clasping my shoulder.

He reminds me that I have to piss like a horse, so I head to the restroom hallway. Of the four unisex bathrooms, the first two are locked. The third opens. It takes a beat for my alcohol fuzz to clear enough to realize what I'm seeing. The hostess's back is against the wall with her black skirt hoisted around her waist. One leg is propped over the shoulder of the man in front of her. Blake's dark head of hair is between her legs. Her moans and his grunts echo off the tiled walls.

"Fuck me, you've got a sweet little pussy," Blake hisses as he reaches up and grabs her breasts.

"Oh my god. Don't stop," she begs.

"This one's occupied," she says, catching my eye. Her hand moves to the back of his head, encouraging him deeper.

Stumbling back, I close the door and stand there, frozen. The only man I've ever loved is about to be balls deep in a girl he met just two hours ago. How the hell did I go from being on cloud nine this afternoon to feeling like my world has been turned upside down in one evening?

West

Seven Years Old

"**H**appy Birthday to you. Happy Birthday to you. Happy Birthday dear West. Happy Birthday to you."

My family cheers and blow in noisemakers at the end of the singing. Mom has made my favorite: chocolate cake with white icing. All of my other brothers and sisters like white cake, so this is special for me. Being the second youngest in a family of seven, I don't get too many special days to myself.

Dad made hamburgers and fries for dinner, another favorite. Donnie, my oldest brother, pours me more soda. This day couldn't get any better. My best friend Blake and I played ball all day today. I love that my birthday falls in August when we're still out of school.

When we moved here from Tennessee, I was worried I wouldn't have any friends. The kids here made fun of the way I talked and started calling me Southie. Right away, Blake stood up for me and now I like the name. When the kids say it now, it's cool. It's not said with meanness anymore.

Summer is about to end. We aren't going to be able to hang out and play ball all day. No more trips to Old Man Jeffrey's pond to fish and swim.

I blow out the candles. While my mom cuts my cake, my dad starts a story about how his boss got his pants caught on the door handle and split them down his rear. Blake laughs so hard he spits Coke out his nose.

There's a knock at the door and Donnie answers it.

"Nora. Would you like some cake? Please join us." My mom smiles at Blake's aunt. She doesn't smile back. She seems like she would be pretty if she weren't so sad all the time.

"Thank you, Mary Beth, but I came to get Blake." She doesn't say why.

"Blake, sweetheart, your aunt is here. Time for you to go home." She wraps a napkin around his piece of cake and hands it to him. "See you tomorrow. West," mom calls to me.

I hug Blake and thank him for coming to my party and for my birthday present. He gave me a really cool rock from this place we found exploring the woods. Blake leaves and I dig into my cake. My dad goes a little quiet, but I hear him tell my mom that he can't believe what goes on at Blake's house. I wonder what he's talking about? I've only been over there once. Blake prefers to hang out here with me. He likes having a big family around.

"What did the sheriff say when you went by there the other day?" My mom tries to whisper, but I can still hear her.

"He said they checked it out, but Nora says they're fine and they don't have any evidence to say otherwise."

"What I want to know is who is going to save that little boy? What were his parents thinking leaving him with that man? Surely if they had known—" Dad cuts her off when he realizes I'm listening.

"More cake sweetheart?" mom asks. I shake my head. I'm not hungry anymore.

I have a room to myself since my brothers turned the attic into their room. They thought they were too old to share their room with a six-year-old. Well, seven now. Which is fine by me. I have my own room and my own bathroom.

It's storming when it's time for bed and mom sends me up to brush my teeth. I tried to ask her what she and dad were talking about, but she said it was nothing I needed to worry about. She just wants Blake to always know he's welcome here and I should always let him know that.

The lightning flashes in my room. I get under the covers and count to four before the thunder booms. I hear the window open. Blake climbs through. He does this sometimes, but he does it more now than he used to. Tonight when he climbs under the covers, his breathing is heavy like he just ran uphill. I'm not sure if it's because of what my mom and dad were talking about or if it's the way his chest is moving up and down so fast, but I'm worried about him. The bed is vibrating. He's wet. I take my T-shirt off and hand it to him to dry off with. When the lightening lights up the room again, I can see it's tears and not water on his face.

"I can't take it anymore," Blake whispers. His voice sounds like gravel.

"You can move in with us." I know my parents would let him. They love Blake.

"My uncle would never let that happen."

"We could run away together. We could go live with my

aunt. My parents could come visit me there."

It grows quiet and eventually the bed doesn't vibrate anymore.

"There's got to be something I can do? You can tell me about it," I offer. I want to make whatever it is better for him, the way he does for me.

"Just—" he lets out a deep exhale, "can I just stay here?"

He asks like I might say no, like he has forgotten that I would do anything for my best friend.

"You can always stay here." I say, and even though I'm scared he'll think I'm weird, I reach out and wrap my hand around his. "We're buds right?"

I don't know if it's because I'm reminding him that we're friends or if he is pulling some strength from me, but his hand grips mine harder and the vibrating is back. It makes me sad because for the first time he feels like something is broken.

Blake

Fuck me, how much does he weigh? It can't be that much, but at a dead weight, it feels like I'm carrying an elephant on my side.

When I got back from my hottie-hostess hook-up, I found West at the bar. Everyone else had left. Fifteen minutes of silence later, West stumbled to the elevator. Five minutes later, I was carrying him into a cab, and now I am carrying him out of it. Pulling his arm over my shoulder, I grab his waist and hoist him against me to carry—scratch that—drag him across the tiled lobby of The Greenwich Hotel to the bank of elevators. The door attendant has the grace to not ask questions or appear as if this isn't an everyday occurrence in the high-end swanky hotel.

I wasn't sure where to take West after he passed out. I could have pulled his driver's license, but this was easier than trying to find his place and get him inside. Plus, I hate to leave him by himself when he's out cold.

He slowly begins to slide down my side as I dig my key-card out of my pocket. By the time we are inside the suite, I am hunched over and pulling him across the floor. This guy. He clearly doesn't overindulge often.

"West." I attempt to rouse him enough to get him on the couch. No luck. In fact, he slips out of his suit coat all together and is now sprawled across the floor just inside the doorway.

"I'm getting too old for this shit," I grumble, pulling West's shoes off and chucking them to the side. I maneuver a pillow under his head and cover him in a blanket before stripping to my underwear and climbing into bed.

The last person in the world I expected to see tonight was West Connors. I had no idea he was living in the city. All Nora told me was he had moved away to go to school, and I barely got that information out of her. That was when I turned eighteen. I was finally free from that house. Free from them. Free from...

Just free.

It's not as if I haven't thought about West. I have. And his family. More times than I can count. For the first few years after I moved, they were all I thought about. Without them, I wouldn't have made it. They were my refuge, my solace.

West's mom, Mary Beth, used to make me my favorite cake for my birthday every year. Chocolate with white icing. All his brothers and sisters that were in town would be there, shaking and blowing into noisemakers. West's parents had seven kids; they didn't have to celebrate an eighth one that didn't even belong to them, but Mary Beth did. Always finding a way to make it special. It was the only cake I'd get all year. She was the only person to kiss my cheek and tell me, "Happy Birthday, sweetheart." It meant the world to me.

I settle under the covers and smile when I hear light snoring coming from the floor. West refused to believe he snored when we were little, no matter how many times we would tell him. His sisters and I finally recorded him one night and played it for him the next morning. He still wouldn't acknowledge it. Stubborn, that one.

There's an unrecognizable sound. It sounds like the donkey from Ryan's parent's farm, but that can't be right. Why would a donkey be in my room?

The sun is streaming across the bed and I force myself to roll over and wake up. When is the last time I slept seven hours straight?

The fog begins to lift. The noise is coming from my room. From the floor. I look over the end of the bed and see West on his back with his arm over his eyes.

"Dude, are you alright? You sound like a damn donkey down there."

Another grunt. He turns on his side. His head falls hard to the floor when he pulls the pillow on top of him, blocking out life.

"Where the hell would anyone get a donkey in the middle of New York City?"

"Sorry, I forget you aren't cut from the same caliber as I am. If I wanted to surprise you with a donkey in the middle of the room, being in New York City wouldn't deter me."

"I'm aware. There is clearly an ass in this room."

"Are you saying I get ass, or are you saying I am an ass?"

"You are an ass. And stop smiling."

West can't contain his agitation, and I can't help but grin. No one whose face is completely covered could possibly know I am smiling. But West does. Even after ten years.

"Ass I may be, but we need to get moving. We're meeting the team in a couple of hours. I'm starving, and not only did you sound like a donkey, you smell like one, too."

"Been around a lot of donkeys, have you?"

"My fair share. Now get your ass up." I rip the pillow off his face and start the coffee maker.

"I only need fifteen minutes to shower then we can head to your place."

"I'll just go." He runs his hands over his face. His hair messy as always.

"Just wait, dude. We can eat before heading to Reid's."

I can't help but feel relieved when I come out of the shower and he's still here, standing at the opened terrace doors, looking out.

"See something interesting?" No response.

"West?" I say his name and he finally hears me. He turns and a blush climbs his face. I wish I knew what he is thinking. "See something interesting?" I repeat, grabbing my clothes out of the armoire.

I've always loved staying in this hotel. Every room is different. This room has a wood-paneled seating alcove with a set of doors leading onto a small terrace.

"This room is great. Although, the hard-wood floor I slept on wasn't too soft." He stretches.

"Yeah, I couldn't get your ass on the couch. This is my favorite place to stay when I have to come to the city. This your first time staying here?" I pull the towel off my waist and run it across my chest, absorbing the last remnants of my shower. I pull on my boxer briefs and my favorite pair of jeans. I've had them for years, and any day I get to bum around in them is a good day.

"This place is a little out of my range," West replies.

"Yeah, I can imagine. Teacher's salary and all," I say tossing the navy T-shirt I'm going to wear on the bed.

"Nice ink," he says, lifting his chin to the tattoo on the left side of my chest. It's a compass.

"How close do you live to here?"

"Meatpacking District. Near Chelsea."

"Let's grab a cab then." I shove my wallet into my pocket and grab a pair of sunglasses.

"I don't even remember taking this elevator last night." West shakes his head as we ride the elevator down.

"Because you didn't take this elevator. You were carried *into* this elevator."

He groans.

"You cannot hold your liquor."

"I can in reasonable amounts. The evening, uh, kind of got away from me." He blushes.

"Does that happen often?" It's been ten years. Maybe he's a partier now.

Growing up, West was always surrounded by people, but never happier than when it was just him and his family—or me and him. Everyone loved him and wanted to be around him, but he never liked being the center of attention. He always left that to me. I was a show hog. Kept people from getting too close, asking too many questions.

"No. It doesn't," he offers as he exits the elevator.

He gives the taxi driver his address and we ride in silence to his apartment. Something is on his mind, but he isn't talking.

Watching him watch the buildings swoosh by, I realize it should seem weird to see West grown up, especially after all these years, but it seems normal. Expected. His bright blond hair from childhood has become dark blond. He has the beginnings of scruff on his chin. He never could grow facial hair. I had a full body of hair at the age of thirteen, and at fifteen, West was worried he never would grow any. I smile at the memory.

"You look just like your dad," I muse. It seems to pull him out of his fog.

"Well, everyone always said he was a brown-eyed, good-looking son of a bitch." He smiles, and at the sight of his familiar dimples, something odd settles in my chest. Comfort.

The taxi drops us off in front of a red brick building with dark-green painted window casings.

"Carvers Do It Better?" I ask of the faded lettering on the brick.

"Meatpacking District."

We turn the corner to access the entrance. "Meatpackers of Manhattan?" I read out loud the wording etched on the window of the heavy wooden door leading to the lobby.

West sighs, greeting the door attendant behind the desk by name.

"Still the same ole' Blake," he says, entering the elevator.

"I told you the blue was the way to go." A sexy redheaded bombshell hops in just before the doors close. She rests her head on West's shoulder. "It looks good on you."

It's obvious she's been out for a run. Her running pants and sports bra fit her just the way I appreciate. She's so hot, I have to shift around in my jeans a little. West exhales another sigh, rolls his eyes, and shakes his head at me. Miss Hot Pants exits on the same floor as us.

"Ari, this is Blake." The way he says it makes me think I have been the topic of a conversation before. "Blake, this is Ari."

"Nice to meet you, Blake." Her questioning eyes move from

mine to West's. She leans up and whispers something in his ear and he laughs. Genuine. Good-hearted. Her breasts slide down his arm and he makes plans to come by and fix her TV for her. It's been stuck on Spanish audio for the last several days.

"I think I would like living here, too," I say as West opens his door, tossing his keys onto an entryway table.

"She's a friend," he says with a titter over his shoulder. "In a committed relationship. Help yourself to something to drink. I'll grab a shower. There's a place a few blocks from here we can grab breakfast."

"Do you have a deck of cards?" I ask.

"Entryway drawer," he yells from the other room.

This place isn't huge by any means, but it's got some great architecture and high ceilings. The kitchen is industrial with bar seating. Cool copper accents. There's a sectional sofa on one side of the room, and a TV surrounded by floating shelves that span the entire wall on the other. There must be a thousand books on these shelves. West always was a reader and smarter than I ever will be.

There's an old beat up caramel leather chair and ottoman in the corner that, even with the throw tossed over the back, I recognize came from the Connors' growing up. I fucking loved that thing. I sink into it, my hands resting on the arms. The coolness under my fingers feels just like I remember, and the smell of the leather immediately triggers a memory of home for me.

"What the…" I yell when a cat jumps into my lap. "You gotta go, dude. I don't like cats."

"He won't hurt you." West says entering the room.

"Since when do you like cats? You were always a dog person."

"Since one of my students made me promise to take care

of the kitten she found. Her grandmother said they couldn't afford it. So, she brought him to me at school. I didn't have the heart to tell her no. Boots and I have been together ever since. He's three."

The cat spends a full minute kneading my thigh, before plopping down in a ball. He's white except his legs are black, like he has on boots.

"See. He likes you."

I harrumph and give him a little push off my lap. He looks up at me, and I can tell I have hurt his feelings. I can't help but lean down to scratch between his ears. "Sorry, buddy."

West walks to the edge of the island and pours a couple of treats into a ball and drops it on the floor.

"There ya go, Kinks."

"I thought his name was Boots?"

"It is. She named him before she gave him to me."

"So, Kinks…?"

"Kinky Boots." He smiles unapologetically. "His full name."

"Your student named her cat Kinky Boots? How old was she?"

"No, dumbass. She was eight. She named him Boots. When she gave him to me and I realized it was a boy named Boots, I added the Kinky."

"People always thought I was the questionable one, but really it's you. They just don't know you like I do." I narrow my eyes with a smirk.

He hands me the pack of cards from the desk. Crap, I had already forgotten.

"Would you say that you still know me after ten years of not even a word spoken?" His brown eyes look directly into mine, and I'm not sure I like what I see. Before I can respond, he turns and pushes open the door. I slide the cards into my back pocket and we head to breakfast.

"Have a seat wherever, West." A pretty girl with a towel tucked in her apron greets us when we walk in to a mom-and-pop diner a few blocks from West's place.

"I'll have the chocolate chip pancakes with bacon, coffee black, and he'll have the chocolate chip pancakes with milk." I hand her the menu and catch the disgruntled look on West's face.

"Actually," he says, "I'll have the oatmeal with cranberries. And a coffee with cream and sugar."

"Since when? You ate chocolate chip pancakes and milk for breakfast every day since you were six."

"Things change." There's a bite to his response and the look I didn't like earlier is back. Thankfully, I'm saved by my cellphone.

"Sorry, gotta take this. Thomas?" I answer. "Follow him. I want to know what he's doing." One of my guys catches me up on the case Elise and I are working on. "He didn't just run into Elise at dinner last night. He's positioning himself. I want to know why. Have Harvey keep digging and get back to me." I hang up.

"What exactly is it that you do?"

"I work for Elise. She's a consultant."

"For what?"

"Anything anyone needs."

"Anything anyone needs?"

"Yep. Strategy. Public relations. Corporate. She runs the gamut."

"So people hire her to give advice?"

"Sort of."

"Vague much?"

"It's hard to explain. She's a fixer. She fixes things. We fix things. People. Problems. Whatever needs done."

"What are some of the things you fix?"

"Mostly things that never happened."

"Because you make them that way?"

"Yes."

"And you handle the security part?" he asks before thanking the waitress for his coffee.

"West, you might as well be drinking a milkshake for breakfast." I frown as he pours another packet of sugar and another cup of creamer into his coffee.

"I like it sweet." He blushes that same blush I saw every day when we were kids.

"Yes. I handle the security part, among other things."

"Is your background in security?" he asks.

"You could say that. I'm ex-Army Special Ops."

"Like a Ranger?"

"Delta 6," I answer, even though I rarely tell anyone. It's not something I like to talk about.

"You don't want to talk about it." This is a statement, not a question. He can act like we don't know each other, but this is an example of how that simply isn't true.

The pretty girl brings us our breakfast.

"I thought the new girl got your order wrong when I didn't see your chocolate chip pancakes." She sets his order in front of him.

"Felt like oatmeal today," West responds sullenly.

"First time for everything, I guess." She winks at him before walking away.

I, of course, chuckle at my validation.

"Ass," West mumbles, reaching his fork over to my pancakes.

West

Blake pays for our breakfast and we walk out just in time to catch the crosstown bus.

"You know the bus route?" He seems surprised.

"Teacher's salary. Cabs are expensive. Plus, the crosstown doesn't take long. From there we only have a few blocks to walk."

He takes a seat by the window and watches the city. "So many interesting people," he mumbles.

We get off at Park and 23rd. Four blocks later we are standing outside of a townhouse in the famed Gramercy Park residencies.

"Man, talk about the other half," I whistle.

"It's good to be Reid Bennett."

"I'm pretty happy being West Connors."

Blake looks at me and smiles. "Always liked that about you."

"What?"

"You guys going in or just hanging out here?" A woman I recognize from last night, Fran, walks around the corner.

Behind her are the rest of the people I met.

"Waiting for you guys," Blake says, climbing the steps to the front door.

"Go on in," Dean says. "They're expecting us."

I was expecting a discussion about the ins and outs of the community center. What I got was insight into the people Blake refers to as his family. They are as unguarded with their comments as I remember Blake was growing up. It's obvious they love each other deeply. A love that is solidified in a deep respect for each other.

They each seem to have different strengths and opinions, yet somehow they make it work. My guess is that Elise is the reason. She seems to be the glue that holds everyone together. I recall when Emme asked me to work with this team, she mentioned with fondness Elise's tenacity and ability to solve problems.

Lunch moves into a card game which moves into colorful conversation that appears to be the norm for this group. But the day goes off the rails at the end of the game when Elise confronts Ryan about his sister who I gather is battling cancer. By the time Ryan storms out, my heart hurts for everyone involved and the tension rolling off Blake is palpable.

"West." Reid pulls me out of the drama. "I'd like to set up a meeting to go over the plans on how we are going to handle your case. I've asked Elise to come up with a plan and a cover for Blake."

"I can swing by your office in the morning if you like. I don't teach my first class until eleven."

"Sounds great." He half-heartedly attempts a smile, but his focus quickly moves back to Elise.

Dean, Gabby, Blake, and I walk down the stoop.

"I'll check on Elise later. You guys check on Ryan." Dean and Gabby nod, and after a handshake with Dean and a kiss on Gabby's cheek, Blake hails a taxi.

"Get in," he says, opening the door.

"I'll catch the bus and head home. Let me know if there is anything…"

"West, get in the fucking taxi." He looks up from his phone long enough to steer me by my arm into the taxi. I hear him say something into the phone to a guy named Theo and then briefly recounts the meeting.

"Where are we headed?" he asks while the taxi maneuvers the traffic.

"I had him drop me off first, then to your hotel."

"You want to get some dinner?"

"You don't need to check on Elise?"

"No. Reid needs to be the one to take care of her. They're already moving at lightning speed. This will be a good test for them and how they handle it. So, dinner?"

I hesitate for a minute. On one hand I'm so relieved to have my best friend back, on the other I'm still not ready to have him back. For all the sense that makes, anyway.

"I have some grading to do," I say. But even after all this time I can still read him. He's upset about what happened between his friends, and I find myself pulled to make it better for him.

"Why didn't you teach today?"

"My best friend, Bree, was sick yesterday so I covered our classes. She covered mine today."

"This is it on the right," I tell the taxi driver, hopping out when he pulls to a stop. "Thanks..." I trail off when I realize that Blake has hopped out of the taxi, too.

"What are you doing?"

"Thought I would help you grade," he shrugs.

"You know anything about Eastern European, Asia, and African countries?"

"Dude, like I said, Delta 6."

"Djibouti."

"What about my booty?"

"It's a country in Africa."

"Fine. Make me an answer key. I know where most countries are. I've been to my fair share of them."

I roll my eyes. Blake follows me into the building.

"Maybe we'll see your little hottie."

"What are you talking about?"

"The hot little redhead from this morning. The one who was all over you in the elevator."

"I told you, it's not like that. Plus, she's in a relationship." I unlock my three deadbolts and pull the door open.

"Worth a shot."

"No, it's not," I glower. "Being in a relationship means something. I'm sure it's hard for you to understand." I hand him a beer.

"Settle down, Southie." He takes a swig. "It's not hard for me to understand."

"But."

"But, just not sure most people have what it takes."

"You're such a pessimist. I'm going to change. I'll make you a key and you can start grading while I make dinner. Or I can grade and you can make dinner."

"Unless by making dinner you mean ordering take-out, I'll take the grading."

The two of us go about our separate chores, and I can't help but notice that, despite the one-sided tension on my part, there's a comfortable rhythm to all of this. There's a completeness in this place that I'd never felt before, even with Jay—before things got bad anyway. I keep trying to remind myself that this man, my supposed best friend, basically ghosted me ten years ago and I should hate him for that, but it doesn't stick. His patience and persistence just keeps bringing me back home.

"This smells wonderful," Blake says over my shoulder. "You take after your mom."

"I like cooking when I have the time."

"How are your parents?"

"They're good." I hand him a bottle of wine and a wine opener. "They're all about being grandparents now. Things we were never allowed to get away with, it's all fair game now. They even allow the kids to eat *in the TV room*," I whisper dramatically.

Blake gasps and clutches his chest in feigned shock. "Man. They are going soft. I remember when Mary Beth had to rearrange the furniture to cover your red Kool-Aid."

"*Our* Kool-Aid stain. Mom said it looked like we had removed the body but left the evidence."

I set our plates on the bar and we eat in a settled silence for a few minutes.

"Damn, West. This is really good." Blake says with a mouthful.

"How long has it been since you've had a home cooked meal?" I watch as he runs another bite of pork tenderloin through the bang-bang sauce I made.

"Usually a while, but we had our retreat a few weeks ago and Elise always cooks for us."

"So, what's with you and Elise? You said you'd check on her later."

"Elise and I have a special relationship. There are things that only the two of us know. Things we'll take to our graves. Plus, she saved me."

"Saved you from what?"

"Myself." He says after a slight beat.

"What does that mean?"

He shrugs. It's clear he doesn't want to talk about it, and I let the resentment creep back in. We were best friends, and now there are things he can never talk to me about?

When he left without a word, without a goodbye, I was devastated. I had no idea what had happened to him or where he was. I thought he was dead. It's the worst thing a family can go through, losing someone and never finding out if they're alive or dead.

I try to reign in my anger and move to easier topics. While I do the dishes, Blake starts on his third stack of papers.

"All I'm saying is some of these countries are not the easiest to spell. If they at least get close, it shouldn't count against them. I mean, when are they ever going to need to know how to spell Bosnia-Herzegovina? I think they're doing good to know it's in Eastern Europe."

"I made you a list. Unless the kid's names are on that list, they get counted half off for spelling."

"I didn't count all of them," he says under his breath.

I stop scooping the vanilla ice cream I'm putting on top of the peach pie I made and give him my best "stern teacher" look. "Dude, you have to be constant. These kids don't need handouts, they need consistency."

"Next time. Is that Mary Beth's peach pie?"

"Yep."

"Fuck yeah. Cut me a bigger piece." I swear I see drool running down his chin.

"You can get seconds if you're still hungry," I say, sliding him an already large piece.

"You always were a disciplinarian. I guess it shouldn't surprise me you would count off for spelling."

Blake

Who knew grading could be so time consuming? Although, something about the monotonous action helps to clear the mind. I liked it.

I knew I didn't want to go back to my hotel when I left Reid's. Truth be told, for once I wasn't sure what to do. I'm a solider. I fix things, make things better. But this thing between Ryan and Elise I can't fix, and its tearing me up inside. Besides the Connors, these people are my family. They've been the only family I've known since.

When the taxi stopped at West's place, I invited myself up before I even realized I was going to. I could have called hostess hottie from the other night, but I wasn't in the mood.

Grading. Grading is apparently what I needed.

I had the Nets game on low volume while I learned how many countries I had never heard of. And in this moment I have a beer on the coffee table, I'm sitting in my favorite leather chair, and my best friend is in the kitchen. I feel like I'm home, which is something I haven't felt since I left the Connors ten years ago.

Blake

Sixteen Years Old

Ten…eleven…I count as I climb the trellis up to West's room. There are seventeen steps from my front door to his window. Seventeen steps. I've counted them thousands of times since I was six. Mary Beth finally stopped re-planting her flowers on this side. West's parents gave me a key almost ten years ago, but I rarely use it. I don't want to wake up the family. Plus, I don't want to risk running into his dad. If he sees me I know he will call the sheriff, who will just take my uncle's side like he always does. That just makes it worse for Nora. I take one last deep breath to holster the pain and push the window open before hoisting myself over the window sill. Seventeen. I made it. I wish I had used the key.

This room hasn't changed much in the last ten years. It's been a constant in a sea of turmoil for me. No matter what is going on in the world outside of these walls, this is my solace. My safe place. It's the only one I have.

It's a little after midnight. West snores lightly. He's so used to hearing his window slide open that he sleeps through it now. I climb into my side of the bed. I've slept in this bed more than I have my own.

He mumbles something unintelligible. He's always been a little bit of a flailer when he sleeps and when his arm shoots out and lands heavily on my bare chest, the pain is more than I am prepared for.

"Blake?" West says sleepily.

I try to hold it in, I really do. I want to be tough in front of my friend but I can't anymore. This is more than I can take. I don't answer but the emotion I've been holding in has no-where else to go and it pours over the edge of the dam that I've kept pieced together with duct tape and super glue.

"What the hell?" West is suddenly sitting straight up, alert.

It doesn't surprise me. He's known for a long time that something was wrong. I could tell by his frequent, pointed questions that have become harder and harder to avoid. I don't know why I have tried so hard to hide and lie about what's been going on.

"What's wrong?"

"Nothing. Same ole bullshit. Go back to sleep."

"Talk to me man." He playfully hits my arm but the pain is excruciating and I cry out. West cuts the lights on.

"What the fuck!" The heat and anger in his eyes when he sees me makes my heart soar, but it also confirms what I thought: I look as broken as I feel.

I've been able to outsmart my uncle and avoid most of his threats by staying away from the house until the alcohol had time to wear off. Tonight I wasn't so smart.

"What the fuck, Blake. What happened? Who did this to you?"

When I don't answer, he hops out of bed and is steps from opening his door. I know he is headed to his dad's room, but I can't have that.

"West."

He pulls the door open.

"Weston." The use of his full name stops him.

"Please," I plead.

He pauses, but he doesn't immediately turn back to me. His hand is still on the door knob.

"Blake." He finally turns around, but I can tell he's finding it hard to look at me. Tears are forming in his eyes. "We have to get you medical attention. You're beat to hell."

"Thanks, man."

"I'm serious."

"Just help me up. If I can clean up and get some sleep, I can work the rest out tomorrow." When he doesn't move, I add, "Please," in a soft voice that finally breaks his resolve.

West

Sixteen Years Old

B lake winces when I help him out of the bed. He must have broken ribs.

"How did you climb up here in this shape? You should have used your key."

"I couldn't risk your parents seeing me like this. Your dad."

"My dad? If my mom saw this, there would be no stopping her."

I set him on the toilet in my bathroom. He squints at the brightness of the room, and now, in the direct light, I can really see the extent of the damage.

There is dried blood everywhere.

"What the fuck. Did he cut you?" I ask through gritted teeth and barely contained emotion.

"It's that fucking ring he wears. Every time he threw a punch it sliced my skin."

I inspect his hands. They're clean.

"Didn't you fight back? At least protect yourself?" I ask incredulously.

"It was me or her."

I shake with rage.

"Just help me cleanup will you? I don't think I can lift my arm by myself."

I turn on the tiny shower before helping him out of his blood-stained shirt, careful to mind his injuries.

The wind rushes out of me when I see his chest. It's an array of smoky blacks and blues. Jesus. How many punches did he take? I see an honest-to-God shoeprint outline on his side. To contain my anger—to remind myself that I have to take care of Blake first—I bite my lip so hard that I draw blood. Right now, he's my priority. Retaliation will have to wait.

"I can't do it anymore, West." His head falls forward and rests against my hip. "I...I can't do this anymore." He finally breaks under the weight and begins to sob as though a weir of pain and heartache has broken inside of him. That's the thing about a friendship—you trust someone enough to come out from behind the façade.

My hand rests on the back of his head in an attempt to calm him. To show him the love that I feel for him every day, the love he deserves. How could anyone raise their hand to someone as kind and caring as Blake? Jesus, he's letting himself be abused to spare his aunt.

"Let me help you up," I say.

He wraps his hand around mine. His legs wobble slightly, and I hold him until I'm sure he has his balance. Once he's standing I have an even better view of the damage.

He drops his sweats and uses my hand to steady himself as he climbs into the shower.

"Blake." My voice breaks.

His instinct is to alleviate the tension with a bad joke. "Like what you see?" That cocky bastard winks and attempts a smile. A tear slides down my cheek.

"Don't." He looks away.

"Shut the fuck up, man. If I want to, I will."

While he does his best to wash himself, I touch the bruises on his chest and side. When he lifts his arms, I glimpse a faint yellow-gray bruise. This isn't the first time he's suffered this kind of abuse. Unbridled anger courses through my body and I have to remind myself that Blake needs me controlled.

"How long?" I growl in a voice I barely recognize.

"West." His whisper carries regret and unease. And shame.

"How long, Blake? How long has he been putting his hands on you?"

His eyes fall and I know. Immediately, I know. I choke back the bile that rises in my throat.

Always. Since he moved in with them. I can see it in his face, which suddenly seems older, world weary.

"Help me?" He lifts the shampoo with his good arm and hands it to me. I pop the top and squirt it into his waiting hand. His legs give a little and I reach out my arms to steady him as he rinses his hair. When he tries to wash the rest of his body, his eyes screw up tight and he winces as he runs a wash cloth over some of the injured spots.

The cloth lowers between his legs and my eyes involuntarily follow. I catch myself and force my eyes up before he sees me. He turns his back to me and the same ass that has mooned me more times than I can count suddenly has me aroused. I shake the thoughts away. What fucking creep gets a boner at a time like this? He comes to me in his time of need and I can't be appropriate for even a minute. Blake's not the only one who's been keeping a secret. And like Blake, I'm finding it harder and harder to hide it.

I look away, but hold my hand up just in case he falls.

When I hear the water shut off, I hand him a towel and make sure he's out of the shower and steady on his feet before I leave to grab him some of my clothes.

"Dude, you know your underwear cuts off the circulation to my nuts. Not enough room." I roll my eyes. Even at a time like this…

We've grown up together. We're dudes. We've practically had dick measuring contests since we were seven. There's nothing about this guy I don't know or haven't seen, from how he sounds when he's dreaming, to what his shits smell like. I am a private person, but you can forget that with Blake around. He just barges in and starts brushing his teeth no matter my state of undress. And, like a dude, he's perfectly comfortable pretending he has a bigger dick than I do. I hand him a pair of basketball shorts and he pulls them on, commando, declining the T-shirt I offer.

"What, are you gonna tuck me in?" he asks when I pull the bed covers back for him. "I'm not completely useless."

"Get the fuck in the bed. I practically had to wash your dick for you in there."

He crawls in and gently lies back, trying to find a comfortable position. I turn the light off and climb in on my side. We lay there for a long time, listening to the rain on the tin roof of our house. It's played a major part in the soundtrack of our childhood, and now its soothing melody helps to settle both of us.

"Thank you," he says in a weak voice.

"Blake, you have to let me tell my parents. You can't keep letting this happen. I know you want to protect your aunt, but that is not your job. She should be protecting you. Getting you help might force her to get help. Please, Blake." I'm not above begging. "You're my best friend. You're too important to me." I finish in a quick rush of words as my anguish comes back with a vengeance. I don't attempt to hide it. I won't pretend I'm okay with this.

"Hey, I'm going to be fine. I have been all this time." He pats my arm. That's Blake, always trying to protect those around him. Only this time it's costing him. More than I'm willing to let him pay.

"Blake. Please, man. Please don't go back over to that house. Please let me help you."

West

I've been in this office once, but it's still intimidating. You would think after working with the Taylor Organization for a while now I would be accustomed to offices such as this, but nope. This level of money will always be foreign to me.

"Sorry, I'm late," Blake says, walking in with his head in a folder. He flips up a page and fires off some directives to Gabby who nods and leaves.

"Where's Reid?" he asks, realizing I'm in here alone.

"Right behind you." Reid enters and takes his place behind his desk. He looks a little miffed and more like a self-made mogul than I remembered. Talk about a fuckable man. Jesus, he's fine.

"Sorry I am running late. I have a deal going awry in LA and need to catch a flight."

"How's Elise?" Blake asks.

"She's fine. On her way to Memphis."

"Did she seem—"

"Blake, I'm not a camp counselor."

"Fuck a priest," Blake groans with visible frustration. "I left her with you. Have you already fucked this up?"

"Blake," Reid warns.

"Nah, man. You seem like an up-front kind of guy. You need to know. I would give my life for Elise every day of the week and twice on Sunday. So, telling you you're acting like a dipshit doesn't faze me in the least. You hurt her and I am not going to be happy."

"Well, I live to make you happy, Blake."

"Fix it."

"Blake."

"Fix it or I will."

The testosterone in this room, between these two men facing off—I mean, come on, I am just a mere mortal.

Reid runs his hand down his face and takes a deep breath. "I only have a few minutes and we need to talk about the community center. I spoke with Emme this morning and there appears to be a couple million missing from the books. Elise is running the case and emailed me the setup this morning. Blake, you're going to start off as West's boyfriend who's looking for a job. You'll help him coach his basketball team. After you get to know everyone, Emme will open a position at the center. You'll apply and win the spot. From there you'll have access to any area you need. Elise will email you the rest of the details." He hands a folder to Blake.

"This isn't going to work," Blake says, flipping through the file.

"Elise is the one who came up with the cover, and you're the one who says she knows what she's doing," Reid replies.

"Then she must have been more upset last night than you are letting on, because Elise wouldn't make a tactical error like this. She knows the best cover is a believable one. No one is going to believe West suddenly has a boyfriend when he's always dated women."

Reid has the civility to not look shocked. I can tell that he's trying to decide whether or not Blake is messing with him or really doesn't know that I'm gay.

"Blake, this is a believable cover. No one will question if I have a boyfriend," I interject in an attempt to help the clearly befuddled Reid.

"Dude, I appreciate your willingness to go with whatever, but I've done my fair share of undercover work. We'd start behind the eight ball if we have to work to convince people that you're gay, too. They need to believe it for this to work."

"God, you're a dipshit. Listen to me."

"I am lis—"

"This cover will work because I'm gay. No one will question that I have a boyfriend."

He studies me for a minute like he's still not sure I'm telling him the truth.

"You're not gay."

"I'm pretty sure there are some men who would say I have done some pretty gay things."

"You're gay?" he asks flatly.

"Yes."

"Why didn't you tell me?" This time there's a hint of accusation in his question.

"Because I didn't think it mattered?"

"It doesn't *matter*, but isn't that something you tell people?"

"Do you tell people you're straight?"

"I have a flight to catch," Reid interrupts after clearing his throat. "Elise said she'll call Blake this afternoon to go over the remaining details." He shakes my hand and pats Blake on the shoulder before he leaves us in his office.

Several minutes pass and Blake doesn't say a word. Just when I think I'm going to have to be the one to speak, he starts again.

"How long have you been gay?"

"All my life. You know, born this way. Lady Gaga wrote a song about it and everything." I attempt a smile, but it's hard to hide my disappointment. I never thought he'd be bothered by this.

"You have classes to teach. I need to do some work," he says and abruptly stands up to leave the office.

"Elise is on the conference room system for you two," Gabby says from the doorway. After a beat of silence, she raises her eyebrow at us, clearly picking up on the strange vibes coming from Blake who brushes by her on the way out of the room. I give her a polite smile and follow Blake into the room with a projection screen on the wall. Elise is sitting behind a desk on what must be a private jet. She looks chic as usual, but when she looks up from her papers, it's impossible not the see the tiredness in her eyes. I haven't spent more than a few hours with the woman and even I know she's struggling.

"How are you?" Blake asks.

"Not gonna lie, bud. I've been better," she replies.

"We just left a meeting with Reid. He said he's headed to LA."

"That's what he said," she says impatiently. But her impatience doesn't seem directed at Blake.

"I had a conversation with him."

"I don't need you fighting my battles for me."

"What did you want to talk to us about?" he asks, ignoring her comment.

"I know Reid went over your covers for the community

center. I talked with Emme. She'll have the position opened in two weeks. We did some recon in the area and something feels off."

"Like what?"

"I don't know. It just doesn't make sense. I just feel like there is more going on here than missing money. I was looking at the local statistics Emme sent me and crime should be going down with a center like this in the neighborhood, especially the broken-windows areas."

"Broken windows?" I interrupt.

"Areas where they police petty crimes," Blake explains. "The theory goes, if you punish the 'small' things, you can divert kids from the larger ones. These crimes are more prevalent in areas where kids don't have anywhere to spend their time. No after school activities, etc. So, when you have a center like this, or provide kids with something to occupy their time, you typically see a decrease in petty crimes and thus overall decrease in the larger ones. Elise is saying the statistics aren't following this path."

"I'll know more after I get into the day-to-day at the center," Blake adds. "I agree it sounds like there's more going on."

"I've emailed you access into The Foundation's files on everyone at the center, along with all of their background checks."

"Is that how you knew I was gay?" I ask.

"Yes," Elise answers. "It's the best way for us to explain Blake's presence. He's already been seen with you at your building, so it shouldn't seem like a stretch that you would have a live-in boyfriend."

"What?" Blake and I cry in unison.

"I'm sorry, did you say live-in?" I ask, hoping I didn't hear her right.

"Yes. Didn't you read my email?"

"Elise, we just left the meeting with Reid. So, no, we have not looked at an email," Blake answers with a little bit of a bite.

"I don't think this is going to work for me," I say. And clearly Blake is not okay with this. "When I agreed to help Emme, I didn't understand it would mean I would have to turn my whole life upside down."

"It's already in motion." She looks to us both, and I swear I see a touch of mischief dancing in her eyes.

"What do you mean in motion?"

"I mean Gabby has already added items into your social media. We have a few pictures of you that we snapped at dinner and at Reid's. Those are online as of," she looks at her watch, "about ten minutes ago."

"My social media? What?" I pull out my phone and I have 103 notifications congratulating me on my relationship. I have a missed call from my mom and texts from my sisters wondering why I haven't said anything.

"West, I'm afraid you are going to have to keep this from Bree," Elise adds.

"Why? She wouldn't say anything to anyone. We don't keep things from each other."

"I know she's your best friend, but we need this to look authentic. We can't risk anyone seeing you two for anything other than your cover. If Bree were to make a mistake, it could put everything in jeopardy."

"Don't you have anything you want to say?" I ask Blake who seems to be way too involved with something on his phone.

"What's the story on this guy who runs the center?"

I am so dumbfounded by his response that when I open my mouth, nothing comes out. Damn, this guy's avoidance-skills are expert level.

I stand to leave and as I walk out the door, I hear Blake tell Elise to "give him a minute." *Give me a minute?* Me. Like I'm the only one unjustly freaking out about this!

I stomp back in—which I realize doesn't help my case—to tell him to go fuck himself, only to find him counting down. I'm directly in front of him when he reaches number one. This asshole. This was something he would do when we were kids, count backwards from ten thinking he knows what my next move is going to be by the time he hits zero. He thinks he knows me. I guess this part, he still does, because it works. I'm not sure which pisses me off more, that I haven't changed that much in ten years or that my life is being uprooted.

I hold back what I really want to say and instead tell Elise to have a safe flight. I leave without so much as a backward glance.

I'm out the door and on the subway ten minutes later. Fuming. Fuck this. You know what? Fuck him. He didn't even know I was gay, but he thinks he knows me. I know, I said that already.

I climb the subway stairs to the street and stomp the two blocks to school. Apparently, I'm five and stomp everywhere.

"Coach." My kids greet me as I take the stairs to the door two at a time.

I stop and turn around. "You guys know the rules. Either get in class or off school property."

There's no response as they leave except for some mumbles about my bad mood.

"Mr. Connors." Beverly, our school secretary, greets me.

"Hi, pumpkin." I give my traditional greeting but not my usual smile.

"How's the salt to my pepper?" she asks.

"I've been better."

"Come tell me all about it." She stands and walks around the desk enveloping me in a hug that forces me to smile. Beverly has love to give everyone, and everyone loves her back. But they respect her. You can mess with a lot of people but Beverly isn't one of them. She'd grab a gang member by the ear and have him saying "yes ma'am" before they'd know what happened.

"There's the sweet little dimple I love." She grabs my left cheek.

"I'm just having a little bit of an off day."

"How's that? Yesterday, I could light the sun with your smile and today I see you have a new man. What do you possibly have to be sour about?"

"Just woke up on the wrong side of the bed, I guess."

"Well then, sleep on the couch, and I'll wake up on your wrong side cause that man in your pictures is F-I-N-E, fine! He's so fine he could jump my battery just by holding the cables."

I raise my eyebrows at her, feigning jealousy.

"Don't worry, you're still the milk to my cookie." She winks and pops some kid on the back of his head. "Get your feet off my desk. This ain't your mamma's house."

Beverly keeps it interesting around here.

"Sorry I'm late," I say to Bree who is covering my classes this morning during her free time. "Feeling better?" I kiss her cheek and roll my eyes at the students' cat calls.

"Someone pass out the books," I instruct.

"How was your appointment?" Bree asks.

This girl. How she hasn't been swept off her feet yet I'll never know. She's got a heart of gold and a body you wouldn't believe. If that did it for me, I would be the luckiest man in the world.

"Fine. Glad it's over," I mumble.

"You owe me," she grins.

"I know. I'll take one of your classes next week to make it up to you."

"No. You owe me an explanation. Blake?"

"Don't. I can't even right now."

"Blake is back in your life and you don't tell me?"

"Hey, Coach," Marius interrupts.

"Yes, Marius?"

"I wanted you to be the first to know. I got my letter."

"That's great, now have a seat and wait for...hang on. You got your letter?"

"Yep." He smiles and pulls a piece of paper from his pocket that already looks like it's been folded and re-folded a thousand times.

I snatch it from his hand and see the insignia on the top middle of the page. University of Virginia.

"You got in!" I shout and hug him in celebration.

"Can you help me understand the financial aid?" he asks, clearly a little worried.

"We'll figure it out. The hard part was getting in. The rest is details."

"Details with a lot of zeros, Coach."

"Details we can work out," I assure him.

He goes to his friends and shows them his letter. Marius had a GPA practically in the negative when he was in middle school. One of the teachers helped turn him around. She realized he couldn't read. In two short years, she helped him get his GPA up to a 2.8. We got him to take the ACT, on which he scored well enough to apply to four state colleges.

"So." Bree brings me back to our conversation. "Blake?"

"Blake." I have to remind myself that I'm doing all of this—the ruse, the lying to my best friend—for students like Marius. Without the community center… yeah, keep telling yourself that Connors. There's another part of me that knows that I'm about to play house with the man I have loved since I was in elementary school.

"And you planned on telling me…"

"I'm sorry. I'll fill you in tonight. Come over for dinner?"

"Fine. But only because I have to go teach my classes now. And you're making me chicken spaghetti."

By the time the end of the day rolls around, I'm ready to be home. Ready to have a minute to think through what this is going to entail and what my next steps are. Eventually, that means a conversation with Blake. His response to my telling him I'm gay wasn't exactly what I was expecting. Not that I had an expectation. Maybe I did. I'm just not sure what it was.

"Why didn't you tell me?" Ari sidles up to me as she exits a bodega two blocks from our place. I reach for her bags and she pulls out a juice drink before handing them over.

"It's still new."

"New?"

"New."

"Since when do you make ten-second decisions?"

"What does that mean?"

"You don't switch laundry detergent without thinking about it for at least a month. And you're telling me you're moving in with someone *new*?"

"We've known each other since we were six."

"Friends before lovers." She nods like she understands, even though I want to shout that she has no clue.

"Something like that."

"He's yummy," she says over her shoulder as we enter the

lobby. "Although my gay-dar must be off because I didn't think he was. Also, I thought he was looking at my ass."

"He was," I admit. I mean there's no use trying to hide it. She's already met the man. The man who oozes sex from every pore in his body. "He's bi."

She frowns. "You've already had one wanderer. Don't tell me I'm going to have to cut his balls off, too?"

"Blake isn't a wanderer." Why am I defending a fake relationship? "But he loves asses. So, he looks." I shrug like it's no big deal.

"Well, I guess the fact he loves ass is good for you," she chides, pushing the elevator button for our floor. "Greg and I have a similar understanding. He's a boob man. I let him look." The doors open and I carry her bags into her place for her.

"Dinner soon? The four of us."

"Sounds like a plan."

I can feel the stress of the day finally lift as I unlock my door, when I notice the panic bar is the only one locked. That's weird. I don't remember the super saying he was going to come by today. I brush the thought away, too tired to care. The door closes behind me. I throw my keys on the table and drop my backpack under it. I grab a beer from the fridge and drink half of it with one tilt of the bottle.

"I think Kinks is hungry."

"Jesus Christ." I spill nearly the rest of the beer down the front of my shirt. Wiping my chin, I turn to see Blake standing on the other side of the bar. He's in basketball shorts and an Army T-shirt. I force my eyes to stay glued to his. A feat all on its own.

Because basketball shorts.

On Blake.

Christ, I am not going to survive this.

I ignore the thickening behind my zipper and ask the obvious question: "How did you get in here?"

"I let myself in."

"Through three deadbolts."

"Like it's hard?"

"What are you doing here?"

"I live here."

"So, we're really doing this?" I ask in disbelief.

"We're really doing this," he says with resolve.

"And you didn't think I needed a heads up that you were moving in today?"

"You had a heads up this morning. At the office."

"Not sure that is an accurate depiction of the meeting. Either way, a text telling me you were breaking in would have been ideal."

"You used to be so easygoing."

"Changing the subject isn't going to work with me."

"Since when? It always worked when we were kids."

"Yeah, well, a lot of things have changed since then."

"You don't say." He takes the bottle out of my hand and drinks what's left.

I let Blake finish settling in while I prepare dinner.

"You're really not going to talk about this?" Blake sits on a stool at the bar while I add the finishing touches to a dish and slide it in the oven.

"What's there to talk about?" I ask.

"Uh, I don't know. Maybe that you like dicks and never told me."

"It never came up."

"Never came up? Are you serious—no, you know what?" Blake closes his eyes and takes a deep breath. "How long have you been gay?"

"All my—"

"—life. I get it. When did you *realize* you were gay?"

I pop the tops on two beers and hand him one.

"When I was fifteen."

He doesn't comment, but it's clear by the ticking in his jaw that he's not thrilled with that information. Even after all this time, I still know his tells. Like they were my own.

"Just say what you're thinking."

"I'm thinking my best friend went through a hell of an identity crisis and didn't tell me, his best friend, about it."

"Admitting you're gay isn't an identity crisis—"

"You know what I mean." He looks none too happy with the brush I'm attempting to paint him with. Yeah, I'm being an asshole. I know his core. Me being gay isn't the issue, but it's easier than dealing with what I'm really feeling.

Before I can finish my lecture on the complexities of coming out, the sound of someone opening my front door stops me. Jay comes to a stop when he sees Blake sitting at the bar.

"Who are you?" he demands, looking from me to Blake. Anger lights up the fire in his eyes—a look I haven't seen since the night he got drunk and raised his hand to me.

"Jay, what are you doing here? You're going to force me to change the locks, aren't you?" My even response adds to his irritation. He hates when I'm calm and he's not.

"I'll ask you one more time." He takes a step forward, and with one fluid and barely perceptible movement, Blake is standing in front of me and I can see the butt of a gun sticking out of his waistband.

"Technically, you're breaking and entering," Blake says. "I believe you've been asked to leave your keys."

"Seriously, who is this guy?" Jay asks, sizing up Blake.

I push on Blake, but it's like he's been cemented to the

floor, so I step around him.

"Why are you here?" I ask Jay.

"It's Bree Night. I came for dinner." He finally pulls his eyes from Blake to meet mine. His are empty. They hold nothing for me anymore.

"You don't even like Bree. And she sure as hell can't stand you. Give me my key and leave."

He shrugs. I see the coolness settle in his eyes, and I know whatever is coming next is going to piss me off.

"What can I say? She's a bitch."

"Yeah, you need to leave. Before this gets nasty," I warn. He knows the surest way to get me to lose my shit is to attack Bree. I hold out my hand and he purposefully drops the set of keys on the floor.

"Mature." I roll my eyes and bend to pick them up. From there several things happen and I really have no idea in what order. At some point I think I saw a knee flying towards my face. Then Jay landed flat on his stomach with Blake's knee in the middle of his back. Now there's a gun cocked at his head and there's some animal-like growl coming from Blake.

"I live here," Blake says from his end of the gun. "Being a fancy lawyer, you should know I legally have the right to use excessive force to protect my house and my partner. I would remember that the next time you think it's a good idea to come in uninvited." Blake grabs him by the shirt collar and thrusts him against the wall. "We'll be filing a restraining order in the morning."

Blake shoves him into the hallway and pulls the door shut.

"What's the point of having a doorman if he's going to let any asshole up here?" Bree asks. With all the excitement, I didn't notice her come in. "Yeah, I'm here. Walked in just in time to hear that asshole call me a bitch and see your man here take him down." She high-fives Blake. "Kudos, by the way."

"Was that really necessary?" I ask Blake.

"You're welcome." Blake drapes an arm over Bree's shoulders. She looks like a midget compared to him. Benedict Arnold looks happy as a lark next to him. It's clear she is not to be trusted.

I cross my arms and glare. "I don't need protecting. I can handle myself."

"Yeah, I can tell. Another inch and his knee would have cracked your head open."

"I've changed a lot since high school. I can throw a punch."

"Being able to throw a punch has never been your problem, Southie. I've been on the receiving end more than enough times to know that."

"But?"

"But, being a softy is your problem. You see the good in others to a fault."

"We're not sixteen anymore, Blake. That was dick measuring and you know it."

"Yeah, well, mine's bigger and now he understands that."

"Bree." I catch her looking at Blake's crotch.

"What?" she says, looking up slower than necessary and with a grin that's difficult to resist.

"I need to introduce you to Gabby. You would make great friends." Blake offers her a beer before taking another swig of his.

I'm never going to win with these two, so I focus on something I can control: dinner.

Bree is in chicken spaghetti heaven. This is her guilty pleasure. She's a cheese and pasta girl and this has it in spades.

Blake takes to the leather chair after getting his third helping.

"How can you not get seconds?" Bree asks.

"Or thirds," Blake says, shoveling in a heap of noodles.

"Seriously, man. Where do you put it all?" I ask.

"You of all people should know," he replies with a naughty wink. I shake my head in irritation (it's going to take a while to get used to this), but Bree smiles thinking she is getting insight into us as a couple. I know this player better than I know myself, and I know Blake is just being Blake. He was always a cocky son of a bitch with all his friends, everything was always an inappropriate comment. Despite my exasperation, a corner of my heart cautiously thaws towards him.

"So, how did you two meet?" Blake asks.

"Bree tried to pick me up on the study lawn outside of Low."

"The library," Bree clarifies. "He told me he was gay, but I didn't believe him. I thought he was trying to blow me off."

"So, she got mouthy, of course, and we've been together since."

Bree blows me an air kiss.

"Why didn't you believe him?"

"Well, look at him. He's not what you picture when you think of a gay man."

"Is there a picture I should be aware of?" Blake asks, suddenly serious. "Gay guys run the gamut just like straight guys. Both come in all sizes, styles, masculinity."

"That's not what she meant. Don't be a dick," I snap.

Bree just studies him for a minute and then a smile stretches across her face.

"I like you."

"I like you." Blake smiles back at her, breaking the tension and making them both chuckle. "I wasn't trying to be a dick. I served next to guys who were gay, and there was never a question to me about their masculinity."

"What?" He catches me staring at him. I can't answer him because I'm not sure what is going through my head. He's caught me off guard. I'm tilted, foggy. I'm not sure yet if that's good or bad.

When I don't respond, he takes our plates to the kitchen. Bree finishes the last bites on hers. I follow him into the kitchen to help him clean.

"I got it. You cooked. We'll clean," he says gently.

"So, my friend here has been a little secretive, I must say," Bree says, rinsing her plate and handing it to Blake.

"How's that?"

"Well, for starters, he didn't tell me you are gay or back in his life."

"He didn't know until we ran into each other again. And we weren't sure if this was going to work, so we were waiting to see before we told anyone. Plus, I don't like labels." He tries to take her plate, but she keeps a firm hold on it. She looks up at him with the kind of look that could bring a grown man twice her size—like Blake—to his knees. She doesn't like his answer. She knows I wouldn't invest in someone who was non-committal about being in a relationship with a man. But as a testament to her restraint, she says nothing and let's go of the plate. Blake gives me a quick look, and I can tell he isn't sure if he's tripped up or not.

"Well, I'm turning in early. I'll let you two talk." From the corner of his eye, he notices Bree observing us. His large hand splays across my stomach and he plants a soft kiss on my cheek.

Nope, not going to make it through this. On all that is holy, when his fingers brushed my stomach, I had to bite the inside of my gums to fight back a moan. That's all it took, a brush of his fingers and I wanted to climb him like he was a tree.

My eyes follow him back to the bedroom where he slides the door closed.

"I call bullshit," Bree says. "But I like him. A lot. So, I'm going to let it go for now." She hugs me tightly before whispering, "Just be careful."

We go over our lesson plans for the last two weeks of school. We are trying out some co-teaching experiments to keep the kids interested and the lessons fresh. When she leaves about an hour later, I lock up and grab a glass of water before heading into the bedroom.

"Sorry. I didn't do that great with her tonight," Blake says not looking up from his laptop. "I won't leave myself so open-ended next time. I'll be better prepared. Do you think she'll be a problem?"

"No. If I'm happy, she's happy. The couch doesn't pull out, but it's still pretty comfortable. I'll grab some sheets," I say pulling off my shirt.

"For what?" He sees my confusion. "Dude, we slept in the same bed just about every night for ten years. It never bothered you."

"I just thought—"

"What? I'm not sleeping on a couch for six weeks. Get in bed, Southie. I've slept beside you more than anyone in my entire life. Another six weeks isn't gonna make a difference."

I slide under the covers on my side, thankful this room was big enough for a king-size mattress, and turn off my light. Something about his comment causes another piece of my heart to thaw, but it has nothing to do with lust. The tapping of the keys on his laptop relaxes me.

"Goodnight, Blake."

"Night, Southie."

Blake

When I left Delta, my body started a tumultuous love affair with sleep. It craves it, but it often leaves me just out of reach of what I want. Sure, I sleep, but I can never totally close my mind off from the images of when I was a Delta.

One of the things I was taught during training is how to control my body's desire to sleep. It's an important arsenal when you are on a mission. There were times eight of us slept in a space meant for two people. There were times we slept back to back. Times we slept in a tree. Some of the guys struggled with it. Me, not as much. I had already had some pretty hard core training.

After dinners when I was growing up, my uncle would start drinking and by the time the news came on, he'd be wasted. Sometimes he'd pass out. Sometimes, he'd just be sloppy drunk. But when he became a mean drunk, I knew I couldn't stay in that house anymore. That was the first night I ran. I wasn't sure where I was going, I just left the house running.

After the first time my uncle hit me, I got out of the house, but I didn't run. I stood there in the dark shadows trying to devise a plan. When I saw West's window open, I knew that was where I was going. Where I would be safe. That's when I started sleeping at the Connors' every night.

I didn't have to sleep half awake at West's house. I didn't have to sleep with my back to the wall to keep an eye on the door. I never had to wonder if this was the night my uncle was going to be a mean drunk.

I never got pulled out of bed to clean an already immaculate house. I never got pulled out of bed and made to do push-ups until I couldn't feel my arms. Never pulled out of bed to learn to fight like a man, at the age of seven. Or to wash the car at three in the morning in forty-degree weather. Once I started sleeping at the Connors, I slept.

Until West would start flailing about. Then I had to learn to adapt to that. I never knew where West was going to be when I woke up. Sometimes he would be on the floor. Sometimes his head would be at the opposite end of the bed. Sometimes, the covers would be piled on me, sometimes he would have them all. Sometimes I'd get an elbow to the gut. Other times he'd be plastered against me like we were glued together. The boy never slept the same way two nights in a row.

So tonight, when he finally realized there was no fucking way I am going to sleep on a couch for however long I'm on this case, he got in bed, and I am interested to see where Adult West would end up by morning.

But he's only pretending to sleep. Tension is radiating off him, I can tell by his breathing. I let him stew for a while, and then I finally put him out of his misery.

"Dude, I don't care if you're gay. I mean, I can't believe you didn't tell me but I don't care. I'm not worried you're going to roll over and try to hump my ass or anything. Just go to sleep."

What was wrong with that? I mean, just lay it out there. Address the elephant in the room and move on, right? Evidentially, it was the wrong thing to say. West looks over his shoulder at me with incredulity, then punches his pillow hard a couple of times. He lays his head back on his pillow and an hour later I hear his breathing finally even out.

An hour after that, I close my laptop and turn off the light, amazed that he hasn't moved an inch. Not an inch. I think this fucker is playing mind games with me. His stillness throws me off, and it's another hour before I am finally asleep.

I learned early on in life how to control my depth of sleep and adjust it to my surroundings. What I didn't learn is how to turn it off when there's not a reason to be guarded.

Like clockwork, two hours later I sit straight up, breathing like I've run a mile and soaked in sweat, trying to shake off the same images that haunt me every night. Before I can start the calming process the therapist gave me, West slaps his big hand against my chest. "You're okay," he mumbles and pushes me back down to the mattress before folding his arm back under his pillow. He hasn't opened his eyes and, other than his arm, he hasn't moved. And just like that it comes crashing back.

Many nights at the Connors', I would wake up in a terror. I would suddenly realize I had slept without caution, without anticipation, and then I would wake up, disoriented and scared, scanning the room for my uncle. Then West, still asleep, would put his hand against my chest, push me back, and tell me I was okay. It was my first memory of truly trusting someone when they told me something. West never let me down. He always kept his word. I'm not sure if he was even aware he was doing it. But then I would remember I was at the Connors', where parents loved their children and Mary Beth would kiss me on the forehead to wake me up.

The memory settles in my chest, and I'm back to sleep within minutes. No calming techniques necessary.

The bedroom door is closed, but I can hear music and smell food. Specifically, syrup. The clock tells me it's seven in the morning, which means I've had four full hours of uninterrupted sleep. I climb out of bed and toss on my Army T-shirt.

I don't know if I am on a familial sensory overload after last night or what, but as soon as I open the bedroom door, I'm immediately hit with a sense of home.

All the windows are open. It's still early, so the heat of the summer day hasn't yet sunk in. The industrial ceiling fan is more than enough to cool the room. The Killers sing through the speakers and a stream of sunlight warms my leather chair.

"Good Morning," West says behind a cup of coffee. He doesn't look up from his laptop. "Pancakes are in the warmer."

The pancakes might be warm, but his tone is cool.

I walk around the bar to the oven and plate a stack of five pancakes with a tab of butter between each one. Warm syrup and a coffee cup are waiting for me next to the coffee pot.

"How are you not with someone?"

"What?" He finally gives me his attention, and when he looks up, I notice he's wearing glasses.

"How are you not with someone?" It started out as a rhetorical question, but now I'm genuinely curious.

"I don't understand the question?"

I pull up a bar stool across the island from him. I spread a tab of butter across the top pancake before licking the knife.

"So good," I murmur.

"It's grass fed butter from the Saturday Market on 23rd."

"Grass-fed?"

"Yes. The cows only eat grass."

"As opposed to?"

"Bad stuff," he says, like I should know.

"It's savory." I drip syrup down the sides and across the top before taking a huge bite. "Seriously," I say with a mouthful, "how are you not with someone? You cook. You keep a great place. You make a great cup of coffee. You're nurturing. You're kind. You teach. You're the whole package. Who wouldn't want that in a partner?"

"You know my mother. She was determined all of her children have the skills to take care of ourselves. Except Donnie. That dicknut can burn coffee."

I'm finally seeing a humor and easiness to him that has been missing since we reunited. It makes me happy.

"There's butter in the coffee. That's why it tastes so good."

"Really?" I look into my cup of black coffee. "Yours must taste like a fucking dessert, then, with all the milk and sugar you add."

"What can I say? I'm sweet." He hits a few keys on his laptop.

"What's the story on this Jay? The background said you've been out of a relationship for a while now."

"Background?"

"Yeah. The report Elise sent me."

"There's a background on me?"

"Yes."

"I want to see it."

"It's in your email."

"It's not. I've been reading the email this morning. All it discusses is your role and our cover."

"Fine, I'll send it to you. So, you plan on answering the question?"

"You plan on giving me information?"

"What do you want to know?"

"Oh, I don't know." He shrugs and tries to play off his tone like he's calm, but I know he's not. Even after these years apart, I still know his tells, ticks, and cues. He takes his glasses off and sets them on the counter. "Maybe where the hell you've been for ten years?"

"Well, for the last five, I've worked for Elise. Before that I was a Delta."

"That's it? No details? No information?"

"Not a lot of details. I can't discuss most of what I did as a Delta, it's classified, and I can't discuss most of what I do for Elise."

"Fine, if that is how you want to play this. That's how we'll play this."

"It's not like you're Siri or anything."

"What does that even mean?"

"You're not exactly giving out information either. How do you think it felt to hear my best friend is gay from Reid?"

"For the record," he pins me with a glare, "*I* told you I was gay. Not Reid. And best friends? Really? I wouldn't say that's an accurate depiction."

"Why not?" It takes a lot of restraint to keep my voice from revealing how much his comment stings.

"I haven't seen you for ten years, friend. Ten years of not knowing. Ten years of wondering what happened to you. Ten years of thinking that crazy bastard finally did something stupid enough to harm you."

His eyes glisten and the last comment comes out sounding like gravel.

"Hey, Southie. I'm here. I'm okay." My words are meant to reassure him, but they just fan the fire.

"It never once occurred to you?"

"What?"

"That I lost my best friend! Without a trace. Not one word." He stands up and punctuates with a single finger. "You come to my house beat to hell. You're gone the next morning. You didn't even say goodbye. Who does that?"

"When you emailed and said you didn't want to be long-distance friends while you were in college, I respected it. I mean you weren't beating the door down to fight for our friendship either, if you recall. It took a year for you to write me back, so it doesn't sound like you were looking too hard. As for not saying goodbye, I didn't know when I left that morning that I wouldn't be coming back."

"What are you talking about? I sent you hundreds of emails, texts, voice messages—begging you to contact me. I didn't even know you were alive. When you weren't waiting for me to go to school that morning, I went to your house. Nora said you had left in the middle of the night. I knew that wasn't true because you were at my house. Your uncle was gone for two days. My dad had the sheriff from the next county investigate because he didn't trust ours, being buddies with your uncle and all. I was convinced he lost his temper and hurt you.

"The sheriff said he wasn't allowed to give details but he didn't find any evidence of foul play. When your uncle got home, I confronted him. Told him what I thought of him. He acted like I was lying about the shape you were in, said you had gone to live with relatives and if you had wanted to get in touch with me, you would have. That he couldn't control who you were friends with. But I just knew. I knew you wouldn't cut off our friendship if you were still here. Guess I was wrong."

Several minutes of silence pass before I can bring myself to respond.

"West, when I got home that morning, I took a shower, and when I got out, there were three men in my room. They explained that they were there to escort me to my 'new school'. When I protested, they told me we could do it the easy way or the hard way. By the time they had me in the van, I had a broken hand, a dislocated shoulder, and a fractured eye socket. The eye socket was curtesy of my uncle.

"They took me to a rehab camp for troubled teens. They put a cast on my hand and I was given some Advil, then they put me in confinement for weeks. They wouldn't let me out until I agreed to live by the rules of the school. And agreed to be trained to go into the service.

"We were allowed to email our families. I emailed you every day for a year. When your first—only—email came, I was so ready for anything from you that it didn't matter it had taken you so long to respond. When it said you didn't want to be friends, I got so angry that I threw myself into being a solider. If I could be a great one, I could bide my time and never look back once I graduated. Six months later I heard you got into Columbia. I was already leaving for the Army. I had just accepted it by then."

All we can do is stare at each other. We are at an impasse. We both have different stories. We are both forced to take the other at his word. This is something we've never had a problem doing, but this time, it's more difficult. There's more at stake.

And that's it. No matter how hard we try, we can't turn back the clock. We can't change what's past.

"Evil. That man is pure evil." I rake my hand through my hair in disbelief. Him, the school. They orchestrated all of this. Used it to break me. And it did. Worse than that, they broke something that was beautiful and pure. Unadulterated. My friendship with West. "Fuck! I can't believe it." I kick a stool on my way to the bedroom. Seconds later I've got my running shoes on and I'm out the door. I gotta get out of my head or I'm going to go crazy. West calls my name as I burst out of the front door, but I ignore him.

I run along the banks of the Hudson. The midday sun beating down, and I'm covered in sweat before I'm even a mile into the run. I have no idea where I'm going, I just need a release. A way to get rid of the hatred that threatens to take hold. Everything I am, even now, is influenced by a man I hate to the very core of my being.

West

D ammit to hell! That son of a bitch left me again. I know it's not fair to expect a sixteen-year-old Blake to know how to handle what was happening, but if he had just stayed at my house, if he had just let me help him, let me handle something for once, he wouldn't have gone home and essentially been kidnapped. I wouldn't have, and my parents surely wouldn't have, let that happen.

But how do you expect a sixteen-year-old in crisis to act rationally?

Blake leaving pisses me off but it's not unexpected. He's always been like this. When something gets hard, he leaves to gain perspective. I've only ever wanted him to stick around long enough for us to talk things out, to get perspective together. We were supposed to be a team. *Are* a team, still, I guess. Even now, when I want to hold something back out of spite, I can't. Flowing back into a friendship with Blake is like stepping into my own skin.

I text him to get his ass back and talk to me, but it's moot when I hear his phone chime on the bedside table.

"Fuck it." I move our breakfast dishes onto the counter. His pancakes are swimming in butter and syrup. This guy is going to have a heart attack by the time he's fifty if he doesn't stop eating like he's twelve.

There's a knock at the door. I check the peephole hoping it is Blake having forgotten his key, but instead I see Elise. I push the panic bar to let her in.

"Hi, West." She greets me with a hug and a kiss to my cheek. We've spent very little time together, but there's something about her that's inviting. Like if you tell her your problems, she'll fix them.

"Elise, come in. How are you?" The last time I saw her she looked devastated over her disagreement with Ryan. "How was your trip?"

"Short. I wanted to check in with you guys and see how you were adjusting after all the changes you've been through in the last twenty-four hours. Where's Blake?"

"He went out for a run."

"Well, then, guess it's just us. So, let me ask you," she locks eyes with mine, "how are you?"

"I'm…adjusting."

"I'm sure. It was a lot to take in. I wasn't there when you talked with Emme, but I'm guessing you never imagined your home life would be uprooted, or you'd be lying to your friends about a fake relationship."

"When you put it like that, it sounds like a lot to take in, doesn't it?" I chuckle. "I admit, I got a little more than I bargained for, but there isn't much I wouldn't say yes to when Emme asks."

A beautiful smile spreads across her face. "I have yet to meet anyone who can say no to her."

"Have you eaten?"

"Unfortunately, I haven't," she says with a hint of surprise, like she's just now realizing this might be something she needs to do. She takes a seat at the bar, with slow and careful motions. She seems tired.

"Let me make you some pancakes. I have plenty of batter."

"Sounds awesome. So how's the new roommate working out?"

"Well, it's just been the one night."

"It must have gone off the rails somewhere if Blake is out running."

"He doesn't usually run?" I ask casually, hoping that I don't confirm her suspicions but also hoping to get more information about Adult Blake. If push came to shove, a part of me would even admit to some irrational jealousy towards Elise. After all, she's had my best friend for the last few years.

"Only when he has something on his mind. He usually favors a workout that involves sprints."

I flip the pancakes and she continues without missing a beat, but there's an uneasiness to her voice, like she's unsure how I'm going to respond to the information she's about to offer.

"When I first met Blake. He ran a lot. He ran every day during our first two years together."

"Why did he stop?"

"He finally found some peace. He still has trouble sleeping, but he finally found the pieces to his heart he didn't think existed anymore. That he didn't think he was worthy of."

"So, you helped put his heart back together?" I ask, sitting a stack of pancakes in front of her.

"No. He's the only one who can do that. I just reminded him there were reasons to want to."

"Reminded me there were reasons to want to what?" A

deep voice startles me. I didn't hear him enter.

"To heal your heart." She doesn't pretend we weren't talking about him and he doesn't seem bothered. It's easy to see they shoot straight with each other. He leans down and kisses the top of her head.

"Want some juice?" he asks, grabbing some from the fridge for himself. Elise shakes her head and holds up her coffee cup, which I top off.

"Ryan?" Blake asks.

Elise shakes her head.

"Reid?"

She shakes her head again.

"The men in your life need an ass kicking."

She sighs. "I'd rather concentrate on the one that doesn't need it. At least I hope you don't. I was asking your roomie how you two are adapting."

"You know, it's like riding a bike." Blake takes the plate with the remaining pancakes and drowns them in syrup. I take the bottle out of his hand mid-pour and place it on the other counter. Elise's eyes move from me to Blake. Yeah, he's not fooling her. She knows it's strained in here.

"I had a few accounts I wanted to go over with you. Thought we could do it this morning if that works?"

"I'll leave you to it," I say, excusing myself.

"Before you go, I'm meeting some people for dinner. Would you two like to join me? We're meeting at Ten Thirty Eight downtown. The bar area. Drinks. Light food. I have a perspective client coming also."

"I can be there if you need me to be. Southie?" For the first time since walking out, Blake's eyes meet mine.

"I'll be there, but I'll be serving the drinks. I work tonight."

"What?" Blake asks.

"That's right. I forgot Emme told me that is how you two met," Elise says.

"Yep. She worked there before she met and married Graham. From bartender to half-owner of Taylor Organization."

"You work two jobs?" Blake looks surprised and, if I'm not mistaken, a tad miffed. Is it wrong that I'm happy not everything about me is in the background profile? He's the one feeling off base now. Good.

"Doesn't every teacher?"

"Wouldn't you rather just live outside of the city?" he asks.

"I have one of the few remaining rent-controlled apartments in Manhattan. I don't work two jobs because I don't live within my means, I work two jobs so I can buy books for my classroom, and supplies and food to send home with the kids who are hungry. Whatever they need. It's usually crowded on Saturday nights, so make sure to give them my name at the door if you can't get in." I look at Elise, "Text me how many you are going to have and what time. I'll block off a table."

"Oh, awesome. Thanks, West."

"Of course." I grab my phone and keys.

"Where are you going?"

I turn to answer and am met with those same old blue eyes. But this time I see in them…I don't know, regret? Anger? Disappointment?

"I'm tutoring my seniors who take the ACT in two weeks, then practice with the boys. Then I close, normally around two."

Blake

"Don't start, Elise."

"All I'm saying is if you don't talk to him, how do you expect to repair the friendship?"

The door has barely closed behind West.

"Our friendship doesn't need repairing. We're thick as thieves."

"Sure. Let me just introduce you to my friend, her name is Reality. To fix this you need to tell him."

"I did. This morning."

"You told him? Everything? What you've been through since you left him ten years ago? All before breakfast?"

"I gave him the abbreviated version, yes."

"Also known as a tenth of what you should have told him."

"Elise, no one needs that shit in their head."

Her hand falls gently on my arm. "Blake, if he's your true friend, he'll continue to be your friend even if you're honest with him. You always think the worst of yourself."

"I'm not the only one. I know what others say. That I'm reckless. Hell, I know Theo thinks it." I challenge her to deny what the current owner of our company has said about me. "And I know he's mentioned it to Reid now that he's taking over. I'm a liability. You can't tell me he hasn't."

"Like I give a shit what either of them think when it comes to you. You work for me. With me. I know who you are. I know you don't leave a man behind."

"Yeah, well, I wish it were that easy for everyone. West thinks all I do is leave."

"To be fair, that's all he knows. If you want this friendship, like I believe you do, you're going to have to show him you're not that person anymore."

"How do I do that when he clearly has his mind made up?"

"You stay, that's how. And for the record, I didn't see someone who had his mind made up. I saw someone that doesn't understand."

"You knew he was gay?" I study her when she doesn't answer. I know a couple of her tells, but not many. You don't get to where she has by giving much away. I do, however, know her heart, which happens to also be her biggest tell.

"Were you going to tell me?" I ask.

"Does it bother you?"

"No, of course not. I just think it's something you should have told me. You know, 'hey, by the way, you're going to pretend to be gay and live with a man for weeks unknown.'"

"It was the best cover I could come up with. Give me a break. Graham Taylor reached out to Reid who gave me all of a five minutes heads up to throw a plan together. Look at it this way, you get your friend back."

"For how long?"

"I don't think that is something you have to be worried about. West seems like a good guy."

"You're right, he is. Too good to have someone like me around him."

"Give him a chance. He might surprise you."

"Let's go, fellas. There will be times we won't be the most talented team on the court, but we will be the hardest working. For thirty-two minutes, we will outrun and outplay our opponents."

The gym looks like it's been here since the early 1900's. This is my first time being in this part of New York City. The big red tour buses don't make it to this area. There's scaffolding around the building and it's obvious The Foundation is still making renovations. I think they'd be better off knocking it to the ground and starting fresh, but what do I know.

West blows his whistle and the boys push off the baseline, sprinting in increments up and down the floor. I'm not sure if he knows I'm here. Part of me hopes he doesn't. I don't want to distract him, I just want to—I don't know, watch him, I guess. To be in the same room with him without causing a fight.

When they finish the full court, he blows the whistle and they all but collapse.

"Fuck! If one of you motherfuckers complains again, I'm gonna beat your ass."

"Malik."

"Sorry, Coach."

"He's not sorry at all," West says under his breath. He never acknowledges me, he just knows I'm here.

I just want to be sixteen with him again, when we were

inseparable. We could finish each other's sentences. We knew what the other was thinking. We were one person in two bodies. It took me a long time to become numb to the loss of my best friend.

"Circle up," West says. A few of the boys make a show of passing out on the floor.

"Next time I give you a curfew, stick to it," West says.

"At least keep your mouth shut," one of the boys warns the others.

"Gym will be closed while they renovate this end of the building. I will be checking in with each of you over the summer to make sure you are working out like I expect you to. I won't be teaching the second summer school, but I will be around to tutor for those of you needing help. Steven, I expect to hear from Beverly that you were in class every day, or you'll be benched the first five games and not allowed to start the five after that."

"Come on, Coach. That's my whole summer."

"You should have thought of that before you failed Spanish."

"I can barely read English. How I'm supposed to pass Spanish?"

"You gotta be there every day. We have to get your GPA up if you're going to play ball at the next level. Plus, I promised your mama. And everyone here knows you—"

"Never break a promise to your mama," the guys say in unison.

"Hands in," West says. "Count it down, Myles."

A kid that I swear has to be almost seven-foot tall throws an arm easily the length of my body into the middle of the circle. Hands pile in on top of his and start moving up and down as Myles shouts, "Panthers on three. One, two…"

"Panthers!" All the guys yell at once.

As the kids separate, I walk over to West, secretly bracing myself for his reaction.

"How'd you find the place? Never mind," West rolls his eyes. "I forget what you do for a living."

"Hey, Coach." One of the players raises his chin in my direction, "Who's this?"

"This is Blake. My boyfriend," West says, dribbling a basketball between his legs before shooting and making it from outside the three.

"What? Since when?" Malik asks. Some of the guys circle me. Some my size, most of them taller and leaner.

"It's new," West answers and winks at me when he sees the boys sizing me up. His signature cocky smile, the one I haven't seen in ten years, makes its first appearance. West leaves me standing there while he collects basketballs.

Myles moves next to me—I think he's trying to be intimidating—and I literally have to throw my head back to see his face.

"What are your intentions with our coach?"

"Come on guys, leave him alone." West is back at my side.

"As long as he's better than that last dude, we won't have any problems." Malik says.

"What was wrong with Jay?" West's brow furrows.

"Everything," Steven says before giving me a one-armed bro hug. "Nice to meet you, man."

I get handshakes from some of the guys, but others clearly aren't so easily won over.

West fist-bumps, hugs, and shoulder squeezes as the guys finally exit the gym. One kid lags behind.

"Where you staying?" West asks the kid.

"Around. You need me for something Coach?"

"I just need you off the streets, Marcus. Where's Mickey been?"

"I ain't seen—"

"Haven't."

"I haven't seen Mickey in a few weeks."

"Let him know I'm looking for him, and if you don't have a place to stay you can always stay on my couch."

"Nah, you lovebirds need your space." He winks at me with a goading smile, and for the first time I realize these kids think I'm gay. It's odd.

"Alright. Call if you need me. See ya Monday at school. At school," West says with a little more force when Marcus groans. "It's only one more week. You don't have second summer classes."

Marcus heads out and West throws a bag of basketballs over his shoulder. He tosses the bag in a closet and locks it before turning to me. "What—"

"How was practice?" A voice over my shoulder cuts West off. I turn to the man behind me. He's regular height, stocky. I don't like this guy. Something about him...

"Good. I think the boys will miss it. I'm going to try to get us into another gym while this one is closed."

"Sounds like a plan. If you need help, let me know."

"Thanks, but Blake is going to assist me for now. Blake, this is David. David, this is Blake."

David offers his hand, giving me a once over before asking, "How do you two know each other?"

"Blake—"

"I'm his boyfriend," I respond curtly, returning a firm handshake. West raises an eyebrow at my behavior.

David nods, but he's looking at me like he doesn't believe me. Yeah, I don't like this guy.

"See you in a few weeks," David says before looking me over one last time.

"What was that about?" West asks.

"Something about that guy. I don't like him."

"You just met him. How can you know if you like him?"

"Trust me, my gut reaction is never wrong."

"Whatever," he laughs and leads us out of the gym.

"Don't mock the gut."

"Wouldn't dream of it. Why are you here?"

"Elise and I finished early so thought I'd come check out the place first hand. Get the lay of the land before I start. Ever have a problem with the boys accepting your preferences?"

"Preferences? Like this is a choice?"

"I mean, do you like only guys? Swing both ways?"

"My swing only goes in one direction. And no, they've never had a problem with it," West says before swiping his MetroCard. We make a run to catch the 1 before it pulls off.

The car is empty so we take a seat. It's a thirty-minute sub-way ride to Midtown.

"Just ask what you want to ask, Blake."

"It's just that you never once said anything. We were inseparable, we told each other everything. You never said, 'Hey, dude, I'm thinking I might like dick.' I thought we were best friends. Didn't you think I deserved to know what you were dealing with?"

"I guess I could ask you the same thing."

"How so?"

"Your uncle. You never talked about how bad it was. Guess our friendship wasn't as solid as we thought. I mean, it happens, right? Friends grow apart."

I stare at him for a minute, trying to decide if he's sincere or if he's just trying to start a fight.

"Yeah, I guess." I answer tartly. But I don't like the way he just dismissed the friendship that has always meant the most to me.

West showered and went to work, and a part of me is relieved he's gone. I can't shake my soured mood at his easy dismissal of a friendship that, for me, was everything. Love, acceptance, safety.

I have a few hours before Elise and I meet some potential clients, so I might as well dig in and unpack. I'm going to be here for a while.

I've been reading a lot of The Foundation's surveillance reports on the community center, but there's something that doesn't match up. None of the people who have access to the funds have spent any of the money as far as I can tell. Two million gone and there's no trail.

The doorman calls to tell me that he's sending up the delivery I am expecting. The hotel was holding the bulk of my luggage while I got settled. I put my overnight bag on the bed and answer the door.

Reid has asked me to move to New York, but I haven't quite made up my mind. I like the guy, and I think he is good for Elise, but I don't want to make any decisions until I see how things are going to turn out. I get the feeling he isn't down with Elise being in harm's way, but that's the nature of her job. There are times she is mixed up in some crazy things, sure. The things that woman knows about some of the most important people in the world would shock Reid. I don't know if he can handle it.

I'm sure this is a good-size place for Manhattan, but I'm surprised by how well the space is laid out. I open drawers and check out West's closet, a walk-in off the bathroom which is a rarity in most apartments this size. I tell myself I'm poking around to get the lay of the land, but who're we kidding, I'm just being nosey. I run my hands over his shirts. As always, there is no rhyme or reason to his closet. I swear, he's like a mullet. Neat and tidy on the surface (kitchen and living areas), crazy as hell in the back (closets and drawers).

I go to work. Three hours later and it looks like a professional organizer got hold of his closet. Some of this comes from my time in the service, but most of it comes from a childhood where nothing was allowed out of place.

With West's things organized, I now have half the closet and two full drawers for my clothes. The bedside table holds the two books I brought with me, along with my iPad and the laptop I left there last night. I shove my suitcase under the bed and fix myself some chips and salsa.

"You want some, Kinks?" I ask the curious cat that has jumped in my lap. He smells the salsa I have balanced on the chip then takes off. I wonder where he spends his day. There can't be too many places he can hide in here.

I clean up my mess and finish the last little tour of West's place. I walk along the wall of shelves and look at the book spines to see what he's collected. I recognize some of the books as his favorites growing up. Plenty of new things. Pictures of him and his family. Babies I assume are his nieces and nephews.

Then I see them. On top of some books he has laying on their sides are two frames. The first is a picture of us when we were eight. It was after a soccer game and we're both covered in mud. We have our arms tossed over each other's shoulders. I remember his dad taking this picture. Our team lost the tournament that night, but we didn't care enough to be upset. We had both played our best and that was all that mattered to us and to his parents.

The second picture is when we turned sixteen. We celebrated our birthdays together that year. I have my arm draped around his shoulder. West's head is thrown back in laughter at something I've said and I'm looking at him with mischief. That West could so easily dismiss this sits heavy in my chest. Strike that, it pisses me off.

Kinks watches me get ready and I give him a little rub under his chin before leaving to meet Elise. I need to remember to ask West where he keeps his food and water.

It's still early when my taxi pulls up at Ten Thirty Eight, but already there is a line forming behind a rope that blocks off the front door. I give my name and am granted entrance, no problem. I have no idea if it is because of Elise or West. Either way, I'm shown to an area with four club chairs around a low circular table. I'm the first to arrive, so I take the seat with my back to the wall. Old habits never die.

It's a Saturday night, and the place is hopping. A waitress greets me and I order a drink for me and Elise, who walks up as the waitress leaves.

"You look beautiful." I kiss her cheek, giving a nod to the security I have tailing her. "Have you talked to Reid or Ryan?"

"Nope." She takes a seat next to me. The tone of her response lets me know she's not interested in this line of questioning, so I change the subject.

"I never got the dossier on the people we are meeting tonight?"

"I know. I got busy and didn't email it."

"You know it makes my job easier if I know who we are meeting."

"We talked this morning. You know who and why."

"But without the background check I don't know exactly what we are walking into. I'm not as prepared as I need to be."

"We're just meeting to consult. We aren't going to work this case."

"Unless we can talk you into it." Two men come to stand beside Elise. We stand to greet our guests. I have to resist the urge to move myself in front of Elise. If it weren't for the fact that I respect the hell out of this woman or that she'd cut my balls off, I would. I learned the hard way not to put Elise in a position where it looks like she needs protecting. She needs her clients to see her as the answer to their problems. A woman can't do that standing behind a man. Beside one, possibly.

"This is my associate Blake Thomas," Elise says, waving an elegant hand my way. "Blake, this is Walt and Finn Nelson of Nelson Financial in London."

"Nice to meet you. You're brothers, right? Seems like I remember reading something about the origin of your names in an article."

"Ah, yes," Finn says. "Our mother named Walt after her favorite poet and I was named after her favorite childhood book."

A new waitress brings our drinks and fuck me, this is the kind of girl I'd like to wrap around my cock. Her legs go on for days and I find myself imagining what it would feel like to slide my dick between her breasts. With a smile and the bat of an eyelash, I'm sporting a semi.

Elise gives me a look that says, "Stop eye-fucking the waitress." Not that it matters. As soon as she hears the English accents from our guests, she's a goner. It takes her longer than necessary to take Walt's order, but Finn curtly orders his gin and tonic with a lime, expertly brushing off her subtle advances.

"So, what can we help you gentlemen with?" Elise asks once the waitress has left.

"We hear you have some connections with the SEC," Walt says.

"I do." She offers nothing else. Elise never gives people more than they need until she has all the information.

"We've thwarted three hostile takeovers in as many months."

"I didn't realize you were vulnerable."

"We weren't. We've had a run on our stocks lately, but we still own the lions share, and we have a family share that we can tap into if necessary. Someone has created three dummy companies in an attempt to buy a majority of the available stocks. We understand they've been paying a pretty hefty price. More than it's admittedly worth."

"Sounds like vengeance," I say.

"Seems so," Finn says. "We need to know who it is and what their intentions are. We're hoping we can buy back some of the stocks, if we can prove the sellers felt coerced. We'd like to find the parent company and have the SEC level sanctions against them."

"Any ideas who it could be?" Elise asks.

"We looked into Reid Beckett," Walt says. Immediately, I shift my weight to the end of my chair.

"Easy there, bloke." Walt says correctly gauging my protective gesture. "We've come in peace. We know it wasn't Beckett Enterprises, and we know you're involved with Reid," he says to Elise.

"Well, then, you get a gold star for figuring out something that's common knowledge. Get to the point gentlemen."

"We meant no disrespect, but I'm sure Beckett crossed your mind, too. Our intention is to help eliminate who isn't involved, subsequently determining who is."

"Sorry, it's been crazy." West unwittingly interrupts the tense conversation. Elise stands, and the rest of us follow her lead.

"Finn Nelson." Finn extends his hand and a charming smile to West. Well, that explains the waitress.

"I didn't mean to interrupt. I just saw you two and wanted to say hello," West says to Elise and me.

"Please, join us," Finn offers.

"Thanks, but I'm working the bar tonight and it's a packed house."

"So, you're a bartender?" Finn says. "I guess the American movie portrayals are more accurate than one realizes."

West glances at me and I have to wonder if he's thinking the same thing I am. What is this fucker going on about? Looking back to our guests, he explains he's a teacher and this is a side job to buy supplies for his students.

"A rare breed."

"How's that?"

"Cute altruist. You're a rare breed."

West smiles wide enough that his dimple makes an appearance. Are you kidding me? His long lost best friend can't get him to crack a smile, but this fucker practically breaks his face for the first asshole with an accent who comes along.

Jealous, party of one.

And why am I even looking at his dimple. And why do I care he's getting hit on? Well, if I can't have pussy, he damn sure can't have dick. And if he does have dick, it's not going to be Finn's.And...and...

And if I don't shut this shit down, I'm going to say something out loud that I'll regret.

"Let me introduce you," I say, stepping between the two of them. "This is West. My boyfriend."

West

"I would offer my sincerest apologies, but the way you were eye-fucking the waitress a few moments ago, I wouldn't have guessed," Finn says, shoving his hands into his pockets. He oozes sex appeal. His lips are the perfect shade of pink and they'd look delicious sliding over my cock. His suit is practically painted on, and he's rocking a serious watch. Something I've always loved on a man.

Despite the need to shift my tray to hide my obvious appreciation, I know this is not a fight Finn will win. This may be a fake relationship, but Blake is never going to be out-pissed.

"It was nice meeting you both." I shake Walt's hand and, yeah, I admit it, I leave my hand in Finn's a moment longer than necessary. I leave Blake with a look that says, "This isn't over, shithead."

"What the hell was that?" Bree asks when I get back to the bar.

"When did you get here?" I mix a Manhattan and place it in front of her.

"Oh, about the time Thor and Captain America decided

to make you their trophy."

"Saw that, did ya?" I smile at her as I mix the next drink. "That man is…"

"Fine? Hot? Yummy?"

"Yes. All those work."

"I don't know how you can sleep next to him every night and not jump him." Bree's comment causes me to over-aerate the drink I'm mixing.

"Keep up Bree. Thor is the British Bombshell."

"I know. Captain America can't be British."

"I'm not sleeping next to Thor. At least not yet," I wink. "Speaking of bombshells, you look hot tonight."

"Don't change the subject." She attempts to chastise me.

"I will if it's ridiculous."

"Why is it ridiculous?"

"Because Blake is not gay," I admit. "He's just looking for a fight. Wants to be in charge."

"Why lie to me?"

"It's a long story and you can't say anything to anyone. It has to do with figuring out what is going on at the community center. I was going to tell you," I add in response to her disgruntled look.

"You know Captain America wins."

"Bree."

"I'm just saying. Thor tries to put his hammer in your ass and Captain America will start Civil War 2.0."

"Bree, he's not gay. He's just mad that he can't get any so he doesn't want me getting any."

She throws the rest of her drink back before she stands. "Just be careful. You've been in love with that man since you were six. I don't want to see you hurt."

"You can't really love something that can't love you back."

"I love these shoes, but they can't love me back. So, yes, I think it's even truer if a real person is involved."

"You just compared my love life to shoes," I call out to her as she heads to the restroom.

It's a busy night and the bar is four deep for the next two hours. Some guy has been chatting up Bree for the last hour, and I have a feeling she won't be going home alone tonight.

"Connors, why don't we switch for a minute? Stretch your legs and work the floor."

"Gladly." I clear the screen of drinks I've made and let my co-worker take the next orders.

"West Connors." I offer a hand to the guy hitting on Bree. He has to remove his from her thigh to accept it.

"Are you together?" At least he has the decency to look apologetic.

"Nope, I'm just the best friend. Don't give me a reason to be your worst enemy," I threaten.

"We're going to fuck tonight, West. Not buy a house and a golden retriever."

Shaking my head at Bree, I turn toward the breakroom. As I punch in my code, a warm, hard body leans into me. His lips brush against my ear.

"When a man looks surprised he's in a relationship, I don't feel ashamed about pursuing him." Finn's strong hand skims my side before sliding into my front pocket as deep as it'll go. "Call me." With a squeeze to the crevice between my hip and thigh, he pulls his hand out of my pocket and leaves.

It's three in the morning when I finally make it home. A soft light is streaming in from the surrounding buildings. I turn off the TV and stand over a sleeping Blake. He's sitting in the leather chair with his legs propped up on the ottoman that doubles as a coffee table. His head is leaned back and I want to run my fingers through the stubble along his jaw.

I have to admit I'm surprised he's here. After his display tonight, I really expected him to be inside a hostess by the end of the evening.

I nudge him awake. "Bed."

He runs a hand down his face. "I was waiting up for you."

"While you slept?"

"I didn't say I was successful. What time is it?"

"A little after three."

"Where have you been? You got off at two."

"No, the bar closes at two."

"Were you with Finn? You two looked pretty cozy in the hall." I can't see his eyes, but I can hear a snit in his voice. How did he know about that?

"Are you high?"

"No. Do I have to be high to not want you out there dickin' around while you are supposed to be in a relationship with me?"

"No. But you would need to be gay."

"I need to be gay because I don't want you fucking Finn Nelson?"

"Yes."

"Then I guess I'm gay, 'cause I don't want you fucking Finn Nelson."

"Really?"

"Yep."

"I see, 'cause I think this is about you not wanting to be challenged?"

"You challenge me all the time."

"I should, I'm your friend."

"You sure about that? You dismissed our friendship rather easily earlier today."

I'm tempted to turn on the lamp so I can see his face, because his words aren't giving anything away. I think I detect something in his voice. Hurt?

"Seriously, are you high?"

"Fuck you, West."

"Fuck me? You'd have to be gay for that, too."

The sound he emits is a cross between a growl and a grumble. "Until we're done, Finn Nelson isn't on your radar."

"Was that meant as a question? Because I know you aren't telling me what to do."

"Telling, dictating, insisting, enforcing. Whatever the fuck you want to call it, Finn Nelson is a no."

This fucker has tried the last of my good graces today. I straddle his legs suspended between the chair and the ottoman and place my hands against the cool leather on the arms of the chair.

"I'm only going to say this once. You don't get a say in my life, Blake. You lost that right at sixteen."

"Fuck me. You don't let anything go do you?"

"Fuck you? Fuck you?" I say again when he doesn't respond. "Is that what this is about?" I slide a knee between his thigh and the side of the chair, repeating the move on the other side of him. Straddled over his lap, I lean forward and skim my lips over the abrasive hard line that forms his jaw until my lips graze his earlobe.

"You want to be fucked alright, just not by me." I bite his earlobe. "But you know who does want to fuck me? Finn Nelson."

I push myself off of him and look down at the man in my chair. "Fake relationship or not, don't tell me what to do again."

I've just made it to the bedroom door when my hips are pinned against the wall, my arms raised above my head. Blake has both of my wrist pinned. I put my forehead against the wall and attempt to push backward, but he's an immovable force.

Shifting my wrists into one hand, he brings the other down to my chin and tugs until my cheek is against the plaster.

"You think if you say the word 'gay' enough, I'll react? Fine. You might have easily dismissed our friendship today, but I call bullshit. You know it and I know it." He starts to pull away but leans back in. "And don't insult me by acting like I give two fucks that your gay. I've got a job to do and you signed on for this." He runs his lips along my jawline and bites my earlobe in an attempt to regain the power I took from him moments ago. "Until that's done, this," he finds my dick and gives it a squeeze, "stays put."

Blake

It wasn't my intention to grab his dick. It really wasn't. I just wanted to prove a point. I don't know what I was expecting, but it wasn't what I got. He was hard. Like hammer-nails-into-a-two-by-four hard. Before I even realized it, I gave him a squeeze. Just enough to remind him who was in the room with him.

Me. Not Finn. And all I could think was, "Damn, someone sure has grown up over the last ten years."

Skeezy, Blake.

Jesus Christ, what is wrong with me? Before I could stop myself, I was telling Finn that West was my boyfriend. It was surreal, like watching the scene from above and wondering who I was. But his solicitation of my best friend was so blatant that it triggered something in me—something like possessiveness. What's more is that West was into him. I just got him back, and I'll be damned if some dude walks in and takes him away. Not when I thought we had at least six weeks to be together again. Forced as it may be, it's hopefully enough time for him to forgive me.

Being away from West the last ten years has been like walking around with my arm cut off. Being in the same room as him and still feeling like I might as well be on the other side of the world, is torture.

I make a living preparing for the unexpected. But this kind of unexpected is just…unexpected.

I can't deny I felt something just now. He was hard and it turned me on. Scratch that, it turned me *the fuck* on.

Unexpected.

I've never been attracted to a man before. So am I attracted to West? To men? Does that make me gay?

Unexpected.

I'm hard.

Completely unexpected.

When I close my eyes, and will the hardness away, I only see West.

West is in the bathroom with the door closed. I'm sure he's angry that I manhandled him, about what I said. But I also know for a fact that he's also turned on.

His bedroom is a collection of blues, woods, and metals that play off the brick wall behind his bed. West likes light. He is light, I think to myself. But it's already four in the morning and I'm exhausted. I slide the bedroom door closed and hit the button closing the shades. I would not be happy being woken up in two hours by the sun.

I'm in bed by the time the shower cuts off. West stumbles through the dark room before the covers lift and the mattress sinks on his side.

"What was that Blake?" He cuts through the silence after several minutes. When I don't answer right away, he turns on his side, facing me. And waits.

There's just enough light to see his features. There's no

anger. No judgement. Just West waiting for me to talk. Like when we were kids.

"I…fuck it." I run my hand over my face before turning to face him. "I don't want to share you. I just got our friendship back. I guess I just thought since we're both stuck in this situation for the next several weeks, it would give me time to convince you to forgive me. I know it's selfish, but I didn't want you giving a part of yourself to someone else. Not right now."

"I forgive you, Blake."

"No, you don't. I know you want to, but you haven't yet."

"I'm trying to," he admits. "I understand you didn't have control over leaving. But that was eight years ago. Once you were free from that bullshit, you didn't even contact me."

"I thought you wanted—"

"To be left alone. I know. You've said that. I know it's irrational, but I just thought you knew me better than that."

"I know it's not an excuse, but that's the way those places work. They manipulate you until you don't even recognize what you know anymore."

"Tell me about it, then," he says curling his arms under his pillows.

"You don't need that shit in your head."

"I am so sick of the way you see me, I could vomit."

"The way I see you?"

"You think I'm weak and need protecting. You could never trust me with what was going on in your home or in your head."

"Not weak. Wholesome."

"You really didn't know me."

"You know what I mean. Untainted. You had a family that adored you, who would never want to see any harm come to you. I had an uncle who beat me and an aunt who let it happen. I wouldn't wish that on my worst enemy, much less my best friend. When I was with you, I just wanted what you had."

"If you had let me help you maybe you could have."

"I couldn't leave Nora."

"The aunt that let him beat you." His anger is comforting, but he just can't understand what it felt like. Nor would I ever want him to understand. Seeing the bruises and knowing the physical pain is bad enough. Showing him the real damage, the emotional abuse, I never want him to see that. No one should ever have to see that.

"I've learned to forgive her. She was doing the best she could."

"Doesn't excuse it." I don't blame Aunt Nora that way, but something about the anger in his voice, to have someone give a damn with such fierceness, touches something in me.

"I'm not, but the fact is I have forgiven her. It cost me thousands of dollars to say that, but it's true."

"And him?"

"I'm not sure there's enough money in the world."

"How long have you been in New York?"

"Only a week before we saw each other at dinner. I have a place in Chicago, but I'm gone more than I am there. I usually go where Elise goes, or I'm on a job that has me all over."

"How long have you been back in the states?"

"Four years."

"Before that?"

"I was in Delta. We weren't in one place. We went where they needed us. It would change on a dime."

"You don't want to talk about it." It's not a question but a statement, and yet another gentle reminder that he still knows me.

"No," I confirm.

"Will you one day?"

"Maybe."

"With me?"

"If we're still friends. Maybe. One day."

He lays back and crooks his arm above him. He doesn't like that response.

"I wasn't wholesome. Hell, you were with me for all the shit we pulled."

"And now that I know you were spankin' it to boy bands…"

He chuckles. "Yeah, well, it didn't seem fair to throw my hat into the pussy ring. You wouldn't have gotten laid until you were well into your thirties."

"I see. Doing a solid for all of mankind, huh."

"Something like that."

"Since we're on the subject of trusting each other, why didn't you tell me?"

It took him a long time to answer. I wasn't sure he was going to, but finally he says, "I wasn't sure what I was feeling. I had known for a while, I just wasn't sure how to come to terms with it."

"It wouldn't have mattered."

"I know this is going to be hard to understand, but me being gay wasn't about you."

"Asshole."

He laughs and I'm struck by how the sound of it lands on my heart. It's a familiar feeling. Growing up, West was always so carefree and easygoing. I never wanted to change that. I was afraid showing him how bad the world could be would taint the simple and easiness that was West. Hearing that same laughter now only proves that wasn't true.

"How did your family take it?"

"Like I asked for chocolate ice cream instead of vanilla. It was as simple as that."

"God, I love your parents."

"Blake?" he says softly.

"Yep?"

"I forgive you. I just need time to get used to it."

"To what?"

"To you being back. Being here. I went from thinking you were dead to sleeping next to you. Within the span of, like, twenty-four hours. I'm just suffering from a little whiplash. But I don't want you to go another day thinking I don't forgive you or that I'm not grateful you're okay."

This fucker, always with heart. Par for the course, West says exactly what I need to hear. Like he already knows.

I attempt to clear my throat of the lump that has formed. "Guess I'll grab some shut-eye."

"Better than grabbing my dick."

West

I'm in a motel room. The walls are muted and the bed has a dark purple polyester spread on it. I'm not sure where I am or why I am in this room, but I keep hitting the box on the nightstand, the one you put quarters in and makes the bed vibrate. Magic Fingers. Why won't this thing turn off?

My brain finally registers that I'm dreaming. There isn't a box on the nightstand, there is no Magic Fingers, so why is the bed still shaking. I sit up and try to pull myself out of the fog of sleep. I notice that I have one leg draped over Blake's calf. Blake is shaking so hard, it's vibrating the bed. Suddenly, he sits straight up, sucking in short hard breaths.

"You're okay." I place a hand to his chest and push him back towards the bed. His heart beats wildly under my palm, and he's dripping with sweat.

"He's here," he whispers, eyes wild.

"No one's here. Just us."

I have a true hatred for his uncle. How horrible it must have been for him to still have dreams this many years later. He's had these dreams every night since he moved in.

"West?" he says, still disoriented.

"You're okay. Go back to sleep."

"West?"

"I'm okay, too. Sleep." I wrap my hand around his bicep so he can feel my reassurance.

When his breathing evens out, I let myself go back to sleep.

"Let me." I swat Blake's hands away and make the loops to form his bow tie. He's wearing a navy blue Tom Ford tux that fits like Tom himself molded it to his body. If sex had a look it would be Blake Thomas.

Tonight is the Taylor Organization's annual event where they highlight their selected charities and introduce people to ways they can spend their money. Emme asked me to be there since the community center will be showcased, but I already had an ACT study session set up with the guys, so I told her I couldn't make it.

I pull the edges of the silk fabric and the tie takes shape. Leaning forward, I position my head into the crook of Blake's neck so I can look behind the knot to pinch the loop tighter. His aftershave tickles my senses and I have to hold back a moan. Somehow I manage to keep myself from running my lips along his jaw.

Jesus Christ, I have to pull it together.

"Something the matter?" The cocky son of a bitch asks with a raised brow, knowing damn good and well the effect he is having on me.

"Nope. Just making sure it's tight."

Blake is only a smidge taller than I am, so we stand eye-to-eye. When mine meet his, he smirks. "It's a tight fit alright," he winks.

He fucking winks.

Blake shifts slightly to my left to see his reflection in the mirror and lifts his chin, fingering his tie.

"How'd you learn to tie a bowtie? This is good."

"Life lesson #1032, courtesy of Mary Beth Connors."

"So, how do I look?" he asks, tugging the cuffs of his dress shirt so they peep out perfectly from his suit coat. Blake and I have been in a decent place the last couple of days. I'm learning to forgive and he's learning to let me.

"You'll do," I shrug.

"Thank you." He plants a chaste kiss on my cheek before whispering into my ear, "Don't wait up dear."

This can't be good, but I don't even hiccup at the feelings swimming inside me right now. There's a part of Blake back with me that I never thought I'd have. A new part. Like we're finally seeing each other the way we are now and not always hitting the same sixteen-year-old speedbump that we seem to hit so often lately. Cautiously, I know it's still out there, but for now I just want to enjoy the few moments when he was just my best friend who needed help with his bowtie.

Checking my watch, I start putting together some snacks for the boys and making some sandwiches. I know some of these kids go far longer between meals than I'd ever want them to. Bree enters with the kids as I'm making the last one.

"So, this is where the magic happens?"

"Marius," I warn.

"This is a nice place."

"Thank you."

"Dude, sit your ass down," Steven says.

"It's just not what I was expecting," Marius says, dropping to the floor. He's the only one of my students who hasn't been here before.

"Want Mr. Connors to gay it up for you?" Bree asks, handing out drinks.

"I'd have to renew my gay-dude card first," I tease, setting a large platter of sandwiches and chips on the ottoman. "Plates." I slap a hand away before grabbing plates and napkins.

"You seem pretty up-to-date on your gay-dude card," Marcus says, rubbing his hand before taking a plate.

"You don't have to be gay to take pride in your home."

"How's everyone doing without the gym being open?" Bree asks.

"It's hard. There's nothing to do to pass the time and some of the kids are getting restless," I reply.

"Well, I got permission for you guys to use St. Phillip's gym until the center is open again. Spread the word will you?"

"When's the last time anyone has seen Mickey?" I ask. "I've been calling him and he hasn't picked up. I haven't seen him in at least three weeks."

"His mama kicked him out. I think he's on the streets. Got caught up in smack," Marcus explains.

"Since when?" Bree's eyes shoot to mine.

"Don't know."

"Well, let's get started. If you see him, let me know. I want to get him some help." I try to ignore the sick feeling in my stomach. Mickey was always a good kid, heart as big as his ears. His mom worked hard to keep him off the streets. Of all my kids, he is not the one I expected to go down this road. "I'll give his mom a call in the morning."

We quiz and study for a little more than an hour when the door opens.

"It's the boyfriend. In a penguin suit," Myles says, shoveling popcorn in his mouth.

"What are you doing here?" I ask looking at my watch. I wasn't expecting him for a few more hours at least.

"I live here."

I make the mistake of looking up. He's loosened the tie I tied for him. Its hanging on each side of his collar and the top two buttons of his dress shirt are undone. His hands are in his pocket and he's leaning back on his heels. I have to remind myself to breathe.

"Smart-ass," I manage.

"Coach!" the boys yell.

"Emme went into labor. Reid fired Elise today. So, I called it a night. Sorry I forgot you were tutoring. I'll leave you to it."

"Wow. That's a lot of information."

"Come on, man. Hang with us."

"As painful as that sounds, Myles…"

"We'll be good. We swear."

"I'll be back in after I change." Blake looks to me to make sure it's okay before he slides the bedroom door closed.

Fifteen minutes later he's sitting cross-legged on the floor in his Army T-shirt and sweat shorts.

"I can't believe Boots is letting you pet him," Blake tells Steven. "That cat is conceited."

"It was my sister's cat before Coach took it in. He remembers me."

"Where's your sister now?"

"She's in school. Got a full ride to St. Louis University thanks to Coach and Miss Latham."

"You going to college?"

"If you quiz me enough I will." He drops a notebook in Blake's lap.

Two hours later the last question has been asked and answered and the kids head out. I watch Blake start the cleanup in the living room. I have to remind my heart this isn't what it thinks it is, but damn, watching him with my kids, loving them where they are… I feel in love with him even more tonight. I never imagined that was possible.

I make myself get a grip and make my way to the kitchen to clean up the bowls I left there earlier.

He hands me the last of the dishes to rinse and put in the dishwasher. I hear the locks on the door and the clicks of the lights as Blake makes his way around the room.

"I keep meaning to ask you, where do you keep Kinks's food?"

"There's a little alcove under the entry table. I think they used it for wood. I put a cat door on it. His litter box, food, and water are in there. I have dispensing bowls, so I only have to feed him once a month. When the jug of water runs out, an alarm will beep."

"Fancy," he mumbles, walking over to inspect it.

"What's this?" There's a cool sharpness to his voice.

I look over my shoulder to see what he's pointing to, only he isn't pointing. He's holding a card. The white embossed card with Finn Nelson's personal cellphone on it. I had dropped it in the bowl on the entryway table with the keys.

"The card Finn gave me Saturday night," I answer, turning back to the sink.

"I see that. What I mean is, why do you have it?"

"I told you, he gave it to me. You were there."

"Why did you keep it?" he says with increasing impatience.

"Blake, I told you. I won't call him while you are working the case, but he's good-looking. He's nice. He's a philanthropist. Why wouldn't I give him a chance if he's still available then?"

"How do you know he's a philanthropist? Did you look him up?" Blake asks, coming up behind me.

"So what if I did?" I shrug, wringing out the dishcloth before turning to face him.

"I thought I told you—"

"And I know I told you. This isn't your decision. You don't get a say in this."

Blake plants a hand on each side of me, gripping the counter. "That's where you're wrong." He all but presses his body against mine.

"Stop fucking with me, Blake."

"You sure about that? He looks down, and the sweats I have on ensure there is no hiding the hard-on I'm brandishing. "Because I think your body wants me to fuck with you."

"Blake."

"Get rid of the card."

"No."

"Yes."

"You're not even gay."

"So. Is there a rule that says I have to be?"

"I'm pretty sure there is."

"Well, I've never been one to play by the rules." He shifts his weight, pushing his pelvis into mine. I let go of a soft gasp when his cock inadvertently rubs against mine. He's hard.

"Blake, this is my life. I'm not someone you pick up and fuck in a bathroom. And the only reason we're having this conversation is because I'm caught in a pissing match."

"Get. Rid. Of the card," he mandates again with more force.

"No. You're really starting to piss me off." I really have no idea if I said that out loud or not. All I know is his lips are wrapped around mine in a rough battle to gain entrance.

Mine part in a feeble attempt to tell him to stop, but he takes the opportunity to slide his tongue against mine. And yeah, there's no way I am strong enough to resist this. A sound I didn't know existed within me echoes off the walls. He has one hand pushed through my hair, maneuvering my lips where he wants them, while the other hand is splayed across my jaw and neck.

He tastes buttery from the popcorn he ate earlier. His lips brush mine over and over and an imbedded desire runs through me. I lower my hands to his ass and pull him to me, causing our cocks to rub together again.

It feels fucking fantastic.

I say his name on a hiss and everything stops. As if someone turned off running water. The only thing left is heavy breathing and heart pounding.

"Fuck." Blake's eyes meet mine. I'm immediately filled with dread, because his are filled with regret.

I overslept. Even though the clock told me it was seven in the morning, I didn't believe it and rolled back over, ignoring the sliver of daylight creeping under the door.

Blake likes to sleep like he's in a cave and it's throwing off my natural alarm clock. Thankfully, this is the first day of second summer school, so I don't have to teach. I'm gloriously off the next eight weeks.

Blake grabbed his keys after the kiss last night and was gone before I could say three words. I texted him to point out that once again, he left. But I never got a response. Not that I expected one.

I figure he's having one hell of a conversation with himself over this. Kissed a man out of, what, boredom? Horniness? Curiosity? I can work with curiosity.

When I woke up at seven, he pretended to be asleep next to me. When I woke up at nine, he was gone. I assume to the office. There was no more dick grabbing, or kisses that curled my toes last night.

Sigh. I absolutely know it's a bad idea, but not only have I not been able to think of much else since, I've been rock hard remembering what it was like to have his tongue in my mouth and his dick against mine. The feel of his hands on me. The scratch of my rough cheek against his soft one.

Overall, the one thing that has my hand on my dick, jacking it in long, unhurried strokes, is that he was hard, too. There was no mistaking Blake was as into that kiss as I was.

I let myself linger here. If I think about the reality of what happened, I won't get off, and right now, I really need to get off.

The smells, sounds, and tastes of last night fill my senses while my hand works my dick over, and as I shout Blake's name, my body convulses and come spills all over my hand.

Running my clean hand through my hair, my breathing finally begins to recover. There really is something wrong with me, I think, on my way to the shower. I'm still hard, even though I came like a freight train not even ten minutes ago.

Yes, I have always been in love with Blake. It was just different kinds of love that evolved as we got older and I came to understand who I was. I realized I might be gay when we first went skinny dipping in seventh grade with the girls in our class. It didn't faze me to see what the girls had, I was more interested in the boys jumping in the pond. This indifference to the opposite sex was mistaken for confidence. That bought me a few years, until I felt comfortable enough to come out the month after Blake had disappeared. I had lost all desire to pretend anymore. I was heartbroken. I had lost my best friend.

This leads me back to the question at hand, why am I still hard? Blake is straight. There is nothing that can come of this. There is nothing that will change that.

I cut off the water and dry off before stepping out of the shower. I come to the conclusion I have to fix this. I can't let Blake ignore what happened.

Blake

"We need to talk."

It's the first thing West says when I fly through the door. He follows me into the closet where I pull an aluminum suitcase off the top shelf. I'm not surprised he wants to talk, but I can't. Not now anyways.

"It'll have to wait," I tell him, throwing the case on the bed before placing my thumb to the thumbprint reader. The case unlocks, and when I open it, West goes from determined to concerned.

"What's going on?"

"I don't have time to talk." I strap a leather holster around me and secure my 9mm in the holder. I check the battery on a burner phone and program it.

"Thomas." I all but shout into my cell when it rings. I place it on speaker so I can continue prepping a to-go bag.

"We located both men."

"Send me their locations. I want someone on them until I say otherwise. Where's Elise?"

"She spoke with Emme Taylor. She is on her way to the

Taylor's beach house in the Hamptons."

"Stay with her. My guess is Taylor has his own security there. If they do, fine. If not, I want someone with her at all times."

I disconnect the call and before West can say anything there's a knock at the door.

"Did you buzz someone up?" I ask.

He shakes his head and I cut off his path to the door. I glance through the peephole and release a sigh of relief when I see the man standing on the other side of the door.

"Mr. Donovan, please come in. I was just headed your way."

"I assumed as much Blake. I'm on my way to see an old friend and wanted to stop by. Elise gave me the address. I hope you don't mind."

"This is West Connors. West, this is Miller Donovan, Elise's father."

"Nice to meet you." He nods to West before focusing back on me. Blake, I'm handling this. You are not to touch these men in any way."

"Sir, I appreciate—"

"No, you don't. You'll not touch these men."

This is Elise's doing. "I can't sit around and do nothing."

"That's exactly what you will do. Elise wants time to herself. No matter how much we want to be with her, you and I both are going to give her time to herself."

"I can work with giving her time. What I can't work with is those men walking around like they own the right to put their hands on her."

He raises his palm, halting me. "I need you to stop talking. I just got my blood pressure back to normal. When I saw the handprint on her face..." he trails off, but the look that remains is lethal.

"I didn't realize her birth father was in the picture?"

"He wasn't. And he won't be again. By this time next week, he'll be bankrupt, disbarred, and arrested for embezzlement. That's a fate far worse than what you could ever do to him."

"I don't know that I agree. I plan to take the only thing that matters to him: his life."

West gives a nervous laugh, but it stops when he realizes I'm not joking.

"Blake," he says softly.

"Son." Miller steps up and puts a hand on my shoulder. "I'm grateful for all the times you've protected my little girl, but this is her battle not yours. This is for her and Reid to figure out. She has her emergency phone with her. Reach out to her in a couple of days."

A long minute passes before I finally answer out of respect. "Yes, sir."

"I need your word, Blake."

"Please don't make me give it to you. I don't think I'll be able to keep it."

"Son, vengeance is no longer your path. Elise would be devastated if you backslid because of this. You have my word. Neither of these men will ever bring any harm to Elise again. Ever."

I nod my head and accept his terms.

"I'm afraid I'm going to need you to say it out loud, or I'm going to have to take your guns."

"You have my word. I won't kill them."

"Or bring them harm in any way. You won't interfere with my plans."

"I won't kill them, bring them harm, or interfere with your plans."

"Good. You're a good man, Blake."

"Thank you, sir." Elise's father knows everything about me. His approval of me as a person is deeply satisfying, especially in a time like this where I know he is concerned I won't deliver on my promise.

"Now that that is settled," he clasps me on the shoulder. "You can't tell Reid or anyone on the team. You know they will go straight to Elise and, honestly, she needs time. I'm not even telling our family where she is."

"What about Theo?"

"No one."

"Yes, sir." I can't help but think of the shit storm that is about to hit.

"You handle the team, I'll handle everything else. Nice to meet you, young man." He shakes West's hand. "You're a lucky fellow."

With another nod of the head, he leaves. What does he mean by "lucky fellow"?

"Are you okay?" West asks.

"I don't have a choice. I guess I have to be. Giving up control is like cutting off my arm."

"Why don't we get some lunch and you can talk about what happened," West offers softly.

"That sounds—hold that thought." I dig my phone out of my pocket and answer it. "Mr. Speaker…No, sir. Elise is unavailable. What can I do for you?"

I listen as he tells me the case Elise and I thought we had wrapped in a pretty bow for him this weekend is now unraveling.

"I'm sure he's bluffing. I'll take care of it…I don't want you doing anything. You go about your day like you normally would. I don't want you to acknowledge the letter. I'm in New

York, I'll charter a flight. I can be there in ninety minutes."

I decline his offer to have someone waiting for me. If this is going off the rails, I can maneuver quicker on my own. I hang up and when my head falls back in frustration, West steps in front of me and pulls down on my shirt between the two bottom buttons.

"Are you sure you're okay to go somewhere?"

"I'm fine. I'm sorry, but I have to go. We'll talk when I get back, I promise." It's the best I can do right now.

"What time will that be?"

"I don't know. I hope tonight."

"I'll wait up."

I nod and a sudden desire to lean in and kiss him sears through me. I shake it off and head to the room to grab my bag. I buckle my back-up pistol around my ankle and when I stand up, I'm met with a frown on West's face.

"It'll be fine," I assure him.

"It's never fine if you need to carry a weapon. Much less more than one."

"Better to be prepared than have regrets."

He's propped against the doorway between the bedroom and the living room. His legs are crossed at the ankles and his thumbs rest in his back pockets. His jeans look like they are a hundred years old. Worn, soft, relaxed.

"I'll let you know something as soon as I can," I offer and start towards the door, but something stops me. I turn back to him. I mimic his earlier move and grab the front of his shirt near the bottom hem.

I lean toward him. "I want to kiss you."

"You're going to miss your flight."

"It's chartered. Trust me when I tell you they aren't going to leave without me."

"I think we need to talk about a few things."

"Before I kiss you?"

"Before you kiss me."

"Alright then." I release his shirt.

Ah, screw it.

My mouth takes his before he has the chance to protest. His lips part for mine and my tongue slides into the wet heat it's craved since last night. He's hands find my waist and when I attempt to deepen the kiss, they move from my torso to grab my hair and pull my head back. West shifts his stance and, just like that, he's taken control. I give it to him. Willingly.

By the time he pulls away, I'd lay in front of a moving train if he asked me to.

"You need to go. This won't happen again," he says with one last press of his lips against mine.

"You sure about that?"

"I'm sure."

I can tell he wants to say more, I can almost read them within him, but he doesn't. He holds them close to the vest. That's probably a good thing because I should have left already.

"Go," he says, with a touch of sadness.

I'm horny for another man. Five words I never imagined I would say. In that order.

It's been four days since I left West standing there in our apartment when I had to catch—Wait. *Our* apartment?

Jesus, I even have us playing house.

Now I'm in D.C. trying to minimize the fallout from a case Elise and I thought we had so perfectly wrapped up.

D.C.…where some of the worst kinds of humanity exists. What would make someone want to get into politics, I'll never know. I've seen enough corruption, hatred, and evil to last me a lifetime.

It's always a difficult case when political careers are involved, but this one was especially volatile. Power is the beast that drives people to do things I doubt they ever imagined they would do. And on some level, when I see people falling victim to that power, part of me thinks, well, you knew what you were signing up for. What I can't rationalize is how people can make a meal out of someone's family for their own advancement. Which was the case with the Speaker. They were going after his daughter, who had had an abortion. If he hadn't reached out to Elise, that fifteen-year-old girl would have found herself either the poster child for the pro-choicers or a symbol of the senator's depravity from the right. Neither of which a fifteen-year-old should be in the middle of. No matter who her father is. By the time I finished with those fuckers, they regretted ever even thinking the exploitation of a minor was an option. But apparently some of our fixes didn't quite take. Since I couldn't do what I wanted to do and handle Elise's situation, I channeled all that frustration into managing the Speaker's crisis.

I slide my key card into my hotel door and am grateful for the bed that awaits me. The only thing that would make it better is to have West in it. And not because I'm horny. It's only been a week since he's been back in my life, but for the first time since I was sixteen, my life feels like it has balance.

I had no idea that West was working through his sexuality when we were kids. We shared a bed almost every night for ten years and there was never even an inkling of something sexual. It was just like two best friends camping every night. Staying up until the light crept in, even after his dad had threatened us within an inch of our lives if we didn't go to sleep. There were nights where we didn't speak a word, nights where we got on each other's nerves, like brothers do.

No matter what kind of night it was, it was always safe. I knew no matter what happened before I went to sleep, West would be there when I woke up. Nothing was going to change that. Of course, my sixteen-year-old self didn't have this type of deep reflection. I spent a lot of time grumbling about sharing a bed that was too small and trying to get West to sleep in a vertical position.

Leaving a trail of clothes, I undress on my path to the bed. I'm exhausted. I don't think I've slept more than an hour or two a night since I got here.

I texted West when I first arrived to let him know I made it and I have made sure to send a text each day. Sliding under the covers I dial his number. He answers on the first ring. The first fucking ring. My heart shimmies.

"Hey." His sleepy voice crawls through the phone and lands on my dick.

"Hey," I whisper back. "Sorry to wake you."

"Don't be. I've been waiting to hear from you. Everything okay?"

"It is now. I'm sorry I haven't called. It's been full force since I stepped off the plane."

"Yeah, I figured."

"I thought you'd be pissed."

"I mean, you said you would call as soon as you could. You're calling now. I figured things have been crazy. You know, two-guns crazy."

Something about his understanding makes me feel...I don't know, safe again, I guess.

"I'll be home in a bit. I don't like to wake pilots up at

three in the morning or I would be on my way there now."

"I think I prefer that, too. I'd rather your pilot be well rested."

"Aww. You care."

"Blake?"

"Yep."

"Shut the fuck up."

"You miss me?" I say this to irritate him more, but as always West has to throw me off balance with his honesty.

"Every minute." When I can't think of a way to respond, he continues. "How does that happen? A week ago, I had my shit together. Now I don't know if I'm coming or going."

"Say what you mean." I tease.

"Well, I've had some time to think about it these last four days. That happens when someone kisses you like they were starving, then sends a one sentence text for the next four days."

"You said you understood."

"I did. Doesn't mean I liked it."

"What did you want me to text you?"

"I don't know…"

"West."

"What?"

"Check your text messages." I send him a message that just says,

Hi

"That's deep. Exactly what I needed to hear," he says, but I'm only half listening to him because I'm pushing send on my next text.

"West."

"Blake." The way he says my name makes my dick twitch.

"Check your messages."

I hear a light chuckle through the phone when he reads, my dick misses you

"Is that more along the lines of what you were looking for?" I ask.

"I had no preconceived notion of what the communication should have been. I was just hoping for some."

"Communicate. You have my full attention."

"Tell me about your day. Is the case totally wrapped?"

"Let's talk about your day. I don't want to think about mine. What did you do?"

West takes me through his day. He hung out with Bree and went to his favorite used book store before checking out a new restaurant. His voice is still deep and raspy from sleep. Sexy. He tells me Kinks has been walking around looking for me, and I hear a rustling of the sheets as he sinks further into his bed. I imagine the way the sheets outline his body, and involuntarily my hand slides into my underwear.

"Blake, what are you doing?" It's clear he already knows. The heat in his voice gives him away.

"West."

"Blake."

"Check your messages." I push send on a close-up of the tip of my dick pushing through my fist.

"Jesus Christ, Blake. What are we doing here?"

"Nope. No questions. This is my call." I tug gently on my balls, letting out a slow moan. "Put your phone on speaker and set it on your chest so you can use both hands." When I'm met with silence, I say with a little more force, "West, I expect a response."

"Stop bothering me." His voice is raspy.

"West?"

"Yes."

"Stop."

"What?"

"Stop. Grab the bottle out of your nightstand."

"How'd you know about—"

"Open the cap and pour some in your palm, but don't warm it up." I hear the click of the top being closed. "Now, run the cool liquid over your cock. I've been so fucking hard since I boarded the plane. Four days, I've been walking around trying to close this case so I could call to tell you."

"To tell me what?"

"That I'm so fucking hard for you, I'm dripping."

"God, Blake."

"West?"

"Yes?"

"Stop."

"*What?*" he breathes.

"Stop. I don't want you coming yet. I know you. You're about to blow, aren't you?"

"Blake, finish or listen to me as I come all over this bed."

"Run your hands over your balls and pull them towards you."

"Blake." He moans my name and something in me finally clicks. I'm having phone sex with a man. With West. Even though until a week ago I had never had a sexual thought about him, I can read him through the phone like I was next to him. He's close.

"Fuck, Blake, come on."

"Trust me." My hand speeds up at the thought of him coming on my command.

"Tell me," West begs. But before I can utter a word, he erupts in a cry so connected with my cock that it's like waking a sleeping beast. My back arches off the bed as my come hits my chest and shoulder. Falling back on the bed, I try to bring my breathing under control. "Holy shit."

West moans his agreement.

"What are you doing?" I ask.

"Licking the come off my fingers. Imagining it's yours."

West

I have no self-control. I'm just lying here wondering what the hell just happened.

"See," he says brightly. "Just like when we were kids."

"How is this like when we were kids?"

"Everyone always thinks you're the good one. But I always knew better."

"Because you knew the real me."

Silence. I almost push him into saying something, but I want him to have the time he needs.

"I'll text you when I know what time my flight is."

"Be safe."

There's another moment of silence before he clears his throat and ends the call. I hug the pillow Blake uses and inhale deeply, letting his scent swim through me.

I find it almost impossible to sleep after our phone call, so when dawn gives me an acceptable reason to finally get out of bed, I feel like a skier who's flying downhill at an uncontrollable speed and I don't know how to stop. This has disaster written all over it. No way I survive this unscathed.

I spend the day picking at the house, arranging and re-arranging, cleaning and re-cleaning, trying to find some way to dispel this nervous energy. Dinner is a complicated lamb dish that takes a couple of hours to prepare. I figure Blake and I can talk over dinner, get some things figured out. I add the last ingredient to the marinade and put the meat in the fridge when my phone beeps. I wash my hands and swipe the screen to unlock.

Blake: Delayed… home tomorrow

I look at the screen and wait for the next message. The one with an explanation. An apology. Something. But it never comes. What does come is a call from Beverly.

"Hello, Pumpkin," I smile.

"How's the milk to my cookies?"

"Good. Enjoying my eight weeks."

"Don't rub it in."

"My apologies. Where's my manners?"

"Yes, well, don't let it happen again."

"Yes ma'am. What can I do for you today?"

"Principal Riley wants to know if you'll be coming in to disperse the supplies you had delivered."

"I didn't have any supplies delivered. Must be someone else."

"Nope. Your name is sharpied all over these boxes. I had them put in your room."

"Thanks. I'll come by and take a look." Supplies? Who would have sent me supplies?

"All right, dumplin'. See you soon."

"Thanks, Beverly."

"Hello?" I switch over to answer the incoming FaceTime.

"West!" Bree looks like a kid who's been given the Christmas of a lifetime. She turns the camera to my classroom and it's filled with boxes. There must be a hundred of them. There are already some opened and Bree is opening another one.

"They're filled with books and school supplies. There's a projector, and the packing list says there's a few dozen laptops."

"Is Oprah doing a special no one told us about?"

"No." The camera spins back around to her pretty face. "This gift came from Thor."

"Who?"

"Thor. The British bombshell. Maybe Thor does beat Captain America." Her eyes are dreamy. The way to Bree's heart is through her students.

"How do you know these are from Finn?"

She shows me the print on the packing list. The sender is Nelson Financial of London.

"I'll send you a picture of the packing list so you can see everything you got. I have the electronics being locked up. Tell him I said thank you! We have books!" She squeals and disconnects the call.

A minute later her text arrives, actually three texts, because, holy shit, it's a three-page packing list. Everything from pencils to backpacks to projectors to laptops. This is the holy grail for a public school in the projects.

When the shock wears off, I find the crumpled card Blake threw on the counter before he left for D.C.

"Finn Nelson's office, this is Samantha."

"I'm sorry. I was trying to reach Finn. I thought this was his cell number."

"Yes, it is. He's in a meeting. I'm his assistant Samantha. May I help you?"

"Um, sure. Could you ask him to call West when he has a moment? My number—"

"Yes, Mr. Connors, I have your number. I'm afraid he's in back-to-back meetings, but he anticipated your call. He asks that you meet him for lunch at one o'clock at the King Cole Bar in the St. Regis." When I don't respond, she presses for an answer. "May I confirm you'll be there?"

"I'm not sure. I'll do my best. Thank you." I disconnect the call.

Kinks walks across the back of the couch in judgmental haughtiness and evident disapproval. "Don't look at me like that," I snap at him.

Three hours and I admit two outfits later, I'm being greeted by a host at King Cole Bar, who freakishly knows my name.

"Mr. Connors."

I check behind me to verify he is truly speaking to me.

"Mr. Nelson is waiting for you." He shows me to a table in the corner. Finn stands when he sees me.

"I was hoping you'd make it." He pulls out the chair next to him and waits for me to sit. I do finally.

"May I get you a drink Mr. Connors?"

"I'll have what he's having."

"Yes, sir." The waiter leaves, but before I can say anything to Finn the chef greets us and offers to make anything we have a taste for. On the menu or off.

"Thank you, Phillipe," Finn nods. "I'll have the strip. Medium."

"And I'll have the same. Thank you."

"I'd ask if you were always this easy and agreeable, but I already know the answer." Finn gives me a look that feels like a long sip of a warm drink on a cold day.

"I have to admit I'm a little out of my league when a host

I've never met knows my name."

"This is Table 55."

What is it about British accents? I could listen to him talk all day. He could read me the obituaries and I'd be slightly turned on.

"Which means?"

"It's $2500 just to reserve the table. They make a point to know who's going to be served."

"That explains the chef."

"Another perk." Finn smiles, crosses a lean leg over the other, and leans against his chair. It's a relaxed pose, but there is no mistaking that he is in complete control.

"You don't have to spend money to impress me."

"No, I don't. It wouldn't work anyway. You aren't the kind of man impressed by a table. It is however a quiet, secluded table, and it is more than worth the extra money to have the privacy and your undivided attention."

"Thank you." I take a sip of the drink placed in front of me. It's smooth. Expensive. "You always order a $3000 glass of whiskey?"

"Only when I have something to celebrate."

"Samantha said you were in a meeting. I take it things went well?"

"My meeting did go well, thank you, but that's not what I'm celebrating."

"What are you celebrating?"

"A boy I like finally said yes to lunch."

It's a line. I'm falling for it. I'm only human, so yeah. I like that. "And that's cause for celebration?"

"It is when that boy is West Connors."

Okay. I like that a lot. And he knows it.

"So. What made you finally say yes?"

"I wanted to thank you for your generous donation to my school. Someone with integrity might have refused the gift, but there's no way I would let pride get in the way of helping my students."

"That's nice to hear. Especially since I didn't send the supplies to get you to lunch."

"You sure about that?"

"Positive. Just as you don't want to be manipulated with gifts for your students, I don't want to be liked for being able to provide those gifts."

We pause while our food is delivered and Finn orders us each a water.

"I'm not sure if your—boyfriend—told you or not, but Walt and I are one of nine that sits on The Foundation's board."

I ignore the way he said boyfriend. "With the Taylor's?"

"Yes, among others. That's how I knew about your school and its needs."

"Well, it was very generous of you. Thank Walt for me, too, please. Some of those kids have never had a textbook, much less a new one that isn't ripped and missing pages."

"Like I said, you're welcome. You seem to really enjoy teaching."

"I do. I love these kids. I'm hoping some of them will be accepted into college or the Taylor's intern program."

"Yes, that's a great program. We have three interns in our office here that we will be sending to college and employing once their internship is completed this fall. Not sure how familiar you are with the program, but Emme created a screening process that has been spot on when it comes to matching the right intern for the right business."

"Hopefully some of my guys will match."

I take a sip of water and I notice that he's looking at my

Adam's apple.

"You know there are other perks to being on The Foundation's board."

"Really? Like what?" And now I'm the one watching his jaw as he finishes his bite of steak.

"Like knowing what projects we are involved with."

"Sounds like you guys are involved in ones that are really making a difference."

"I'd like to think we are, but I'm referring to the less than pleasant aspects of the projects. Like the fact that we have a community center that is missing a couple million. We've hired Elise Donovan to work the problem, and my understanding is she has her right-hand man playing house with a coach from that center." He studies me, expecting a response. When he doesn't get one, he smiles and continues with a more direct approach.

"So, not only did I register your surprise when—Brian, is it?"

"It's Blake and you know it."

He smirks. "Not only did I register your surprise when Blake announced you were dating, but I now know it's just for show."

"Blake and I have been best friends since we were six."

"That's endearing. But you were estranged, right? And he's not gay, is he?"

For the life of me I don't know why this question is so hard to answer. Blake isn't gay, but lately he's done some very gay things.

I decide to avoid the question. "So, how long are you in the states?"

"I have a place here. Walt and I bounce back and forth between here and London. I have to leave tomorrow, but I'll be back the first of next week. I'd like to take you out again."

"This is me meeting you to thank you for your generosity. This isn't a date."

"You sure about that?" He leans forward and lays his hand on my thigh.

I don't answer. And I don't move his hand.

"I like you. A lot."

"You don't know me."

"I know more than you realize. You don't get where I am without being able to read people and find ways to learn about them."

"Do tell?"

He gives my thigh a slight squeeze, and the heat from his palm moves up my leg. "I know you're an excellent teacher. You were awarded Teacher of the Year two years ago. You coach basketball. You tutor your students. Since you've started teaching your school's graduation rate has increased by 22%, which is nearly unheard of in that community. You come from a large family. You graduated from Columbia. You're just shy of finishing your doctorate. You're an all-around nice guy. Shall I go on?"

"Sounds like you read a report someone pulled together."

"Since you're still here, I'll let you in on something that wasn't on the report."

"What's that? The size of my dick?"

His good-natured laugh has the corner of my lips curling up. He stops laughing and stares at me. I'm just about to ask him if there is something on my face when he leans in.

"That dimple." He shakes his head as if to clear it. "What is not in that report is you are sexy as hell and I want to fuck you. And so there is no confusion, I *am* gay and this *can* go somewhere."

"Sounds like you only want a fuck buddy, so I'm not sure where you would see this going?"

He leans close enough to my ear he could trace it with his tongue.

"Make no mistake about it, I want to do dirty things to you. Very dirty." He leans back, removes his hand from my thigh and crosses his legs. His long fingers run down the front of his tie, smoothing it back into place. "I also want to get to know you. Date you. Spend time with you. I like you, West. Very much."

Our waiter brings us dessert I didn't know we ordered and a cup of coffee. He tells me about London and what his family is like. It's obvious he has a great amount of respect for his brother who I learn is guardian to his best friend's kids. All around he seems like a good guy and I'd be crazy not to spend time with him.

We stand to leave and he nods to a few tables that have business men. He buttons his suit coat and his hand rests on my lower back as he escorts me out of the bar.

"Thank you for lunch."

"The pleasure truly was mine. I don't remember the last time I enjoyed a meal so much. I'll text you. Maybe we can meet again next week."

He doesn't wait for a response but leans in and brushes his mouth against the corner of mine. Reflexively, my lips pucker and it's all the invitation he needs. In the lobby of the St. Regis Hotel, Finn Nelson kisses me slowly and deeply. His hand finds mine and gives it a light squeeze.

"God, I want you," he whispers before placing one last kiss on my lips. As I watch him walk away, a pretty blonde quickly joins him, handing him a stack of notes. Samantha, I assume.

My lips tingle and I run a finger lightly over the bottom

one. It takes me a minute to gather my wits, and as I force my feet into a walking motion, I unintentionally bump into someone.

"My apologies."

I get no response, but I'm met with stormy blue eyes. Blake's stormy blue eyes.

There are a hundred emotions ticketing across Blake's face, but the one that seems to win out is anger, although I'm certain I saw hurt in there, too.

Oddly, I feel a bit embarrassed and ashamed. Which then leads to resentment, because, I mean, Blake is fucking straight. And not really my boyfriend.

He walks around me and has a conversation with a girl at the desk. He signs something and then he's back. "Follow me."

Though I should protest, I follow him across the lobby. There's a set of elevator doors open and Blake stops next to them.

"Get in," he says in quiet anger. I hesitate and he says again, "West, get your ass in the elevator. Now."

I take a step forward and Blake wraps his hand around my upper arm and practically lifts me off the ground, pushing me into the car. The operator gives us a glance before Blake gives him a floor number. Blake looks forward, never taking his eyes off the door, not saying a word.

I can't stop staring at him. Fuck me running he's a sight to behold. He's rocking the ultimate trifecta: a fitted suit, simmering anger, and sexual prowess. With all occupants in the elevator facing forward, I steal a second to push a palm against my dick in an attempt to calm it.

The doors ding announcing our arrival to the eleventh floor, and with a hand still firmly around my bicep, I am escorted to the end of the hall.

"Blake." I attempt to pull free of his hold. He says nothing and slides the card in the door. After shoving me through first, I'm whipped around and before I can protest, breathe, or acclimate, Blake has pinned me against the wall. The table we bumped is still swaying and there's a clatter as things tumble over.

Again he has drawn my arms above my head, wrists trapped in his grip. His free hand is working the button on my jeans while his mouth devours mine. He lowers my zipper and I'm so grateful for the relief he's provided my cast-iron cock that I find myself deepening the kiss in gratitude. His hand dives into my underwear and I hiss as his fingers wrap around my dick, giving it a rough tug.

"Blake."

"Again," he demands. "Say my name again."

"Blake," I moan, leaning my head against the wall as his lips devour my neck, biting its way from my Adam's apple to my jaw. "What are you doing?" I attempt to bring us back to reality, but he is having nothing of it.

"What did I tell you about staying away from that guy?"

"Blake, you're not gay. We're not—"

"I may not have a label, but I know what I'm feeling." He straddles my thigh while he continues to work my dick like a pro, applying the right amount of force and roughness it craves. Pushing his hips forward he rubs his cock against me and I can feel his hardened length.

The thought of the only man I've ever loved but never thought I could have getting hard for me is enough to make me lose my senses. It wraps me in a sexual haze. But I have to focus. His mouth takes mine again in another bruising kiss and I'm sucking in oxygen when he finally breaks away.

"Blake," I just manage. "We just can't." It's all I have to offer.

Blake looks me in the eyes, and my jeans fall to my knees. He releases my dick and slides my underwear down. "You're going to have to come up with something better than that, Southie."

He drops to his knees.

"Blake, what the fuck are you doing?"

He leans forward and runs his tongue from the base of my dick to the tip before taking me into his mouth.

"Fuck. Fuck. Fuck." I swear as my hand finds a home in Blake's hair. My protests have flown out the fucking window, because nothing could stop me from sliding my dick further into his warm, wet mouth. I've had dreams about this, if I'm being honest with myself, since I was thirteen. And the dream doesn't hold a candle to the reality.

I push my hips forward, forcing Blake to take me deeper than he's ready for. "Breathe through your nose," I say in an attempt to help him, but he doesn't need it. He's opened up his throat for me, taking me in deeper, and a feral sound escapes me. When I look down at him, his eyes are on me. Even though he's the one on his knees, there is no mistaking who is in control.

His eyes lower and his other hand cups my balls. My hips are bucking back and forth and I'm mindless with the need to come.

"Blake, I'm going to come," I warn, but he doesn't let me pull off, and there in the middle of a hotel room that costs more a night than I pay in rent a month, I come harder than I ever knew was possible. He gags but stays with it until the end, licking me clean, giving me a slow, sexy wink. I've been blown by guys that wouldn't swallow, but, like everything Blake does, he goes balls to the wall.

My breath is coming in strong waves, and I think I'm

seeing double. Blake stands and adjusts himself before straightening his suit jacket. Pulling on his shirt cuffs, he leans forward and runs his mouth over mine. The taste of myself on his lips is enough to have me ready to go again.

He straightens to his full height and with eyes locked on mine he speaks. "I have a meeting." He takes a step towards the door before stopping and turning back to me. My pants are still around my ankles and my dick is hanging out like a flag in the wind.

"I won't tell you again. Stay away from Finn Nelson."

Blake

All I had wanted to do was surprise West by getting home a day early. Instead, I had gotten a text from Elise this morning asking me to take a meeting for her, which is how I found myself at the St. Regis. I'm the one who got the surprise.

I mean, I sucked a dick today. The big surprise is how much I enjoyed it. When West came down my throat, I almost creamed my pants. It was single-handedly the hottest experience I've ever had. And I've had some pretty extraordinary experiences.

I hadn't planned to do it, but when I walked into the lobby and saw Finn escorting him out of the bar with a hand on his lower back, I almost lost my shit. I completely lost it when I saw Finn's lips kiss the ones that I haven't stopped thinking of since I left for D.C. When I got West into the hotel room, when he protested, I knew it was because he thought this is just all one big experiment for me. Maybe it is, I don't know. What I do know is that this experiment, if that's what it is, is nowhere near over.

I just finished my meeting and I hail a taxi to take home. Home? Christ, I did it again. What the fuck am I doing? The last person on this earth I want to hurt is West. Not after what I unknowingly put him through the last ten years. I'm not intentionally trying to play with his head. At least, not the one on his shoulders.

I pay the taxi driver and the doorman has taken to greeting me by name. Ari is getting her mail in the lobby. On the ride up, we chat about a party at her place this weekend and I make a note to tell West we're invited. This is as domesticated as I've ever felt.

Standing outside our door, my body releases a deep sigh before heading in. I toss my keys and the mail on the table and drop my bag. West isn't in the living area and the bedroom is empty, but I can hear the shower running in the bathroom.

Since "fuck it" seems to be my mantra today, I enter the bathroom to grab some fresh clothes out of the closet. West has his back to me, but I can see him clearly through the shower door. He has one hand above his head leaning against the wall. The water is raining over him and my eyes follow the droplets down the curve of his body. He has a tight round ass and…seriously? You saw that ass hundreds of times growing up. What's different now?

I pick up the clothes West dropped on the floor and put them in the laundry basket in the closet I added earlier this week. I'm standing in my athletic briefs, unbuttoning my shirt when he walks in.

"Jesus Christ. You scared the shit out of me," West yelps. There's a towel wrapped around his waist that with a flick of a finger, my finger, would be on the floor. I resist the urge.

"Sorry, I was getting some clothes. I really need to freshen up." I'm suddenly bone tired.

"Water's still warm." West says before grabbing some clothes. "I'll change in the bedroom."

I nod but don't say anything.

"You look exhausted. Why don't you lay down for a little whi—"

I curse when my phone starts to ring. West looks on with disapproval, but looks relieved when I say Elise's name. We've both been waiting to hear from her.

"I'll be there in," I look at my watch, "about an hour and a half."

Disconnecting the call, I'm met with a frown. "Dude, you can't keep up this pace. Can't you wait and go up tomorrow?"

"No. Elise—"

"Will understand."

"You're right, she would. But she needs me."

"I know she's important to you."

"She saved me, West. And has never asked anything of me in return. Not as a friend, anyway. Never. She needs me, I'm going."

"Fine, but I'm going with you. I don't want you driving off the road."

"Okay," I answer softly. Damn, it feels good to give him the reigns.

"There's a rental place on 30th that I've used a few times. It's on the way, we can leave from there." West says as we exit our apartment building and hail a taxi. I instruct the driver to drop us at Pier 6.

"We're not driving. We're taking a helicopter."

"If you're taking a helicopter, then why am I going?" West asks. He's wearing green chino shorts that look soft, like he's had them for ages, a white T-shirt, and flip flops. He's sporting a two-day scruff and a pair of tortoise-shell Wayfarers. His body is defined, but not overly muscular. The hair on his arms and legs matches his blond hair. It also matches the dusting of hair trailing under his towel that I saw earlier. My mind lingers on that memory, and I'm so distracted that it takes me a second to realize he's saying my name.

"Blake."

"Yeah?" I finally respond, thankful he can't see my eyes behind these aviators.

"If you're not driving, then why am I going?"

"Because you offered and I'd like for you to."

"Okay." A soft smile spreads across his lips as he looks out of the window at the city buzzing by. I slide my hand on top of his and, without turning his head, he spreads his fingers so mine fall between his.

Yeah. I like that.

West

"I need a helicopter, please. Landing at a private heli-pad. These are the coordinates," Blake tells the pretty redhead behind the counter. She blushes when he removes his aviators and slides them into the opening of his shirt. He's wearing a white button up with the sleeves rolled up and khaki shorts that hug his ass just so. In fact, I stand slightly behind him so I can enjoy the view.

"We have a private service available. Will you need a return flight?"

"Yes, tomorrow, 2:00 p.m."

"Passport or driver's license, please."

Blake hands her two passports and she types some information into the system. "Round trip comes to $3850."

The blood drains out of my face but Blake doesn't even bat an eye. He pulls a wad of cash out of his wallet and hands it to her. She picks up the phone and makes a call.

"Mr. Ben Greene, here's your passport and ticket. And Mr. Jack Goff, here's your passport and ticket. Your flight will be leaving in fifteen minutes." She points us to a first class lounge.

I follow Blake to the lounge, opening my passport on the way. It has my original passport picture, but none of the information is the same.

"You made me a fake passport?"

"Wanna say it a little louder? I'm pretty sure security didn't hear you." Blake whispers sharply, pulling the passport from my hands and placing it in his messenger bag.

"Why do I have a fake passport?" I whisper.

"We make one for every operator for every project. You never know when you'll need one."

"And we need one now because?"

"Because even though Reid Beckett says he's giving Elise time, I know he's looking for her. Theo, too. I don't want them pulling a manifest and seeing my name, or yours, on a helicopter rental heading to the Hamptons."

"And you gave me the name Jack Goff because?"

"It's funny?"

"Why are you walking around with that much cash?"

"It's the nature of my job. There are times that I need quick access to things."

"So, you just have $4000 laying around."

"I typically keep between fifty and a hundred on hand."

I choke on my water. "Just laying around?"

"In places."

"Like my apartment?"

"Yes."

"So, there's fifty grand in my apartment right now?"

"Closer to ninety." He flips through a magazine on the table next to us.

"Do you think that's wise?"

"I installed a safe."

"You installed a safe?"

"Yes. What do you want for dinner? I'm starving."

"Will you show me?"

"Sure." He flips more pages in the magazine.

"Seafood. Seafood in the Hamptons."

Forty-five minutes later we are landing on the Taylor property. It's magnificent from the air. I can only imagine what it's like from the ground.

I watch the helicopter take off and I ask Blake, "Can you fly one of those?"

"Blake can fly just about anything," Elise says from behind us.

Blake throws his messenger bag around to his back and pulls Elise in for a long hug. When he releases her, she has tears in her eyes and leans in for a kiss on her forehead.

"Want to see how the other half lives?" she jokes before walking over and hugging me. "West, I'm so glad you came."

"I hope you don't mind."

"Not at all. Let me show you where you can leave your things."

We hop into an old blue Harvester, and Elise drives us to a different part of the property.

"Emme and Graham have two guest houses. This is yours," she says, pulling to a stop outside a small house that looks like it should be in *Architectural Digest*. It's modern, but in keeping with the spirit of the area. We enter the front door and it's impossible to notice anything but the view from the wall of glass windows across the back.

"Holy shit." I set my bag on the chair. "Why would anyone leave this place?"

"It gets better. Also, you should see the main houses."

"Houses?"

"Family property. Graham's parents have had a house here

for years. Graham built one a couple years ago. They just added the guest quarters. You guys are in this one and I'm in the other."

She pushes a button on an iPad in the wall and the doors open and slide apart. The warm air and sound of the waves roll in. I walk to the balcony that overlooks the ocean and know that is exactly where I am headed.

"I think I'll go to the beach. Let you two talk."

"Taking one for the team, huh?" Blake teases.

"Something like that." There's a flash of heat that crosses over his face when I smile his way. It makes me want to forget the beach and stay with him, but I know he and Elise need their time together.

I slide out of my flip flops and take the stairs down to an empty beach. How is there not someone here today? Every day? I could stay here all summer and never miss the city. Especially this time of year when the heat in the city can be brutal.

I walk the water's edge for about an hour, then head back to the guest house to grab a book. It won't be dark for a couple more hours, so I should be able to get a few pages in on the hammock I spied. It's hidden under some large trees, but it still catches the breeze off the water. It takes me two tries to maneuver myself inside the little cocoon until I'm just right.

"You're looking pretty relaxed." Blake's voice slides over me like my favorite T-shirt.

"Dude, how do I become a billionaire? I don't even need the big house, just this, a little beach cottage on the water. This is the dream."

"Scoot over."

"No way! I had a hell of a time trying to get just me in this thing."

"Pussy."

"Missing it?" I smirk.

He gives me the finger and then begins a painfully awkward climb into the hammock. We sway wildly for a minute, and just when I think we are going to topple off, he settles in the only way we'll fit: on his side with one leg thrown over mine. I lift my arm to give him more room and he shimmies into my side, resting his head in the nook of my shoulder.

"Blake?"

"Yeah?" He removes his aviators and sets them on my chest.

"Whatcha doin, bud?" I attempt to keep it light, but there's a lot to my question. Because there's some honest-to-God cuddling going on.

"I wanted to lay on the hammock."

"I would have given it to you."

"I wanted to lay on the hammock with you." He drapes an arm across my stomach.

"Since when did you become a snuggler?" He doesn't answer, and there's an air about him that seems heavy.

"Read to me?" There's something in his voice—desperation, need? It has the same tenor as that night when he climbed into my window, bloodied by his uncle.

So here, on a borrowed beach, swaying in a hammock, I read to him and he sleeps.

Blake's phone buzzes a few times and, without moving, he digs into his pocket and picks up without a greeting. After a beat, he says "okay" and hangs up. He's stretches his body, trying to wake up, and when he turns his head up at me, he looks peaceful. Carefree.

"Hey."

"Hey." I don't give my mind a chance to overthink it, I lean down and place a soft kiss to his lips. Not meant to arouse, but to show my enjoyment of holding him while he slept. His free hand cups my jaw and he lazily runs his thumb in a repeated pattern over my cheek.

"That was Elise. She'll have dinner ready in thirty minutes."

"Blake?"

"Hmm?"

"What are we doing?"

"Going to dinner."

"No, I mean this. What are we doing?"

"Just going with it."

"With what?" There's an edge to my voice that I didn't plan and I feel his body tense up.

"With whatever comes each day."

"I'm not asking for a roadmap, but I need more than that. If you're just messing around to try something different, tell me. If you're doing this 'cause you can't get pussy till this is over, then tell me that. But tell me something."

He pushes up to his elbow and looks at me with—

Plop. Plop. Plop. Something warm and wet runs down my face.

"What the fuck?" I look up in time to see a bird flying off the branch above us.

Blake bursts into uncontrolled laughter and leans back a little too far. Before we can stop it, he's landed hard on the sand and I'm tangled in the hammock above him upside down.

"Blake!" I growl. "Get me the fuck out of here."

But it's no use. There are actual tears streaming down his face and only every fifth word is intelligible. He's holding his stomach like he's in actual pain. "You...lying there...so serious...roadmap...bird shit... burrito."

"I do not look like a burrito. Get my ass out of this." Every attempt I make to free my arms twists me up in the fabric even more.

"Blake, I have bird shit running down my face."

"Okay, okay, okay." He pulls his shirt over his head and wipes the shit off my face.

"That was hysterical," he chuckles, but when he sees my face, he freezes. This is the first time I've really seen him up close without a shirt, and he realizes what's left me speechless.

It's the tattoo on his chest, the compass I caught a glimpse of at the hotel that first day. It only points in one direction.

Blake

I look down at the tattoo, finding it strangely hard to look him in the eye as I say, softly, "You were always home for me, West."

And it's the truth. Even now, I have a condo in Chicago, but it might as well be a hotel. The only home I have ever known was the Connors'. And in this short time, West's apartment.

Before I can reach up to unwind him, he swings his body out of the hammock and lands with an "oomph" on top of me, long limbs splayed in every direction.

Without giving me a chance to catch the breath he knocked out of me, his tongue dives in my mouth with only one intention: to claim me. And who am I to deny him? Even if I don't know what the hell has been going on with me this last week, I know for sure I'm ready and willing for the person on top of me right now. I've only shared a handful of kisses with this man and already I'm needy for it.

West's left hand grasps the back of my neck while his right hand palms the hard bulge in my pants. I protest when his mouth leaves mine, leaving a trail of nips and licks down my throat as he makes his way to the tattoo that started this. His tongue traces the ink on my chest before he bites my nipple.

"Holy fuck." All the bullshit I come with doesn't matter to him right now. It's like he's on a mission to show me he'll always be home if I'd let him be.

West sits up and makes quick work of the fly of my shorts. "There's nothing holy about what I want to do to you, but if I do it right, you'll see the light."

"West?"

"Hmm?"

"If you're going to make bad puns, at least do it with my cock in your mouth."

He bites his lip, and with a sexy as sin wink, he leans down and takes me in.

"Holy fuck," I cry as his lips tickle the curled hair on my groin.

He works my cock like it's an idol he's fucking worshipped forever. He massages my balls while his finger strokes the skin beneath. Releasing me, he runs a flat tongue around the head before taking me back down his throat.

His other hand is at my neck, and in a choreographed move, he hums around my dick, pulls my balls, and gently squeezes my throat. The mix of sensations and act of dominance from my mild-mannered West is enough to shove me over the edge and I come so hard and so long that I see bright spots. The fucker actually did make me see the light.

He stays with me until I've given all I have and then kisses his way back up my body, his rock hard cock rubs against my now sensitive one. He watches me, waiting for my trademark smart-ass comment, but I got nothing.

"Well this is a first. Blake Thomas, speechless?" His smile

gets cockier and more confident as I take in long inhales of oxygen to calm myself.

"Dude, you might have sucked out my brains through my dick. I can't even think right now."

He leans down to kiss me and tasting myself on his lips sends a thrill through me that has me ready to go again. How is that even possible? I've tasted myself on many a lips, but I've never had this reaction.

West stands, and then pulls me up with one arm. I shake the sand out of his book and head inside.

"I need a quick shower. Won't take me a minute. I just want to wash this bird shit off me for good. Could you text Elise and let her know?"

"Off you? You just rubbed your face all over my body."

"It's not like you're gonna get the bird flu or something. Plus, I didn't hear any complaints out there."

"No. No complaints," I tell him pulling him to me.

I do as I'm told and tell Elise we need another thirty minutes. It occurs to me, finally, that this is a one-bedroom cottage. I can't tell if Elise knew that or if she's the conspirator I think she is. But how can she know when I don't even know? Come on, Blake, do you *really* not know? My conscious taunts me.

West's backpack is on the bed and I notice he's laid out a change of clothes. I drop mine where I stand and make the easy decision to join him in the shower.

West has positioned himself in the middle of a shower made for two. Water sprays him from all directions. He's rinsing the shampoo from his hair when he turns around at the sound of the shower door closing behind me.

"Can I help you with something?" His cock swells the second he sees me.

"No, but I think I can help you." I wrap my fingers around the steel rod projecting from his body.

"Blake, we're on the clock."

"I bought us thirty minutes."

I position myself behind him. My dick has found a home in the crevice of his ass, and it's the happiest I've ever known it to be. I wrap one arm around his chest and the other strokes his cock. He pushes back and grinds against me. He moans when I run my thumb through the slit on the tip of his cock. My fingers find the hard nubs on his chest, and I match the rhythm of my strokes to the twisting of one of his nipples.

I rest my lips on the curve of skin between his neck and his shoulders and within seconds his ass sheaths my cock, massaging it with each pass. My teeth sink into his neck and he cries out as his release, covering my hand while I milk him to completion. I don't give him much time to recover before I station his hands on the wall, bend him at his waist, and use his ass to finish as the water washes his come down the drain.

"Fuck yes," West groans as I slide up and down between his cheeks. His approval arouses me further, and in a few more strokes I'm coming all over the small of his back.

He leans his forehead against the wall and I'm certain I'm the only thing holding him upright. I show no mercy leaving him bent over so that I can lick the come off him. Before I have a chance to swallow, his lips are on mine, taking what he wants. And, dammit, I'm hard again.

"So, how are you liking your cottage? Pretty spectacular, isn't it?" Elise asks us over a glass of wine.

"It's perfect. I can't imagine what the rest of the property is like," West says.

"I can show you around tomorrow if you like. How long are you planning on staying?"

West looks to me, so I answer for both of us.

"I have the charter scheduled to pick us up tomorrow afternoon."

"You and Jack Goff should change your schedule and stay a couple more days."

"Well, we only have one change of clothing each—"

"So go into town tomorrow and pick up a change of clothes, since you clearly don't know how to use the washer and dryer in your cottage." She points to a door off the kitchen that I assumed was a closet or pantry.

"Whadaya say, Jack Goff?" I grin. "Think you can slum it here a couple more days?"

"I blame you," West says to Elise. "You could have stopped him."

"He already had the passports made up when it came to my attention," she laughs, throwing her hands up in surrender.

"You look good, kid."

"I'm getting there. More and more."

"You plan on talking to Reid, so he can call the blood-hounds back home?"

"Not yet. I need a little more time."

"For what?"

"Why don't I give you two some time to talk?" West says, but before he can get up from the chair Elise waves him back down.

"Nonsense. There's nothing private about what we are dis-cussing. I need time to decide what it is I want. Reid might have done me a favor by firing me. I need to figure out what I want to do in this next phase. What do you want to do?" she asks me.

"This is your decision."

"Bullshit and you know it. Besides, I'm not your boss anymore."

"That's true," I concede.

"So, what do you want to do?"

"I'm ready for a home. Not a white picket fence or anything, but also not a hotel room."

"Me too," she smiles. It's refreshing to know we are back on the same page.

We're interrupted by a knock at the door, and as I reach for my bag to grab my pistol, she picks up the iPad next to her.

"It's Emme's security. Put the gun away, Rambo."

"I'm better looking than Rambo," I yell as she goes to open the door.

"Holy shit, I'd know that voice anywhere. And I know for a fact you're one ugly son of a bitch."

I'm frozen for a moment by both disbelief and a rush of memories. Once I get my bearings, I practically sprint across the room and slam myself against the wall of muscle that is Teague Sanders. He pulls me to him in a fierce embrace.

I can't speak. I want to, but the words won't come. I have to use every tool I've been given to control my emotions. Teague seems to be doing the same. Very few people make it through the things Teague and I have survived.

We pull away and when our eyes meet, he pulls me back in for another hug. Eventually, I clear my throat and we separate, giving one another a second to recover.

"You dumbass," I growl and give him a hard shove.

"Those are the first words you choose to say to me?" He still has that same stupid grin I had to look at for six years.

"I can't believe you're here. I searched two years for you. What are you doing here man?"

"I'm security for the Taylor's. Specifically, Emme."

"Since when?"

"Almost a year."

"And before that?"

His eyes darken. "The streets."

"How long?"

"Since we got back."

"You fucker. You could have reached out to me. I know you were checking in, I got the reports."

"It wasn't your job to save me. Not twice. I had to save myself the second time around." He pauses before adding, "Well, me and Emme."

"What are you doing here? Are the Taylors on the grounds?"

"No, they want to wait a few more weeks before traveling with the new baby. Since Emme won't be leaving the house, Smith who is Graham's security, has them covered. Joy and I came up for a little vacation."

"Joy?"

"My wife." He smiles like he's won the lottery. There's an odd feeling settling in my chest.

"I'm so happy for you, man. I can't believe it."

We stand in a comfortable silence, adjusting to each other's presence. Teague breaks it by acknowledging the others in the room.

I turn around to gesture to Elise and West, only West is the only one in the room.

"This is West. My best friend growing up."

"We know each other. He's working with Emme on the community center." Teague reaches out to shake West's hand.

"Hold up! You're *that* West?"

"Apparently." I'm not sure if West looks pleased that I talk about him or not.

"Well, now that I know you're *that* West, I'm gonna need your mom to make me one of her peach pies. He tortured us with stories about her cooking every time we were hungry. Which was all the time."

"I see how it is," West smirks at me. "I'm *that* West."

"Where did Elise go?" I ask.

"She excused herself for a minute," West says.

"Emme asked me to look in on her. There's supposed to be a pretty big storm coming through, so I wanted to stop by tonight. How do you know Elise?"

"She's my boss."

"You're Elise's guy? Makes sense."

"How so?" West asks curiously.

"Elise's team has a certain…reputation. Especially her handler. Jesus, what a small world."

"You'd have known if you had kept in touch," I grumble.

"He said he was sorry," Elise says re-entering the room. "Thanks for checking on me Teague. Blake and West will be here for at least one more day, hopefully more."

"That's great. Maybe we can catch up. I'd love for Joy to get to meet an old Delta 6 commander."

"I'd like that." We exchange a handshake.

When Teague leaves, Elise looks at me with concern. "You okay?"

"Yeah, it's just crazy. How long did I search for him? Man, am I grateful he's okay."

"Thanks to you," she says, squeezing my arm.

I clear my throat and turn to West. "Ready?"

He nods.

"You want to stay at our place or us stay here?" I ask Elise. "Teague said it's supposed to storm pretty good tonight."

"Nah, I'll be fine. I'm in the middle of a book and I have a couple of cases I need to work on. Which reminds me," she turns to West. "I got an email from Finn. Sounds like he made a rather nice donation to your school."

"He did. A very generous one."

"He's hot. You should go out with him. Are you going to say yes?"

West doesn't give anything away. "It didn't occur to me it was really a possibility right now since people think Blake is my boyfriend."

"I mean Finn knows. He's one of the nine on The Foundation. He would be discreet."

I want to call bullshit since he tried to face-fuck West in the middle of the hotel lobby, but I refrain. Elise frowns at me. "What? He would be. He's not going to do anything to jeopardize the case." She misinterprets my frustration.

"I'll think about it," West says, darting his eyes to me.

"Don't let him dissuade you. He's never going to like who you date."

"I like Reid," I protest.

"You tolerate Reid. You try to like him because I like him. And you never like the guys Gabby and Fran date."

"Can we really call what Gabby does 'dating'?"

"Fair enough. The guys Gabby has slept with."

"That's more like it."

"I'm just saying you're protective. It's your nature. But Finn truly is a good guy. He's the real deal and a catch. West would be lucky to be with him."

West gives me a pleased smirk that I want to fuck off of his face. He must see it in my eyes, because it drops from his lips like a brick, and in an instant I see the heat in his eyes I saw this afternoon.

"We should go. Sure you don't want us to stay?"

"I'm sure. Go."

West and I each get a hug before we leave. It's about a fifteen-minute walk to our cottage and there's a pronounced breeze in the air announcing the approaching storm. Both of our moods darkened the minute Elise closed the door. Even lost in my thoughts of Teague, I can feel West's surliness. I slide my hand in his, but there's a hint of hesitation before wrapping his fingers around mine. It should feel odd but it doesn't. It feels natural, like a second skin.

We jog the last few yards as large droplets of rain start to fall. We just make it inside the house before the heavens open, letting loose a symphony of rain on the tin roof. Without a word, West makes for the bathroom and emerges a few minutes later wearing a pair of pajama pants low on his hips. I like what I see, despite my unwarranted sour mood. My eyes travel from the V at his hips, up his sun-kissed torso that reminds me of warmed toffee. When my eyes finally reach his, it's clear we are not having the same thoughts.

West clears his throat and slides a "Taylor Organization" sweatshirt over his head, cutting off my little daydream.

"Found it in the closet," he explains.

The doors between the master bedroom and the screened-in porch are pushed aside, letting in the ocean breeze. Even in the dead of summer, and with the storm coming in, it's nice and cool. I follow West's lead and change into the T-shirt and bottoms I stowed in my bag this morning then take a seat at one of the two large cushioned chairs on the porch outside of the bedroom sinking low into it and resting my legs on the ottoman in front of me. West joins me a minute later, setting down two beers on the table between us.

We watch the dramatic display outside. The flashes of lightening and the steady tempo of rain and thunder and waves, lulls us back inside our own heads.

"Were you and Teague a couple?" he asks before taking another swallow of beer.

"A couple?"

"Yeah. Or did you ever hook up?"

"West, what part of our interaction made you think that was even a possibility? I have never been with a man or even looked at a man before this week with you. To be honest, I don't know what the hell is going on. I even watched some gay porn to see if that would give me some answers but it didn't. Didn't even make me hard. But every time I think of you…"

West doesn't say anything. Did I say too much? Admit too much? I can't help it. He and I are the only ones who know what we are doing right now. I mean, maybe Bree or Elise have some suspicions, but no one knows what is truly going on besides us.

A part of me likes knowing it's just me and him.

He mumbles something I don't catch.

"What?"

"How long, Blake?"

"How long for fucking what?" I snap frustrated by the chasm of distance I suddenly feel between us.

"How long did you look for me? You told Teague you spent two years searching for him. Did you even think to contact me? To look for me?"

"No."

I watch the two-letter word land like a punch to his gut. Cursing myself for not doing this better, I circle the front of the chair and sit on the ottoman facing him. But looking him in the eye is harder than I imagined. If anyone else had caused the pain I can see there, I would have dismembered them.

"I didn't look for you because I knew where you were. I knew you went to prom with Allie Brooks. I knew you went to Columbia. I knew you graduated Magna Cum Laude. I knew when you moved to the city and lived in that crappy place in Hell's Kitchen and when you moved into the place you have now. When you started teaching. I knew how your parents were." I release a breath.

He shakes his head slowly. "You knew. This whole time." His voice is slow, restrained. It's almost frightening. "Every day for a year, I would go to your house and ask your aunt for information. Beg her for it. Every day for a year, I would beg my father to hire a private investigator to find you. I just knew you were somewhere, that you needed help." There's a sheen in his eyes when he finally faces me. "I knew in my heart my best friend needed me."

"We talked about this, West. There's nothing I can do to change what happened."

"So, that's it? No explanation?"

"I already—"

"Bullshit!" He stands up with such a force that he almost knocks his chair over. "You know and I know it. So, I'm going to ask you again, do you have an explanation?"

"No," I answer. I hang my head, unable to look up at him. "No, I don't."

He nods and walks into the bedroom. "Goodnight, Blake."

I watch him walk away. The part of me that has always wanted to go to West wants to stop him now. But how can I admit to him that the best friend he had is gone? How do I explain to him the monster I had become?

Blake

Sixteen Years Old

"Cadet Thomas."

"Yes, sir." I stand straight as a board, even though exhaustion has seeped into every thread of my being. My muscles constrict and I will my mind to control the tremors rolling through my body.

"Cadet," Sargent McGuire says with disdain dripping from his words. "Once again, you've fallen below standard. What do you have to say for yourself?"

Vomit rolls through me. I force it back into my stomach.

"Sir, I'm a disgrace, sir." That's all he wants to hear. Excuses don't matter. What we encountered doesn't matter.

"You are two hours late to your rendezvous point. Are you really that selfish that you would put your entire unit in jeopardy?"

"No, sir."

"I think you are, cadet. I think you are exactly that selfish." His nose is touching mine and he's yelling at a decibel point that splits my head wide open.

My unit just finished our fifth excursion in as many weeks. Each excursion is designed to make us fail. Each one designed to break us. I've been here 378 days.

"Why were you late?"

"I got lost," I lie.

Before I can even see it, his fist connects with my jaw in a force so brutal it drops me to the ground. He pulls me up and I stand as straight as before.

"I'll ask you again, cadet, why are you late?"

"Sir, it's my fault, sir," Teague says from my right. "I fell down the chasm. Cadet Thomas had to work his way down to rescue me then carry me out." Teague sways and I know his broken ankle has to be screaming in pain.

"What was your objective, cadet?" McGuire asks in an eerily quiet voice.

"Reach rally point A before Sargent Townsend's unit, sir."

"Cadet Sanders, you are dismissed to sick bay. Cadet Thomas," he looks back to me, "you are to spend a week in the box. Longer if needed."

"Sir, it wasn't his fault. It was mine. I fell. He came back for me."

But it doesn't matter. He's done listening. Someone grabs my arms and escorts me to the box while two cadets literally have to drag Teague to the infirmary, kicking and screaming.

The box is a four-by-four wooden structure with two inch drilled holes on all four sides. It's hot during the day and cold at night. The smell from its previous occupants is pungent. I am given one nutrition bar and one canteen of water. That's it. No bathroom. No shower. No one is allowed near the box when it's occupied.

The first three days go by more slowly than I could have imagined. I'm hungry and thirsty, but I try to keep my wits about me, keep my mind sharp. By day four, time ceases to exist. My mind begs me for the rest of my protein bar and canteen instead of rationing them. I can't stretch my legs. I'm bent over the entire time. There's no ability to control where I relieve myself.

It is somewhere between day three and four when West joins me in the box. We talk about going for a swim in the pond. He tells me Mary Beth has a cake all ready for me. We talk about all the stupid things we will do every day when I get out of here. He says we'll go to Jimmy's Diner and get a shake. West has always paid me a visit when I needed him. In my dreams, in my imagination, he was always there. Just like now. He is in the box with me, reminding me that I can make it, that I will be eighteen soon and that I can move in with him and his parents. That they want me, that they're looking for me.

On day five, Sargent McGuire brings his steak and eats it next to my box. "You know, your uncle is a friend of mine." He takes a long drink of water and takes a bite of his hot, buttered roll. "He said you were going to be a problem. Said you were weak and would need training."

I don't say anything. I stopped pushing back by the end of my first two weeks at this place. All I was getting was bruises and low-level torture. Teague was the first person I met. He arrived a few weeks before me and learned the hard way how to best survive this place. He taught me the ins and outs as quickly as I could learn them. He's become a brother to me.

"He called today. I told him you were in the box. Told him why. He was disappointed to say the least." He looks at his roll. "This one doesn't have enough butter on it. I hate it when they do that." He brings it close to one of the holes as he sets it on top of the box, leaving it there.

"Mail came today," he chews. "You got a response from your friend. Finally. What's it been, a year and he's just now writing? Sounds like he's having a good time. Took some girl named Allie to the prom. Made captain of the basketball team. Applying to colleges."

He takes another long sip of water.

"Said he was sorry he just wrote you back, but he's had a lot going on. He sounds like a real charmer that one. With friends like that who needs enemies, am I right? Well," he pours his water on the ground and rubs his stomach, "I'm stuffed." He puts his plate of half-eaten food on top of the box and leaves. When I look back to the corner, West is gone.

Blake

Twenty Years Old

"You've been given clearance," whispers a voice in my earpiece. I push the button at my throat to ask Teague if he's in position. He answers affirmatively, and I check the elevation and wind speed on the scope of my rifle. We have a one-minute window to accomplish our mission. Teague's team will create a distraction, I'll shoot. It's a near-impossible shot to make under normal circumstances, and these aren't normal conditions.

We see movement. The convoy coming to make the exchange is at the gate, and as soon as they are given entrance, Teague's team does its job. Men with guns pour out of the building to see what is going on. Teague's unit takes on heavy fire, and finally the man we've hunted for sixteen months shows himself in the doorway. I can't get a clear shot at first but then he steps into the courtyard and bends over, obstructed by a wall that comes just above his waist. I wait until I see the top of his head as he begins to stand back up.

We've got our man, I think as I tap the trigger, knowing that, at this distance, the bullet will make contact with his heart by the time he is fully upright. It's too late to change courses when the toddler he bent over to pick up appears in my scope.

West

I pull on Blake's shoulders with enough force that he sits up in the bed. His eyes are wild, searching, lost.

"Jesus, Blake." He's shaking and unable to catch his breath. I straddle his hips and take his face in both of my hands, forcing him to focus on me.

"You're okay."

"West?"

"It's me. You're okay."

"You're here? You're really here?"

"I'm here." I pull his hands up and place them on each side of my face. I need him to feel me. To feel the fierce desire I have to protect him. Even from himself. "This is me. I'm not going anywhere." And the minute I say it, I know it's true. I'm not going anywhere. I've loved this man since I was six. I'm certain of it. Enough is enough. I told him I forgave him, now I have to mean it. To show it. And the best way I know to do that is to give him time. It's clear he's dealing with years of trauma and that isn't something that is tackled in one night. It's going to take patience on my side. Patience he deserves, whether he feels he deserves it or not.

"I'm so sorry. I'm so sorry." His arms encircle me and he buries his face in my neck. I wrap my arms and legs around him and hold him in a vice.

"It's okay," I whisper into his hair, pulling him tighter, rubbing my hands over his back. "Whatever it is, it's okay."

"I thought you left me. When I was at camp—they tortured you until you don't know what's real and what's not. Until you believed the lies. You were always the light at the end of my tunnel. When the light got dimmer and dimmer, I thought it was because you were leaving me. Now I can see it was their manipulation that pulled me so far away from it, I couldn't see it anymore. I thought you left me. I was so angry and I wanted to hate you for that, for leaving me, but I couldn't. I just hung on to my memory of you even tighter. I wanted to see you when I came home, but I didn't know how. How was I supposed to look you in the eye after what I went through? The lives I've taken? You were light and I was dark. You were everything good in this world, and I was everything that was wrong."

"Blake."

"No, let me finish. Teague was at the school my uncle sent me to and after that we were in Delta 6 together. Teague had my back when no one else did. We made decisions together no person should ever have to make. When we got back to the states, he went under. I couldn't find him. All I knew was he was out there and he was in trouble. He needed me. You don't know it, but you needed me to stay away.

"When Elise found me, I was a mess. I did things I can barely admit to myself, and that made it even harder to find you after I got out of the service. I had to get help first. Elise helped me find it, helped me become the man I am now. Being with you these last couple of weeks, though, has made me want to be better than that, better than I am now, but nothing, nothing can make me the friend you deserve. I am broken, West," he sobs, clinging tighter to me. "Too broken for you. You deserve so much better than me."

Tears pour down my cheeks for the man I have never stopped loving. Tears for everything he has been through. Tears that he's had to live like I have, thinking his best friend left him when he needed him most. And all the animosity I have been feeling toward him crumbles away and the places in my heart he has always occupied begin beating for him again. I decide then and there, I don't care what it takes, I'm going to be the best friend he deserves, whether he can admit he deserves it or not.

I say his name. When he looks up at me I lean forward and press my mouth against his.

"You deserve me, just like I deserve you. You deserve to be loved and cared for." I pepper words of love and tenderness in-between kisses. When I tell him he has a good heart as my lips again land on his, he fists his hands in my hair and he pulls me tighter to him for a deeper kiss. This isn't about sex. This is cleansing. Acceptance. Forgiveness. About giving ourselves to each other.

My hips shift forward and Blake pulls the hoodie over my head, his hand roaming every inch of skin they can reach. He kisses his way down my neck, his lips latching onto one of my nipples. He gives it two gentle bites before sucking it into his mouth.

His fingers knead my ass, controlling the movement of my cock against his. I rest my cheek against the top of his head. "Fuck yeah," I moan.

"West. I need you."

"Blake, I'm yours."

In one motion, he has me on my back, pulling my pants off. He leaves me on the bed and digs in his bag on the chair. Before he climbs back on the bed, he drops his clothes and stares at me.

"Jesus Christ, West." He begins to stroke himself. "You're a fucking dream."

"Get down here," I say, but in true Blake fashion, he isn't going to do this on anyone's time table but his.

"Cup your balls," he says in a deep, authoritative voice. I do as I'm told.

His tongue traces his bottom lip. "Run your thumb over the tip."

I slide my hand up my shaft and run my thumb over the tip as he instructed. Lifting my thumb to my mouth, a visible strand of arousal follows.

That's all it takes to get Blake on the bed and between my legs.

"Are you sure about this?" he asks. But he's not asking me, he's asking himself. He needs me to tell him. He never made it inside me in the shower earlier, so this is going to be new to him. His first time inside another man.

"God, yes. There's Aloe Vera in the bathroom. Grab it, we can use it for lube."

He holds up a bottle. "Delta 6. Always prepared."

"Sure of yourself?" I tease.

"I had hope."

The honesty of his statement catches me off guard and reminds me this isn't just some one-night fuck. This is Blake. This is going to mean something to me. Will it to him? Blake's mouth envelops my dick. His hand works me from the root. There's no teasing, no tentativeness. Just full-on blowing my mind.

"Blake," I warn. I'm one good suck away from exploding in his mouth. He sits up and I watch as he rolls a condom down his length. The wondering eyes find mine again, and as he rubs lube on himself, he waits for me to guide him through this.

"It's been a while for me, Blake," I admit. "You're going to need to prep me a little."

He pushes my thighs to my chest and I feel cool liquid run down my crevice then his fingers begin skating over my hole, rubbing and massaging. His middle finger runs in a circular pattern over the puckered skin and right when I think it's truly his goal to make me grovel, he pushes his finger in and I release a breath.

"God, that's hot," he says. I grit my teeth as he carefully adds another finger.

"Wait till it's your dick," I gasp, pulling roughly on my cock.

"It's gonna be so fucking tight in your ass, I'm gonna want to stay in there forever."

Oh. My. God. I am not going to survive this. This is how I'm going to die. My obituary will read "Death by Blake's Dirty Talk."

The images of my funeral leave as quickly as they came when Blake adds a third finger and unknowingly runs it over my prostate. My back bows off the bed and his head shoots up.

"What did I just do? What was that?"

"Oh, fuck me. That was my prostate."

"That's a good thing? You like that?" he shifts around for a second and finds it again. My toes curl and my ass clamps around his fingers, answering for me, Blake gives a naughty grin and pulls them out.

"Now. I have to be in you now," he says with a singular focus.

I can feel the tip of his cock as he lines it up with my entrance. His eyes find mine, asking for permission, and when his tip breaches me, my head falls back with a loud groan.

"Eyes, baby, I need your eyes. I'm flying blind here. Does that sound mean keep going or stop?"

The look I give him is all he needs to continue. He carefully thrusts his hips, sliding his steel rod in and out of me a few times until he's seated fully in my ass, his strong thighs against mine.

"Go," I tell him.

"I can't." He closes his eyes in an attempt to gain some control. "I'm about to blow and I haven't even deep dicked you."

His word choice makes me chuckle and when I do his eyes shoot open.

"I felt that. Like your laugh just shimmied down my dick. Fuck that's hot."

It's all the encouragement he needed. He pulls up to his knees and pushes his weight against my legs, driving in and out of me in long, deep moves. There is no question he is in control and needs no further guidance.

Blake sees me moving my hand to my cock to provide some relief to my throbbing flesh, but he swats it away and wraps his hands around me.

"Let's get something straight. This is mine, got it?"

When I don't answer audibly, his hand swats my ass. "Answer me."

Aww, fuck. Bossy Blake.

"Yes. I got it." I answer before intentionally reaching for my dick again. He rewards me as I had hoped and slaps my ass again with a grumble about not learning the first time.

Oh, I learned alright. When I bite my lip and smile, he notices.

"You sneaky little biscuit. You did that on purpose."

"Did you just call me a biscuit?" I can't hold back the laugh. Leave it to Blake to add laughter to sex. Dirty talk. Bossiness. Laughter. Blake. This is what it feels like to have sex with your best friend.

He leans over me, and captures my cock between us. "Your dimple is quickly becoming my new aphrodisiac." He dips his tongue in it before leveling me with a scorching kiss. His fingers entwine with mine and he pulls them above my head. Picking up his pace, he drills in and out of me as he chases his ending. Every muscle in his beautiful, sculpted body flexes with each measured movement.

A current like I've never experienced rips through me, an orgasm so intense, my body would levitate off the bed if Blake wasn't holding me down. My come lubricates our stomachs as Blake continues to work me through the spasms. Once he's sure he's gotten everything from me, he pulls out, flicking the condom off and moving his fist down his cock in rapid speed. His hand comes to rest firmly on my chest as he hovers over me, adding his come to mine. His body shudders before collapsing on top of me, sealing the evidence of what just happened between us.

"Holy shit," he whispers. Our hearts beat rapidly against each other. I wrap my arms and legs around him. We lay like this for a long time, saying not a word.

"I promise to move in a minute," Blake mumbles.

I tighten my limbs around him and kiss the top of his head. "No rush." His lips brush the skin in the valley of my neck before he burrows back in.

And I mean it. I am in no hurry for this to end. I love

feeling his weight against me. I brush the tips of my fingers up and down his spine.

"I just had sex with a man."

My fingers pause, then resume. "You're welcome?"

He laughs and shakes his head before resting his chin on my chest, watching me. There's something raw in his eyes, vulnerable. Just because he had sex with a man, doesn't mean he understands what the hell is going on with him. It's a lot to take in.

"I know you think I'm going to freak out."

"Are you?"

He runs a finger across his chin in thought.

"It's you. So, no."

"Maybe give me a little more to go on? I speak Blake, but it's been a while. I need a few more words if you have them."

"I just...I don't know. It just feels," he looks to me for a word.

"Sorry. You gotta do this one on your own."

"How about we start with what it doesn't feel like?"

"Okay."

"It doesn't feel wrong. It doesn't feel weird."

"Okay." I can work with that.

"It feels unexpected. It feels like I'd like to do it again. It feels...like home." He tilts his head to me and his eyes own everything he's saying. He's not trying to run or hide behind anything.

"It feels like home. You're my home, West."

He lays his head back down and I think about what that means. Do I want to be his home? Yes, with every fiber of my being. It's something I understand. Blake feels like home to me, too, but, do I want to be a sentimental trip down memory lane?

"What are *you* thinking?" he asks me.

"I'm just focusing on this moment."

"That's how you're playing this?"

"Yep."

"Okay."

He rolls off me, releasing a sigh. "Let's see if we can't move you onto another moment then." He stands and yanks my arm, pulling me off the bed.

"Dude. What the hell."

"Shower."

"Shower?"

"Yep. I know you're an old man at this, but this is my first time and I want a few more experiences to add to it."

"I'm not a Putt-Putt."

"What?"

"You know, let's see how many fun things you can tap your balls into."

"West, stop talking. I want you to take a shower with me. I want to wash you clean so I can come all over you again. I want more experiences."

Dick: hard.

"Sounds like a plan."

"Yeah?"

"I can definitely get behind this."

"Not sure if that's in the plan just yet." He winks at me.

"Trust me, your ass will be mine."

I wrap my hand around the rigid flesh that lets me know he's not totally put off by that. Leaning in close to him, I whisper in his ear, "And Blake?"

"Yeah?" he answers in an aroused whimper.

"You're gonna love it." I give him a squeeze and walk into the bathroom.

Blake

Fuck me.

He's a cocktease.

How did I not see this coming? You're losing your touch Thomas, I think to myself, because West is nothing if not consistent.

Growing up, West was always the first one to suggest we do something stupid, something we weren't allowed to do. Everyone always thought I was the crazy one, but really West is the one that was uninhibited. He never felt the need to be anyone other than who he was. He was always comfortable in his own skin.

That gets me to thinking. "You said you were fifteen," I say as I enter the shower. West is already washing away the evidence of our tryst. Oddly, I'm not sure how I feel about that.

"I was."

"Why didn't you talk to me about it?"

"I don't know."

"Bullshit. We talked about everything."

"Not everything," he reminds me, but not unkindly.

"Shit, we gotta get off this merry-go-round."

"You're right. I'm sorry."

"Here, let me." I massage the shampoo into his scalp. He moans his appreciation. I move closer to him and when my cock comes to rest in the crack of his ass, he snakes his arms behind him and takes hold of my hips.

"So, you were fifteen."

"I was fifteen when I admitted it to myself. But if I'm being honest, I knew before then."

"You didn't think you could admit it?"

"I think I just didn't understand it."

I rinse his hair and reach for some conditioner. He sighs as my fingers begin the massage again.

"Keep going." I want to hear this. I want to understand this side of him he never showed me growing up.

"You remember the first time we went skinny dipping with all the kids in our class?"

"Wasn't that seventh grade?"

"Yes."

"We were thirteen."

"I wasn't sure then, but that was the first time I felt something, only it wasn't for the girls. It was for the guys. I wasn't sure what it meant or if it was just a weird one-time thing. To tell you the truth, I thought maybe I was bisexual. But when I was fifteen, I knew for sure."

"What happened when you were fifteen?"

Besides being in love with my best friend?

"I did the research. I watched porn. I kissed girls and felt nothing. I just knew."

"Did you kiss any guys?"

"No."

"Good." He turns and faces me and decides to return the

favor and wash my hair. My hands fall to his hips and I relax into him doing what no one has ever done for me before, cared for me after sex. I've always had wham-bam-thank-you-ma'am sex.

"I didn't have to. By the time I was fifteen I just knew."

"So you came out?"

"The month after you left. I was sad and depressed. I was struggling in everything. I just didn't care enough to pretend anymore. I had this regretful feeling like I had lost the chance to tell you who I really was."

"I'm sorry I left you," I whisper.

"Shh." He kisses the tip of my nose. "This is about me remember?" I nod and he continues.

"A couple of weeks after you left, a new kid started at the school. Shawn. He played hockey. He was out and proud and I walked up to him in the hall and kissed him. In front of all our friends. Asked him if he'd like to go out. I was nervous. Jesus, I thought I would actually throw up. But he said yes and we dated until I went to Columbia."

"Have you seen Shawn since?" I ask with an irrational jealousy running through me. He puts his hands on mine and squeezes, and it's only then I realize my fingers were digging into his hips.

"No. He went straight from high school to pro."

"Pro?"

"He's in the NHL."

"The NHL?" Then it dawns on me. "You dated Shawn Baker? The forward for New York? Shawn Baker was your first kiss?"

"No. Jenny Jones was my first kiss, remember?"

"Smart ass, you know what I mean."

"Yes. Shawn was my first boy-kiss."

Why does that grate on me? Would I have felt something for West in high school if I had known? Would I have been strong enough to act on it if I did?

"If I hadn't left, would you have kissed me?"

"You aren't gay."

"I just did some pretty gay things." I wiggle my brows at him, which only makes him roll his eyes.

"You're telling me you're gay?" he asks in the same manner he'd ask a student who just failed a test. *"You're telling me you studied?"*

"I'm definitely attracted to you." I take a step closer to him, and when my hard dick rubs against him, his immediately takes notice.

"For six weeks anyway." He winks to play off the fact that he's being a little serious.

I want to reply, "for always," but something stops me. "I've learned not to look to tomorrow. You never know what it will hold."

"I'm a planner, Blake."

"I know." I kiss him. Pushing his back against the wall, I take both of our cocks in my hand. The feeling of his dick against mine makes me tremble.

"Blake," he breathes, his head falling back, his hand finding my ass.

"Say it again."

He does, knowing exactly why I am asking. His breathing picks up and in minutes were both coming on my hand.

West

"Will you tell me one day what it was like at the school your uncle sent you to?"

I run my fingers through his dark locks as we sway in the wind. I live a great life and have no desire to change it, but spending time in the Hampton's, living like the Taylors live, is pretty sweet. I could get used to living in a bubble with Blake.

"No."

"Why not?"

"Because I don't want you anywhere near that darkness."

"You know I've seen some pretty tough things with the kids I teach. I can handle it."

"Can and need to are two different things."

"I'm just saying."

"No," he says, looking me square in the eye. When he lays his head on my chest, he softens it. "No."

"Will you tell me why you left Delta?"

The breeze pushes us back the other way. After several minutes, I decide he's not going to answer, and I'm ok with that. Really, I am.

"I just couldn't kill anymore." He answers so softly I almost miss it. I kiss the top of his head and tighten my hold on him, hurting for the things this man has had to endure.

We've stayed an extra two days. Two days of beach, sun, hammocks, and sex. Lots of down-and-dirty sex. But this has been my favorite part, swaying in the wind, just the two of us spending time together.

"I told Teague I would stop by later today. I think we are going to shoot some hoops."

"Elise is going into town. I might hang with her while you hang with Teague."

"You can come if you want."

"No, you two should catch up. I'll go next time."

"Back to reality tomorrow."

"Yep."

"Mint chocolate chip," I tell the girl behind the counter. She hands Elise her waffle cone with three scoops of chocolate, and a few minutes later, we're enjoying our ice creams under a striped umbrella.

"I like a girl who'll eat."

"Then you and I will truly get along." She gives me an easy, comforting smile. Being with her makes me feel like everything will be okay.

"So, how's the hiding going?" I ask her.

"I'm not hiding."

"Come on, you made your mind up days ago."

"And you would know that how? You and I have spent

maybe a total of twenty-four hours together."

"I don't know. I feel like I know you from all the things people tell me. Emme, Blake, Reid. You don't seem to me like a person who needs two weeks to make up her mind about something. I mean for crying out loud, you're a fixer. You make decisions on a dime. Like, big ones. Ones they make movies about."

"Well, I don't know about that, but yes, you're right. I know what I want to do, but I'm just taking some time for me. I've always figured things out with my best friend, Theo. He was my safe place. Now Reid wants the job. I don't want to jump from one to the other. I just needed a minute to breathe and know that I can do this on my own. And that I'm not just replacing Theo with Reid, but that I am asking Reid to take part because I want to share it with him."

"I get that."

"Do you?"

"Yep. That's why I broke up with my first serious boy-friend. Even though we were young, it could have worked. Easily. I just knew I was using him to replace someone else and it just wasn't fair to him. I loved him, but not in that I-can't-take-another-step-without-you kind of love."

"All-consuming love."

"Yes. Only sometimes I wonder if people realize all-con-suming love shouldn't devour your light, it should reflect it, make it shine brighter. Corny, I know."

"No, it's refreshing. And true I think. I totally get what you are saying. When someone loves you with all they are, it should add to you, not take away from you." She steals a bite of my mint chocolate chip.

"So, are you going to tell Blake?" She asks.

"Tell him what?"

"That he's your all-consuming love."

"He's not—" She shoots me a "don't fucking bullshit me" look.

"Okay, so maybe he is. But I'm not going to tell him that."

"He might surprise you."

I give Elise a look that says "give me a break."

"Look, love is love and Blake knows love. I've seen the way he looks at you. He covers it well, but I know Blake."

"Just a few nights ago you were encouraging me to date Finn."

"That was before I was around you two. And if Blake doesn't step up, I think you should."

"He says you saved him."

"He always says that. Really, he saved himself, I just gave him the hand up."

We eat a couple more bites before I press to see if maybe she'll give me some insight into our ten years apart.

"Blake has said that the school was strict, but they must have been hard-core for it to have affected him the way it did."

"I don't think I would call it a school. It was a 'camp for troubled teens,'" she says, throwing up her fingers for air quotes. "Only it wasn't, it was programming. It was abuse. The men who ran that camp were the vilest men I've come across, and let me tell you, I've known some scum."

"He doesn't tell me about it."

"He never told me his story, always said he didn't want that in my head, but when we went to trial, the stories those boys told…I've seen prisoners tortured more humanely than what they put those kids through."

"Trial?"

"When Blake was working through things, he told me he wanted to get the camp shut down. So we went to work and found the evidence we needed. Ten of the twelve men running the camp were convicted on dozens of counts of child endangerment and abuse. Blake's testimony put the nail in the coffin. Those men will never see the light of day again. They will die behind bars for what they did."

There's another chip at the anger my sixteen-year-old self was holding on to and it's the last to go. The only thing I have now is remorse that I didn't find him. Didn't go to him. Didn't save him.

"You couldn't have known," she says, watching me over her cone.

"What?"

"What was going on, how to save him."

"How did you know that was what I was thinking?"

"Because that's what Theo felt when I was attacked in college. Gabby, also. When you are a victim of a heinous crime, those around you suffer, too. Only no one wants to be called a victim. Least of all me. Least of all Blake."

"No, he doesn't."

"It's his uncle I really wanted to take to trial, but Blake wouldn't let me."

I'm about to respond when a shadow falls over us.

"Connors. What are you doing here?"

I'm shocked to see David outside of the city.

"Hey, David. We're spending a few days hanging out. A friend has a place here. David, this is Elise. Elise, this is David. I volunteer at a community center that David runs."

As expected, Elise never misses a beat. "Nice to meet you. That sounds like rewarding work. Is it for kids? Seniors?"

"Like the community itself, it's a melting pot. A little of everything," David says. "West here works with the kids from his high school, but we have programs for all ages. The center is getting the second part of a face-lift, so it's closed for a few weeks. Two more and we get to open our doors again."

"That's exciting. You're such a good guy," Elise winks at me.

"They don't get better than West. So, how long are you in town for? Want to grab some dinner? Maybe catch a movie?"

"Do you have a place here?" I ask him to avoid answering his questions.

"Investment property."

"You need to teach me how to invest then," I joke.

"There are probably several things I could teach you if you're interested."

Is this guy hitting on me? Seriously?

"He's already an ace student," Blake says, sitting on the bench next to me. Before I can answer he has his lips on mine, his arm around my waist. When he finally releases me, Teague is watching from the bench next to Elise and David looks like he's swallowed something sour.

I hand Blake the rest of my ice cream and he eats what's left.

"Well, I'll see you next week," David says and excuses himself.

"You dipshit," Elise says to Blake. "We need him to want to hire you."

"He will."

"Not if he thinks you're the competition."

"That's exactly why he'll hire me," Blake tells Elise.

"Exactly," Teague confirms. "It's the way a guy's brain works. Dude, you totally sold it. If I didn't know you, I would totally think you were into West."

"See? I know how to do my job?" Blake says.

It's like a punch in the gut to be reminded that what's

happening between us is a job to him. I've tried to remind my-self this was temporary, but I allowed myself to lose sight of it over the last two days.

"What?" he asks Elise when he sees the look on her face.

"Never mind," she says with a bit of disgust and frustration.

Blake

I hold a beer in front of West. He takes it without looking up from his book. I take a brief moment to drink him in, because yeah, he's wearing his glasses.

"Come on. Let's take a walk on the beach," I say, kneeing him gently on his leg.

"Think I'll finish my book," he says without looking at me. Something has been bothering him all afternoon. He's given me nothing but one-word answers. I should be happy we've at least moved on to whole sentences.

"You can read that in the city. This is our last night."

He hesitates, but eventually he stands and, with his beer in hand, heads out to the water. The moon is full and high in the cloudless sky. The tide is coming in.

"You plan on telling me what is bothering you?" I ask, sliding my hand in his. His fingers hang loose for a moment before he gives in and folds them around mine.

"Nothing is bothering me."

"Sorry, but that's not gonna work for me."

"What do you want from me, Blake? You have me all over

the place. You act possessive, then you act like this is just a job. Then you hold my hand walking on the beach. Behind the scenes, you've had your dick in my ass four times now. Is that part of the job, too?"

"Forgive me for needing a little time to adjust and for not wanting to invite the world into our bedroom."

I turn abruptly and head back towards the cottage.

"Walking away again," he says and it stabs through my heart. It's his go to protection mechanism and I hate that he feels like he needs it.

"This time, you're coming with me. I may not know what to call this, I know enough to know I want you, West. So, house, now." I pull him in the direction we came from, but he stands his ground, his feet literally sinking into the sand with each wave that fizzes around his ankles. Before he can protest, I throw him over my shoulder like a sack of potatoes.

"What the hell are you doing?"

I carry him up the stairs to the house, pull the string to rinse our feet then into the bedroom where I deposit him. We're going to settle this once and for all.

"Take off your clothes."

"I don't think so." He tries to move around me, but I block him.

"Do I look like I'm going to repeat myself?"

Our eyes clash and it's more than clear that a challenge is being given. I know this man. I know he can't refuse.

"Now." I pull the T-shirt over my head then drop my shorts, freeing my erection. This is happening. He wants it. I want it.

Slowly he undresses, his eyes never leaving mine. When the last stitch of clothing hits the ground, I'm on him before he can blink.

I make the first move but he fights for dominance and wins in the end.

"Yes," I moan as he works his way down my back. I've been waiting for this West. Everyone thinks he's easygoing, and he is, more than anyone I know. Put he's also protective. In control. It's easy to be fooled by his laid-back personality.

There's a force behind his hold on me, and for someone who's always been the aggressor, being taken is turning me the fuck on. He knows it. I know it.

His lips work their way back up my neck and bite my ear.

"You forget, Blake, I know you like I know myself. I know exactly what you are doing, so be very sure this is what you want."

"You know shit," I hiss as his hand squeezes my dick. I'm so hard for him. I can't remember a time any woman made me this hard.

"I know you're dripping for me, aren't you?" His tongue brushes my ear again. "You want me in there don't you? My cock in your ass. Taking what's mine."

Fuck me. West is not here to play.

"West." I've pulled the pin on a live grenade only instead of throwing it, I kept it in my hand and it's detonating. A shimmy of an orgasm starts to climb, but he squeezes the base of my cock, holding it off. His lips are back on mine and I'm seeing stars from the heat of his desire.

"On your knees, Thomas," he says with his brown eyes on mine. His dimple makes an appearance, and he has to squeeze the base of my cock again. This fucker knows exactly how to handle me.

I sink to my knees in front of him and try to take back some of the control. Just enough to remind him who he's in this with. He holds my face steady and uses me to pleasure himself. The tip of his head hits the back of my throat. I gag and he pulls out.

"Relax your jaw and breathe through your nose. Tilt your head ever so slightly." His thumb skims my cheek. He's asking me to trust him, and I do. We've done this dozens of times over the last week or so, but this time he wants something different. I nod and do exactly as he tells me. On the third attempt, he slides into my throat. He has one hand resting on the wall above me and the other cupping the back of my head. He doesn't hold back and I love it.

I can tell West hasn't been with someone where he hasn't held back a piece of himself. Neither of us have. Until now.

My lips hit the trimmed, honey-colored hairs at the base of his dick. He's close and is just about to pull out of my mouth when I hum around him. His body convulses and his come roars down my throat. I pull him out of my mouth slightly so he can finish on my tongue.

His breathing is erratic and as he takes a beat to compose himself, I take a minute to appreciate the Adonis standing above me.

"On the bed," he commands.

I stand at the foot of the bed as he grabs the lube and a condom. I don't have to tell him because this is West, and he knows exactly what I want.

"On your stomach."

I comply without hesitation. He puts a pillow under my hips and presses his body against mine.

"You're sure this is what you want? 'Cause once I get in there, it's going to change things for you. And for me, too. You've always carried my heart, Blake."

"This is what I want," I softly assure him.

He sits up, straddling me. I hear the click of a top, and I

take a deep breath in. He begins to rub lotion into my skin, only it's on my shoulders. My shoulders, my arms, my back. He takes his time. I realize he's helping to ease me into this, and I have to fight back the tears. This is my West, my best, friend, the kid who always tried to fight off whatever demons were biting at my heels.

He moves his body down mine, and his strong hands work the lotion into my thighs.

"You have a dimple I love, too," he says. I feel his hand follow the curve of my muscle between my hip and my butt. He leans forward, flattening his tongue against the crevice between my thigh and my butt cheek. He repeats the move on the opposite side. My hips begin to undulate against the pillow beneath them. The massage moves slowly to my cheeks, and he gently spreads them apart, exposing my private places to him. I'm more relaxed than I can ever remember. And that's when I feel it, a wetness against my hole.

It feels indescribable. I prop up on my elbows and lift my ass for him to feast on. He chuckles and gives me a pinch. I shift closer to him, my dick dragging across the pillow it's pinned to. And that's when he blows my fucking mind and enters me with his tongue.

"West," I moan. By the time he's done, I am so hard I could chop wood.

Another click of a top and this time I feel a cool liquid running down my crack. He rubs in a circular pattern over my entrance, helping me to relax. He breeches me with a finger. I was expecting it to feel foreign, unwanted, but my body accepts the intrusion without much complaint.

He leans up and kisses my shoulder. Another finger added. He's scissoring them, stretching me. By the time he's added a third finger, I'm close to exploding. The bottom of my feet feel like they are on fire. Walk across burning coals, fire. He must have found my prostate.

"Roll over."

I barely recognize his voice, but I obey and do as I'm told.

"I want to see you, Blake."

West rolls on a condom. I don't think I've ever seen him so hard or ever thought a cock could be so appealing. West's is. It's long and thick, and I love seeing the tip turn a deep purple for me.

He's so steady, and his motions so fluid and in control. He knows this is what I need from him, because I sure as hell have no idea what the fuck I'm doing. Being on top, that's easy. I'm a pro at that. I haven't the first clue about being on bottom, other than what I've seen from West. But this, this feels natural. It feels like being cared for.

West leans over me and kisses me while his fingers trail back down to my hole. "This is mine. No one else has been here. I don't share what's mine. Understood?"

Who knew a possessive West would get my rocks off? Truth is, I love that someone feels possessive of me. West has always made me feel valued. His friendship always made me feel like I had won the fucking lottery.

"Understood." I answer and he tickles the dimple on the side of my ass, liking my answer.

The head of his cock lines up with my entrance. "Breathe, baby," he says as he pushes just inside me. The pressure is intense, but only for a minute. He watches me and when he senses I'm ready, he slides in and out in small increments. "Just relax and let me in."

In and out.

"This is us. Just you and me."

In and out.

My legs rest against his shoulders. He leans forward and his lips capture mine. He's holding himself back, giving me time to adjust.

I purse my lips and let out a slow exhale, willing my body to relax. This is West. He's not going to hurt me. I hear a swoosh right before I feel a sharp slap on the side of my ass. While I'm distracted, West slides all the way in. My hands fist his hair. He's fully seated within me and what I thought would feel wrong feels right. He's not fucking me, he's making love to me.

I can see in his eyes what he's about to say. Don't say it. Please don't.

"No. Please don't," I say. There's a wetness on my eyelashes.

"You're going to have deal with it. Because I do."

"You can't."

"I can." He kisses my chest, exactly where the west side of the compass is placed. Right over my heart. "You're used to taking care of everyone, fixing things, being in charge. You can take a load off, because I'm in charge now."

He lifts my ass up and his dick slides against my prostate. I close around him like a vice.

"Shit, Blake, if you keep doing that I'm gonna blow."

I look him in the eye and purposefully tighten around him again. West begins to fuck me.

Hard. His hand works my dick in time with his thrusts and within minutes he's warning me to get there. His penis has just the right curve to it, and as it works my prostate, I explode, coming in long streams in his hand. I've never experienced an orgasm of this intensity.

West shouts my name through his release, collapsing on top of me.

West

Blake's been gone a week and I miss him. Like feel-it-in-my-bones miss the guy. He flew to Indiana to be with Ryan and the team. Ryan's sister had taken a turn for the worse and passed away the day after they arrived. I know it's got to be incredibly difficult on all of them to see their friend suffering.

I can hear it in Blake's voice. The exhaustion, the need to fix when there is no fix for this.

We've been talking every night and texting every day. Time apart has given us a chance to reacquaint. Each night is a different conversation. They've run the gamut from the heartache Blake feels for his friend to things we've missed about each other over the last ten years to things we did together as kids. Last night we had some spicy hot phone sex before arguing about my lunch date today. With Finn.

I've had to remind Blake more than once that there is, one, nothing to be jealous of and two, I'm to be trusted. He easily agreed with the latter, but he still struggles with the first. Finn is a total flirt, mostly in front of Blake, but he no longer hits on me. I get the feeling Finn could use a friend. I'm not sure what it is, and I am still getting to know him. I've learned he and his brother are close, but his inner circle is limited. I think he hides behind the flirt.

I grab my ringing phone thinking Blake is calling to say they are taking off.

"Hello?"

"Hey, kid. You going next weekend?"

"I'll be there, Donnie."

"Mom says your Facebook says you're in a relationship. Please tell me you did not let that jackass Jay back in?"

"No, Jay is not in the picture."

"Good, 'cause I would hate to have to kick his ass."

"I can kick ass on my own, you know."

"Of course I know. You could kick my ass, but that's what big brothers are for, to kick ass for their siblings. Ran into Bree the other day. I hear you have a billionaire chasing after you. Gotta say, I'd spread my legs for a man with that kind of money, too."

"I swear Mom and Dad dropped you on your head when you were a kid."

"Gotta go kid. I'm being paged. I'll see you soon."

I blow my whistle. "Marcus, what was that?"

The center is still under renovation, but the gym is finished so we can at least practice.

"Come on, Coach," Marcus whines.

"What did I ask you to do during that play?"

"Pass."

"Right, pass. And what did you do?"

"Shoot the ball?"

"Yes, you shot the ball. Did you make the shot?"

"No."

"So not only did you screw up the play, you didn't score. And Steven was left wide open in the paint. We would have had two points. Two points that could have won us the ballgame."

"Sorry, coach."

"Think about it while you all run 8's until passing is second nature to Marcus."

The team grumbles their disapproval and hits the line. I blow the whistle and they start the drill. Marcus does the first one, but before he gets back in line he jogs over to me.

"I saw Mickey yesterday."

"Where?" I turn eagerly towards him. "How is he?"

"He didn't look good, coach. I asked him if he was coming back and he said it wasn't safe for him."

"What does that mean?"

"Don't know," he shrugs.

"Did he say where he was staying?"

"The streets. Said I could find him in that old subway station off 12th."

"Thanks. Hit the line."

"Who's staying in the 12th?" I turn to see David walking up behind me.

"One of my students I've been trying to find."

"Do I know him?"

"I doubt it. His name is Mickey."

He gives me a look like he doesn't know who I'm talking about. "Tell me about this Blake. I got a call from HR saying he applied for the open position."

"Yeah, he could use a job."

"You don't seem like someone who would be with a deadbeat."

"He's not. He just got back from serving oversees. It's taking a while to figure out what he wants to do."

Something about this guy gives me the creeps. I can't put my finger on it, but there's something off about him. I know he's involved in the missing money, I just don't know why or how to prove it.

"I tried to reach him to come in. I'll get him set up."

"That would be awesome. I appreciate it man. He had a funeral out of town. Should be back any day now."

"Sorry to hear it. Want to maybe grab some dinner tonight?"

"Thanks, but I have somewhere to be after practice. I'll tell Blake to give you a call." I blow the whistle, putting the boys out of their misery.

Myles collapses on the floor. "Finally."

My phone dings.

Blake: Hey babe—how was lunch?

Corny as hell, I know, but my heart flips when he calls me babe. Even if he's fishing for something.

Me: Good. Finn said hello.

Blake: I'm sure he did.

Me: LOL. Don't be like that. Have you left yet?

Blake: In the air. What about you? Still at practice?

"Alright Coach. We all know what that smile means." Steven teases.

We set up a time for the next practice and talk about how summer school is going. By the time I close the gym it's after

five. I text Blake back while I head over to the abandoned station on 12th. I want to see if I can find Mickey.

Me: Just left. Someone saw Mickey. I'm going to see if he's
still there.
Blake: Where is there?
Blake: ?????

My phone rings, but I silence it. Easier to ask for forgiveness than permission.

The smell at the bottom of the stairs is pungent. It's been
used as a bathroom too many times, and in this heat I'm surprised anyone would come down here. The door has been broken and its obvious people have been living down here for a
long time. This hasn't been an active station for years by the
look of things.

When I move further down the platform, I have to turn
on the flashlight on my phone. I find a guy and show him a
picture of Mickey on my cell. He points me in a direction. It's
only now I realize this might not have been the smartest idea.
It's too dark and hard to see. I can either illuminate where my
feet are walking or I can see where I'm headed, but not both.

I make myself ignore the rats and needles and keep my
eyes up. I can hear someone behind me and his steps mimic
mine. When I walk, he walks. When I stop, he stops. I turn
and look, but the light is only so strong and I don't see anyone.
I continue on another twenty or thirty yards, and when I turn
a corner, I see Mickey fighting with someone. I yell and run to
him, but whoever it was moved into the darkness where I can't
see him.

Mickey falls to the ground, there's blood coming from his
stomach.

"Hang on Mick."

"Coach." He's terrified.

I try to call 911 but there's no signal.

The last thing I remember is telling him I was going to have to carry him out of there to get him help.

Every time I try to fall back into a deep sleep, something sticks me. I will myself to wake up, but my body doesn't seem to respond. I can hear voices. Loud ones. Angry ones.

My arms feel like lead, but my eyelids finally cooperate and open. My vision is blurred, but I make out Blake at the end of the bed. His arms are folded across his body and he's having a heated conversation with…Finn? Is that Finn? I try to speak, but nothing happens. I blink my eyes thinking the movement will capture their attention, but it's dark in here.

"If you two don't lower your voices, you're going to be asked to leave." I recognize that voice. Elise.

"Like that is gonna happen," Blake says.

"Why are you so pigheaded? Are you that threatened that you would say no to me even when it is the best thing for West?"

"Elise, tell him."

"Finn, I have to side with Blake on this one. There is no one in the business better than him. Ask whoever you would hire and they will tell you he's who you need."

"You're not worried he's too close?" Finn asks.

"No. Blake is not reckless. If he was too close he would say it. He's not going to take chances with West's life. I'm more concerned about his directive."

"I didn't put a hit out on him, Elise. I have my guys looking for him with a directive to bring him in alive. Not dead."

Finn shakes his head in frustration but relents. "Fine. But if something happens, I'm taking over."

"Why are you here?" Blake asks him.

"Because I care about West."

"You've spent an hour with the guy."

"And you've spent years with him. Not sure that gives you anything but a head start."

I try again to say something but it's no use.

"West is a friend. Something I don't have a ton of," Finn admits and I see some of Blake's resistance fade.

"Fine, be here for him as a friend. But where West's safety is concerned, I'm telling you, step the fuck off. West is mine to look after and care for."

"Care for him and we won't have any issues." Finn runs his hands through his hair. "But my men stay on the door and my doctor stays on the case."

"That I can work with," Blake concedes.

I can no longer keep my eyes open. My head is splitting.

"I talked to Emme today," Elise says. "She was roommates with the trauma surgeon who saw West in the ER and with the neuro resident following him. She trusts them both."

"That's great, but my guy is head of neuro. He stays," Finn mandates. "I'll be back in a couple of hours. We have a Foundation meeting to decide how we want to clean up this mess."

A minute later I feel cool lips against my forehead and my hair being swept to the side. The hands are soft, but large. I know Blake's touch. This isn't it.

What feels like only a few minutes later, I pull my arm back with a grimace. Someone is using me as a pincushion again.

"Looks like someone is back with us."

Slowly, my vision comes into focus and there's a friend-ly-looking woman in scrubs leaning over me.

"West?"

I look to the left and Blake is there. He runs his hand gently down the side of my face and it feels so good I lean into it. This is Blake's touch.

"I'll let the doctor know he's up," the nurse says on her way out the door.

Before she's even out of the room his lips are on mine gently kissing me. When he pulls back, his blue eyes are stormy.

"You are in a fuck-load of trouble. When you're better, I plan to take the last twenty-four hours out on your ass."

I must be ok, because I immediately feel myself begin to stir under his threat.

"What happened?"

"Glad to see you back with us, Mr. Connors." A handsome man comes in the room. Blake stands, letting him have access to me.

"I'm Kyle. I'm one of your doctors. I'm a friend of Emme James." He sees my confusion and laughs, "Taylor. Emme Taylor. Sorry."

He shines a light in my eyes and moves to the foot of the bed. Lifting the covers, he runs a metal thing down the bottom of each foot making them twitch. He does several more tests, asking me questions and making me follow his finger. When I'm squeezing his hands, he tells me that I have a concussion and have been out for a little more than a day.

"We ran tests. There was no skull fracture, but you do have some bleeding on your brain. It's slight and should remedy itself. Our bodies have a way of healing the bumps and bruises we get. Your bump just happened to be in the right spot to knock you out for a while. I want to keep you one more night for observation." He turns to the nurse. "Let's remove the IV and catheter. He can have a light diet. If you have any nausea, vomiting, or blurred vision I want to know about it. Understood?" he looks to Blake who nods his answer. "Good. How are you feeling?"

"My head hurts."

"Sarah here will bring you some pain meds. You can have them every six hours and I'll send you home with some. Get some rest. I'll be back to check on you later."

"Thank you, doc." Blake reaches out to shake his hand and he and the nurse leave.

"What happened?"

"What do you remember?" Blake asks, sitting on the side of my bed.

I think for several minutes trying to recall.

"Mickey!"

"Is in recovery. He was stabbed twice. He lost a lot of blood, but the trauma doc was able to save him."

"How? Who found us?"

"My security. I was having you followed."

"What?" I try to sit up, but Blake stops me. He helps me into a sitting position, propping me up with pillows.

"I was having you watched while I was out of town."

"Why didn't you just tell me?"

"Easier to ask forgiveness than permission," he grins. "Apparently you were hit on the head when you found Mickey. By the time my guy got to you, you were out cold. He carried you and Mickey to the street and called for an ambulance. Somehow Finn found out and had you both brought to NY Pres, so his doctors could take care of you. I landed about an hour after you got here."

"Who did this?"

"David."

"Why?"

"Details are still a little sketchy. He's still on the run. Mickey woke after surgery and best we can piece together is David was using the kids from your school to sell and distribute drugs. He took the money to create a diversion. Sounds like Mickey's brother was involved and Mickey was working off a debt. That's all I know right now. Lots of drama and not many answers."

"So, it's over? You don't have to work at the center?"

"It's not over. David is still out there, and until he's caught and we know who he was doing business with, I'm not going anywhere."

Until? Does that mean once this is over he's going *some*where?

"How long has Finn been gone?" I say in an attempt to change the subject. I don't have what it takes to deal with this right now. Blake's eyes are like a kaleidoscope. They go from surprised to hurt to irritated in a matter of seconds.

"Two hours. How did you know he was here?"

"I remember hearing you two arguing, but then I slipped back asleep."

Blake stands and looks out the window.

"Blake?"

He doesn't answer me or look my way. Instead a nurse comes in, hands me two white pills, and takes out my IV and catheter. Not a fun experience, I must say, and it makes me have to use the bathroom. When she leaves, I push off the bed to stand. When I do, the room spins and I probably would have fallen if Blake wasn't by my side.

"You don't get up without telling me," he says. He gives

me a minute to recover and then basically carries me into the bathroom.

"Do I have something besides this hospital gown?" I ask, looking down and feeling ridiculous.

"Yes. Bree dropped off a bag for you. Pee and I'll help you shower," Blake says, pulling on the string holding my gown up. It falls to the ground. I try to pee in a straight line, but it's not easy after a tube is pulled out of a place a tube should never be. And my hands are shaking. Blake reaches down and steadies my hand, helping me aim into the bowl. Once I'm done he lowers the shower seat and sets a towel down for me. I take a seat, because standing is not an option the way my head is swirling. The water feels remarkable and Blake bathes me, taking extra care with my head that is still pounding.

"I'm exhausted," I admit as he helps me step into a pair of shorts and pulls them up. He sits me in a chair and calls for my bed to be changed. Ten minutes later I'm under the covers and asleep.

I wake to a knock on the door. It opens and Finn comes in carrying flowers and a take-out bag from a deli off 5th. One of my favorites.

"Hey, handsome." He leans down to kiss my forehead. "Bloody happy to see those brown eyes."

I glance questioningly towards Blake, who looks away.

"Thanks for texting me," Finn says, offering Blake his hand. To my surprise, Blake shakes it and clears his throat.

"I asked Finn to pick up a soup and sandwich from the Deli you like on 5th."

Ah. So, it's not a coincidence. What I can't figure out is why Finn? Why not Bree?"I carried in for you, too." Finn says, by way of a peace offering.

"Thank you, but I think I'll stretch my legs, give you two time alone." Blake still hasn't looked in my direction.

"Where are you going?" I ask.

"I'll be back. I'm staying here tonight."

"I can stay if you need a break," Finn offers.

"Thanks. I know your guys are on the door, but I feel better being here to make sure nothing happens."

"Am I in danger?" I ask Blake. He finally looks at me.

"Oh, I don't know. A man you worked with tried to kill your student and very well meant to harm you. We don't know where he is. We've cut off his resources and he's on the run. Won't be long before he's truly desperate. I'd say there's cause to be cautious." There's a bite to his tone. He's still pissed, but there's something else there, too. Whatever it is, I don't like it.

Blake leaves without a backwards glance.

"I ordered your favorite," Finn says, rolling the hospital tray to my bed and sitting down next to me.

Blake must have told him. No way Finn knows my favorite anything.

"You didn't have to do this."

"Sure I did. Hospital food will kill you." He opens containers and hands me a spoon for the chicken and pasta soup. It smells delicious and my stomach growls on cue.

"You not eating?" I ask.

"It's hard to eat when I'm distracted," he says. I feel a blush creeping up my cheeks when I realize he's referring to me not wearing a shirt. He smiles when he recognizes the faint markings all over my torso: love bites. Love bites or sex bites? Sex bites, I decide with a dim heaviness in my chest. My heart hurts and I rub my sternum as if that will soothe it.

"Looks like I need to get Blake a dummy."

"A huh?"

"I believe you Yanks call it a…" He thinks hard for a minute and his perplexed look makes me smile.

"A pacifier!" he says, snapping his fingers.

"I really appreciate you bringing me dinner, but I'm alright. I go home tomorrow. I hate everyone is making such a fuss over nothing."

"This isn't nothing. I know Blake has probably read you the riot act so I've held off on adding to it, but I don't know what you were thinking going into a place like that by yourself. No matter who was down there. How is that logical?"

"I know. I was so focused on getting to Mickey that I didn't think it through."

"As for making a fuss, it's not. People care about you."

I don't respond and he doesn't push for it. When I finish eating, he cleans up, leaving the food for Blake on the tray he's rolled into the corner. He returns to my bed, sitting at my side, his arm on the other side of my legs propping himself up.

"So. You don't want to talk about it?"

I'm considering it when Blake comes back in. He takes one look at Finn's position but doesn't say anything.

Finn gives me a cocky smile and winks. "I'll go so you can get some rest. I'll check on you tomorrow."

Finn says his goodbyes, and Blake stalks around the room for several minutes before finally plopping down in the chair. It's obvious he doesn't want to talk and I'm more exhausted than I should be just from eating. Blake must notice because he finally gives in and walks over to me. Pushing the hair off my forehead, he releases a lungful of air and tells me to sleep. "I'll be here when you wake up."

I would be his if he would have me, but something's changed. I don't think we want the same thing.

Blake

"You plan on telling me what is going on?" West asks as I stand over him, telling him to sleep. He's leaned his face into my touch, and I have to fight the urge to kiss him.

"Isn't it obvious?"

"Not to me it isn't."

"You could have been killed."

"But I wasn't." He studies me for a minute. He looks lost and confused, and I hate that it's because of me.

How do I tell him that I've watched him since I got here, begging for him to wake up? Promising that, if he did, I would do everything in my power to surround him with light and not darkness. To do all I can do to make sure he has a life he deserves. I've risked my life for others, but I've never understood what it meant to sacrifice yourself for someone you love and the pain that comes with it until now. Now that it's clear I have to let him go.

"Rest. You can barely keep your eyes open. I said I'd be here when you woke up, I meant it."

I can tell he doesn't believe me. He moves to his left and pats the bed next to him.

"I'm good," I say, shaking my head.

"In a plastic chair?"

"I sat in it all night last night." I don't use the word sleep, because I didn't get a wink of sleep last night.

West's large brown eyes take me in and I know he knows. "If you're leaving me, the least you can do is sit with me."

"I'm not leaving you," I lie.

"You've never lied to me before. Don't start now. This has always been until the job was over. Hasn't it?"

My resolve to be an ass to him and try to make him not love me anymore crumbles when one lone tear falls down his cheek. Letting him go is going to be the hardest thing I've ever done. It was impossible at sixteen. It's harder now.

"You will be okay," I whisper into his hair.

"Why are you doing this? I know you weren't pretending at the beach. I know you felt what I felt. You've been in this just as much as I have. We don't need a cover."

"West, you deserve so much more than what I can give you. You deserve someone like Finn."

"Bullshit and you know it."

"There will never be a friend for me like you. Never. It's always been you for me. I love you. You have to know I do. You're my best friend. That's why you need to give Finn a chance. He can give you things I can't." Like a heart that isn't scarred beyond recognition.

West

The dam that has shored up my emotions since I was sixteen breaks.

How is it the person who broke me is the only one who can put me back together?

I'm angry. Angry that he's wrapping his "I love you" up in friendship when I know it's more.

"I don't care about his fucking money," I lash out.

"That's not what I mean and you know it."

"No, I don't. I honestly don't know. You're spewing so much damn bullshit that I don't fucking know anything anymore."

"He can give you his heart."

I physically double over from the emotional blow Blake just hit me with. It's worse than being hit over the head with a two-by-four. Rage courses through my body. How dare he? How fucking dare he?!

I stand faster than my body can accommodate, my vision blurs and I stumble. Blake is by my side in an instant, but I push him away.

"What the fuck are you doing?" he yells.

"Leaving. You're an expert at it, you should fucking know what it looks like."

"I'm not leaving!"

"You're right. You're not leaving, I am."

"West, I swear to God, if you don't get your ass back in bed." He comes toward me.

"What? What are you going to do?"

"If you so much as take another step, I promise you, before you can take your next breath, I'll have you restrained to the bed."

"I'm leaving."

"Your insurance won't pay if you leave AMA."

"Good thing I have a hot new billionaire boyfriend. He can pay the bill."

"West, you're pissing me off."

"Don't start showing emotion now."

"Sit down," he says, and I hate the look on his face. With every piece of toxin that spews from my mouth, he looks like I'm twisting a knife deeper and deeper into his heart.

"You can stop this," I plead with him.

"Stop what?"

"You can stop this, Blake. Admit what we both know to be true."

"I have no idea what you are talking about."

"Bullshit. Admit that you love me."

He doesn't respond.

"Fine." I take a step forward and reach for a shirt out of the bag Bree dropped off. Before I know what's happening, Blake grabs the shirt out of my hand and lays me out on the bed. He knots the T-shirt around my wrist and the bedrail, and as I attempt to unknot the knot he's tying, he pulls my free wrist to the other side and holds it in place as I struggle against him. He finds a tourniquet on a shelf and uses it to secure me to the bedrails.

"I said calm the fuck down."

I give up, leaning back, exhausted. My blood pressure is through the roof, and I can feel my pulse vibrating through my skull. "My head is splitting."

"You don't say." He's pissed.

My head is exploding. I close my eyes against the double vision. The dinner I ate is threatening to reappear.

"You better not throw up," Blake says, and just as quickly as he can grab a basin and hold it under my chin, I puke. "I'll go get the nurse."

"I'm fine," I say, laying my head back again. "I just overdid it arguing with a dumb ass and the movement made me spin a little."

Blake rinses out the basin and brings a wet washcloth to run over my face. I keep my eyes closed. I have to bite my bottom lip to keep it from quivering under his touch. I hear him in the bathroom and when he's back he taps my mouth. I open my eyes and he's holding my toothbrush.

"Just untie me."

"No. Open. Your breath smells like vomit."

I open my mouth and he brushes my teeth then gives me a sip of water to rinse and spit. When I'm done, he leans over, and kisses me deeply, like he's starving for me.

"When I got the call that you were being brought here and I couldn't get to you right away, I swear, I thought my life had ended."

Is that what this is about? He thought he was going to lose me?

"You are my best friend and I will always love you, but

I am not the man for you." This time he's the one with water-filled eyes.

I don't know what else to do or say. I can't be the only one to fight for us. He has to want this. I can't want it for him. I won't force him to be with me. Without a doubt I love him, but I love myself, too. And I won't trap someone into being with me. I close my eyes and lean back. There's nothing left to say.

The lowering of my arm jostles me awake. Finn reaches across me and unties the other one and tries to massage feeling back into them.

"I thought I was pig-headed, but you two take the cake," Finn says.

"What are you doing here?" I ask, sliding into the T-shirt he just removed from my wrist.

"Blake rung me. I was a block over at a meeting. He asked me to come sit with you."

"You didn't need to leave your meeting."

"Well, in all fairness, he told me he tied you to the bed and I felt like you probably shouldn't stay this way too long. So, I came over."

"How long have you been here?"

"I just walked in. Blake called me about twenty minutes ago."

"I swear, I feel like I've slept hours and I'm still tired."

"I didn't mean to wake you, but I figured your arms might get sore. Your body is trying to heal itself. That is why you are still tired." Finn sets the item Blake used to secure me on the bed and gives me a stern look.

"He told me you were trying to leave. I don't blame him for restraining you. And don't think for a minute I would have paid the bill. I don't pay for things I don't condone."

"I wouldn't have let you pay my bill."

"That is not the point. The point is you trying to leave at all. You have blood on your brain. I'm going to get the nurse and make sure you are okay. Blake said you mentioned blurred vision and that you vomited."

"Only because I was upset and moving too fast."

"Still, I'm getting you checked." He leaves and comes back with Kyle, the doctor who examined me earlier.

"If you refuse to take proper care of yourself in here, how can I be sure you'll do it at home? I'll keep you here if I need to," Kyle warns.

"No, I'm ready to go as it is."

"Then follow my orders and you can go home tomorrow. If not, you'll be in here longer."

"He'll follow them," Finn says, arms crossed.

I give myself a minute to take in the man in front of me. He's beautiful. His pants hug him in all the right places. His shirt sleeves are rolled up, showing his forearms, and he has on that watch. His eyes sparkle as he stares into mine. If my heart wasn't with another, he would have it.

"Got it?" Kyle asks. Finn answers in the affirmative. He knows I didn't hear a word that was said.

"Good. Now rest and home tomorrow." He leaves and Finn laughs.

"I have to say, if I wasn't in love with Blake, you would be off the market."

"Thank you, I think? Are you always this smooth? Turning someone down while stroking their ego? Because I must say, it just makes me want you more."

"Finn." I want to make sure I'm really clear. I would never want to take advantage of him.

"There is no way I would act on it, though. Blake is the one person who could make me disappear and no one would ever know what happened to me."

"I would miss you," I tease and am rewarded with another chuckle.

"That man is in love with you."

I must have a look on my face that says I'm not so sure anymore.

"Trust me. I'm telling you the man that came after me this morning when I threatened to take over is a man in love. No way a friend acts like that."

"He's a good friend."

"I don't know if you're being deliberately obtuse or if you're just delusional."

"I thought you were here to lift my spirits?"

"I'm here to take care of you until that blighter can see for himself what he wants."

"I don't think he knows what he wants."

"Only a man that loves you more than he loves himself would call me to come look after you. I could hear it in his voice."

"Finn, this is not your problem. Seriously. I appreciate everything you've done for me, but this isn't your mess."

"Piss off. You're my friend, right?"

"Of course."

"Dandy. Since you're in a bad way and we're having a moment, I'll admit to you that I don't have many friends and I'd like to keep the few I have. Even if they did drive a stake through my heart," he says with a smile.

"You look devastated."

"Disappointed. But as a friend, I'm going to help you out."

"I'm certain I am not going to like this."

"Nothing helps someone decide what they want more quickly than the green-eyed monster."

"Finn, I really don't like playing games."

"That's not a problem. I'll do all the playing."

"Why?"

"Like I said, we're friends. Plus, I get to kiss you whenever I want over the next few days. I'm thinking by the end of next week, we'll have our answer. I'll probably have a broken nose, but we'll have our answer. Now, scoot over. I promise I'll be here when you wake up."

"Dude, you can't even keep it in your pants while you're in the hospital?" Donnie's voice wakes us up. Sunlight streams through the windows.

"I haven't slept this long in a while," Finn states absently, looking at his watch.

"Still got the moves, huh little brother? Put them straight to sleep," Donnie teases.

I throw my legs off the side of the bed to stand. He hugs me tightly and I can feel the tension drain out of him. "What the fuck man? What were you thinking? You could have been killed."

"Please. I can't take another lecture."

"Well, prepare yourself 'cause Mom and Dad know and so does the rest of the crew."

"How?"

"Blake called."

"You talked to Blake?"

"Yep. Called me last night. I caught the first train here. Forgive my manners." He extends a hand to Finn who's trying to finger comb his hair. "I'm Donnie, this idiot's older brother."

"Nice to meet you. Finn Nelson."

Recognition flashes in Donnie's eyes, but it's gone as quickly as it came.

"I'll go get some coffee." He points to Donnie who says he takes his black.

"You're not planning to really drink it in front of me are you?"

"Of course," Finn answers.

"But I can't have any."

"Exactly," he winks. "That's what makes it fun."

"Holy shit. That's the billionaire." Donnie points to the door Finn just exited.

"His name is Finn."

"Damn, little brother. He's into you."

"We're just friends."

"Trust me. I know."

"Yeah. How so?" I point to my bag and he brings it over. I dig out a clean T-shirt.

"Blake called me."

"And?" My arms and head poke through the openings.

"And you've been in love with him since you were six. No way is he around and you're with another guy. Why didn't you tell us he was back? I assume he's the one who left the polka dots on your chest." He lays on my bed. I take the chair.

"You know Blake's not gay."

"Not for just anyone, maybe, but for you, he's totally gay."

"What are you talking about?"

"Exactly what I said."

As if on cue, the door opens and Blake saunters through.

"Why is *your* ass in the bed? You weren't clunked over the head."

"Hey man!" Donnie jumps up and wraps him in a long embrace. "I couldn't believe it when you called me. I am so grateful you are okay. Mom broke down when I told her."

"Shit," Blake and I say together.

"Yep. That's on you, dumbasses. She has plenty to say about it, too."

"I'll call her," I say.

"Call her? I'm staying with you two until we go up for the weekend."

"What?" Blake asks.

"The party for Maggie. This weekend," Donnie says, glancing between the two of us.

"I can't go."

"Blake Thomas. I can and will kick your ass if you make me back out on a promise to my mom. You're going."

"Donnie—"

"She deserves to see you. You'll break her heart if you don't."

Donnie is pulling out the big guns, but he's serious. He's also right. I've been so caught up in our bubble that I haven't talked to my parents in a few weeks. That's unusual.

"Good news. Kyle is signing the discharge papers. We can go," Finn says, handing Donnie and Blake a coffee.

Three alpha males clink their cups together as a toast, each raising a brow before they take a sip.

"This is so fucked up," I moan.

Blake

Leaving West in the hospital with Finn was more difficult than I imagined, but it was necessary. I let this get out of control. I got caught up in the role we were playing and told myself that it was okay, because we were supposed to look like a couple. But I was only kidding myself. I knew it was going to end. I just never thought it would be this hard. I mean, this is West. He's been my insides since I was six.

Growing up, I had no idea he was gay. To me he was West, my best friend, my solace. I didn't feel anything physical for him, but he was always home for me. I resist saying he's my soulmate, but there are large parts of my heart that only West will have.

Dammit. My glove-covered fist connects with the punching bag in front of me.

As soon as we got West settled back into the apartment, I made an excuse that I had to meet Teague. And I did—right after I called him on my way to the gym. I just couldn't stay in that place. Donnie glaring at me like he wanted to kick my ass. Finn swooning over West. I have to give it to him, he looked uncomfortable, but he let Finn take care of him.

The image of Finn kissing West flashes through my mind, and I hit the bag so hard Teague has to take a step back.

"Dude. When I said I'd hold the bag for you, I didn't know you were in this kind of mood."

"I'm not in a mood."

"Want to talk about it?"

"Nothing to talk about."

He spares me and doesn't say anything else, but he knows I'm lying. I hit for another ten minutes and he puts a stop to the work out.

"You won't be able to move if you keep that up. Come on. I know somewhere we can go that will take your mind off things."

"I'm not up for a titty bar."

"No, fuckwit. I'm a married man. Plus, call me stupid, but I don't think there's anything at a titty bar that would interest you."

"Meaning?"

"Exactly what I said."

"I like tits," I say, but even I can admit, it wasn't very convincing. Still, when he gives me that "oh, please" look, all that anger that was just below the surface starts to bubble up. "What are you saying, man?"

"I'm saying, get your head out of your fucking ass before you lose the best thing that ever happened to you."

"You know shit."

"Fuck you, Blake." He's in my face and his irritation catches me off-guard. Teague isn't one to show anger very easily. "Don't you fucking stand there and lie to my fucking face. Not after all the shit we've been through. You dishonor yourself and you dishonor me when you do that. We don't hide."

"You hid. For two years, I had no idea where the fuck you were. I spent months trying to find you."

"At least you knew I was alive. You hid from West for ten years. He had no idea you were alive."

"That's unfair and you know it. I wrote him every day for a year. You know how they worked. I didn't know they never sent the letters. They cut us off. Made us think we were alone."

"That was the first two years. What about the other eight?"

"We were Delta 6. No one even knew we existed. What would you have me do? Send a note via courier pigeon from the Middle East?"

He shoots me a look that lets me know I'm close. Real close.

"Fine. Let's go with your reasoning. No matter how stupid as shit it is. You've been home almost five years."

"Teague..."

He gets in my face again. "Blake, just say it." He shoves me.

"Stop pushing me," I shove back.

"Stop being a pussy and say it."

"Say what? What do you want from me?"

"I want you to stop hiding."

"West knows where I am. I'm not hiding."

"God. You're a dumb shit. Not from West. From yourself. Say it."

"I swear I don't know what you want me to say."

I'm angry, it's Teague, my guard is down. That's the only reason I can account for the fact that I didn't see the fist flying to my face before it connects with my eye. As soon as I hit the ground, I jump to my feet only to be pushed back down again.

"You stay down there." He pushes against my chest. "Say it."

"Teague." It's part growl, part pleading.

"Say it, Blake. You know you'll feel better. No one else gives a fuck who you love. Say it."

"Since when have I ever given a shit what anyone thought of me? You want me to say I'm gay? I'm not gay. That I might be bi? I'm not attracted to men. Only the one. I have no problem with that. I have no problem saying I'm in love with a man."

"Then what is it?"

I sit up and Teague sits on the floor next to me.

"He has no idea the things I've done. He deserves someone who can give him their heart. Not someone who has no heart to give."

"Bullshit. You have a heart as big as the sea. Why else would you have looked for my sorry ass for two years? You were always the one that took care of all of us."

"Of course I did. You were in my charge. It was my job."

"Maybe, but that wasn't the only reason. You cared. You still do. Blake, I've seen you offer yourself up to be tortured in place of another person. You've put your life on the line to save others. No way does a man do that and not have heart. Don't let your uncle and the bastards at that school win by making you believe you are less than you are."

"I see you're still watching Dr. Phil."

"Hey, that man has real answers for real people. I didn't think I was worthy until I met Emme. She gave me purpose and led me to my wife. Not only did she literally bring Joy to me, but Emme reminded me that I deserved love. And you do to, Blake."

"I'm not saying I don't, but West deserves more."

"Have you asked West what he thinks he deserves? Don't you trust him to know what's best for him?"

Teague stands and reaches down to pull me up.

"Go be the man I trusted my life with."

"I can't believe you hit me."

"Next time, I'll just shoot ya."

"What the hell happened to you?" West asks when I walk into the kitchen.

"Teague."

"Did it work?"

"What?"

"Did he knock some sense into you?"

I grumble under my breath.

"I gotta run to a dinn—oh, sorry. I didn't know you had company," Finn says coming out of the bedroom. I have to bite my lip to keep myself from commenting that I'm not the company, he's the company, but I remind myself why I'm doing this and leave it unsaid.

"Thank you for spending time with me," West says.

Finn walks over and places his hands on West's hips. He stands slightly taller than West and it makes me nauseated to see West tip his head back to look him in the eye.

"Remember, you promised me you'd behave."

I gag, and West cuts his eyes to me before looking back to Finn.

"I remember."

"But feel free to disobey. That would be fun, too."

Pink. West's cheeks visibly pink at the sexual promise radiating off of Finn who cups his hands around West's jaw. Finn leans his body against West, and I almost shatter the bottle in my hand when he kisses him. West's hands pull Finn's hips closer and, that's it, I can't take anymore. I set my beer down with enough force that it fizzes out the top and walk to the bedroom to take a shower.

"God, you're an idiot," Donnie says from the couch.

Yes. Yes I am.

West

I am one-hundred percent in love with Blake. I have zero doubts about that. But fuck me on a Sunday, Finn can kiss. And I am only human, after all. Blake keeps pushing Finn on me. He's shut me out. I'm at a loss what to do, so I'm going with the only thing I know left to do: give him what he's asking for.

"Sorry," Finn whispers in my ear. "Got a little carried away."

"We need to stop this. This isn't fair to you."

"Please. This is the most fun I've had in ages."

Blake steps out of the bedroom looking like he is about to say something. Before he can, Finn leans forward and pulls on my bottom lip with his teeth. "See you tomorrow."

"Can I see you for a minute?" Blake says with a calmness he clearly is not feeling. "Now," he adds with a little more force.

Donnie's lip twitches as he reaches for the remote and turns on the TV. I close the door to give us some privacy. When I finally enter the bathroom, Blake has a towel wrapped around his waist and the shower is running.

"You know there are people who don't have running water," I say, reaching in and turning the handle to the off position.

"I've dug wells for those people. Don't tell me about those people."

"What can I do for you?" I ask.

"If you like Finn's face the way it is, I suggest you keep his lips off yours."

"I'm sorry, but you no longer have a say so."

"West, don't fuck with me," he growls, but then immediately tries to regain his composure. "I can't go to your parents this weekend," he says.

I shrug. "Yeah, I don't know what to tell you. Mom already thinks you're coming."

"Well, fix that. Call her and let her know it's not going to work out."

"No."

"Excuse me?"

"You made a commitment."

"I didn't make a commitment. Donnie committed for me." His voice is rising.

We're at a stalemate so we just stand there staring at each other.

"I'm not going."

"Well, I'm not calling."

He enters the shower stall mumbling all sorts of things. He has his back to me, and I can't help but take a minute to study each line and ripple in his arms and his back. The water trails down his torso like a stream down a mountain. It takes every bit of willpower I have not to follow him in there.

I close the bathroom door and walk back into the living room with Donnie.

"Dinner when Blake gets out of the shower?" Donnie asks, steering clear of a deeper conversation.

"Sounds good." I lay on the couch, fluffing a pillow under my head. "What inning?" I ask. The Yankees are playing.

"Bottom of the first. It just started."

Blake's voice pulls me out of the light slumber I was in waiting for him to get out of the shower.

"There's a Thai place on 11th that delivers. Why don't we stay in so he can sleep?" Blake suggests. He covers me with a blanket and runs a thumb along my jawline, almost like he can't resist touching me. At least that's the story I'm going with. I consciously stay in the land of sleep a little longer. They don't need me to make dinner decisions.

I'm worn out. The doctor said it was to be expected for a few more days, but I'm still surprised by it. I pull the blanket under my chin and shimmy deeper into the cushions.

"That's fine with me." Donnie says. "I was going to suggest we go somewhere that had the game on anyway."

"What's the score?" Blake's voice sounds far away and I hear the fridge open. Kinks walks up my legs, his feet clawing at me until he's pleased with the space and curls up on my hip.

"Sox are up one in the bottom of the 5th."

Blake orders enough food for a small army. I really have no idea where he puts it.

I'm just about to drift off again when Donnie starts talking.

"So, who do I have to thank for the black eye?"

"Dude, shouldn't you be kicking his ass?" Blake says.

"Not this time, kiddo."

When Donnie pulls out the "kiddo", a lecture is coming. Blake must remember because he grunts a little. "This is gonna hurt, isn't it?" Blake sighs.

"Nah, I think you're hurting enough. You don't need me to add to it. But I gotta ask you, what are you doing man? You're really gonna walk away from the best thing that's ever happened to you?"

"You haven't seen me in ten years. How do you know this is the best thing that's ever happened to me?"

"Oh, come on, Blake." Donnie's tone shifts. "I love you like a brother, but if you really are gonna leave West, you need to do it sooner than later. Don't play games with him. It was years before he recovered the last time you left."

"Stop, man. I can't listen to this."

Yeah, stop, Donnie. I'm not sure I'm okay with what he's about to say.

"You will listen. You will be a man and listen. When you left the first time, you had no control over it. I know there is a part of West that resents you for it, and that is something he has to let go. But this time is on you, not your uncle. This is your choice."

"Donn—"

"I wasn't sure I would ever get my brother back. It took years and, to be honest, I don't think he's totally back yet. He mourned you. And not well, I might add. He tried with Shawn, but he always held pieces of himself at bay. They were young and I don't think Shawn knew how to fix it."

"West doesn't need to be fixed."

"No he doesn't, and neither do you. Stop treating yourself like you do."

"Donnie, man. You have no idea."

"No one is without baggage. West loves you. Let him."

I keep my breathing steady, not wanting to alert him that I'm listening, but I'm really interested in his response.

"What happened to the protective older brother?"

"I am being the protective older brother."

"Then why are you pushing West to stay with me?"

"West doesn't need protecting, Blake. You do. From yourself. You despise your uncle. Why are you letting him be your internal voice? Let West be your voice until you can hear your own again. Trust him. He won't let you down."

By the time I wake up again, the Yankees are gone and Donnie has switched over to a west coast game while he works on his laptop. I roll over to an irritable Kinks.

"Why don't you get in bed? You'll rest better," Donnie says, tapping on his keys.

"I'll make up the bed for you," I stand.

"I'll sleep on the couch." Blake says from the chair. "Donnie can take the bed with you."

"Nope. I haven't slept with him since he was eight."

"I'm not that bad anymore."

"Blake?" Donnie looks his way over the top of his screen for confirmation. A slight smile dances across Blake's face, and it's so carefree that my heart skips a beat. More than anything in this world, I want Blake at peace.

"You're better, but only by a smidge."

"Smidge? Who says the word smidge?"

"Mom," Donnie answers. "Right before she licks her thumb and wipes the smidge of chocolate off your face."

"Let's go, old man. Let Donnie get some sleep."

"You should eat something," Blake says standing and steadying me.

"Nah, it's late. I won't sleep if I do."

I slide the bedroom door closed, and as usual Blake lowers the shades. I use the bathroom and strip down to my boxers before climbing under the sheets.

It doesn't take long for me to succumb to exhaustion, but just as I fall into the abyss of my unconscious, I think I feel something warm and safe falling over my body. I want it to be Blake, but I'm scared to hope.

Blake

One of the things Delta taught me was patience and steadfastness, which means I have a strong resolve. But even I don't have the strength to push West's taut ass away from me when, after a rather comical bout of kicking and flailing, he comes to rest his back against me. Instead, I concentrate on controlling my body, which takes every bit of restraint I have. My dick has a mind of its own, and right now it wants nothing more than to be buried deep in the ass that's cradling it. His breathing eventually settles to an easy pace, and I give in and blanket my arms around him, relishing in the moment of holding him and knowing he's safe.

When we got the call on the way back, I turned over a thousand scenarios until I could get to the hospital. I made a vow then that I would love West more than myself and walk away. Do what is best for him. And in my heart, I know that's not me. West deserves someone whose mind isn't always looking for the most strategic exit from the bar we stopped in for drinks. Whose mind isn't looking at the people in coats to see if they're hiding a weapon. Someone whose first thoughts aren't trained to see the worst of humanity. First thoughts. They say a lot about a person. I want more than this for West. I want someone whose first thoughts are pure and sunny and warm.

But for now, he's stuck with me until I can guarantee he's out of danger, so I maneuver my arm under his and pull him tighter against my chest. Even in his sleep, he reaches out to me and wraps his hand around mine. I'm not sure he's even aware of it. Our fingers entwine and I sleep with a peaceful-ness I haven't felt since boarding the plane to Indiana.

"You can't drive worth shit."

"Get in the car, Blake."

"No, West. I'm driving."

"Fine, walk there." He closes the driver-side door and locks it. The SUV starts and he pulls his seatbelt. He honks to shoo me out of the way and starts to pull off the curb. By the time I reach the other side, I'm jogging to reach the door.

"How come you get the back seat?" I look back to Donnie after I've jumped in. His feet are kicked up and he's playing a movie on his iPad.

"I rented the car," he shrugs, untangling his earbuds.

"I can't believe I'm going when I said I wouldn't."

"You're the one who said I needed protecting." West mocks, "'Where you go, I go.' That's what you said."

"You did say that." Donnie says, with an irritating smirk in his voice.

"Pay attention, Southie." I snap my fingers. He's frown-ing at me instead of watching the road. "Can't drive for shit," I mumble under my breath.

An hour into the drive we are far enough from the city that we are finally making some time. I make West pull off to use the bathroom before grabbing a drink and snacks.

"Can I help you?" I ask. He's at the urinal next to me, eyeing my dick. He looks at me, shrugs, zips up, washes his hands, and leaves without a word.

"What happened to Modest West?" I ask. He's filling an 84-oz cup with cherry Slurpee.

"He made up his mind what he wants." He takes a big sip of Slurpee, showing me his dimples and winking.

"Oh." He reaches out and steadies himself on my arm. I reach out to balance him. He's only been out of the hospital for a few days. "Brain freeze," he says with a puckered face.

"Asshole." I snatch the keys out of his hand before paying for the snacks.

"You act like we're driving all day. We're just going to upstate New York." West says, digging through the bag of snacks.

"Hit me," Donnie says from the backseat, louder than necessary before removing an earbud. I toss a bag of chips his way. West hands him a bottled water.

"What do you want first? The foot-long rope of candy, the king-sized candy bar, or…" West digs to the bottom of the bag, "the oatmeal crème pie?"

"Why are all your snacks phallic euphemisms?" Donnie smirks. "Foot-long, king-size, crème?"

West turns to him, points to my crotch, and then holds his hands a foot apart. Donnie grumbles something about "smart-asses" and "having no respect", to which we laugh.

West turns up the music. His feet are propped up on the dashboard. He seems relaxed and his smile is so familiar and easygoing that I once again feel a tightening in my chest. I had my license almost a full year before I went away. Was taken away. West and I used to drive on the weekends for hours, just exploring the hills. We'd listen to music, talk about everything and nothing. West would always end up with a Slurpee, Hot Tamales candy, and his feet on the dashboard.

Fuck me does he look good. He's usually preppy, but I love this side of him. Hair all askew, he's wearing cutoffs and a worn T-shirt. I'm in his wayfarers, so he's wearing my aviators. And my dick is very appreciative.

"What's on your T-shirt?" I ask, offering him a chip and keeping the conversation light and easygoing. It feels good to be with my best friend.

"Old New York hockey shirt I've had for years. It's one of my faves. Baby-butt soft," he says patting his sleeve, trying to be silly, but my mood is immediately doused.

"Years, huh?" I mumble, but he's not watching me so he doesn't catch my annoyance.

"Yeah. It was in a hotel welcome basket when Shawn went first in the draft. I stole it," West babbles on, like I give a fuck about this baby-ass T-shirt. He's completely oblivious to my surliness.

"Taste like vinegar, doesn't it? Your man in someone else's shirt," Donnie says from the backseat, having had his eyes on me.

"I thought you were watching a movie," I snap.

"Selective hearing," he says loudly, tapping at his earbuds.

"What?" West asks clueless.

I wasn't a 4.0 brainiac like West, but you'd think it would have occurred to me before pulling into town that I was about to be next door to a family I haven't seen since I was sixteen. I was so distracted by the thoughts of seeing Mary Beth and the rest of the Connors that it was like that part was erased from my mind.

I pull to a stop at a red light and the car grows quiet. West gingerly slides his hand over my thigh and pats it a few times in a show of understanding and support. When we pull up to the Connors, I try not to even glance at the house I grew up in.

"We're here," Donnie calls out, the screen door slamming behind us. There's a loud roar that crashes over us like a massive wave. I'm in the back of the pack and when Maggie and the other sisters release me, I come face to face with the only real parents I've ever known: Jim and Mary Beth Connors.

"Son," Jim says in a voice choked with feeling. He wraps me in his arms. Mary Beth joins us and the three of us stand in their kitchen, crying over lost time. Or a little boy who no longer exists. I'm not sure which.

West

When Blake and my parents finally separate, the kitchen is empty save the four of us.

All the animosity that I was feeling towards Blake evaporates. All the bullshit games I was playing with Finn, done. All of it. I'm not leaving here without the Blake I've loved since I was six.

"Forgive me?" my father asks Blake.

"For what?"

"Not taking you out of that house sooner. Not fighting for you, not demanding better for you. I was afraid to push too much into someone else's family. I've regretted it every day."

"The three people in this room are the only reason I survived as it is. There was nothing more you could have done."

It's clear Dad doesn't see it that way, but he lets it go.

"We have special plans for dinner tonight, but you boys must be tired. Why don't you nap and clean up? You are in West's old room."

"I can sleep on the floor," Blake offers. "Let someone else have the bed."

"No one else will sleep with West," Mom smiles patting my cheek. "Don't roll your eyes at your mother."

Blake takes my bag out of my hands and carries it up the stairs. It's been a while since I've been here. For a long time, it was too painful to come back. It felt like Blake was around every corner. So I chose to stay away, opting for my parents to come into the city instead.

"Rest. You're still recovering," Blake says, setting our duffle bags on the floor.

I slide out of my shorts.

"What the hell are you wearing, Southie?"

"Bree." I answer, looking down at the navy blue boxers dotted with tiny pink penises. I yawn, more tired than I realized, and pull the shade down before climbing in bed. Blake turns on the ceiling fan and lays on the bed.

"Did they change out this bed?"

"No."

"How did we fit?" he asks.

"We were sixteen."

I wake sometime later. It takes me a half a beat to remember we are at my parent's house. I sit up and stretch and Blake enters the room quietly carrying a juice bottle.

"Here," he says, seeing that I'm up. "Mary Beth asked me to wake you. Dinner will be ready in ten minutes."

"I can't believe I napped that long."

"They said that was to be expected."

I nod, taking a large swig of cranberry juice. Blake looks down at me and nods to himself as if making a decision. He pulls something out of his duffle bag. He walks back over to me, stands in between my legs, grabs the hem of my T-shirt, and yanks it off me with an unexpected force.

"Dude, what are you doing? A little heads-up."

Just as quickly as my shirt came off, he pulls another one over my head. I pop my arms through the sleeves and look down. It's his Army T-shirt.

"Now, let's go eat." He turns toward the door, but as he opens it my hand closes it. I place my other hand on the other side of him, boxing him in.

I rest the front of my body against his and lean in, grazing my lips along his stubbled jaw before placing a light kiss behind his ear.

"You belong to me, too."

Blake

I open my mouth to speak, but he doesn't give me the chance.

"Whatever lies you're about to spout, you might as well stop." West leans his chest against mine. His hands are on my biceps, immobilizing my arms, denying me the ability to touch him. He nuzzles his nose against my neck and leaves light kisses across my skin, sucking on my Adam's apple. I close my eyes and imagine putting just the tip of my shaft between his lips.

"Just so we're clear, you'll be mine before we leave here. No more dicking around. No more of Finn's lips where only yours should be. Man the fuck up, Blake, 'cause I promise you, no one's lips will ever touch you the way mine do. Not as long as there is breath in my body."

The more West takes charge, the more my body aches for him to fulfill his promises. The soft moans that escape me make it clear how I feel.

"Fix this will you? There are children downstairs." His hand wraps around my cock, and the tight-fisted squeeze he gives it is almost enough to have me coming in my shorts.

In my state of stupor, he easily pulls the door open, propelling me forward. And just like that, I'm left standing in his childhood room wondering when he became a force to be reckoned with.

Dinner is how I always remembered it growing up, only with more people. All seven Connor kids are in attendance with their respective spouses. Four of the seven have kids, making for a very active home.

"How are we all going to fit in here?" I ask.

"We built out the basement. Between there and the additions in the attic, we've squeezed in three more bedrooms. The large ones go to the kids with kids and the smaller ones, like West's, go to the couples who are still free from—"

"Tyranny," Sandy says. "Free from tyranny." Maggie slaps the back of her head while Sandy clinks wine glasses with West and Donnie, congratulating them on being child free.

"Remind me not to leave my children with you," Maggie quips.

There are about four different conversations happening at once, everyone following each one and commenting in random places. It's like watching a choreographed play and I love it. West reaches over my plate to pass the beans and when his hand drops, it falls to my thigh where it remains for the remainder of dinner. I watch him laugh and tease his siblings. His smile is easy and his dimples are on full display tonight.

"What?" he asks when he catches me observing him. But I don't have an answer for him. I just shake my head. His brown eyes knowingly drink me in and with a warm smile, he says, "Me, too."

Without missing a beat, he throws himself back up into a conversation about a ball that may or may not have gone through a window and may or may not have been my fault and not West's.

The oldest daughter, Maggie delegates duties once dinner is over, each person with a task to accomplish the end goal: a clean table and kitchen before we start dessert.

My task, giving six-month-old Flora her bottle.

"Wouldn't you rather I scrub the pans?" I ask Ken's (the third brother) wife as she puts Flora in my arms and wraps a horseshoe pillow around my waist.

"You'll be fine," she assures me. She sets us up in a rocking leather recliner, leaving Flora and I to rock out while I give her a bottle. She has West's eyes, so it only takes me a half a second to fall in love with her. We talk about all kinds of interesting things, like what kind of season the Yankees are having, when I hear a roar of laughter from the kitchen.

"You are the luckiest little girl, did you know that?" I watch her plump little lips pucker around the bottle, her eyes taking me in. "This is the best family. You will never want for anything with them around. They will always love you for who you are." As if she totally understands me, her tiny hand reaches up and comes to rest on my cheek. And because my emotions are on edge, my eyes water as I kiss her fingers.

"You're so beautiful." I tell her.

"So are you." West squats beside the chair and gently rubs Flora's head. She smiles at him and goes back to the bottle. When he looks up at me, without a second's thought, I place the softest of kisses on his lips. "I love you," I say.

"Finally," West says before kissing my forehead and leaving me with Flora.

Ken lifts Flora from my arms, and while he puts the "last scraggler" down, the others prepare the table for dessert.

"Donnie rented a pontoon. We're going on the water tomorrow," West says, plopping down in my lap. I wrap my arms around him and he rests his head in the crook of my neck.

"How are we all going to fit on a pontoon?"

He shrugs. "We'll make it work."

"Aren't both of you, like, eight-feet-tall? How is that comfortable?" Donnie says as he and Ken grimace from the doorway.

"Just because you don't have any romance in you, don't deny them theirs," Ken's wife says.

"I have romance," Ken argues. "I'll show you romance right here, right now." He winks and grabs at his crotch.

"Nice," Sandy says with a gag, while Ken gets a high-five from her husband.

"Kenneth Andrei," Mary Beth disciplines from the other room. "Stop touching yourself. I raised you better than that."

"Thanks a lot." He gives Sandy a noogie and pulls her into the dining room.

I look at West. "Andrei?"

"Great Uncle on my mom's side. Russian," he explains.

"Blake, you and West are here." Mary Beth points to two chairs before heading into the kitchen. Sandy walks out with a dessert that has congratulations written on it in chocolate. Everyone sings the Happy Birthday song, replacing the "happy birthday" with "congratulations." She places the dessert in front of Maggie, who blows out the candles. When I start passing out plates,Maggie points to my left and a second chorus starts, and everyone sings "we lo-ove you, Blake." Mary Beth enters with a second cake and sets it in front of me. Chocolate with white icing.

"You okay, babe?" West asks, pulling back the covers. He's asked me about a hundred times tonight. Can't say that I blame him. I've been one walking ball of emotion. When Mary Beth set my favorite cake down on the table, I nearly tipped my chair over trying to embrace her. The hug was so tight, I might have squeezed her to death, but she never once complained. She just held me and told me she loved me, told me how proud she was of the man I had become.

"Your parents…" I say with a lump in my throat.

"Our parents. And I know. They are pretty awesome."

We both lie back, hands behind our heads, looking up at the ceiling. Even though we took a nap in here earlier, it's different going to bed. I'm flooded with memories, and, as if my spirit summoned him, West rolls over and drapes his leg over mine and his arm across my stomach.

"Sleep." He places a light kiss to my chest.

A couple of hours go by. West has long been asleep. He mumbles a little when I move out from under him, but he's out for the count. I go to the window and count the seventeen steps I used to sum every night to get to West. Seventeen steps to get to my safe place, where I knew I was loved and nothing would happen to me. Seventeen steps from the monster living inside my walls. The house is dark, and I wonder if they even know I'm here. I doubt it. I don't see the Connors saying anything. I finally give up and lay back down.

Still asleep, West puts his hand back on the center of my chest and says, "You're okay. I love you."

"Blake and I are going to the marina to get the boat set up."

"Here." Ken's wife walks up to West and wraps him in some scarf thing.

"What the hell is this?"

"You have so much to learn, little brother," Ken says, walking up and sliding Flora into the wrap, which has now become a cocoon against his chest.

"She's gonna fall." I reach out to catch her.

"She's okay, big guy," Ken laughs. He checks the set up and gives West a pat on the shoulder. "We'll round the others up and meet you there."

Lake Erie is only about a hundred feet from the Connors' front door. It's one reason these houses are close together, to make sure each one has a great view of the lake. West and I head left to walk the half-mile to the marina where you can store or rent boats.

West looks completely at ease with Flora wrapped around him.

"What?" he asks, dipping his head down, looking at me over the top of his Ray-Bans.

"You'll make a great father one day."

"Thank you. So will you."

I can't imagine West saying something he didn't truly believe, especially something as important as this. But…would I?

I open the door to the rental office and West steps through.

"Reservation for Connors," West says to the guy behind the counter.

"Can twenty-one fit on the rental we have? Are there twenty-one life jackets on board?" I ask.

"It will be a tight squeeze, but we were told six of the twenty-one are young kids?"

"They are," I confirm.

"Have them stop by the shack at the end of the dock, and they will get them fitted for their life jackets. Adult jackets are on board," the guy says, putting a picture of the boat we are renting on the counter.

"That's not our boat," I say to the guy, matter-of-factly.

"I believe it's what was reserved." He flips through some paperwork.

"I'm not taking twenty-one people out on that."

"Blake, it's fine. We'll take it."

No way in hell am I taking us out to the middle of Lake Erie in this little boat weighed down with twenty-one people. "What else do you have for a party our size?"

"Unfortunately, most everything is booked." He flips through his book. "We have this." It's a yacht.

West scoffs and rolls his eyes. "No way are we renting that."

"Technically, you can't. It only holds eighteen. For the twenty-one of you, you'd have to take this one." He points to a picture of a larger yacht.

"Know your customer, bud," West laughs good-naturedly. "Do we look like we can rent that?"

"We'll take it." I pull my wallet out and place my card on the counter. "I assume it comes with staff?"

"Yes, it comes with two people to pilot the craft. We can provide additional wait staff if you like?"

I look at West, who hasn't said a word.

"I think we can make it on our own. Maybe a steward just to help if we need it."

"Certainly, sir. The boat is fully stocked for meals.

The steward will give you a tour. There is a 24-hour rental requirement."

"Perfect. Also, can you throw in T-shirts please?" I point to the marina T-shirts behind him, rattling off how many of each size. "Did I get everyone one?" I ask West, who is still staring at me like I have two heads.

"You just spent in T-shirts what we were renting the pontoon boat for."

"But I upgraded us. You're gonna give me the T-shirts for free, right man?" I turn to the guy behind the desk. "I mean I just dropped some dimes on the upgrade."

"Of course." He hands me a brown shopping bag filled with shirts. "Slip 3," he says and picks up the phone to let someone know we're coming.

"What are you doing?" He's annoyed. "Dude, the pontoon was fine."

I peer into the cocoon he's wearing and look at a sleeping Flora.

"Sorry, but that thing was at least ten years old and too small for a group our size."

"Blake, it's too much," West says, walking through the door after me. "You just paid more for a 24-hour boat than I pay in one-year's rent."

"Only because you have a ridiculous rent-controlled space."

"That's not the point."

"West, stop. I'm not putting this family at risk. You've heard the same stories I have about this lake. It's not happening. Enough!" I add, probably louder than necessary, when I see him attempt to protest further.

He stares at me, his jaw ticking. I wish I could see his eyes.

"I'm s—"

My apology is cut short when West grabs my shirt and pulls me to him, shoving his tongue down my throat. My hand automatically reaches for Flora to make sure she isn't smashed between us.

"You're so fucking hot when you drop the hammer," he says coming up for air. He grabs my hand and leads me down the dock. "Holy fuck," he says stopping to look at the boat in front of us. I have to admit it's impressive. This boat in a city like Miami would cost triple what we are renting it for today.

We walk up the ramp and deposit our flip flops on the deck.

"Good morning, Mr. Thomas," the steward says. If he has a problem with West holding my hand, he doesn't show it. "Let me give you a tour before your guests arrive."

Twenty minutes later we've toured the entire craft. There are sleeping quarters: eight below deck, one on this level, and one on the level above. The main level houses a full-size kitchen and casual dining seating for twenty-eight. The ceiling over the seating area can be opened or closed.

"I'd like to meet both the captains, please," I tell the steward as I sit down at one of the laptops in the cabin. I research the marina, and when the captains introduce themselves, I pull up their license history and verify they are active with no violations. After a short discussion, I learn they are both retired Navy. Jim joins us aboard and shakes both captains' hands. They're old friends.

"We're in good hands, son," West's dad assures me.

"This is insane," Donnie says, lifting a beer to his lips.

The day was perfect. I really had no idea what this vessel could do when I asked for it. Once we were on the open water, they opened a deck below and there were four personal watercrafts that each accommodated two people. We took the younger kids on a few passes, and then the adults decided to have a little race. Losers had to cook dinner and clean up. We damn near lost when West wrapped his arms around me, but my competitive nature kept me focused and we pulled it out in the end. West taunted his brothers and sisters with a victory dance, but I interrupted it with a little shove that sent him for a swim.

"Glad you won. I would have felt bad making you cook and clean after you rented this," Donnie laughs. "Well, not that bad," he adds when West gives him a disbelieving look. "So, lil' bro, I can see why it wasn't a hard decision to drop the billionaire. I mean, looks like your man here has enough to keep you satisfied."

"More than you know," West replies with a cheeky wink.

"Ugh. Can we not?" Sandy says curling into her husband.

"Seriously, Blake. How do you make your money? You're a contractor, right?"

"Something like that. Also, I have an inheritance."

"You have an inheritance?" West asks.

"Yep. My uncle spent a good amount of it, but there was a portion that was only accessible to me once I turned twenty-five. He tried to fight it, but Elise made sure it was moved to a secure location when I turned twenty-two and had his name removed so he couldn't steal it, too. I mean I make more than enough money doing what I'm doing, so I never touch my inheritance, but it's there if I ever need it."

"Dude, how much money do you have?"

"Donnie!" Mary Beth chastises.

"It's fine. My mom was an only child so her parents left her everything. I was the only child, so I got it all."

Donnie stares at him, waiting for a magical number.

"I gave half of it to a foundation, the one West coaches for. There's enough in there to do things like this, and I bought my place in Chicago with it too."

"If I had known that I wouldn't have tried to drown you in the race today." Ken says.

I laugh. "No harm. You would have been covered. If something happens to me, West is the beneficiary."

West chokes and coughs to the point that I have to pat him on the back.

"I am?"

"Yes, you are."

"Since when?"

I shrug. "Since I was able to take control over my own money."

"I don't want it," he says, but I can't quite read him or figure out how to take his comment.

"Then donate it. Do something good with it. Whatever. But it's yours."

"Are you going to see your family?" Mary Beth asks softly.

"My family is on this boat with me. Sans my team at work."

"I think we'll turn in," Sandy says softly, kissing the top of my head and then West's before heading down below. Others follow her lead until it's just us, Donnie, Maggie, Ken, and their parents.

"Does that mean you aren't going to see them?" Maggie asks once we've settled back in.

"Have you told anyone I was in town?"

"No," Jim and Mary Beth answer in unison.

"I haven't really thought about it." Which they know is a

lie. I've thought of little else since I've been back in the prox-
imity of a man who made my life a living hell for more years
than I want to admit. "Maybe?"

"No," West says.

"Honey, this is Blake's decision."

"Like hell it is, mom." My easygoing West looks like he's
close to exploding just at the thought.

"Hey," Jim and I quickly chastise at the same time.

"Sorry, mom." West looks at me. "But the answer is no."

"I should check on Nora. I'm not a sixteen-year-old boy
anymore. I'm a man now. Nothing is going to happen that I
don't want to happen."

West is incredulous and at a loss for words.

"I'm going to bed," he says, finally. "Good night, everyone." He doesn't look my way. I watch his legs disappear as
they climb the stairs.

"You know you have to do what you think is right for
you," Donnie says. "West will come around."

"Yeah. He's had to do a lot of adjusting lately. Since I
came back into his life." I make a feeble attempt to excuse his
behavior.

"He knows it wasn't your fault," Donnie says.

"He does," Mary Beth agrees. "But he grieved for you for a
lot of years. There was a time Jim and I weren't sure he would
ever get his spark back."

"I'm sorry. I promise I will do everything in my power not
to hurt him again." A little quieter I admit, "I'm in love with
him."

"Finally, dumb ass!" Donnie says, tilting up the last of his
beer.

I say my goodnights and leave the group on the deck.
West and I are in the only room on the upper level. It's small,

but it has a private deck and a phenomenal view. West is so deep in thought when I enter, he doesn't notice me come in.

He's on the small balcony, backlit by the full moon. The wind blows his hair. He's beautiful. Inside and out. I walk over to stand behind him. I need to be near him.

"I'm sorry," he says when I wrap my arms around him. He relaxes into my chest.

"You have nothing to apologize for." I tighten my hold.

"Yes, I do. I support you no matter what you decide."

"West?"

"Yes."

"I love you. You are the first person I've ever wanted to say that to. When this is over, it's still going to be us. You and me."

West

"Mom wants us to grab some tomatoes," Donnie says.

"How many?" I ask, heading in the direction of the vegetable stands. Donnie and I are on a run to the grocery for mom while the others take the kids to the park.

"Three."

"Three," I say to myself, searching for the best-looking ones.

"Don't squeeze the vegetables," says a warm voice in my ear. I'd recognize it anywhere.

"Tomatoes are a fruit," I smirk, turning to Shawn. "What are you doing here, man?"

"I'm in town for a few days. You know mom, she likes me to be around when it's not hockey season." He's all teeth when he smiles for me.

"Shawn." Donnie gives him a friendly embrace and asks about his family. While he and Donnie chat, I take the opportunity to study him. I have nothing but good feelings for the man in front of me, but it ends there. At one point, I thought

I might have loved him, but even then, I was so in love with Blake. Shawn knew it, too. He wanted more and knew I couldn't give it to him. It wasn't fair to him or me. That said, there will always be something special between us. Shawn got me through some difficult times.

"Maggie made partner, so all of us are home to celebrate," I tell him. "You should come by."

"I'll try to do that. How long are you in town for?"

"We leave tomorrow."

"We?"

"Blake." I can't help but smile at the admission, and I appreciate his big smile back.

"I'm so happy for you, man. Truly." It's easy to tell he means it. Shawn is very genuine. He's competitive and cocky as hell, but he's also kind and considerate of others.

"Thanks. Come over tonight, you can meet him. I know he'd love to meet you."

"Blake?" Donnie says with doubt. "Have you met Blake? The guy is more possessive than a dog with a bone."

"True, but still, come by. He'll eventually settle down," I smile, but with little confidence in my words.

"I'll try to make it happen. You look great, West. I'm so glad you're happy."

"This will be fun," Donnie smiles, dropping an onion in the basket.

"That's everything." I put the last of the groceries in the fridge. "What time are we eating?"

"I thought we'd eat later. Give your brother and sisters

time to give the kids their baths and get them in bed."

"Sounds good. Think I'll go find Blake and see if he wants to get out for a while."

"Blake is next door," mom says, hesitantly.

I shake my head at her as if I didn't hear her right. Blake is next door with his uncle? After he said he wasn't going over there? After what that man did to him? To us?

"Before you get worked up," my mom starts, "he has the right to go over there."

"I never said he didn't, but I do think I deserved to know. And I'm not getting worked up."

"Honey," she says gently, "Nora came over and asked him to lunch."

"Fine. I'll go over there." I push off the counter, waiting for her to say that I shouldn't. She glances into her coffee without a word, and I take that as a sign that either she doesn't want to interfere, or she doesn't have a problem with me going over. Hell, it doesn't matter what it meant, I'm going over.

When I get outside, I take a deep breath. In that moment, I realize for the first time that, from the outside, our large four-square houses are almost identical. But inside, they couldn't have been more different. My heart aches for the boy that had to grow up in the lesser of the two. Blake told me once that he would count the steps from his house to mine because it gave him a calming sense of comfort knowing he was one step closer to safety, to acceptance, to love. Seventeen steps until he was in his real home, my home, with me.

I counted the same seventeen, knocked, and waited for an answer.

I wait what feels like an eternity before knocking again. Leaning to the side, I can see lights on. I know there is someone home. My heart beats faster and I bang on the door one more time, ready to break it down, until I finally hear a gruff voice yelling its arrival. The door swings open and there stands the man I have despised for a decade. Only I wasn't aware how deeply rooted within me that hatred was until now.

"What can I do for you?" his uncle asks. It takes a beat, but I see when the recognition hits him.

"I'd like to see Blake please."

He looks around and there's an abhorrent twitch to his lips that matches his eyes.

"Even after all this time, you don't give up do you? Still the same cock-sucking fairy you were ten years ago. Why don't I save us a trip down memory lane? I don't know where Blake is. If he wanted to get in touch with you, he would have."

I can feel my temperature rising. "Blake is here and I want to see him, now." I shove my way through the door, knocking him back a step with my shoulder.

"Who do you think you are coming into my house?" he yells, pushing me back. The fear and panic I felt ten years ago comes crashing down like a boulder. Only this time I'm not a kid without a voice.

"Blake?" I yell out and head towards the kitchen, he steps in front of me, cutting off my path.

"I'm not going to tell you again, leave my house now, or I'll have you removed. Blake doesn't want to see you."

"Bullshit. Blake is with me." I take gratification in the hint of surprise and displeasure that flashes through his expression. "Get him now."

With a trail of derogatory slurs, he pushes me towards the door. I'm expecting to land on my ass, but instead strong hands grab my arms, and Blake throws me behind him.

"What the fuck is wrong with you?" Blake stands toe-to-toe with his uncle. They're matched in builds, but Blake has a solid two inches on him. His voice is eerily quiet and he issues a threat full of promise. "Put your hands on him again, and it will be the last thing you do." He turns to his aunt. "This is why I will *never* step back in this house."

Tears fill Nora's eyes, but instead of anger or defiance towards her husband for what he has done, there's only defeat. I know this woman will never stand up to her husband.

"Don't talk to your aunt like that. This is how you choose to repay us, after we spent thousands of dollars to get you away from this queer? I should have known it was too late to save you from his fag ass."

"Trust me, there's a long list of things I love to do to his ass."

"Blake," Nora says, covering her mouth in shock. His uncle uses Blake's diverted attention to his advantage, and I see the backhand coming in time to step in front of Blake. It's like a brick to the face. Everything moves so fast, I barely register what's happened. Donnie is scarcely containing Blake, while my dad threatens his uncle within an inch of his life.

"I should have put a stop to it then. I knew you were putting your hands on my son, only I couldn't prove it."

"I never touched that boy."

"Not West. Blake," my dad spits back.

"He's not your son."

My father is not to be intimidated and with his nose mere inches from the man in front of him, he growls, "He is my son and will be until I take my last breath. How long until you take yours depends on your ability to follow directions. You don't put your hands on my sons. You don't talk to them. You don't look their way. You don't so much as say their names."

He turns his back, dismissing Blake's uncle. "Let's go."

Blake steps forward and Donnie attempts to hold him back, but he makes it clear he's reaching for me. His fingers entwine with mine and without a backwards glance, we walk the seventeen steps home.

Blake

"If you would have told me those things then I wouldn't have let him go over there," Mary Beth tells Jim. She is not happy and like the saying goes, if Mary Beth ain't happy, no one is.

"Honey," Jim kisses her forehead, "I didn't want you mixed up in all this."

"What if he tries something crazy? The man is not all there. How could you be and then treat your own flesh and blood the way he has?"

"He's not stupid. Plus, he cares more about himself than he does anyone else. There's no way he'll retaliate or fight back. He won't risk his reputation."

West pulls the ice I have against his mouth away. "My lip is fine." I'm standing between his legs, so he has to gently push me away to slide off the counter. "I'll be down in time for dinner," he says, leaving the kitchen.

"I'm sorry," I tell his parents.

"You have nothing to be sorry for." Jim squeezes my shoulder.

I take a deep breath and go in search of West. When I enter his bedroom, I hear the shower running. My hesitation keeps my feet planted until I hear what I am certain is a light sob coming from the shower. That's all it takes. I strip and open the shower door. It's a tiny bathroom and we barely fit in the small stall together.

"Hey," I say softly. West rests his head against his arm propped up on the tiled wall. I wrap my arm around him, sliding my hand across his belly. I turn him toward me and hold him while he releases ten years of emotions. His arms are wrapped around me like I'm the only thing he needs in the world.

"Shh. It's okay, babe. Just let it out." I run my hands through his wet hair and give him a tender kiss. Our hands chart each other's body but there's nothing sexual about it. It's a reassurance. To him that I'm here and to me that I deserve his love.

"I just…" He hiccups through his tears, his emotions taking over him again.

"Everything's okay," I say again.

He hiccups softly again and I hold him closer. Any questions I might have had about what we've been doing are gone. I am one-hundred percent in love with this man. There is no doubt in my mind.

"It was like I was taken back to that day. Mom told me you were there and I didn't want you to be in that house alone. When I got there, he was so belligerent and you were nowhere to be found. I know it doesn't make sense, but immediately I thought he had sent you away again."

"I'm here. I'm not going anywhere."

"I can't lose you again, Blake. Even if you don't want to be with me after this is all over, I just can't lose you. Promise me you will always let me know where you are and how you are doing."

I lift his chin so he has to look at me. His red-rimmed eyes are still the most beautiful I've ever seen. "I'm not going anywhere." I kiss his palm and lay it over the compass on my chest.

"You're my home. It's true, I love you, but more importantly, I'm in love with you West. I think I have been since we were kids and I just didn't know it."

My declaration stirs his emotions once again and I can't hold back a smile. For the first time in my life I've found peace. In a four-by-four shower.

"Oh, now you come down. Now that everything's already done," Donnie grumbles, setting the last plate on the table.

"You're doing a great job," West teases, and Maggie slaps him on the back of his head.

"Grab the wine, dumbass," Donnie barks. "And the salad," Maggie adds.

Mary Beth sets her legendary lasagna on the table. I pick up the spatula to cut myself a larger-than-necessary piece when we hear a knock at the door. Everyone at the table looks confused as to who it could be, so I stand and head that direction. There's a guy about my age holding a bottle of wine. He's dressed in jeans and a NY hockey shirt and it only takes me a split second to figure out who he is.

"Shawn." I half-heartedly offer my hand. I realize we had a few things going on this afternoon, but West could have given me a heads up.

"You must be Blake. Nice to meet you." He gives me a firm

handshake. It's no comfort that he knows who I am. I'm still miffed.

"Everyone's at the table," I point towards the dining room, but it isn't necessary. He clearly knows where he's going.

"Shawn," Mary Beth sings, genuinely happy to see him. He hugs her, offering her the bottle of wine he brought before shaking Jim's hand. I'm finding it harder to temper my annoyance.

"Your mother didn't tell me you were in town."

"You would be the only one then," he laughs and takes a seat at what I now realize is an extra place setting. I glare at Donnie who beams back at me with a shit-eating grin. He winks at me and I flip him off. His raucous laughter draws attention to our end of the table.

"Sorry, don't mind me," he says.

"I should have known when West was picking out tomatoes at the grocery that you were making your famous lasagna. This will be worth the extra work out tomorrow," Shawn says, taking the plate being handed to him.

Which is funny because this fucker doesn't have an ounce of fat on his body. And now I'm imagining that body under West. Or over. I'll be sure to badger the details out of West later.

West shifts his chair towards me and places his hand on my thigh. I like it. Of course I do. And I take pleasure in the fact that West is in *my* Army T-shirt. But if he thinks this is going to get him out of trouble later, he's seriously underestimated my pettiness and grudge-holding skills.

"He's just a friend," West says with a wide grin when we step into his room, clearly anticipating my irrational jealousy. I know West would never give me a reason to doubt him, but the idea of him being with another man makes me crazy. How I survived pushing Finn his way I'll never know. His eyes drift to the doorknob when he hears the click of the lock. I don't respond, but I know my look is predatory to match how I'm feeling.

West bites his lip with dirty intent and he begins to strip. The room is dark, neither of us bothering to turn on the light when we came in, but a street lamp sends a strong stream of light through the window.

I stand there, with my arms crossed as he saunters to-wards me, butt naked. His firm arousal is visible. By the time he reaches me there's a pearl of pre-cum dripping from his tip. He wipes his finger along the underside of his cock, and by now I've learned his intentions. He places the finger in his mouth and sucks, moaning his desire. I watch this show without moving an inch, other than the steel rod in my pants jumping at the mere site of the man I love in front of me.

"Knowing you're jealous is hot. I wanted to fuck your brains out since the second he walked in and I saw it all over your face. I didn't think he would ever leave."

"The only one doing the fucking tonight," I say ominously, "is me. On your knees Connors."

West palms my dick and his lips brush against mine be-fore he whispers, "Exactly what I was hoping for." He drops to his knees and I unfold my arms, sliding my hands in my back pockets. West unbuttons my jeans and lowers my zipper, free-ing my painful erection.

He slides my pants and underwear down my thighs, my dick pulsing in anticipation. With his eyes locked on mine, he sucks the bulbous head in between his lips and hollows his cheeks sucking my juices like he's sucking a fucking popsicle. A wickedly sexy smile forms on his lips before he takes me to the back of his throat. His eyes tell me everything. He wants me to be in control.

"Jesus Christ, your mouth." My hands take residence in his hair and my hips take on a mind of their own when I slide into the back of his throat. It takes every ounce of self-control I have not to release a sound so untamed it would wake the house.

I pull him to his feet and when my mouth possesses him, I can taste my arousal coating his tongue. I stop the kiss and clutch his jaw with both of my hands, blue eyes locking on brown.

"You belong to me."

We must be on the same page because he wraps his fingers around my wrist and with a look of sincerity and possession that mirrors mine. He boldly agrees, "Only you."

"On your back, on the bed," I demand. West follows without hesitation. I pull him by his armpits so his head is tilted back, slightly off the edge of the bed. Guiding the tip of my cock into his mouth, he takes me to the root, my hands wrapping around his throat. My thumb skims his Adam's apple and I give his throat a slight squeeze when my dick slides deep into it. I'm seeing stars from the intensity I'm feeling. I pull out to give him a chance to catch a breath before I shove my way back in. This is something I could never do with a woman, be this forceful, this open with what I want.

I can only ride this out a few more strokes or I'm going to come sooner than either of us want. Sensing this, West pulls me out of his mouth. He lightly licks and kisses his way across the smooth skin underneath my balls, and I almost full-on lose my shit.

West's eyes track me as I walk to the other side of the bed. I pull on his hips until they are aligned with the end of the bed. I reach into the nightstand drawer and grab just lube. My eyes on West, I wait for his permission. He knows I would never have unprotected sex with him if I wasn't certain I was clean. And he wouldn't let me if he wasn't certain he was.

Massaging the liquid onto my cock with one hand, my other hand works on prepping West.

"Get on with it," he says, heat crawling up his neck and shoulders, his face full of desire and lust.

My head breeches the tight ring of muscle, and I stop to give us both a minute to acclimate. I've never had sex without a condom and the sensation of skin-on-skin is unlike anything I could have imagined.

"Fuck me," West exhales, echoing my sentiments.

I show this man my intentions, my love, and my heart with each stroke of possession. West pulls on my nipples before giving them a pinch. The bite of pain causes my dick to jump, which in turn causes his eyes to roll back in his head, our bodies in tune to the other. I bat his hand away from his engorged dick. *I* make him come. No one else.

"I'm there, Blake. If you go, I'll go with you."

The sincerity and love in his expression undoes me. Leaning over him, I capture his mouth in a kiss I know has no way of conveying everything I'm feeling, but it doesn't stop me from trying. The change in position and skin-to-skin contact has me hitting his prostate dead-on. He comes in a full-body shudder, toes and fingers gripping the sheets. Watching him is erotic, and as his orgasm ripples around my dick, I come inside him.

West

W e finished breakfast at the diner around the corner from our place. Our place. God my heart skips a beat just thinking it. Blake and I have been home from my parents for a little more than three weeks. He's been working in the New York office and I've been coaching and enjoying the last of the summer before school starts back next week. We spent Labor Day weekend in the Hampton's at the Taylor's cottage. It's funny how attached you can get to something that isn't yours.

I love that little cottage. It has quickly become a place where we are making so many fond memories every time we go. The Taylors are so gracious to let us stay there. Blake and I wanted to show our appreciation, but what do you get a family that has everything they could ever want? Well, we kept their kids. I don't think Graham was too sure about the arrangement, but Emme didn't even think twice, happily pulling her husband out for a night with their parents. Watching Blake hold a 6-week-old baby was one of the sexiest things I have ever seen. Something I spent plenty of time imaging over and over when I bent him over the couch and fucked him into oblivion the minute we got in the door to our place.

It's still warm in the city so we're both sporting shorts and T-shirts. Blake has a ball cap on backwards and my tortoise shades. He looks relaxed. Content. Just the thought of him being so happy makes my heart swell. He comes to a stop at the light, and when I stop next to him, his hand wraps around mine. Blake isn't hiding, but I know he hasn't told his team yet. Not that he has to, but it still surprises me that he's so open in public. Before I can think better of it, I lean into him and place a kiss on his neck. The light changes and he pulls me forward to the subway stop.

Thirty minutes later, he meets Beverly.

"You know I can pay someone fifty bucks to make sure your body is never found if you hurt my boo," she threatens with a seriousness that I am sure Blake wonders is possible.

"I have no doubt. I promise you won't have to do that."

"Good. It's only after a lot of prayer that the last one is still breathing."

She gives Blake a sly wink and I pry us away and head to my room. I should have been in here already this summer, but I've had so much going on it hasn't happened.

"Wow. This is a lot of stuff. Where are you going to put it?" Blake asks, looking in an opened box.

"That's a good question. It has to be locked up or it will get stolen. Looks like the principal took the AV boxes already."

"She did," Bree says from the door. "In fact, it's already installed in the AV room and is being used."

"Sweet."

"You guys need help?"

"Not unless you're done with your room already?"

"Ugh. No," she answers, looking into another opened box.

"Bree. You can't use my room to procrastinate about your room…"

"Fine. But you boys are fixing me dinner tonight."

"Deal," Blake answers distractedly.

"Babe, what are you thinking about?"

"That." He points to the empty wall at the back of the room. He opens his phone, makes a call to Gabby, and by the time we have unpacked all the boxes, four lockable cabinets are being drilled to the wall.

"The world of Blake and Elise. Make a phone call and," I snap my fingers, "it's done."

Two hours later and the cabinets are filled.

"God, it makes me hard watching you organize things." I kiss his neck.

"Yeah?" he chuckles, lifting his chin giving me better access.

"You're still around? Wasn't sure you were gonna last," Marius says walking into the room with a couple of the other kids from the team. West and I separate, forcing ourselves to be appropriate adults.

"For real. Hate to have to take care of you."

"Beverly already gave me the lecture. Why does everyone want to do me physical harm?" Blake asks like his feelings are hurt, but I know better.

"Coach is our boy," Marcus explains.

"You guys headed to the gym to shoot?" I break the last box down and add it to the stack for the custodial team to pick up.

"Yep. I wanted to drop this off first," Steven says. He hands me a rock the size of my palm. It's a mixture of pinks and purples. It's quite beautiful.

"I love it!"

He beams.

"Where did you find it?"

"There's a creek that runs behind my grannie's trailer in Pennsylvania. We play in it every summer. I found this one in the middle of a whole bunch of brown ones."

"That's cool. Thanks, man." I give him a one-armed hug, then make a spot on the window sill for it. The kids head out and I call to Blake over my shoulder as I lock the cabinets.

"These cabinets are great. I really appreciate them."

"Uh huh."

"Everything okay?" I ask. He's at my desk holding a rock.

"You kept it." When he looks up at me, I see the little boy that I fell in love with all those years ago.

"I did. It's my favorite. It's what started this whole thing. I had it on my desk and one day they asked me about it. I told them someone I cherished very much gave it to me from a trip they went on. Since then, the kids bring me a rock anytime they go on a trip. Which for these kids isn't often. But they get creative."

"I remember the day I got this. I was so excited to bring this back to you. Nora had taken me to her sister's at the Grand Canyon, and I remembered thinking how much fun we would have and how much I wanted to take you there one day."

"You told me. I couldn't even be jealous because you were so happy. Here's the one you gave me for my birthday that year." I hold up a second rock.

"God, we were, what…"

"Eight," I answer. "It was the first time I realized I loved you."

This is one of my favorite times to be in the apartment. It's just starting to get dark outside. The lamps are on, music's playing in the background. I'm sipping on a glass of wine while I cook.

I used to think nothing could make times like this more perfect until Blake saunters up behind me. He wraps his arms around me and rests his head against the back of my neck. It's sweet and comfortable, but there's also an immediacy to it, like he has to touch me or he might not make it. At least that's how I feel about him. He breathes me in and I know this is what I want for my always.

When we hear a knock at the door, he slumps. When he groans into my neck, I laugh. "Don't make her wait all day," I fuss.

He meets Bree at the door with a glass of her favorite wine, and the two of them fall into an easy, laughter-filled conversation while I finish getting dinner ready. My two best friends, my two loves, loving each other. It's a happiness that's almost painful.

"I was always rooting for you, you know," she tells him, "but Finn's gift to the school was almost enough to sway me."

I'm shocked to hear Blake agree that it was a lovely gesture.

"I'm sorry, are you softening to Finn?" I raise a brow in disbelief.

"I'm not exactly over the moon for the guy, but he ended up not being too bad."

"Because he bowed out and let you have West," Bree laughs into her sangria.

"I love you, Bree, but if you think for a minute anyone *let* me have anything, let alone West, you don't know me."

"I think she knows you better than you think," I say to Blake before turning to Bree. "Stop poking the bear."

Blake is in motion to toss a roll at her head when his cell rings.

"Hey, Elise," he answers, and I know whatever it is, I'm not going to like it. I can see it on his face.

"I'll leave here in ten." He's already on his feet and in our bedroom closet by the time I get to the room.

"You're leaving?"

"Yes," he answers, but I know I've already lost him. He opens the safe and I watch as he packs thousands of dollars in cash and at least six firearms into a bag. He flips through what looks like a stack of passports, throwing two into his bag. Four cellphones, two changes of clothes, add one kiss and he's out the door. No explanation. No preparation. No discussion.

Five days. No text, no call, no email. Not a single peep from Blake. Elise has been gone, too. Gabby came over the night after Blake left to check on me. She had zero information to give but explained this was often how it was. Blake and Elise handled the sensitive cases, and there was a possibility they would have to get their hands dirty. I truly did not understand the level of financial and political corruption they dealt with until Gabby explained just how involved they are.

I've been watching the news and reading online to see if I can figure out what they are working on, where they are, who they are with. But there's nothing that would explain why he would walk out without even the vaguest explanation. Anything to prepare me, to make me feel differently than I am feeling right now. Blake is gone. No idea where he is. No idea if he's safe. If he's coming back...

There's a knock on the door, and, considering I'm on my third whiskey, I don't answer.

My phone vibrates and Reid Beckett shows up on the screen.

"Reid?" I answer in a rush, my heart dropping into my stomach.

"Let me in, please." Even in my inebriated state, I know that his "please" is not meant as a request.

"Everything's okay," he assures the minute he sees my face. My shoulders visibly sag and I back up so he can enter. "I know this is your first time going through this, so I thought I would stop by and check on you. Three fingers and a single cube of ice," he says when I raise my glass to him.

"You check on all your clients?" I ask, handing him his drink.

"No. But you're more than a client, and as I haven't heard from Elise, I can imagine that you are feeling the same thing I am."

"I don't know how you do this." I sit in Blake's favorite leather chair and roll my drink in my hands.

"Even with a head start on you, I haven't mastered it. Elise and I are still working out the kinks, but I'm learning to trust her. She promised she wouldn't do anything to put herself in danger." He pauses before adding, "And I trust Blake."

We sit a while, neither of us saying anything. You think it would be awkward but it isn't. And as kind as it was for Gabby to check on me, I have to admit, Reid's fortitude and contained power, and his trust in Blake and Elise, offer me a little relief.

"I had something else I wanted to talk to you about. Elise is still consulting with my team, but since everything is still in transition, she passed off the community center case to Fran before she left. We got word today that David was found in

New Jersey. It appears he's been dead for a little over a week."

"What? How?"

"The local authorities are saying it was an overdose. It's not a stretch considering he's been dealing in drugs."

I sit back in the chair. "So, it's over."

"Looks like it. They found an account in his name with part of the money he stole. I talked to the security team that is following you, and they don't see any reason to keep you under watch. You're a free man."

I have nothing to say to this. I should be happy the community center's problems have been solved. Happy the man who knocked me over the head is no longer out there, but all I hear is "the case is done." What does that mean for me and Blake?

Three more days go by. Radio silence.

"Hot dogs? Really?"

"I thought you American blokes loved your wieners."

"Not touching that."

"If I buy you another beer will you?" Finn winks and pays the guy behind the counter for our hotdogs. We take them and our beers across the street to the park and sit on a bench.

"There is no better hot dog than Gray's Papaya," I mumble around a mouthful.

"Agreed."

"I didn't take you for a hot dog kind of guy."

"There are a lot of things you never gave me the chance to show you."

Finn called last night and I think he could tell by my voice that I needed to get out of the fucking house. I was making myself crazy.

"So, you must be pleased to be able to do as you wish without security around you?"

"I am. Although, when Blake isn't here, the security is in the background. Sometimes I feel like I am being followed, but most of the time I'm not even aware they are there."

"Yeah, I get it. My team is great at giving me a wide birth. Something I insist on."

"You have security?"

"Over your right shoulder. Red hat." He points to a second guy across the way in a blue shirt and then shows me a panic button that looks like a leather bracelet.

"Guess I shouldn't complain."

"Wail all you want. You're entitled. Your life was turned upside down for the last several weeks. That's not easy. Add Blake into the mix and it's definitely not easy." He props his ankle up on his knee, shielding our beers from the officer walking by. "You know I hear things in our Foundation meetings."

"Do you know where Blake is?"

"No, but I know whatever is going on is major. I hear rumblings amongst the crowd we run with. Whatever is going on is being kept under wraps, which is near impossible with this group. Someone eventually says something."

It's a little past one in the morning when Finn's driver drops me off at my building. Spending some time with Finn got me out of the house, but I'm still feeling the same. The only person who will be able to calm me is Blake.

Blake

How did this man become my everything? When did it happen? When I was six? Sixteen? Just this year? I rub my hand across the tightening in my chest, and it reminds me of my tattoo. He was my everything long before now.

As usual, West left open the shades, and the lights from the city cast in just enough light for me to see him asleep in the bed. It's cool enough that he left the windows open and faint hums of the city join me as I watch him sleep. Fuck me, I've got it bad.

It's been an exhausting eight days and I have to fly out again at noon tomorrow, but I had to see him. I feel like shit the way I left and that I haven't had even a second to communicate. That's how it is on some cases. I have to block out everything else and focus on the task at hand. I can't afford distraction. Distraction leads to mistakes, and in my line of work, that can be the difference between life and death.

I take off my clothes and climb into the bed.

"What—" he awakens, startled.

"Shh. It's me, babe."

"Oh my God." Strong arms wrap around me, his emotions on the cusp of release. "I know I shouldn't need you like this, but I've felt so lost without you this week. Are you okay?" He pushes me away from him, scanning my body. I guess he's checking to see if I have any bullet holes, or that all my limbs are still intact.

I take his chin in my hands and shower him with kisses. "I'm really sorry. I couldn't call."

He doesn't say anything for a long time, and I'm tempted to fill the air with awkward conversation just to alleviate the silence.

"I don't know how to deal with this. I really want to be okay with you having to leave at the drop of a hat, but I..." he pauses and his long eyelashes fan across his cheek as he closes his eyes. "I'm not," he admits. "And I don't like the way that feels. I don't like being that person. Needy. Out of control. Untrusting."

"You think I would cheat?" I ask, staggered by the word "untrusting."

"No, I don't think you would cheat."

"Then what is it? You have to say it so I can fix it."

"I didn't trust you to come back." His voice is like gravel. "And," he adds stopping me before I can speak. "And, I don't want to be that person. I don't like that person."

His words are like a knife to the gut. I'm not a relationship guru by any means, but I do know that without trust there isn't much to go on.

"I'll fix this."

"You can't, Blake. I'm not something you fix. I want to be your partner and you aren't ready for that."

I panic. Even though he isn't saying it, it sounds

like—something I'm not prepared for.

"I am. What more do I have to do to show you that I'm ready for this, that I want us?" I climb out of the bed and stand in front of him. I'm keenly aware that this is as real as it gets, standing naked, physically and emotionally, before the person you love.

Not ready to face this, I do what's been engrained in me since I was sixteen: I quell the panic with something I can handle, something much more familiar—anger, denial, blame.

"I fundamentally changed who I was for you." My voice rises and I jab my finger in his direction. "I've never been with a man before. Do you think I would change that for anyone other than you?"

He stands and turns on the light. There's no hiding now. The bed between us might as well be a valley when I see the look on his face. I'm sure I fucked this up with what I just said, but for the life of me I don't know how.

"Maybe I didn't convey that in the best way." I try to back-pedal seeing this is going to get us nowhere fast.

"Ya think? Why don't you try that again, because it sounded an awful lot like you think you have given every part of you to this because you've had a dick up your ass."

I run a hand down my face in frustration and take a deep breath to balance myself. West is engraved on my heart, my soul. He brings me back to center.

"I love you." It's all I know to say. It's what I know to be true. For once I don't know how to fix this.

"I know you do."

"Then what are we arguing about?"

I'm tired. I've flown fifteen plus hours to get here. I don't have the stamina in me to monitor my temper and West is aware. His body language tells me he is drawing on all his patience to make me understand.

"I know you love me. I know you opened yourself up to a love you had never considered before—"

I interrupt him because I want to be clear on this part, if nothing else, "I don't know if that's true. I was watching you sleep thinking that I've loved you since I first saw you that day in your yard. Clearly, I didn't know it would be like this, but there was a part of my heart that you took that day that no one has ever had. It's only been you. Why can't you see that?"

"I love you. You love me." He's shouting now. "That is not the problem. The problem is trust. Love isn't enough sometimes."

"Love is always enough."

"This isn't a fucking soup commercial, Blake. It doesn't matter how much we love each other. You leave."

"I can't help—"

"Don't you think I know that? This is your job. It's who you are. You didn't ask to leave when you were sixteen, either. I know all these things, but it doesn't stop me from feeling like this."

I cross the room and stand in front of him. Maybe if there isn't a king-size bed between us we won't feel so far apart.

"I came home. I'm here." I take his hands and place them on my chest. "Yes, I have to leave. But I will come back."

"And if you don't?" his eyes brim with tears, and it finally hits me what is going on here. This isn't about trust, it's about fear. Fear I can fix. I've known fear my whole life. And in this moment our biggest fears are the same: the fear of losing each other.

"Then dig a hole and pour my ashes under the hammock at the Hampton's, because that's the only reason I wouldn't come back to you." I pull him to me, casing myself around him, giving him the protection he needs to ride this out. "I'm not going to ask you to marry me right now because it hardly seems like you are in a place to say yes, but as sure as I am standing before you, you are my lifetime, West. I will always come for you."

I strengthen my hold to calm his trembling body. People, books, movies, they always make love seem like it's the happily ever after. Like it's rainbows and glitter and musical numbers. The truth is love is hard, sometimes ugly, and takes work.

"We can work through this. Don't give up because you're scared. But the only way I can prove it is over time. Take the chance, West. I promise I'm worth it."

I forgot to close the blinds before falling asleep, and now the sun glares through the window after I've had less than three hours of rest for a total of ten over the last nine days.

"Babe, hit the button." West's fingers fumble over the bedside table before he finds the magic button that sends the room back into darkness.

It took some doing last night, but I finally convinced West to give this relationship some time. I had to remind myself how raw he is still. I underestimated what it was like to be the one left behind and carelessly thought the breakdown he had at his parents had settled this. I made a promise to him that I would never leave again without checking in with him. The nature of my job pulls me into things in a moment's notice, but I need to remember it's not just me now. I have to think about the kind of man I want to be for him. Priority number one is to be reliable.

My body responds to the closeness of his, but I'm too exhausted to let it have what it wants. After we both agreed on how to move forward, we spent the better part of the night making slow, lazy love to each other.

"Baby, your alarm is going off," West says sometime later.

Shit. I have a plane to catch. "I hate to tell you this," I moan, rolling onto my back and pulling him to me.

"How long?"

"Just a few days. The team is going to Ryan's parents' farm to spend some time together. I promise to call and text every day. I'd take you with me, but I know you have school this week."

"Fine." He kisses my chest. "What time is your flight?"

"Noon."

He leans over and hits the button to raise the blinds. "Then we better get up."

"Shower with me?" I ask him. West joins me and we take this time to talk.

"It's okay," he says. I know he's trying.

"I'll be back," I promise.

"Where were you last week?"

"You know Sir Randolph?"

"The crazy billionaire guy?"

I nod. "Someone kidnapped his three-year-old daughter."

West stands there, dumbfounded, the soap slipping from his hands.

"And you got her back?"

"Elise and I did," I smile.

"How do you keep something like that quiet?"

"By not having any contact with anyone. Flying under the radar." His face falls and I know him well enough to know what he's thinking. "Don't. You're entitled to your feelings no matter the reason I'm pulled away."

"I'm bitching because my boyfriend left me for eight days to rescue a kidnapped three-year-old girl. God, I'm a dick."

"I'd ask you not to talk about the love of my life like that, please." I roll my body against his before capturing his lips in a kiss that practically brings me to my knees. West's hand wraps around our cocks, gently squeezing them together and, with an already conditioned hand, he begins to slowly, tortuously jack us off.

It's funny, I used to travel more often than not. I think the entire time I lived in Chicago I stayed at my place fewer than a dozen times. In the short time I've been living with West, I've come to dread traveling. Or, more accurately, being away from West. From home.

We touch down in Reid's plane, and the closer I get to my man, the more my body begins to hum. One night in two weeks wasn't enough. But as much as I hated being gone this past week, it was good to be with the team and spend some time with Ryan's family. I had plenty of opportunities to tell them what is happening between me and West, not that they don't already know. This team, after all, makes a living at reading people. But I didn't, I decided to wait. It didn't seem right to do it without West and, to be honest, I wanted to make sure West was still okay with trying to make this work. He's been struggling with his fear of losing me again. A part of me wants to make sure he wasn't going to try to push me away.

Elise offers me a ride, but I catch a cab, wanting to have a minute to myself before getting home. West and I have been talking and texting every day, and he does seem more settled than he was the week before, but I just need to be with him, see him, touch him, love him.

A smile spreads across my cheeks when I see the now-familiar "Carvers Do It Better" painted on the brick. I'm home.

"You look beautiful," I smile as Ari and her guy enter the elevator when I step off.

"Hope you're back for a few days. I was worried he was going to decompose," she laughs as the elevator doors close, but it's too late. Her comment has kicked my ass in gear. Did I misread him on the phone this week? I don't know how to move us forward if he's not honest with me when he is feeling this way.

I faintly hear a bass beat and when I pull the door open, it's clear its coming from our apartment. I set my bag in the entry and watch, enthralled with what I'm seeing.

The twilight outside is showing through the iron windows, opened to the cool air. There's an open bottle of wine on the counter and West is standing at the stove—cooking something that smells fantastic as always—wearing only tight-fitting briefs that stop a few inches down his muscular thighs.

This man. My man. My heart.

A mischievous smile spreads across my lips. The music concealed my entrance, so I have a minute to watch him get his groove on. He's uninhibited and I fucking love seeing him like this, knowing he's mine. All mine. Only mine. Did I mention he's mine?

I sneak up on him and place my hands on his gyrating hips. He yelps, dropping the pan, but I quickly put my mouth next to his ear, reassuring him it's me.

"Stand right there. Don't fucking move."

Blake

I wasn't made to resist West. On every level, he calls to me. Sexually, spiritually, emotionally.

It's like he's my insides and there's no way to get him out.

Thank fuck.

I have zero hesitation in saying that this time next year, I'll be Blake Connors. Yep, I like the sound of that. West's family is my family and I would love to be a part of it in name.

"I had to throw away a perfectly good jar of coconut oil thanks to you," West says crunching on a piece of coconut fried shrimp and pulling me out of my daydream. He laughs at the horrified look on my face when I realize I had my come-covered fingers all in that jar earlier. "I had another jar," he assures me.

"I'm going to take your name," I blurt out. Then I blush.

West does a good job of locking down his expression, but not before I note his surprise. Or shock. I'm not sure which.

"I think that's the dick talking," he responds.

I furrow my brow. He's being a little dismissive and I think he can tell I'm not pleased with his comment.

"I'm just saying, you didn't even like men until a few months ago."

"I don't know that I like men now. What I do know, is I am in love with one."

"I love you, too, babe."

"But?"

"But I think you are moving fast for someone who's going through a lot of change."

"So, what are you saying? That you don't want to marry me?"

"I would marry you tomorrow in a heartbeat. You're the love of my life."

"Then what's the problem?"

"I only plan on doing this once. Marriage."

"Well, then, we're on the same page," I grumble.

"I just think it's different for you Blake. You need to make sure this is what you want. Me. For always and forever. Till death do us part."

"So, you think I'll wake up in ten years and want pussy?"

"What I think is you need to make certain you're sure."

"I am," I say more aggressively than I intend.

"You've been 'gay' for, what, a few months at the most?"

"What I am is in love with the love of my life."

He smiles at that and the heart that was threatening to beat out of my chest at his blatant refusal, calms down. But only a little.

"So, what are you thinking? Go in the front or back?" Teague asks me, loading his reserve pistol before strapping it to his ankle.

"Let's work our way in from the back."

"Intel says there are five guys. One appears to be injured. There's no info on what kind of weapons they have, and there are mixed reports about hostages," he says, adjusting the Velcro on his Kevlar vest. He pulls his safety glasses over his head and we pick up our weapons. We make our way to the back door and the light in the simulation booth turns from green to red. An alarm sounds. We move to hand signals like we used in Delta 6.

We've been at the FBI's training facility for the better part of the day. Teague trains once a quarter to keep himself sharp, and since it's been a while for me, and it gave us a way to catch up, I agreed to join him when he called.

Five minutes later the lights come on and we assess our damage.

"Delta 6's are the shit." The guy who runs the training center shakes our hands when we turn in our weapons.

"You still got it," Teague says on our way back to the city. He flew us down in one of the Taylor Organization's helicopters.

"If you say so."

"I had to draw last year. First time since I've been back." He goes into how he returned fire on some gang members, killing them, but not before he lost someone.

"I got Emme down, but I wasn't able to save Reggie." He says climbing in altitude over a mountain.

"I'm sure you did the best you could. Sounds like you were ambushed."

"Yes but, isn't that part of the job? Recon, not letting anyone get the jump on you?" He sounds regretful. A feeling I understand too well. I've carried it around for years.

"By your own account, you saw the gun and alerted people before the first shot went off. Even Delta 6's can't be in two places at once. I'm sorry you were put in that position."

"I'm sure you've had your own share, being on Elise's team."

"I have, but I've been fortunate. I haven't had to kill since coming back. I've had my fill of taking lives. I hope I never have to do it again."

"Here here."

"How are you coping?"

"Some days are harder than others."

I nod in understanding. "I heard from Colonel Brent last week. Told him we had been in touch. You should be prepared for him to make you an offer."

"I'm happy where I am."

"Bullshit." He glances out of the side of his eye.

"I am."

"I believe you like working for Elise, but you don't seem like a man who is happy with what he is doing. Not today anyway."

I'm not sure how to respond to that. I have been feeling a little unsettled lately, but I don't care for it to be obvious.

"We all have our days," I side-step.

"True," he nods, and we ride in silence for a while, watching the land give way to pavement as we near the city.

"Well, shit. I'm just gonna say it. I don't think you're happy doing what you're doing. And I know you have always been in charge, but I need a partner. Graham and Emme have two kids now and when they aren't together, which, as you can imagine, happens often, it can spread me thinner than I'd like to be. I have a big guy for the fear factor. He's huge and intimidating, but I need someone who's quick with assessment and quick on the draw if, God forbid, it ever came to that. Plus, Graham told me about your work a few weeks ago on the billionaire's kid."

"Word gets around."

"When you're good at what you do it does. Just think about it. Talk to West."

Yeah, West won't be the only one I'll be having a conversation with.

"You don't get to handle me!" A door opens behind me just as I yell my frustration at Elise louder than I had intended.

"Blake," Reid says, shutting the door behind him. His voice is calm but with a hint of threat and a huge dose of reproach. Tough shit, though. This is between me and Elise and the look on her face tells him that she doesn't need anyone stepping in for her. She squares herself in front of me and lets it fly.

"I will handle the fuck out of you if you don't get your head out of your ass and take care of this yourself. I made a promise to put you before business and I won't back down from that," she says.

"If I want to make a career change, that's my call. I don't need you orchestrating my life. You aren't a puppeteer and I'm not your marionette."

"You're crazy if you think I'm going to stand here and let you tell me what I did was wrong."

"What did you do, Elise?" Reid says with a hint of accusation.

"I suggested to the Taylor's that Blake would be a good

addition to their security team."

His eyebrows hit his hairline, and he darts his eyes at me. "That would give you a real chance at a life with West," Reid offers. "You should have talked to Blake first though, Elise."

"Thank you!" I exclaim.

Elise crosses her arms and stares at her fiancé.

"Glare all you want, you know I'm right." He walks to her and kisses her forehead. "I'll leave you two to duke it out. Watch your tone, Blake."

"Are you even ready for this?" I ask her.

"I will be. I plan to contract you from time to time, but I made a commitment to Reid to be more present. And I want to be. And I'm so sick of fighting with him over safety. There are days I'm not sure I'd pee on him if he was on fire, I'm so sick of it."

"I don't need insight into your kinky fantasies."

"Why are you freaking out about this?" She plops down on the couch, and Reid's dog is immediately by her side, head in her lap.

"I just don't like someone planning my life for me. It's *my* life."

"You know, Blake, it's easy for people to think you plow ahead with a fuck-all mind-set. But you and I know different. You've sacrificed long enough. It's time to do this for you. For West. If you're honest with yourself, you've been thinking about making a change for a while."

She's right. "I have been."

"Then what are we arguing about? Meet with the Taylors. At least take the first step."

West

I'm usually the one bouncing around the bed in my sleep, but tonight, it's Blake. He's restless. Has been since he got home from his day with Teague.

Things between us have been better than I could hope for, but there has been an underlying frustration building in him since our dinner the other night. Sure, Blake is ready to jump feet first into this relationship, but I know what it's like to lose him, and I know I won't survive it twice. I need him to be absolute in his feelings before I give this last part of myself over to him.

This is all so foreign to me. I've never been someone who's always waiting for the other shoe to drop, expecting the worst, but it's the only way I know to deal with this. We may have known each other since we were six, but these last few months feel like we've been going at breakneck speeds.

I wrap around him and pull him to me. He lays his head on my chest, and it only takes a minute for our breathing to synchronize. I comb my fingers through his hair. The longer I lay there, the more overcome with need I have for him. I roll on top of him. He's groggy but wakes easily.

"What's wrong?" he asks, clearing the frog from his throat.

"That's what I wanted to ask you?" I softly kiss his lips and lace my fingers through his. He gives my hands a squeeze. "You might as well tell me. It'll make you feel better," I prod.

"I can think of a few ways right now that would make me feel better," he moans and rolls his body around underneath me.

"Start talking, Thomas," I say, nibbling the base of his neck.

"I'm thinking about changing jobs."

That has my attention. I sit up, straddling him.

"But you love your job."

He has to tilt his head back to see my face in the shadow of the night. "There are parts of it I do, but there are parts of it that I am ready to have a break from. I don't want to give up my life to solve other people's problems."

The weight of what he's saying settles over me. "Blake, I don't want you giving up what you love."

"I'm not." In one move Blake has me on my back, his beautiful body laying heavy on mine. "I'm not giving up what I love, I'm going after it."

"We can make this work. You don't—"

"This is what I want. I've already talked to Elise. She's taking a few steps back, too. It's the right time for us both."

"I woke you up because I could tell there was something bothering you even in your sleep. That doesn't make me confident that you think this is the right call."

"I'm not apprehensive because I'm making a career change, I'm worried that even with that barrier between us gone, you still won't want me." His voice catches before he admits, "I don't know what I would do if that was the case. I love you, West. You take the darkness away and give me hope for something I never knew I had the right to hope for. If you need me to be labeled as gay, then label me as gay. Whatever you need. All I need is you."

"This wasn't about a label." I run my thumb over his cheek.

"Then what was this about?"

"I just wanted to give you the time and the opportunity to walk away if that is what you wanted."

"What I want is to marry you. That's what I want. I don't need an out. Stop trying to give me one."

His lips close over mine, and I can feel him pouring every part of himself into this kiss.

"What's on your schedule this week?" I ask, setting two plates of French toast on the bar. I refill Blake's coffee before taking the seat next to him.

"You make me look forward to Mondays. Before you, I would dread the week. There was always regret about what I couldn't accomplish the week before, apprehension about whether or not I could get it done in the days stretching out before me. But now, with you, I'm excited to see what the week will hold. I look forward to Mondays with you."

I can feel my knees buckling at his declaration. He pats my ass with a shit-eating grin. Clearly the tender moment has passed.

"On the agenda today, Elise and I are going to close out some cases. Then Teague and I are hoping to meet up after work, maybe hit the gym."

"If Teague is any good at hoops, why don't you come to

practice? I need a few guys for a scrimmage with the kids."

"Sure. I'll ask him."

"Cool. By the way, did you know Mickey was released on bail?"

He gives me a don't-be-stupid-of-course-I-knew look.

"Well, Mr. All-Knowing, did you know that he will be back in school today?"

"No. But I think that's great."

"Me too. He's not allowed to play for the team yet, but I'm hoping he'll be the team manager. I'd like to see him get back in with the right crowd."

"You're a good guy." He kisses my temple with powdery lips.

"I was kind of surprised that he was released," I muse, never taking my eyes off him.

"Well," he shrugs, cutting into his French toast, "he didn't have any priors, and I'm sure the judge took into consideration the circumstances around his case."

"Do tell?" I narrow my eyes at this man who most certainly got involved and is trying to pass it off like he doesn't know what the hell is going on.

"What? I'm just saying, the judge must have seen the obvious. Which," he continues, anticipating that I'm going to ask, "is that he is better off in school making the grades than in a cell where his chances for a real shot at life are dismal. Plus, like you said, he has strong family support. I'm just saying, if I was his lawyer, that is what I would be presenting."

This man. "I love you."

And if he would look at me he would see every ounce of it in my expression, but he just takes another bite of toast.

Blake

"Who you callin' 'old man'?" I dip my shoulder and nudge Marius who is playing some great defense. I'm not a spring chicken anymore, but I'm at least keeping up with them. I asked Teague before we walked in if he brought the oxygen tanks.

"You, grandpa." He pulls on my shirt a little, trying for the ball.

West blows a whistle and we all groan.

"What are you blowing the whistle for?" Bree asks. Gotta give it to this girl, she can play. She's a helluva point guard. Can hit the three, no problem.

"This is practice. You guys are turning it into a pick-up game. Plus, you know there's no trash talk in my gym."

"Yeah, Marius." I smack him on the arm.

"You gonna sell me out? Really dude?"

"You get to leave when this is over. I'll have to listen to it all the way home."

"Fine, but you owe me one. Guess Coach likes pussy after all," he smirks, and I try to cover my laugh with a fake cough.

"You're funny, kid." Teague slaps him on the shoulder.

"Sorry, Coach," he says, raising his hand. "This one is on me."

"Think about it while you run twenty."

Marius starts his laps.

"Ladders," West clarifies. His take-charge demeanor electrifies my balls.

Marius groans and for a minute I think he's going to sell me out, but he doesn't.

"Blake?"

"Yeah, babe?" I pass the ball to Bree.

"Hit the line."

I look over my shoulder to see who he's talking to.

"Yes, you. Hit the line. No trash-talking in my gym."

"I'm so hot for you right now," I say in a low voice, winking as I walk past him to join Marius. No way am I gonna challenge his authority in front of the kids. I might goof off with them, but I will always make sure to show respect.

"Need me to carry you?" Marius taunts me. Isn't that what got us here?

I laugh because there's a good chance I might really need him to.

"Let's start and finish together," I suggest, setting the stride for our pace.

"You run like ten miles a day. Why are you acting like this is any bigs?" West asks as we run our last lap.

"Keeping the kid off guard. Make him think I'm tired so he changes his game."

"Marius is too smart for that. Just play."

Alrighty, then.

When practice is over, we decide to play a game just for kicks. West joins in. I'm enjoying the hell out of these kids and watching West teach and mentor them just makes me fall more and more in love with him.

"You need a walker? They keep some extras on the senior's side."

I palm Marius' head, pushing it away.

"Leave him alone, man. I like him," Steven says to Marius.

"He knows I'm just givin' him shit."

"He's so much better than that other dude," Steven says to which Marius agrees.

This gets my attention.

"That guy that was steppin' out. What was his name?" Steven asks.

"Jay," Marius answers.

"That was it." Steven rambles on throwing the stuff into his bag. "Mickey's brother never stood a chance. Catch ya tomorrow." He clamps hands with Marius and heads out.

"What did he say?" I catch Marius by the arm.

"Nothin' man. He's just talkin'."

"Jay knew Mickey?"

"Just rumors. Supposedly Jay and Mick's brother were doin' the brokeback thing. We debated on calling in a few favors and having Jay roughed up, so to speak," he glances between me and Teague, not sure if he should have admitted that. When it's clear neither of us are going to comment, Marius shrugs and continues. "But he was mixed in some heavy shit. We didn't want him to think it was Coach. But it didn't matter. Coach dumped him a week later. We didn't even tell him. None of us liked Jay. Didn't want to give Coach a reason to talk to him. Hey, thanks for practicing with us." He shakes Teague's hand and leaves.

"What is it?" Teague asks.

"I'm not sure? When you all first looked into the missing

funds, you looked at all the staff at the center, right? Including West?"

"We did." He looks puzzled.

"Did you look at their known associates?"

"Not unless there was something to make us think we needed to."

"Hey, babe," West enters. "I'm going to help Bree with her practice. Meet you at home?"

"I can hang," I offer.

"Nah, I think we might go back to the school and set up for the program tomorrow."

"Okay. Make sure you're back before dark."

He rolls his eyes but doesn't argue. He and Teague say their goodbyes and when we hit the bottom of the steps, Teague asks me what's really going on.

"I want to talk to Mickey. I'm not sure, but I think the missing piece of the puzzle is Jay."

"The one they said was West's old boyfriend? I'll go with you."

"I got it man. I'm sure Joy's waiting for you for dinner."

"Let's go." He pulls me down the steps and I stop one of the players for directions to Mickey's place. It's only a couple of blocks away.

Mickey's mother lets us in with a hug. She thanks me for the lawyer. Yeah, I didn't tell that one to West.

"I was happy to help. Coach Connors has a lot of interest in making sure Mickey gets his degree."

She smiles at the mention of West. "He's always been so good to the kids. Always helping them after school, making sure they have something to do besides being in the streets. Both were always so giving of their time."

"Both?" Teague asks, his eyes dart to mine.

"Mr. Connors and his partner." She smiles awkwardly like she made a blunder. "Not that I like him better than you. You're much cuter."

"I appreciate that. His partner Jay?" I confirm.

"Yes. He spent so much time with Mickey's brother. Tried his best to keep him on the straight and narrow. But it didn't work. We still lost him to the streets."

"What did he do?"

"Made sure he had some money so he wouldn't feel like he had to join a gang. Made sure no one messed with him. I was skeptical. I didn't think a white, preppy man, would have any pull on him, but he worked at it. Those kids respected him. Still do."

"Do they still see him?" I ask.

"Yes. He was just here a few minutes ago. Took Mickey to the community center to shoot some hoops. Wanted to help him now that he was away from that David." She shivers a little at the thought.

"They're at the center?"

"You just missed them. They left about ten minutes before you guys got here."

A cold chill runs through me. Teague thanks her for her time and declines the offer of coffee. As soon as the door closes behind us, we hit the stairs running down the nine flights. Teague is on his phone calling I don't know who. I'm in a dead out run with him on my heels.

We slow to a walk when we enter the center. We each pull a pistol from our bags and leave them against the wall. Teague glances into the gym and when he turns to look at me, no words are needed. I know who is in there.

"They're both in there," he whispers. "Jay has a 9mm on West and Mickey has Bree's arms behind her back. I can't see if he's armed or not. You good to go in there?"

He asks me again when I don't answer him the first time. "I'm good."

"Give me four to get to the side door. Go on five. SWAT is," he looks at his watch, "eight minutes out. This will be over in three."

I nod. But he doesn't go.

"Focus. I want to get West home to you and I want to get home to Joy." He prods, "Acknowledge or we wait for SWAT." Teague would give his life for mine, but he's not going to run into the fire if I don't have my fucking head in the game.

I can hear Bree yelling and I know it's escalating.

"Go," I order and Teague takes off without hesitation. I clock the four and enter on five. We enter at the same time. Teague is slightly off to my left and as soon as we enter, Mickey pulls his right arm up and puts a knife to Bree's throat. She doesn't look scared, she looks pissed, which makes this more difficult to navigate. I don't need a hostage doing something stupid.

I don't even give a glance to West. I already know he has a gun to his head, but I'm the better shot and Teague knows this. Slowly, we begin to move towards each other.

"Drop the knife," I yell to Mickey. Teague crosses behind me and checks behind us to make sure we aren't going to be ambushed.

"Two." He confirms these are the only two in here and moves to my right.

"I want to, but he'll kill my mom if I do," Mickey says. There's a slight tremor to his hand that makes me believe he really thinks that.

"I won't tell you again to drop it. If you so much as give her a paper cut, I'm taking your life," I tell him, still slowly moving to my left, positioning myself in front of West and Jay.

"You wouldn't shoot a kid," his voice cracks.

"I can and will shoot a killer."

As soon as Teague has a lock on him, I move my focus to Jay, who is escalating.

"It's over for me anyways," Jay says.

"That's up to you," I answer.

"I'm sure we can work something out." West tries to appeal to Jay, but I know it's futile.

"West, don't move," I tell him without taking my eyes off Jay. "There's no way out of this. Drop the gun."

"I'm not your boy like he is," he says with contempt. "I don't bend over for you. You want West? Drop yours."

"Not gonna happen. Last warning, drop your weapon or leave in a body bag."

"You—"

It's the only word he says before falling dead to the ground, pulling West with him.

West

It's been a little more than two weeks since I was released from the ER. Evidently when Jay jerked me down with him, I hit my head in the same place the two-by-four did a few weeks ago.

Blake is waving his arms like a crazy person, but I pretend I don't see him. I haven't been able to hear anything since the shooting. Two whole weeks I've been home. Not teaching. Stuck with Blake. You would think that would be a good thing, but Blake is not only way too attentive, not letting me do anything for myself, he also apparently thinks my ability to have sex is directly connected to my ability to hear. I even had to ask Kyle to have a talk with him during my last check-up.

But Blake hasn't budged. Hasn't touched me other than to hold my hand whenever we leave the apartment. Not that I'm complaining. Okay, maybe I am a little.

The first day I tried to go out on my own, Blake must have followed me because when I stepped off a curb, clearly not hearing the cab honking it's warning, Blake was there to pull me back before I was pancaked on the street. He was livid and thus began the babysitting diaries of West.

When he can't be here, it's Donnie, my parents, or Bree. Hell, he even had Finn in here. I'm so sick of people I could spit. I just want to be alone with my boyfriend. For said boyfriend to have his dick in my mouth. Or my ass. Either one. Beggars can't be choosers and believe me I've begged.

Kyle says the sudden hearing loss is temporary and there's nothing to do but wait. And wait some more.

I have so much to be grateful for, so I've tried not to be an asshole, but we've had a hard time communicating since the incident. Blake says he has no regrets taking another life, after he was adamant he never wanted to kill again. But when I scribbled my concern on a legal pad, he dismissed it saying he would do it again in a heartbeat. That taking a life to save one wasn't the same as taking a life in war. All I can do is take him at his word. He did go back to the counselor he saw when he was first back in the states. I was glad for that.

He's been home from work for a few hours. He brought dinner with him so I wouldn't have to cook, but he doesn't understand that I *want* to cook. I huff and puff and finally throw my book on the table. Blake raises a chastising eyebrow and then goes back to the game on the TV.

The sun has gone down and the windows are open. It's another perfect night in the city and we're sitting inside like some damn old ladies.

"Do you have any plans to fuck me?" I ask from the couch.

Another don't-be-stupid look, then he goes back to watching the game.

Motherfucker, that's it. I slide my sweats off, kicking them across the floor. Did I mention I wasn't wearing a shirt and don't have on underwear?

Blake's eyes glue hard to mine and I think he's asking me

what the fuck do I think I'm doing?

I give my cock a good, hard tug. That gets his attention. He doesn't move an inch, but I can feel his body tensing from here. I hold his stare until I give another yank, drawing his eyes down to my dick where I wipe a drop of pre-cum off the tip with my finger, sucking it into my mouth, tasting myself. It's a move he loves and he's never been able to resist. Two weeks. This isn't the time to play fair. In fact, I'm about to show him it's every man for himself.

I bite my lip and continue to pleasure myself, working my balls into play. When my finger grazes the smooth skin under my sac, I shimmy with a full body shiver. Before I can stop myself, I slide a finger into my ass.

"Oh my God," I moan, but Blake is a wall of fortitude. He's not budging. But he's also in sweats with no shirt, and they are doing squat to hide his arousal.

Fuck it. I think I say aloud. I'm not sure. Either way I move to straddle him. He lowers his feet from the ottoman to the floor. He doesn't touch me. He doesn't say anything. Not that I could hear him. His fingers twitch on the arm of the leather. He loves this chair, says it reminds him of home. I plan to give him something else to remember about this chair.

I grind against his thighs matching the movement of my hand. I'm leaking like a faucet now and the bell-shaped head of my cock is purple in expectation of release.

"Blake," I hum his name. My eyes close in the sheer ferociousness of what I'm feeling. There's a sharp crack against the side of my ass popping my eyes back open. Blake nods his approval. He wants my eyes open. The electricity shooting through my body pitches me forward. My hand rests on his chest as I paint his abs with long ropes of come.

It's only when I come down from my high, that I realize

his fingers are gripping my thighs. He says something that I can't hear but it doesn't matter. The only thing that matters is that he's touching me. And with that touch everything I've been feeling over the last couple of weeks falls squarely back into place.

Blake

My body thrums with pent up desire. It's been too long since I've been inside this man. This man who just came all over my chest and stomach. Have I experienced a sight hotter than that? I don't think so.

The pressure of his hand against my chest is strong and heavy. My arms catch him as he falls into me and, without another thought, I stand, taking him with me. West's legs instinctively wrap around my waist, his arms around my neck. I carry him from the leather chair to the bed, and...seventeen. Fuck me, it took seventeen fucking steps.

What was I thinking, keeping my hands off him? Losing all this time, when we've already lost so much. Being with him right now, listening to his pleasure is pure bliss. Every neighbor on this floor must hear him, and I could give a damn because the name he's screaming is mine.

His ecstatic cries spur me on and I release into him at the same time he comes for a second time. He holds me to him, our breathing erratic as we kiss. He got what he wanted. Now I'm never letting go.

Ali and I smirk at each other in the elevator the next morning.

"Sounds like someone had a great time last night," she sings.

"Indeed." I admit without remorse. I am surprised she heard, though. Ari lives three doors down.

"Maybe next time close your windows," she winks. "Or don't," she says over her shoulder as she exits. "It was hot."

There's a sharp jab to my bicep. "I can't believe you let me get that loud."

"You're the one who jumped me, remember?" I laugh.

"If Ari heard us, you know everyone else did."

"Who gives a…" I stop so abruptly that a woman behind us runs into me. I apologize before moving us to the side, out of the way of foot traffic. "Wait, you heard me? Just now?"

"I did," he smiles.

"How long?"

"Woke up like this."

"And you didn't think to tell me?"

"Thought I would get one more breakfast out of you before I have to get back to work."

I'm so relieved I just hug him to me for several minutes and he lets me. I'm still hugging him when he throws up what little of his arm is available to hail us a taxi.

We've been invited to Reid and Elise's townhouse. The last few months have pulled all of us in opposite directions, so we finally planned to spend the day together. Even if we all had to take off work to make it happen.

Climbing the stairs hand in hand, it hits me this will be the first time we will be here together as a real couple, not just pretending to be one.

"Wiggin'?" West asks. It's like he has mind-reading capabilities.

"No. I couldn't be more honored." Like a magnet, his lips are pulled to mine in a kiss so sincere I feel it in my soul.

A throat clears and Reid takes a step back to let us enter. The blush blooming on West's cheeks just endears me to him that much more.

"Everyone's in the kitchen making their plates. Good to see you both."

West says thank you, and Reid looks at me quizzically, obviously surprised that West could hear him.

"Since this morning. I've only known for about thirty minutes myself."

We enter the kitchen to a chorus of greetings, all turning to cheers when they find out West can hear.

"West, glad you could make it. Please, make a plate," Elise says.

"How are you not the size of a house?" he asks as I juggle a plate full of food, balancing a spring roll on top.

"I'm hungry."

"We just ate."

I shrug and he puts a spoonful of veggies on his plate. "At least put something on your plate that isn't fried."

"Alright, Mary Beth."

"Don't use my mother's name in vain."

I grab a beer and head out to the table outside, choosing a seat in the shade.

"Not hungry?" Gabby says sarcastically, eyeing my plate.

"Right? We literally ate an hour ago," West huffs.

"Can't help it," I say to Gabby. "He's working me out so much at night, I gotta keep up my stamina."

"Oh my God. You'll just say any ol' shit won't you?" West kicks me under the table.

"No use getting shy now, the whole floor heard you last night." I laugh. He kicks harder. "Aww, don't be like that, babe." I lean forward and kiss him.

"Could you not please?" Gabby teases.

"Jealous?" I gibe.

"Nope. For your information, I am getting plenty of the baloney pony."

West chokes on his beer and Gabby gives him a polite pat on the back. It just now occurs to me West is new to the everyday interactions with these people that I love. The people who have been my family. It's going to take him some time to get used to Gabby, that's for sure.

"Who's the guy? I want to check him out," I ask and Gabby smiles.

"Dean."

"Still with Dean?" Ryan asks, taking a seat next to Fran.

"The one and only."

"Wow. Didn't see that one coming. Is he the longest relationship you've had?"

Gabby gives him the finger.

Elise passes around bowls of mint chocolate chip served over warm brownies. Fran places a giant portion of ice cream in front of me. West reaches for it, but I pull it away before he can.

"Get your own, Southie."

"You don't need all that. You eat like a teenager."

"I went out a guy who ate like a horse," Gabby says, around a mouthful.

"Didn't work out?" West asks and I chuckle. He doesn't know. But he will.

"No he ate like one, but he wasn't hung like one." She holds up a pinky for dramatic effect. "Like a hot dog down a bowling lane."

I pat West's leg. I'm sure he regrets asking. He has no idea how to respond to Gabby's analogy.

"Ugh," Fran and Elise respond in unison.

"You should look up Joel while you're in town." Gabby suggests to Fran.

"Nah," she responds curtly. When I left the farm Fran and Ryan were an item, so I'm confused as to why Gabby is asking her about another man.

"What was wrong with him?" Ryan asks. "He was a nice guy."

"He's a no," she says more adamantly.

"Wasn't he the one you said kept blowing air in your goods like you were a balloon?" Elise asks.

"You know, at this point you're just wasting good beer," Gabby says as she dabs a napkin at the beer West spit out again running down his shirt.

"I see now why Blake works so well with this team," he says.

"So the community center case is closed?" Ryan asks. "Did we have any clue it was this Jay guy?"

"No." I'm still pissed I didn't figure it out sooner, but none of the pieces were pointing to him. "We had no idea he was the ringleader. He was using David and the center to launder money and drugs. Paying the kids to distribute. When David started skimming off the center and we found Mickey, Jay knew it was only a matter of time until we put it all together."

"Has anyone else figured out how Theo and Ross kept it quiet they were expecting?" Fran asks. I'm grateful for the subject change.

"You don't get where Theo is without knowing how to keep it a secret," Elise reminds her.

"No I get it, but Ross? This means they were expecting when we were at the retreat. I can't be the only one who's surprised he kept it under wraps. I guess I thought they would wait until Ross finished his residency." Fran says.

"Makes sense though. I mean he and Theo have been married for three years. Maybe this will push them back to New York. Are you an official New Yorker?" Gabby asks me.

"He better be. I'm not going to have a husband who lives in another city," West says casually.

It's made him the center of attention, which I don't think he expected, but I just lean back and watch.

"You asked West to marry you?" Fran chirps at me with excitement.

"Technically, no. He didn't ask. He told me," West answers again.

"Are you going to sell your place in Chicago?"

"Eventually. I have some things to work out first."

"Such as?" Ryan asks.

"There's a chance that I'm going to work security for the Taylor's."

Silence. West moves his hand to the inside of my thigh. His thumb brushes back and forth supportively, but it's making me hard.

"You're okay with this?" Gabby asks Elise.

"I am. I'm pulling back from the type of work Blake handles, and he wants to make some roots."

"You aren't worried it'll be a step back for your career?" Ryan asks.

"It's not backwards, it's just a different direction."

"A baby for Theo. You're getting married and leaving the team," Fran nods at Blake. "Elise is working on her own. That really was our last work retreat."

epilogue

West

Seven Months Later

"**B**abe, I can't get my tie to work," Blake calls out, and when I round the corner into our his-and-his closet, I freeze.

Every time, dammit. Every time I see this man in a tux, I lose my ability to function.

"Good, huh?" he smirks, knowing the effect he's having on me.

"Fucking delectable." I work his tie into a bow.

"We have ten minutes before the car pulls up," he reminds me, pulling my hips against him so I can feel his arousal.

"No hanky before the wedding."

"I'm pretty sure that's only for the bride and groom. And since we're already married, I think we're exempt."

"Elise will have my balls if we're late, and since you seem fond of them, I'd like them to stay where they are."

"Chicken."

"We can't all be gun-toting Delta 6's."

"I never knew I could love anyone as much as I love you," he says to me, fingering my wedding band.

"I love you, babe." I place my lips over his for a quick kiss, but within two seconds we're full-on out of control.

"Jesus Christ we gotta go!" I gasp, reluctantly pulling us apart.

"Fine. We'll put a pin in this until later."

Thank God he has some willpower right now, because I sure don't.

Reid and Elise are getting married at the New York Public Library. We're in a space off to the side that has been draped off for the wedding party. We're here a little earlier than the others, so I steal the moment to continue what we started at home and show my husband how much I appreciate how he looks in a tux.

"Can't leave you guys alone for five minutes." Reid's voice breaks us out of our heated haze.

Holy Shit. Reid is giving Blake a run for his money. Hand in his pocket, he's every inch a god in his own right. Blake pinches my ass, knowing exactly what has me tongue tied.

"Thought you would be with Elise," Reid says, shaking Blake's hand and then mine.

"Nah. Thought I would let the girls have their time."

Reid laughs. "Theo will appreciate the reference." He's Elise's best man.

"Bake!" A familiar voice echoes off the marble pillars,

and we turn just in time for Blake to catch an acrobatic Olivia Taylor flying through the air. If she ever realizes his name actually has an l, his heart will break a little.

"Ollie!" He engulfs her in a hug and peppers her with kisses. The day Blake met with the Taylors to discuss working for them, he fell in love with their little girls. He's phenomenal with them, but he's more protective now than ever.

Watching this man receive butterfly kisses from the curly-haired beauty in his arms puts a knot in my throat. His hand finds mine and gives it a squeeze.

I'm feeling emotional today, but Blake doesn't mind. He doesn't make me feel silly or want me to stop. He just wants me to feel safe so I can be vulnerable with him. If I'm being honest, he's been this way since the first day I met him. Always looking out for me.

I feel a tug on my jacket and I look down to see a beautiful, bashful, younger version of Emme raising her arms to me. She's only been walking for a couple of months, but it was like she went straight into running, trying to keep up with her big sister. I lift her up and she puts her arms around my neck, her head resting on my shoulder. Addie can command a room, she's just happier being quiet about it.

Graham and Emme are steps behind their girls, and both offer their congratulations to Reid before Dean escorts him to another area. Elise is due to arrive any minute.

"You could have ridden with us," Emme says, wiping something off Olivia's cheek.

Blake decided that full-time security just wasn't for him. He would miss fixing things, working on the confidential projects. Elise has had a harder time stopping than she thought she would, too. Blake consults now, giving him the ability to choose what is right for him and us at the time. There are still drop-everything-and-go cases, but I've finally made peace that he will come home to me.

Consulting allows him to cover security for the Taylor's if he's needed, and he's been doing some side work for Emme's dad, who I understand is a fixer in his own right. Even though Blake has only covered the Taylor's once in the last seven months, part of the on-call deal was moving into their building. Smith and his expectant wife live a floor above us. Teague and Joy split the floor with us. It's only blocks from the area we were living in and it has awesome views of the water. Plus, it's huge. Bigger than I can imagine we would ever need. It's three bedrooms with a quaint little outdoor space. It's us.

Donnie has the rent-controlled apartment now. Blake sold his place in Chicago and bought the house next to my parents. I'm still not exactly sure what made his aunt and uncle sell. All I know is that Blake and Elise paid them a visit one day and a week later we were in escrow. I protested until Blake made it clear that he wanted our hometown to be our safe place, where we could go without dealing with them being feet away. He wanted this to be about his love for our family and not about the monster he grew up with.

We completely gutted it—which felt fucking fantastic, tearing down all the ugly—and I have to admit it's stunning. Our extended family uses it when they need it, which is often since the family continues to grow. Now that Maggie is pregnant, we can no longer all fit in my parents' house comfortably.

We spent our first Christmas as a couple there and were married a week later at midnight.

It was a surprise to our guests and to me. I showed up to what I thought was a New Year's Eve Party and left a married man. Blake planned everything.

"Did you have the plane stocked?" Emme asks Graham,

pulling me out of my reverie.

"I did."

"Are you leaving after this?" I ask Blake. Did I miss a trip on the calendar?

"No," Emme responds. "Graham has a—"

"We," Graham interrupts. The respect and love Graham looks at his wife with…did I mention Graham Taylor in a tux?

"*We* have a plane that's built for international flights. Reid is using it for the honeymoon."

"That's right. Europe?" I rub Addie's back as she nuzzles into my neck sleepily.

"It's under wraps, but he's taking her to the Harry Potter World. Then they'll be in…" she looks to her husband,

"Sri Lanka."

"Sri Lanka for two weeks, then Italy, then home."

I whistle. "That's some trip."

For our honeymoon, Blake and I stayed on a private island that Finn and his brother Walt own. An entire island.

The music alerts us that it's time to be seated, and I guide Blake down the aisle to our row. Theo's husband Ross is seated in front of us holding their son, William. We sit down with the girls in our laps. They insisted on staying with us through the ceremony, so Emme and Graham let them.

"I'm ready." Blake's intense blue eyes find mine.

"Okay." I know exactly what he means, and I lean in for a light kiss.

"Yeah?" he whispers.

"Yep. Let's have a baby."

Bonus

This was a sex scene I really loved, but couldn't keep. It broke up the story too much. This is what happened when Blake gets home from his trip to visit Ryan's family. He lands and comes home to find West shakin' his groove thing in the kitchen... the rest is...well, read for yourself. ;)

Blake

I faintly hear a bass beat and when I pull the door open, it's clear it's coming from our apartment. I set my bag in the entry and watch, enthralled with what I'm seeing.

The twilight outside is showing through the iron windows, opened to the cool air. There's an open bottle of wine on the counter and West is standing at the stove—cooking something that smells fantastic as always—wearing only tight-fitting briefs that stop a few inches down his muscular thighs.

This man. My man. My heart.

A mischievous smile spreads across my lips. The music concealed my entrance, so I have a minute to watch him get his groove on. He's uninhibited and I fucking love seeing him like this, knowing he's mine. All mine. Only mine. Did I mention he's mine?

I sneak up on him and place my hands on his gyrating hips. He yelps, dropping the pan, but I quickly put my mouth next to his ear, reassuring him it's me.

"Stand right there. Don't fucking move."

West

"Ah, fuck," I growl, but I know it's lost in the air. Blake is already making a meal of my body, starting with the space between my neck and shoulders. I'm just now getting the love bites he left me with before catching the plane to fade. Not that I care. I fucking love his need to constantly mark me.

He bends me over the island and slowly pulls my underwear down.

"Fuck me," he breathes. "I want your ass for dinner." Literally. He bites down onto one of my cheeks.

Aww fuck. Blake's home.

I've only caught a glimpse of him over my shoulder. He's wearing my favorite jeans, a V-neck navy sweater with a white undershirt, cuffs rolled up his forearms. Jesus Christ, this man does it for me.

"Palms flat on the counter," he says, reaching to turn the stove off. "Move them and I'll tie them up, understand?"

I do. I really do. But his denim-covered cock nestled in the crease of my ass has stolen my ability to respond.

A sharp crack across my ass helps me yelp out a "yes."

He squats down behind me, his hands spreading me

open and vulnerable before him. A wet finger enters me briefly before his tongue skates the puckered edge then enters me. Unable to contain myself I grab his hair and pull him as close as he can get, willing him to unzip my body and climb inside. An honest-to-God whimper leaves my mouth when he stands.

"Last warning." He smacks my other cheek, the heat rising in the shape of his hand. He flattens my palms against the counter once more.

He's bare this time as he nestles between my cheeks. I'm stark naked but he's still fully dressed, only his cock has been released.

I watch him dig his fingers into the coconut oil I was using for dinner. He works his lubed fingers into my hole.

"Your delectable ass should come with a warning. I'm fucking addicted to it. Crave it." His hand is back in the coconut oil but this time he uses it on his cock. His mouth lands next to my ear so that I can hear his excitement each time his hand travels his length. Listening to his arousal is hot as shit, but I want more.

"Blake," I beg.

"Finally," he exhales.

I realize he must have hit repeat on my phone, because the same song has been playing since he caught me dancing in front of the stove. And as the artist belts out "gonna get some dick today", Blake slides home.

Blake

I wasn't made to resist this man in front of me. On every level, he calls to me. Sexually. Spiritually. Emotionally.

It's like he's my insides and there's no way to get him out.

Thank fuck.

I have zero hesitation in saying that this time next year, I'll be Blake Connors. Yep. I like the sound of that, I muse while West moans his pleasure, my dick sliding in and out of him. West's family is my family and I would love to be a part of it in name.

"I love you so much."

Slide.

"You belong to me."

Slide.

"I'm never letting you go."

Slide.

I've been so caught up in my thoughts that I don't know if it's my words that push him over the edge, or that he was already there.

Gripping his hips in a bruising force, I pick up my pace,

pounding him as I take what's mine. Coming soon behind him.

My arms wrap around him, his back to my front. I can feel his heart pounding while I hold him to me, kissing him.

"Welcome home." He smirks as he pops the last of the kisses against my lips. "Your jizz is running down my leg." He pushes me back with his ass. "I'm going to hop in the shower for two shakes, then finish cooking the dinner I had for you." He kisses my nose and leaves me wanting him more than ever.

acknowledgements

Book four. Even now it sounds foreign to my ears. It's been less than a year since Taylor Made was released. I have met so many people along the way. I would be amiss not to mention them.

Blake's story was a bit of a surprise for me. I had no intention of his true love being West, but as Sunday Love progressed and with the consistent nudge from my PA, Amber Hamilton (whom I adore!), to write a m/m book, I knew it had to be him. I never thought I would fall as hard as I did into their love story, but I did. The fact that so many of you have fallen just as hard confirms that Blake and West were meant to be.

As always I couldn't do any of this without some truly amazing women in my life:

My editor—Anna Esquivel—every comment you leave me is like unwrapping a gift on Christmas morning.

My betas –

Ari—The hours and hours of text messages, hot inspiration photos and conversations we have had. Thank God we have locks on our phones.

Jerilyn—You visually let me see the book through your eyes. I love it and wouldn't give anything in the world for it.

Jess—You never forget your first. I love you.

Jessica—You let me pop your m/m cherry. I couldn't be more honored. (Plus you'd let me smell your baby :))

Kristen—Thank you so much for jumping in and reading the book as a whole. Your time means so much to me.

Rachel—I mean… there aren't enough pages or ink. You know what you mean to me. You don't need to read it here. That's not our style ;)

Tracey—The things we get ourselves into… that should be what I write in a book!

My formatter, Stacey Blake, always shows kindness and flexibility. She gives of her art to make my book beautiful.

Amber Hamilton—My PA who puts up with me. A feat far greater than anyone can understand. Her encouragement and desire to help me achieve my dreams means the world to me.
Kell Yarwood—My girl of all trades. The hardest job she has is keeping me on track and constantly reminding me to trust my gut and always showing me that dreams are never silly.

Monique Tarver—My friend. My mentor. My proofer. This woman represents so many things to me.

Frankie and Shawn—You answered every question, and there were some doozies. More than that, you're family and I love you.

Waldo and Wynand—I asked and you said yes! I still remember how excited I was. Your love for each other made this cover beautiful. I cannot thank you enough for selflessly sharing it with me. For those of you that haven't heard the story, I found their picture on Pinterest and knew I wanted them to be on the cover. You couldn't meet genuinely kinder men than these two. They never hesitated in saying yes. They unknowingly had such a huge influence over the love story of West and Blake. While it's a work of fiction and not their story, I really wanted to translate the adulation so evident in their picture onto the pages inside the book.

Lastly, to the people I see making a difference every day to show the world that truly love is love. Frankie and Shawn, Kathryn and Carolyn, and Waldo and Wynand to name a few. You couldn't find a purer example of love than these families.

Excerpt from

taylor
made

ch♥pter
one

Breathe in. Breathe out. *Fuck me.*

How do I get myself into these situations?

For the normal person, flying would not warrant a "fuck me," but when it comes to flying, I am not normal. I have issues. Control issues. Control is my security blanket. I don't like to give it to others. If I cling to it, I know I am going to land on my feet.

The practical side of me understands flying is a safe way to travel, but I've never understood asking someone to put their trust in a tin can, flown by someone they've never met, whose sole intention is to hurtle them down a runway at a ridiculous velocity and propel them into the air. Seriously, what sense does this make to the average person? What person wants to give this kind of control to someone? I barely tolerate being driven by others. But, like always, the convenience of the tin-can of death wins out when it comes to travel, and I subject myself to the emotional torture.

My best friend Jules would call this propensity toward hyperbole "dramatic." Not really a word I would use to describe myself. Drama is for girly girls or bitchy girls. I am certainly not a girly girl. I admit there is a version of me that can be a bitchy girl—a trait the airline employee behind the desk in Memphis is well acquainted with.

The day from hell ended with me running towards my gate, only to watch the airline employee close the door as I was yelling that I was almost there. She had just clicked the door closed when I arrived in front of her, out of breath and barely able to stand. I could see people in the gateway still waiting to board and she refused to open the door. It was the only remaining direct flight. What's more is she appeared to enjoy my frustration. A conversation with her manager, a bump up to first class, a three-hour delay, one layover later, and I am finally on the last leg of my journey.

Feeling my anxiety flare, I take a deep breath and try to focus on what I can control. From the small window on my row, I see the ground crew prepare the plane for our flight. I cannot wait to be home. Funny, I used to say that about Memphis, but if home is where family is, Memphis stopped being home long ago. New York is my home now. I was born and raised a Memphian, but I have become a New Yorker at heart.

I heart New York. I have a true love for my city. Not always an easy love, mind you. New York is a demanding love. New York makes you need it. Want it. Have to have it. New York makes you work for it, and I like the work. I get it. It's something I've never held against it.

With a three a.m. start, my day has been hectic with travel, a missed appointment, more angry and agitated people than I care to count, and, eventually, a missed flight, which is how I find myself in Chicago's O'Hare airport. The only plus to today was being bumped up to First Class. I'd hoped it would tame the growing fear of another flight, an added takeoff and landing. Regrettably, I am sitting here wearing the same fears, wondering the same thing I do every time I fly: *why* and *how the hell?*

I've never flown first class before. I've always been the cattle they march past the people at the front of the plane. A social-caste processional. The airlines have first-class fliers sit first so they can provide them with refreshments to watch from their oversized seats while the cattle herd by to get to their undersized ones. Some don't look at you, like they're embarrassed for you. Others seem irritated that they have to endure this cattle call of people moving by them, as if your presence as you stand there waiting for the line to move is an inconvenience to them personally.

I had decided earlier I wasn't going to give into the classicism I judged the airlines for. I was going to board and be seated after everyone else. But I needed a Diet Coke. Honorable of me, I know. As I sit here watching the procession, waiting impatiently for my Diet Coke, I find I don't like to look at the cattle passing me, not because I am embarrassed for them. But I'm embarrassed the herd might mistakenly think I am part of this first-class caste.

Once everyone is seated, the stewardess returns and, with a smile, picks up my Diet Coke and the orange juice of the little girl across the aisle from me. She can't be more than five. I watched as her mom reluctantly entrusted her daughter to the stewardess and kissed her with a promise her grandmother would be waiting for her when she landed. She's a beautiful little girl with curly light brown hair and dark eyes.

She has her coloring to keep her attention and a stuffed bear that she loyally introduced as her best friend, Walter. Walter wears a blue and green striped tie and has a monocle that makes him look older and wiser than his years. She introduced us when I commented that I liked his tie. I'm pretty sure Walter and his monocle are silently judging me and my nervous foot fidgeting at the thought of taking off.

The door closes and the plane starts to back away from the gate when the familiar panic creeps into my chest. Just as I seek out my happy place, I am granted a short reprieve when the attendant announces overhead that we are delayed for a few minutes and will be returning to the gate. The catastrophe of today replays in my mind. These trips are getting harder and harder. I'm not sure how much fight I have left in me. The selfishness of that statement leaves me frustrated and angry with myself.

I grab a barf bag to keep handy. As I try to concentrate on keeping my breathing steady, my eye lands on the multi-colored circles that make up the pattern on the carpet. My mind moves to my to-do list for work tomorrow. I don't have any clients to meet with, but my team has a lot of shopping to accomplish to ready our client's closets with the latest fall fashions. Mentally cataloging what needs to be done, a pair of brown Berluti shoes come to a stop in my line of vision.

Scanning my eyes up, I process the vision of the man attached to the shoes. His handmade gray suit is tailored to perfection. His legs long and lean. The jacket is buttoned while one hand rests in his pocket. He has on a blue and green stripped tie with a simple silver bar tie clip and a crisp white shirt. I know that the suit he is wearing cost more than I make in a month. His cuff links are small, round, blue dots that look like sapphires with silver around the edges. Actually, based on the fact that I price the ensemble he is wearing at least fifteen grand, my guess is they are platinum. His copper and caramel-brown hair is askew, like his hands have been giving it a workout. His chin is angular and sporting an evening shadow. Impressive. Powerful. I have seen a lot of stunning men in my line of work, but this…this is another level.

"Sorry to inconvenience you, but I believe that's my seat," he points to the empty one next to me.

I run my fingers over my bottom lip to make sure I'm not drooling and to help close my mouth that seems to have unhinged at the sight in front of me. My voice and manners kick in, and I manage a coherent response.

"No problem. I'll move over so you can have more head room. Unless you prefer the window?"

"No. Thank you," he says.

I settle into the window seat, my eyes meeting his as I reply, "My pleasure." Something in my response causes his blue eyes to skip, halting my breathing. They are striking. A medium blue with specks of silver dusted in. Commanding. Illimitable.

A flight attendant makes an announcement that once again the door has been closed, and we are to prepare for departure. He must have been the reason we were delayed. I couldn't get through the door for a plane that was still loading, but this guy gets the entire plane returned to the gate for him?

He punches a number on his phone and announces to the person on the other end that he made the flight they held for him and what time he is expected in New York.

"You know. If you are responsible for delaying an entire flight, I don't think I would broadcast it over a phone call." I unload my misguided frustration out on him.

The plane backs away from the gate as the attendant reviews the safety features of the Boeing 737 we are on. While I am certain most people ignore her, I pull the card out of the pocket attached to the wall in front of me and follow along, determined that, if nothing else, the headlines will read that I, and hopefully others near me, survived whatever catastrophe happens. I count how many rows there are between us and the exits behind us. I make note that the door has a pull handle and that the closest exits to me are in front of me and have handles located at the bottom right-hand side that activates the safety slides. Placing the card back in its pouch, I can never decide if it's better to have the window shade open to see my life flash before my eyes, or to close it for ignorant bliss. Ignorant bliss wins out, and the shade comes down.

"My apologies if I've offended you." His apology is not really an apology. In fact, he seems rather surprised that I said something to him.

"You haven't. But I'm sweeter than most people on this plane." I offer my go-to southern smile to make amends, causing him to cock his head in thought. "Honestly it's not a big deal. Misguided frustration. I'm just over this day."

"I'm having a bit of a day myself." He says absently looking forward, folding one leg over the other and smoothing his tie down his torso. My eyes follow on instinct.

"I'm sorry," I say sincerely with a pat to his arm. Because I am. I am not arrogant enough to think I am the only one who could be having a terrible day. "Anything I can do to make it better?" I offer empathetically. If he's had a day worse than mine, he can use it.

He doesn't respond but gauges me, when the captain announces that we are next in line for takeoff. I remind myself to breathe as my head hits the headrest from the force of the plane propelling itself down the runway. White-knuckling the armrest, a light dew settles over my skin. My eyes close just as the front of the plane comes off the ground. Within seconds, the back of the plane is airborne, and we take that little dip every plane makes once it leaves the ground. *Fuck me.*

A chuckle reaches my ears, and I cautiously open one eye to see him watching me. It becomes clear that I said that expletive out loud and not just to myself.

"Sorry. I don't usually use such colorful language," I blush.

"No worries. Are you ill?" He eyes the barf bag in my lap.

"Severe fear can have a not-so-pleasant effect on my stomach." When we take another slight dip in our climb, my breath catches and my grip tightens. I sip in a deeper breath and then release slowly. I know only a handful of ways to calm myself. That is one. Sometimes it works.

Leaning forward, I check on the little girl and her buddy Walter, only to find they are better than I ever hope to be. She looks at me and I wink at her. Her smile reminds me of wildflowers and fireflies in a mason jar. Sweet. Innocent. Unadulterated. Oh, to be five again.

"Is this your daughter?" he asks.

"No. She is traveling unaccompanied to her grandmother's." It hits me that I am giving information about a little girl to a total stranger, but something about him feels familiar and safe—and dangerous at the same time. I can't put my finger on it...

He greets her with a nod and a hello. She gives him a full-on mega-watt smile that lets me know, even to a five-year-old, this man is handsome. She responds with a small wave, and he leans over the aisle to better hear her.

"This is Walter. Your ties match," she says.

"Walter, you have impeccable taste," he replies. She proudly accepts this as a compliment to herself.

"She seems fine" he says turning back to me.

"I'm sorry?" In the confusion of my anxiety, I'm only half listening.

"You appeared to be checking on her. I was just saying she seems fine. Better than you actually." His tone is one of frustration, as though I should easily be following the conversation.

I'm not sure if I want to smack or lick the smirk off his face.

"Yep. She is taking this flying adventure like a boss." Steady as a rock. Her five years, light-years ahead of my twenty-five. I release another long breath.

"Did you tell her you were afraid to fly?" he asks.

"Previous exception aside, I don't make a practice of telling people my fears."

"Because?"

"Because telling someone what you're afraid of is like handing them a playbook on how to defeat you." And, for some reason, without prompting, I add, "And I don't like to be defeated."

As soon as the words leave my mouth, I regret them. The expression on his face tells me I revealed more than I intended. He looks at me for what feels like a full minute, only turning away when the attendant walks up.

"Another Diet Coke?" She hands me the drink. I smile and nod my thanks.

"May I bring you something to drink, sir? Wine? Cocktail?" She looks at him longer than necessary, her expression changing, as if to say, "Mother, may I?" I recognize the symptoms. I, too, am suffering from the same ailment.

"Bottle of water, thank you." His reply is perfunctory and dismissing.

I search my bag and locate my iPod, placing it and my earbuds on the small tray table that is shared between the middle armrests. My iPod has seen better days. Some days I feel like my iPod, being held together by duct tape. The screen cracked a couple of years ago, but this iPod takes a licking and keeps on ticking. Also like me, I muse to myself.

"Your iPod appears to be in the need of repair."

I nod in acknowledgement. "I've had it for about 10 years."

I pick it up and look at each side. "I think it's a 3rd generation. I don't really know. I bought it used when I was in high school. It has been a good friend. It still works." With the screen so cracked, I struggle sometimes to read what songs I'm pulling up, but it plays. I run my thumb over my cherished friend.

"Maybe it's time for a new one?" He picks up my iPod and turns it over again. A label with my first name and a pink heart is on the back. "Emme."

"Not in the budget. Besides, they don't make the Classic anymore, and I don't really want another version. I like the Classic. Holds more music without all the bells and whistles. Just a good, sturdy, hard-working iPod. All I need."

He nods and takes a drink of water.

"Do you like music?" I ask.

"I do. All kinds." He pauses like he is trying to decide something. He then asks, "What brings you to New York, Emme?"

Distracted by the way his tongue massages my name, I catch myself looking at his mouth, envisioning other things his tongue could be massaging. I'm caught off guard that my thoughts have gone to such a foreign place. *Why is this stranger having such an effect on me?*

"I live there," I stutter, realizing he has caught me staring. Again!

"You? You live in New York?" His incredulous eyes sweep over me, landing a little too long on my chest.

I can't determine if it is a question meant to keep the polite conversation going, or a question of judgement. Like I'm an outsider who doesn't belong. I concede that I am not dressed my best today. It's the middle of August, and I've been in three different cities, with three very different climates, all in one day.

The cuffed skinny jeans I'm wearing are a little too snug for my ample hips and ass, a gift from my mother. The ass not the jeans. Thankfully, she gifted me with a flat stomach and smaller waist to offset the other two. A white tank top and my grandfather's thread-bare, oversized navy blue cardigan pushed up to my elbows round out my travel attire. I know it's only my imagination, but I can still smell my grandfather when I wear it, even though it has been washed a thousand times since I took it as my own. It's my comfort piece. It makes me feel like I am wearing a hug. And after spending the day in Satan's lair, I need all the hugs I can get, even if it's only in the form of a cardigan that's more than forty years old.

Other than a soft-pink matte lip gloss, I am wearing no makeup. I have large, cocoa-brown eyes. The front of my light-blonde hair is braided on one side. It is held together by bobby pins and a tiny, blue metal flower that turns my side part into a messy bun. The only jewelry I am wearing is a long artsy neck-lace and my grandparents' white-gold wedding bands on my right middle finger. My wrist dons the Rolex that belonged to the father we never knew. It has a black leather band with a white mother of pearl face.

"Yes, I live in New York," I reply with bite. "Does that surprise you? I have lived in the city for seven years now. Moved there when I was seventeen."

A look creeps across his face that leaves me feeling like I've been warned about my tone.

"I was taken by your accent," he says slowly as if to clarify. "Where are you from, originally?"

"Memphis. Born and raised."

"Ah," he says, like a piece of a puzzle has fallen into place. I have long become used to comments and occasional snares concerning my southern accent. Despite my time away from

Memphis, I still have it. Truthfully, I wouldn't have it any other way. You can take the girl out of Memphis, but you can't take Memphis out of the girl. Memphians are proud of our southern roots. I don't notice my accent, but rarely a day goes by without someone commenting on it. You would think I was transplanted from another country.

The attendant makes another stop to replace my now empty Diet Coke, halting when he positions his hand to stop her from placing the new glass on the tray table.

"Could you bring her a bottled water instead?" He directs more than he asks.

"Certainly, sir" She retreats without even looking to me for approval. *What the…?* I'm so dumbfounded by the whole encounter that I find myself speechless, and only a small noise of protest escapes my throat when he looks at me. I know by the look on his face that there must be one of shock and confusion on mine.

"That would have been your third Diet Coke since boarding," he says, in a voice that denotes his irritation at having to explain himself. Is he monitoring my alcohol consumption or something? Am I in Diet Coke's Anonymous? Is he my sponsor? "You need to drink water. Flying can dehydrate you, and you stated you've been on a plane more than once already today."

"You do know I'm grown right?" My tone is sharp. His eyes deliberately land on my chest before crawling their way up to my mine. There's a heat in them.

"I'm aware."

"I've been on my own since I was sixteen. I think I can handle a drink selection. In fact, I'm certain of it." My indignant manor is interrupted when the attendant drops off my bottle of water and two freshly baked chocolate chip cookies. I don't know if she intends it to make amends, but they are deliciously warm and gooey. He declines his.

"Actually. I'll take his." I smile sweetly at the stewardess before looking defiantly at him. Two extra cookies almost offset my lack of Diet Coke.

Sitting back, I realize he is watching me. He looks like he is having a conversation in his head and needs no one else to participate or give feedback. Rotating the cap back on his water, I find my ire dissipating and my mind wandering again, wondering what it would feel like to be beneath those strong hands. I like men with strong, firm hands. It's often one of the first things I notice about a man. It is a testament to his striking looks that his hands weren't the first thing I noticed about him.

"What do you do in New York?" He distracts my wayward thoughts. I have to remind myself he's had a crummy day and give him props for attempting polite conversation.

"I work for Jackson Hollingsworth. Are you familiar with him?"

"Not personally, but I know of his business and I'm sure I know many of his clients. What do you do there?"

"I am the styling and personal analyst for his company."

"How long have you worked for Mr. Hollingsworth?"

"We met my first year in New York. I was leaving class one day and ran into *Grays Papaya* to grab a hot dog. He was on the Upper West Side to see a client. I made an unfortunate comment about the shape of my hotdog, and we have been close ever since." I smile just thinking of Jackson.

Like Jules, Jackson Hollingsworth is my life line. I was drowning when he rescued me back to land. He is the successful owner of a very prestigious brand imaging company. He is beautiful in his own right with ebony skin, hair trimmed close to his scalp, broad shoulders, and a sculpted body. He is the epitome of masculinity. Jackson draws the attention of women everywhere we go, disappointing them when they learn he is engaged. To Patrick.

"So you attended Columbia?" His eyes lose a little of their warmth. Why, I am not sure.

"No." Where did that come from?

As if to answer my unspoken confusion, he explained, "You said you were leaving class on the upper west side. I assumed, based on the fact that you work for Mr. Hollingsworth, that you were referring to Columbia."

"Oh, no. Right. Sorry. No, Julliard. I was attending Julliard.

"You went to Julliard?"

"Yes. Then NYU."

"You went to Julliard, NYU, and worked for Jackson Hollingsworth? In seven years, that's quite a resume."

"If that were true, it would be," I laugh and clarify. "I accepted a scholarship to Julliard before my financial responsibilities changed. Once there, I realized that, between required practices and performances, the time frame was too stringent to allow me to work. So, I left Julliard after one semester and went to NYU. Unfortunately, I had to put it on hold, too. I couldn't give school and studying the time required *and* take care of my responsibilities. I've been with Jackson ever since. What do you do?"

"I work in acquisitions." He seems annoyed that I have directed the conversation back to him.

"If finances had not been an obstacle, would you have stayed at Julliard? I thought their scholarship program was competitive and covered all school and living expenses?"

While I don't enjoy talking about myself, I also don't shy away from answering easy questions. It gives people a false sense that I'm an open book. I am transparent about things most people might not comment on, but I hold close the things that matter the most to me. Share my thoughts, not my feelings, a lesson learned in deflection that has served me well.

"You know, I'm okay. Really. You don't have to distract me with questions. I am sure you have more important things to tend to."

"I don't ask frivolous questions Emme, and I never ask a question I don't want the answer to," he pauses. "Expect it actually." His tone is imperious, authoritative, but his eyes are kind and inquiring. "If finances had not been an obstacle, would you have stayed at Julliard?" he repeats. Something I also get the feeling he doesn't do often.

I nebulously wonder how the questions have turned back to me so quickly but find myself compelled to answer him, for reasons I'm not sure I want to analyze. Is it because he is kind, or is it because he demands it? Either way, I wasn't prepared for the question. No one has ever questioned my answer before. They have always accepted my reasoning that money was the issue, and it was. But the larger part was that I had lost my love for playing. Now, holding a cello was like holding a lifeless creature. It has been six years since I picked one up. I doubt I ever will again.

Taken aback by the direction of my thinking and the depth of my feelings in front of a perfect stranger, I opt for a fact that played a far less significant role in my decision to leave Julliard and give him my "blind date" answer to what, at that time, was an easy choice.

"No. I came to realize I didn't want the life of a concert cellist. I didn't want to travel eleven months out of the year. I wanted more roots than that life would give me."

He stares at me with a long canyon of silence that I feel

the need to fill with…I don't know—something. But my mind can't seem to form a sentence. I'm not comfortable with him looking at me like I'm a puzzle where the pieces don't match up. It's like he knows and is waiting for the real story. Sidestepping that mine field, I look forward and take a break to gather my wits about me. It's been a long time since I have even looked at a man this way. Actually, I never have. I have never looked at a man this way, much less someone I only met forty-five minutes ago.

It's in that moment of space that my terror comes roaring back, angry at being ignored. The plane hits an air pocket and drops what feels like a thousand feet, eliciting screams from the rear of the plane. The captain announces overhead that he is turning back on the seatbelt light and asks passengers to be seated. We are beginning to encounter some turbulence from a storm. I hate his calm voice that has no feeling, no understanding that I am being tormented. I know it is meant to soothe us, but I'd rather hear panic and determination, like he is going to fly this plane as if his life depends on it. His calm voice makes me think he has his head back, chillin', and not correctly assessing the death-con level we are clearly experiencing.

He instructs us to stow belongings, put seats in the upright position, and close tray tables, while the attendants come around to clear trash before taking their seats. I close my eyes and concentrate on not needing my barf bag. My hands take a death grip on the armrests while my mind tries to control the pace my heart is beating. I'm stuck in this small space with nowhere to go, forced to endure whatever happens. I have no control. None. My breathing is coming faster now, and I realize if I don't figure out a way to self-soothe, I'm going to hyperventilate and have a full-on panic attack. Every time the plane takes another dip, people cry out. *Why the fuck doesn't someone knock them out? Their screaming is only making it worse.* Just when I have reached the height of powerlessness, I feel it: A calm. An equanimity. My fear is still there, but my breathing comes in deeper droves. My heart slows from a full-on gallop to a survivable canter.

I open my eyes to see him calmly sitting with one leg draped over the other. His suit is still perfectly pressed, as if he has no concerns in the world. Like we are sitting stationary and not about to meet an untimely death. He watches me, and I distantly process that it's not his demeanor that is placating me, but it's his hand—the one that has taken mine as he slowly and repeatedly moves his thumb across my knuckles in a circular motion.

"You're safe." His eye contact offers an assurance that I am far from feeling, but at the same time holds power over my fear. It is such a simple statement. A statement I have not felt or heard since I can remember.

"How much longer?" I whisper.

"How much longer?"

"How much longer till we land?"

"We'll start our decent in about twenty minutes," he assures me.

Twenty minutes. Twenty minutes. It might as well be a life sentence.

The captain, who I am sure has heard the cries of his passengers, comes back on over the intercom in his same steady voice, informing us that he has been unable to find a smooth patch of air to fly in and to expect rough turbulence until we land. All along, he continues to console me by steadying my hand with his. Another dip, another group screaming. Another jostle and crash accompanied by more screams. The fear I think I am doing so well to contain must be showing on my face, because he quickly explains that some overhead compartments have come open, emptying their contents on some of the passengers. It's in that moment that I remember the little girl.

I always thought I would be heroic if the need ever presented itself. I would be Wonder Woman, wearing the stars and stripes, my metal-covered wrists ricocheting bullets. People would tell stories of my heroism and bravery. Yeah, no one will be writing that about me if we die tonight. I kick myself for being so selfish. Shaking my head in frustration, I whisper, "What a dick." My comment stops the traipse of his thumb across my knuckles.

"Excuse me?" he asks with a dip in his eyebrows.

"Sorry, not you. I mean me." I lean forward and ask the little girl if she's ok, her face a mirror of my feelings. She looks at me with big, round eyes, and I have to strain to hear her small voice.

"I'm scared."

Right then and there, I know I need to lock my shit down.

"Come sit with me. It's ok," I say at her hesitation. Regrettably, I squeeze his hand before removing mine to reach across him, making sure she isn't knocked down as we continue to bounce. In a blink, she is in my lap. I undo my buckle, pull the belt around us both, and click it back in place. Wrapping my arms around her, I smile as she lays her head against my chest. Her face towards him.

"You have nothing to worry about," I assure her.

Thunder booms around us, and I see an acknowledgment from him that we are having a rough ride.

"One of my favorite movies is *Sound of Music*. Have you seen it?" She nods while holding tighter to Walter.

"You remember the part where it's storming and they're in

Fräulein Maria's bed, scared, and she sings to them? Well that song has always made me feel better. Whether I'm happy or sad or scared."

Softly, I begin singing "Raindrops on roses and whiskers on kittens…" as I unwind my earbuds from my iPod and pull up "A Few of My Favorite Things" on my cracked screen. I place buds in her ears and hit play. She closes her eyes and listens as I softly rock her side to side, rubbing her back in a comforting repetitive pattern that mimics the one across my knuckles minutes ago.

Still bouncing like a rock skipping across the water, we begin our descent into LaGuardia. Landing. I think I hate it more than take off. One runs a close second to the other. I glance to my right with a smile, to say a thank you for his kindness, and I am met with a heat-filled look.

"What?" I mouth with an inquisitive slope of my eyebrows.

"You." He answers simply and follows with a glance from the little girl to me as clarification. I blush—not a response that is common for me.

I hear the landing gear lowering and feel the grinding of its machinations. I realize we have said fewer than three words to each other in the last twenty minutes of the flight, but I feel like we have had one of those high-school conversations where you talk all night long with your crush.

It feels like the pilot is working overtime to control the plane when the wheels finally hit the ground with a thud. The flaps shoot up with a roar to bring us to a crawl, and the plane erupts in an applause so joyous, you would think we just witnessed a miracle. Maybe we did.

The captain welcomes us to New York and doesn't hide the appreciation in his voice that we have landed. Releasing the breath I was holding all this time, I say to the girl, pulling the earbuds from her ears, "We're safe and we're here!" She throws her arms around my neck and leans up for a kiss before making her way back to her seat. I remind her to stay put until everyone gets off the plane and then the attendant will take her to her grandmother.

We stand when the door opens and he takes a slight step back, motioning me in front of him. I move into the aisle and with a placement of his hand at the small of my back, he ushers me forward.

Walking up the short ramp, it dawns on me that we will be saying good-bye. It unsettles me for reasons I am not sure I want to understand. Deflecting my feelings for light conversation, I declare how happy I am to be on land.

"If I didn't think security would detain me, I would kiss the ground right here," I laugh.

We walk side-by-side to the escalator that moves from the terminal down to baggage claim and transportation. A feeling of sadness and loss lingers around us.

"Do you need help with your luggage?" he offers as we step off the moving stairs.

"Thanks, but it was a there-and-back trip, so I don't have any."

Missing my original flight has me getting home later than anticipated. It's August, and even though its ten thirty at night, it's stifling. I stop to place my oversized Louis Vuitton bag, a vintage that was my mom's, between my feet, freeing my hands to remove my cardigan and knot it around my hips. I watch his eyes canvas my body, finally moving up to my face with no remorse at being caught. A smile plays across his lips.

"What part of the city do you live in? Can I provide your transportation? My driver is here."

Provide my transportation? Why not just say "Can I give

you a lift?" It doesn't surprise me that he has a driver. Some of the most influential and powerful men in the city are my clients. I am used to being around wealth, and he exudes it.

"I live in SoHo, but I'll just take a taxi. I don't want to inconvenience you."

He gives a shake to his head "It's not an inconv..."

"James!" I turn towards the familiar sound and two of my dwarfs, Drew and Russ, walk up each pulling me into their arms, planting a loud, wet kiss on me.

"What are y'all doing here?" I ask, surprised to see them.

"You're in Memphis less than twelve hours and your accent is even thicker." Drew mimics a ridiculous southern accent. Why can't people learn to do a true southern accent? Must everyone make all southerners sound like we are missing four teeth and had a baby with Cousin Earl?

"We were at Kyle's parents' house in Queens for dinner, so we hung around to pick you up," he explains. "You ready? No luggage, right?"

Deep down in a place I shouldn't explore, I am disappointed. I wanted to see where this ride would take me.

"Sure," I say with a smile I am not feeling. "I was just about to catch a ride. We were seated next to each other on the plane." They look quizzically between me and my new friend. "I was bumped up to first class," I clarify.

"Well good thing we caught you before you left. Save him an extra drop." Drew gives him a direct look and then drapes an arm over my shoulders. "Thanks for looking out for James. We'll take her from here."

What the fuck? I look at him like he has lost his mind. *Take me from here. What the hell does that mean?* Like I'm suddenly the unaccompanied minor. *I'm a fucking adult!* I hand them my bag.

"I'll be right there," I say, dismissing them in irritation before turning my attention back to him.

"Thank you for the offer. I should probably go before security makes them move."

"James?"

"Huh? Oh, yeah, Emme James. James is one of the names people call me."

"You live with three men?"

"Actually, I live with six. One more and I'm Snow White. Although we don't have space for one more, so alas, I'll never make princess status. I call the boys my dwarfs, anyway. As a consolation prize," I smile. "Thanks again for the offer."

"Goodnight," he nods to me.

In a move of showing him my true appreciation for his kindness during the flight, I wrap him into a strong hug before he has a chance to respond or anticipate my actions. It's a one-sided hug for what feels like a very long minute. I feel his resolve finally snap, and his arms fold around me. Leaning my head against his chest, I squeeze and breathe him in. *He smells divine, like…him.* Releasing him I reach up and place my palm to his cheek. Idly, I register that he has leaned into my touch.

"Thank you. You are very kind."

His eyes unreadable and jaw rigid, he nods in acknowledgement before watching me walk away.

ch♥pter
two

"What was that all about?" I ask harshly while closing the leather-clad door to Kyle's BMW.

"Uh, you're welcome," Drew replies, like they were doing me a solid.

"I'm welcome? I'm welcome?" My sheer disbelief in Drew's statement has me repeating myself.

"Yes, you are welcome!"

I glare at Russ next to me in the back seat. Then I direct my glare back to the front passenger seat.

"Seriously, Drew! He was completely nice, and you basically peed on me right in front of him!"

We pull onto the Queens expressway, and I catch Kyle's eyes bounce from me in the rearview to Drew sitting next to him, a confused look in his eyes like he's trying to catch up.

"What is she talking about? What did you do Drew?" Kyle asks like he's talking to a child.

"I didn't do anything. I simply thanked the guy and told him we had her from here."

"What guy?"

"The plane guy."

"What?" Kyle inquires in an exasperated "help me

understand" tone, looking at Russ next to me.

"This guy that was on James' flight was being a little too possessive, so we took care of it," he explains without prejudice and a shrug of his shoulders, like he's speaking only the truth, and I or anyone else would be irrational to think any differently.

"That is ridiculous!" I say with enough feeling for the both of us, since they want to play this one off like I'm the idiot for being mad. "He was very kind and very polite. His intentions were..."

"To get into your pants," Drew speaks over me.

"You're ridiculous."

"I'm ridiculous?"

"You're ridiculous!" I state with more force.

"I'm ridiculous?" He's riled up now.

"Yes! What are you a parrot? Did you fall down today and smack your head on the pavement? I don't need you, or any of the dwarfs for that matter, to step in and pee on me in public."

"What does that even mean, James?" Drew grunts, unable to hide his irritation.

"It means, Drew, that I don't need y'all to stake claim to me like I'm something that needs protecting."

"You guys know James doesn't like to be handled," Kyle interjects, trying to contain the situation.

"We *didn't* handle her Kyle," he argues. "We showed her the same courtesy we'd show our sisters. And stop calling us dwarfs James. It's not very manly."

With a deep sigh of frustration, I shake my head and lay it against the head rest. "I am living with baboons."

We're coming across the Williamsburg Bridge now, and the exhaustion of the day has taken the fight out of me.

"It doesn't matter. It's not like I'll see him again. I don't even know his name. I'm just ready to be home," I say a little deflated. Even with my eyes now closed, I can feel them watching me. Drew's the first to break. He always is.

"How was your trip?"

"Long and stressful."

"Want to talk about it?"

"Nope."

"How about some Doughnut Plant?" Kyle always knows the way to my heart. Food. Especially my favorite doughnut place in the city.

"Crème Brulee and Manhattan Cream. Your favorites," he entices. Not that I really need it. I love all things food.

A dozen shared doughnuts later, we are finally home. Home is a classic, white cast-iron facade building, typical of the area. Our apartment is a three-bedroom, one-bath, fifth-floor walkup on Greene St.

Matt, the head dwarf, has been renting this apartment for a few years now. He lived here with his wife while finishing medical school at Columbia, and she was in her first-year internship at New York Presbyterian Hospital. Becca is now an attending physician in Boston, while Matt is in his last year of residency. When he's finished, he will be moving to Boston. Actually, all six of my roommates are doctors at New York Presbyterian. Matt kept the apartment and took on five roommates for extra income.

By Manhattan standards, our apartment is large, at a little over a thousand square-feet. The entry is a small hallway leading into an open kitchen, dining, and living area. The bones are what you would expect from a SoHo apartment. High, open ceilings with cased windows across the front. I place the mail I grabbed on the way up on the kitchen counter as I make my way to my alcove.

Off of the living area are two bedrooms with our only bath in between. On the other side is the larger bedroom and a small, three-sided alcove, two inches smaller than a twin bed. It opens to the living room. The guys stay two to a room, and I sleep on the couch.

The alcove is all mine. I have smartly utilized the square footage to get the most out of the space. Sliding back the curtain I installed, I turn on the small table lamp that sits on the four-drawer teal dresser I found at the Chelsea Antiques Garage for a steal. Its slim profile made it the perfect piece for the space. The back wall houses my closet. It's only three-feet wide, but the shelves above the rod extend the entire height of the twelve-foot wall, some holding clothes, others with decorative boxes, framed pictures, and items from my childhood. A full-length mirror hangs on the wall between the dresser and the closet. Opposite the dresser and mirror is an overstuffed, comfy, white cotton chair, large enough for me to curl into, with a soft, colorful throw across the back. It sits at an angle, leaving just enough floor space to maneuver the closet and get dressed.

I come in here to read and have some alone time when I need it. Even though the curtain doesn't block out noise, the visual barrier is really all I need. I like to still hear the guys. It reminds me that I'm not alone, that I have loved ones near.

Matt and Russ are both married to wonderfully strong women whom I adore. Tim is engaged, Kyle is one step away from engagement, while Drew and Ryan have made an art form out of being single. All six men are smart, capable, and sexy as hell. It's like living in a GQ magazine. Except that the place was a hazard area, and their living habits were atrocious. How they made it before I moved in, I'll never know.

I am closest with Matt. We met at Junior's in Brooklyn

during my third year living in the city. We were sitting next to each other, waiting for our cheesecakes, and struck up a conversation. His wife Becca and I became fast friends. At the time, I was living in the Bronx, and Becca always thought I should be somewhere safer and actually in Manhattan. But living in the Bronx was all I could afford, and I was having a hard enough time making ends meet.

Jackson has always paid me a generous salary and would pay me more if I would let him, but I won't take what I don't earn. So, I picked up a couple of night jobs and with my financial responsibilities in Memphis, I was still struggling to make ends meet.

After Becca moved to Boston and the dwarfs were on their own, she called me and asked me if I would move in, rent-free, in exchange for "overseeing" the apartment, make sure it stayed livable and the guys actually ate a green vegetable at least once a week. She felt like it was the best of both worlds. It's been the seven of us ever since. Some days are more trying than others, but mostly it's like living with six brothers. I get a free place to live, and they get a wife/mother/sister/friend in exchange. The day and need dictate which hat I wear for each of them.

Grateful that it was a one-day trip and I don't have a bag to unpack, I throw on a tank and some sleep shorts and make my way to the kitchen. One of the ways I earn my keep is making sure they each have a healthy meal. I look at the calendar on the fridge and see that four of the guys are working tomorrow. Their shifts are a minimum of sixteen hours. Grabbing the Sharpie, I write their names on their individual brown paper lunch bag with twine handles. I make each of them two healthy meals and a snack to take to work. I put a little note in each bag. I am adding the last orange to the bags when Kyle comes in for a snack.

"The guys picked up an extra shift, so they won't be in tonight. You should crash in a bed instead of the couch."

"I think I will. It's been a long day and I am bone tired."

"Sweet dreams, James," he says as he kisses me on the forehead.

"Thanks. Love you." I start the nightly John-Boy ritual with whomever is awake. Experience has taught me to never miss an opportunity to tell the ones you love that you love them.

"...love you, too," he slurps biting into an apple.

Pulling the covers over me, I sink in and think about the day from hell. I feel like each trip to Memphis is the same. I'm not accomplishing anything. I have the same arguments with the same people. I'm just not sure what the next step is and how much fight I have left in me. My mind moves to the stranger on the plane tonight, and how out of character our conversation was for me. Was it because the day was so horrible that my mind needed idle conversation to decompress? Even as I wonder, I know it was more than that. It was him. Conversation felt easy and safe with him, but also necessary. Like it was expected.

Morning comes earlier than I had hoped and based on his language and the pillow Drew throws at my head, I must have slept through my alarm going off. God bless whoever put the old car horn alarm on cell phones. It's the only noise that wakes me. So maybe it takes a while for me to hear, but what can you do?

I sit on the edge of the bed, allowing my body time to

acclimate to my mind giving it commands. I hate mornings. I am not a morning person.

Grabbing a Diet Coke, my first thought is of him. I wonder what his mornings are like, who he spends them with, what it would feel like waking up next to him? I start the coffee for the group, and the carousel begins. Food, coffee, and an endless stream of people in and out of our only bathroom. We have our routine worked out pretty well. If you get up when I do, you get breakfast. While I cook and clean, the guys start their shower rotation. Once food goes on the table, each person is responsible for loading his dishes in the dishwasher and I'm free to take my shower.

Sharing a bathroom with six guys is pretty interesting. I have learned that they care not if they smell like peaches and cream. If it's in the shower and it looks like something to clean yourself with, they will use it. It's a running joke at the hospital that my guys are the best smelling residents there. I have trained them well. Their wives, current or future, all owe me a debt of gratitude for teaching these men to put the seat down. Now, if I could only teach them to replace the empty roll on the toilet paper holder, I might feel I've accomplished something.

The bathroom is a decent size with a glass shower, a toilet, and, thankfully, a double vanity. We installed a curtain over the outside of the shower door, so one person could be taking a shower in private while others use the bathroom or the sinks. Not ideal, but necessary when sharing a bathroom with seven people.

As I said before, I am not a girly girl. It doesn't take me a long time to get ready. This morning is holding true to the routine. I'm bathing to The Killers, when a movement catches my eye from the corner of the shower. A water bug. Also known as a cockroach. Also known as my arch enemy. My kryptonite. I can pick up a snake, hold a mouse, bait a hook, but do not put a roach anywhere in my radius. Slowly, I start backing up to the shower door never taking my eyes off it. I can hear my heart beating in my ears, my stomach starting to churn. This is worse than flying. This is a full-on panic attack of fear.

Three things happen at once. It shoots towards me at lightning speed. I scream like Norman Bates has thrown back the shower curtain. I run. One second I was in the shower, and the next I am in the living room. Thankfully, somewhere in between my subconscious grabbed a towel.

Matt comes out of his bedroom, walks to the bathroom, and closes the door, like he is out for a morning stroll. Kyle is at my side telling me to take a deep breath and slow my breathing. The door opens and Matt comes out.

"Taken care of."

I can count on one hand how many bugs I have found in our apartment, but the guys know the scream. They don't understand the rationale or the reasoning behind my fears, but they realize the seriousness of it. The first time they encountered what they thought was just a girl being a girl over a bug, they did what guys do. Tease. Act like they are going to toss it on you or run their fingers over your arm like it's crawling on you. One complete meltdown and brown-bag hyperventilation later, they learned I am not that girl. Since then, they have only been my white knights when I encounter a bug.

"Jesus, James. You scare the shit out of me every time." Drew pulls me back into the present when he enters the living room. "You ever going to tell us why?"

"Why what?"

"No one has that kind of reaction without a story."

"There's nothing to tell. It's just an irrational fear." As I say it, I know they aren't buying it, but I am grateful when they let it drop.

Matt touches my shoulder forcing my eyes to him. "You're ok."

I let out a long deep breath. "I'm ok," I affirm.

"Actually I don't think you are," Drew says, turning me around and looking me over. "You're bleeding."

"What?" Matt asks, taking a step back and looking me over.

"She's bleeding. There's blood on the floor." Drew points down at the red spots.

"Here." Kyle points to the back side of my hip. Sure enough, there's a coffee-can size circle of blood on my towel and drops on the floor. "Let me see." He begins to pull the towel back.

"I don't think so," I say dubiously.

"James, you're bleeding. We're surgeons. We've seen it all. Now, let us look."

I roll my eyes and turn my towel so the opening is in that area and pull back the edge just enough for them to see where the blood is coming from while keeping all my girly bits covered.

"Damn, James! You sliced it open. It's deep, too. Didn't you feel that? Wonder what she cut it on?" Kyle checks out the damage while Drew looks around the bathroom.

"She caught it on this metal piece." He points to the strike plate that is connected to the door jam.

Matt is holding the towel to the cut, absorbing the blood. "She's gonna need stitches. Who has their work bag here? Anyone have a suture kit?"

"Really? Stiches? Is that necessary?" I ask.

"Yep," Matt nods once in confirmation. "When was your

last tetanus shot?"

"Two years ago."

"At least you won't need that," he says grabbing a sealed tray from Drew.

"Lay down on the couch," he instructs as he drapes a blanket across it, "and I'll suture you up." The living room has two club chairs that are anchored by a couch on each side. The rectangular coffee table in the middle is currently housing three laptops and bag of chips that, most likely, is empty and needs to be thrown away.

Me and my stupid fears. How do I get myself into these messes? I lay on the couch with the cut side closest to him. Matt leaves the room and comes back with a towel for my dripping hair and one that he later uses to cover me as much as possible while he begins prepping me.

The guys were right. They could care less who is attached to the ass or what the ass looks like, they are have a pissing competition over who is the best man for the job.

"Let me do it," Drew insists.

"You're Ortho. You don't care what scars look like," Kyle says.

"That's true, man," Matt agrees.

"Dude, you're trauma," Kyle says to Matt, like it's a no brainer. "I'm Neuro. I stitch up brains. I should do it."

"I did a stint in Plastics. I'm doing it," Matt argues. He is already gloved and ready to go.

"Now, you're going to feel a little pinch, Emme." Matt puts on his doctor tone. "This will numb the area. After that takes effect, we can have you done in no time."

Twenty minutes later, he's done.

"Hell, Matt. That took fucking forever!" Both of the guys lay into him.

"Well, it took twelve stitches, and I don't want her to have a scar," he pushes back.

"That's true," Drew says. "I'd hate to mess up that luscious ass. My God, James. Your ass..." he trails off. "I can't believe I've been living in the same apartment as that all this time".

Matt and Kyle both slap him across the head as I tighten the towel around me and make my way to my closet to get dressed. "Dude, not cool." I hear them chastising Drew as I close the curtain. The wound is tender to the touch, so I opt for cotton underwear to let it breathe a little.

Every Friday I bring home my outfits for the following week. One of the perks of working with Jackson is the wardrobe he provides. He expects his employees to represent the image of his company. Instead of a clothing allowance, we have a closet of designers that we have full access to. It's the most amazing closet I have ever seen, and I have been in some pretty spectacular closets.

This whole fiasco has me running late, so I go for the easiest outfit: a Missoni Mare striped one-piece. I've wanted to wear these adorable shorts since summer started, and the wound gives me a practical reason. Since the back is cut out in the jumpsuit, I grab a blazer to complete the ensemble. I throw on my favorite long necklace I picked up at a street fair and slide on a pair of Louboutin pumps. I put my hair into a messy bun, add a little mascara and some lip gloss, and I am out the door in less than ten minutes.

Sliding on my sunglasses as I exit our building, ready to haul tail to the subway, I am pleasantly surprised to see Jackson standing with a coffee in one hand and a Diet Coke in the other.

"Hello, beautiful." He kisses me while handing me my drink.

"Hello, beautiful." I return his greeting and his kiss. He twirls me around looking at the day's chosen outfit.

"Love it," he says. "I can't believe it's long enough in the back. It looks great."

I was equally surprised given the hem is sitting an inch higher than what I usually wear.

"I swear your legs look a mile long."

"Pretty sure it has something to do with the four inch heels I am wearing," I smirk.

"Thank God I came to pick you up on my way in. I can't imagine you taking the subway in those."

"Thank you for the Diet Coke," I say, getting into the back of his car and greeting his driver.

"You're welcome. I wanted to make sure you were in one piece after your trip home yesterday. Thought you might need my undivided attention for a few minutes."

"You're sweet, but I'm fine. Tired, but fine." If I say it enough times, will it be true?

"I'll let you get by with that lie for as long as you want to keep it up. When you're ready to talk, you'll talk," he shrugs. "And since when aren't you tired? I don't know how you keep the pace you keep and accomplish all you do. I'm exhausted just thinking about your daily schedule. Today is not going to be any different. I have a full day's session for you. Blaine Moore is coming in today for a new image. The label wants him to be edgier in his personal style and more confident in his interviews. I want you to take the lead. He was runner up for "Sexiest Man Alive," and the label wants him on the cover next year. Start with your questionnaire, but don't let him know you're rating him. The label wants a read on him by end of day. They're about to drop millions on him, and they want to know that he has the goods to go the distance."

"No problem. But I won't do the questions without him knowing it's a rating system. That's the only way my system works. I have to be honest with them so they will be honest with me. If the label wants to know the real deal, they have to let me do it my way."

Jackson ponders this as we pull up to our building across from Bryant Park.

"Okay, I trust you. Don't get it wrong. This is a huge account for us."

"Got it, Boss."

"You know what it does to me when you call me 'Boss.'" His wink turns into a smile.

I give him my best "why, I can't possibly know what you're talking about" innocent smile that I know tickles him. "Get out of the car, Romeo. We're here."

From the car to the elevator, Jackson draws the attention of almost every woman we pass. He is formidable in his stature and appearance. At a muscular six-foot-five, his clothes fit his body like a glove. Jackson is a man who is comfortable in his own skin. Who can blame him when that man is a modern day Frank Sinatra with a slightly edgier style and has the moves of a young Sammy Davis, Jr. He really is beautiful, inside and out.

We exit the elevator on the twenty-first floor. Our receptionist, Amanda, buzzes us through the half-opaque, half-clear glass doors that have "Hollingsworth Imaging" etched out of the frosted area.

Amanda's simple, black desk is situated in front of a seating area comprised of two white leather chairs with a round table between them. Behind Amanda hangs a large, colorful art piece by a local artist. Like the rest of the office, the area is clean-lined and understated. It reflects the same mix of contemporary chic and mid-century modern that Jackson, himself, conveys in his personal style. After a warm welcome from Amanda. Jackson heads to his office, while I head into the workroom.

The workroom is a large, open space that houses my team, Joy and Henry. Their desks are on opposite sides of the room. My office is across the back. In the center of the room is my team's worktable surrounded by six chairs. Behind Joy's desk is a large door that leads to our styling closet. The facing wall, behind Henry's desk displays our image boards. Next to the boards is a platform surrounded by a five-way wrap-around mirror.

"Good morning, team. Let's take five and group before we start our day," I say pulling up a chair to our work table.

"We have Blaine Moore coming in today. Joy, I'd like you to pull three everyday looks, and Henry I would like you to pull three event looks. Make sure to include the Saint Laurent studded boots that I picked up at Barney's last week. Those will be perfect for him. I'll work on our image board. You have an hour to put looks together while I get to know him. After that, we'll do the first run through, then I'll take him to lunch while you each pull ten looks. The afternoon will finish with the last run-through and the cherry. Sound good?"

"Yes," they answer in unison.

When I style someone, I'm always looking for the one thing that makes each person unique, or "the cherry." It's the "cherry on top", so to speak. My questionnaire and our "cherry" technique is what sets our team and Jackson's company apart from any other. Other companies only see dollar signs and mold the person to some pre-fab image that the client—or the client's company—thinks they want, or need, to sell their product. We mold the image around the person.

"Emme, Blaine Moore is here to see you," Amanda announces through the speaker.

"Show time," I say to Joy and Henry. I make my way to the reception area.

"Hi, Blaine. I'm Emme James. Nice to meet you." My brown eyes meet his grey, and they are congenial and welcoming. How did I get so lucky? I am surrounded by beauty. *Smoke and mirrors,* I remind myself.

"Nice to meet you," he shakes my hand. "Sorry I'm running late. Honestly, I'm sorry to be doing this at all. This is the label's doing, not mine."

"Well, hopefully we can make this as painless as possible, please come with me." An edge enters his eyes at my request and a slow, almost wicked, smile sweeps across his face.

"Ladies first," he says pruriently.

I know then that I am in the presence of a player. I give him my best stern-but-amused look, and he throws his head back and laughs a deep, sexy, throaty laugh. I shake my head, "It's going to be a long day," I quip and show him to my office.

My office is in keeping with the look that Jackson has for his company but is also uniquely me. My desk sits to the left. Behind it is a row of floating shelves flanked by two large photos. To the right of the door is a dark purple modern couch and chair with a natural wood coffee table that looks like it was cut straight from the tree.

Above the couch, I have a painting that my grandmother gave me right before she passed away. Other than my father's watch, it is the only thing of value that I didn't sell. It's by a local Memphis artist Paul Edelstein, from his *Lost in Love* collection. This painting has people standing in a group, composed of mostly bright colors, while black—and brown-tinted greys are layered in. Offset to the right is a dark-haired girl in a white dress holding bright blue flowers. Even though the faces are abstract and not defined, to me each one conveys an emotion. I see happiness and sorrow wrapped in what I imagine is a celebration. I love it.

"Please, have a seat," I motion to the couch. I sit on the opposite end and relax into the cushions. I have found in the past that a casual stance helps put my clients at ease. Amanda enters and asks what Blaine would like to drink. She brings him water and me a Diet Coke. Standing there a little longer than necessary, my "thank you" brings her back to the present, and she leaves blushing.

"I imagine that's the effect you have on all women."

"Apparently, not *all* women," he teases.

I give him my best no-nonsense look again, and change the subject back to business.

"So, your label wants to up your image. We are just the people to make that happen. I have a particular way I like to work with a client. I have a set of questions that I would like you to answer so that I can learn a little about you. This will help me not only guide your style, but direct the label in how to best present and represent you. I am being paid by the label for my services, but you are my client. Not them. That's the only way this works. We're a team. Got it?"

"I'm intrigued," he acquiesces.

"Great. Let's get started. Tell me a little about your parents?"

"Your first question is about my parents?"

"Yes."

"Not, how do I see myself, or what is my favorite color?"

"Nope."

"Hmm. Why not?" he cocks his head to the side. Curious.

"Because you don't know the answer to that question, so

how can I expect you to convey it to me?"

"I know my favorite color is green."

"As do I. It was in an interview you did as a favor for a teen reporter."

"My niece"

"Now I'm the one interested. Tell me about her after you talk about your parents."

An hour later, Joy enters the room to notify me they have their looks pulled together. We enter the workroom, and I introduce him to Joy and Henry. Joy and Henry are seasoned veterans with my processes and take control of making small talk to allow me a minute to review their pulls while making several notes.

"Okay, Joy. Why don't you walk us through the everyday looks first, then Henry can do the public event looks. Blaine, I would like you to hold all comments until the end."

My team takes twenty minutes each to introduce their looks and a quick review of their reasoning behind why they made the pull.

The next twenty minutes are really the sum and substance of our meeting. It's where the client responds to the looks, and then, as a team, we review the notes I made on their pulls before their presentation. The idea is to see how well I am matching up with my client. Can I know their response before I take cues from their facial, behavioral, and verbal feedback? If I missed the mark, I have to go back to the question session and ask different ones. In the four years I have been using my system, I have only had to go back twice. I've never had to do a third round, and frankly, if I did, I would release them as a client. I am clearly not the right fit for them.

"Blaine, tell me what you like and dislike about each look and why. Then I want you to tell me your favorite of all six looks and what it reminds you of. Got it?" I cross my legs and his eyes follow.

"Eyes up," I say with the same no-nonsense look I have given him twice already. He responds with a sly smile and moves into his thoughts on each look. He finishes with his favorite look and what it reminds him of.

Every client's favorite look evokes a memory that he is tied to. Something that reminds them where they were, who they were with, and how they felt at a special moment, whether it was a sweet or angry moment with someone or a moment of rebellion. Clients always remember what they were wearing. That is the beginning of helping them understand their image, who they want to be. I never know what it's going to be for that person until I ask my trademark questions. When Blaine finishes, I announce that I am nine-for-nine.

Henry nods, "Let's get busy then, Joy."

I smile at Blaine, and he looks perplexed.

"Why don't we walk over to the grill and get some lunch while they do the next pull. This time it will be twenty looks. You will leave with fifteen today."

"Just like that?"

"Just like that."

"How can you know that you'll have 15 looks for me today?"

"Because I am nine-for-nine. I wrote down nine comments about the looks when I reviewed them this morning, and they matched your nine responses just now. I know that we are on track. I wrote down the direction I wanted them to take in their next pull based off what I thought you would choose as your favorite look, about which I was right again."

"You were nine-for-nine," he says in a supercilious tone.

"Actually, I was ten-for-ten if you count that I matched

your favorite look. See for yourself." I hand him my notepad as I stand.

"Wow."

"You're very articulate," I tease.

"Smart-ass."

I shrug with a smile that has him laughing, when Amanda enters and brings me a package.

"This just arrived via courier for you. You have to sign for it directly."

I apply my signature to the line she points me to and hand her back the pen. The package is wrapped in brown craft paper with a string tied around it. "Emelia James" is written on top.

"I wonder what this could be? I didn't order anything." I frown and shake it for clues.

Joy's and Henry's curiosities pique, and they congregate around me and Blaine at the worktable. I open the package and pull out the telltale Apple box.

"I didn't think they sold the Classic anymore?" Blaine muses.

"They don't."

It is a brand-new 160GB iPod Classic. Speechless, something I am often not, I remove it from its plastic covering. Turning over the iPod, I notice an inscription on the back: *Someone told me there's a girl out there with love in her eyes and flowers in her hair.*

"Zeppelin," Blaine says just behind my shoulder.

"Going to California." I add.

"Why not send the Touch?"

"I don't like the Touch. It doesn't have the memory and it has too many other things than just music. I'm a fan of the Classic. Simple."

I look through the paper it was wrapped in, not really

expecting to find a note, but already knowing it is from him. The thought of him makes my pulse jump, as it has done no less than twenty times since our flight last night.

"Who's it from?" Jackson has entered the workroom.

"An acquaintance. Blaine, I would like to introduce you to Jackson Hollingsworth." I sidestep the question and find my footing again.

Jackson gives his firm handshake and greetings to Blaine, engaging him in conversation over his experience so far, but not without first giving me a glance that I know means "this conversation is not finished."

Jackson has a previously scheduled meeting he has to prep for, so he declines the invitation to lunch. He assures us he will be back in the office for our end of day wrap up.

I grab the envelope clutch I'm carrying today. "Ready?"

"Ladies first," he says with that same sexy, slow smile.

"Really? Is this going to be our thing now?"

"Oh, I hope so," Blaine smiles, entering the elevator.

The day is sunny and beautiful, but the summer heat has me removing my blazer. We cross 42nd Street, making our way to the upper terrace at the back of the New York Public Library to the Bryant Park Grill. Our office frequents Bryant Park, whether we are eating at the Grill or grabbing some food from one of the kiosks by the fountain. We enter the iconic restaurant and are seated upstairs on the rooftop so that we have a view of the park and the surrounding city. This is one of my most loved areas in the city.

The waiter comes to take our drink order.

"Blaine Moore. I'm a big fan," says the waiter as he shakes Blaine's hand. "*Sex with You* is my favorite." My laughter cues a redness that rises to his cheeks when he realizes how his statement sounded.

"No worries, man. You'd be surprised how often that happens." Blaine has the good graces to soothe the waiter's embarrassment.

"What would you like to drink?" the waiter asks me.

"Iced tea."

Blaine says, "She'll have iced tea and I'll take whatever's on tap."

Our waiter leaves, and two young girls come to our table.

`"Can we have our picture made with you?"

"Do you mind?" he asks me.

"Not at all." Looking up from my menu, I watch his interaction with his fans and catch a glimpse of him as a person. He's at ease with himself and comfortable talking with the random people who stop him. He's not short or rude; he doesn't act like it's an inconvenience. And he's thoughtful enough to ask my permission for the interruption.

The waiter returns with our drinks and takes our orders. I order the East Coast Fish and Chips and Blaine orders the Sweet and Spicy Monkfish.

"Also can you bring the bread trio appetizer please?"

"Sure thing."

Adding the lemon to my tea, I look up to start a conversation and find Blaine staring at me.

"What?"

"You're not like most girls I meet."

"Really? How so?"

"Well..." He pauses. "You eat bread."

I laugh. "I eat a lot of things."

"Do you, now?"

"Do you always equivocate?"

"Apparently," he grins.

"I do eat bread. I like food. A lot. I am sure that is very

different from the girls you meet."

"It's refreshing."

"It's going to add another workout is what it is." In my line of work, I have come across my fair share of hanger girls, who are a size two and eat a cube of cheese for lunch. I am not a hanger girl.

The waiter places a plate on our table. I move into telling Blaine what each appetizer is.

"This one is grilled artichoke and cloumage cheese, this one is crushed vine ripe tomatoes and sea salt, and lastly, sheep milk ricotta with roasted butternut squash, dates, and honey. I suggest you try them all," I say, handing him half of the one I bit off of.

Lunch flows like two people who have known each other for years, despite the fact that we just met. We swap stories and spend time talking about where he wants to take the next step in his music.

The waiter takes our plates and, before he can offer, I tell him that I would like to order dessert.

"Bananas for Bananas, please."

"Would you like anything?" he asks Blaine.

"No, thank you."

"Two spoons, please," I interject. "Do you like bananas?"

"I do."

"Then you'll love this. It's their twist on banana pudding. Its banana brioche pudding, salty peanut ice cream, peanut butter caramel, hot fudge, and whipped cream." I hold up a finger each time I announce an ingredient. "Now, tell me why you're resistant to being styled."

"How do you know I am?"

"I told you, nine-for-nine."

"I don't like pretending I'm something I'm not. It doesn't

feel right." He's quiet for a minute. "I want to be seen as an artist, not a sex symbol."

"Everyone wants to be seen for who they are and not the label we put on them. I hope you'll trust me to not present you as something you're not. You can be more than one thing. You don't have to be known as the sexy artist, but there is nothing wrong with being the artist who is also sexy. Remember, you're my client. Not the label. I won't stray from that."

The waiter brings our pudding.

"Alright then. I'll take you at your word."

"Good, now dig in."

We finish dessert, and I pay despite his objections. We are making our way to the stairs leading to the bottom floor when I feel him before I hear him.

"Emelia." He's sitting at the table I am about pass.

I stop. He stands, buttoning his suit jacket, and nods a greeting to me.

"It's nice to see you," I say, not quite believing that I have run into him. His eyes lock on mine for what seems like a minute, but I'm sure it was just a beat.

"It's lovely to see you again. I see you arrived home safely." It's not meant to be a question. He pauses, and his eyes land on Blaine's hand resting on my exposed back. He gives nothing away to anyone else, but I notice the shutters that come down in his eyes.

"Blaine. This is…" I pause realizing I still don't know his name.

"Graham." *Graham. Finally a name.*

"Blaine Moore." Blaine's hand caresses my skin as he lowers it to the small of my back. Reaching around me he offers his hand in greeting.

"If you'll excuse us for a moment," Graham says, grabbing

my forearm. My feet barely touch the stairs as he leads me down, nodding to the bartender before steering me into a small office off the restroom hallway.

"What the hell do you think you are doing?" My voice is louder than necessary. "I am with a client."

"A client? Really? You let all your clients rest their hands on your ass?" he asks, crossing his arms while he peruses my body.

"I write it into my contracts. Adds a little sweetener to the deal don't you think?" I respond flippantly, adding a shoulder shrug.

"You aren't dressed like someone meeting a client."

"I don't work in a business office, Graham. *My* clothing choice is appropriate." I lock my eyes on his, not backing down from his glower—one I get the feeling he is using to intimidate me into his way of thinking. He moves towards me, and I have to work to stand my ground when I realize I am backed into a corner. He's close enough I could run my tongue along his jaw line. The thought sends a shiver through me.

"So you think *this* is appropriate? *This* length?" He runs a finger along the inside of my thigh, tracing the hem of my jumpsuit before following with his thumb, the tip running along the crevice where my leg meets my hip. His touch sparks electricity in me. I know if he skims a little more to the right, he will find me wet for him. My breath catching is all the time he needs to turn me away from him, his thumb now traveling the crevice where my ass meets my thigh. His other hand is plotting a course down my back.

"You sent me an iPod." I go straight to the topic I want to touch on. Avoiding for now my confusion at being turned on instead of angry at his unearned familiarity. Where's the man who held my hand and why is my body equally attracted to this one?

"I did." His voice is heavy in my ear.

"Why?"

"Because I can."

"You shouldn't have."

"I believe the polite response is 'thank you'" he replies.

"Thank you?" I turn towards him. *I don't need a lesson in manners.*

"You're welcome." His reply is authoritative and sarcastic at once. Reading me correctly he adds, "I would think twice before opening that smart mouth Emelia."

"Emme." I cross my arms to put some distance between us. "If you could give me your work address, I'll have it couriered back to you."

"If I say you're keeping it, you're keeping it." The shutters open a little, and I see the smirk in his eyes, baiting me to put a voice to what he knows I am thinking: *Asshole!*

"Blaine's waiting for me." Thankfully, my legs cooperate, and I walk away from him.

Available Now!